AS EASY AS FALLING

THE RAEK RIDERS SERIES

AS EASY AS FALLING

THE RAEK RIDERS SERIES
BOOK 3

MELANIE K. MOSCHELLA

This one's for me—a reminder that I can and should feel proud of my accomplishments.

NOTE TO READER

Dear Reader,

This series addresses serious, potentially upsetting topics. For a full list of sensitive subject matter, please visit my website: melaniekmoschella.com and select the Content Warnings page. I hope you will join my characters in finding the strength they need to overcome their struggles. However, if you feel any of these topics might be detrimental to your well-being, I encourage you to pass on my books and find your reading bliss elsewhere.

With love,
Melanie

AS EASY AS FALLING

1

MEERA

Meera opened her eyes to an onslaught of light and feeling. She thrashed and flailed. Cold water surrounded her, dragging at her limbs and sucking her under. She took one shuddering breath of air before her mouth was submerged. She fought toward the surface, but her body felt strange—her senses confused. Every detail of the blue-green water around her drew her gaze. Every minute particle jostled by her movements caught her eyes. Every shade of color in the bubbles erupting from her nose and mouth invaded her mind. It was all too much!

Then she had a thought, and she clung to it like a buoy: she was in the ocean—the Cerun Sea. A wave had knocked her over, and her father would soon pull her to safety. He would lift her from the water with his big, comforting hands—he always did. Strong hands did grab Meera and thrust her toward the surface. She coughed and spluttered and choked in much-needed air, but her feet didn't touch the sandy ocean's floor. She didn't remember going out so far ... Had a wave dragged her out?

She squinted in the dim—yet harsh—light of morning, disoriented by the steam rising around her in layers of billowing, swirling opacity. It was too much. Shutting her eyes, she tried to tread water, but without her sight, she was all feeling—a jumble of disjointed sensation. The pores of her arms and legs prickled. Her body buzzed with pulsing muscle. She kicked and paddled, but her movements felt wrong—jerky and ineffectual. Her head went under again, and she panicked, opening her eyes to another invasion of light and color and movement. What was happening? Where was the beach?

An arm wrapped around her middle, pulled her above the surface, and towed her through the water. She gasped in air and shut her eyes in relief: her father. Her father always pulled her from the tumbling waves of the ocean. Meera lay back and let herself be dragged to shore. She clutched at the arm around her middle, glad that she was not alone in her confusion. Then her nails scraped against the bare skin of her stomach, and her mind reeled: where were her clothes? Did she lose them in the current?

Groping frantically for her missing clothes, she found—breasts? Her full, naked breasts breached the surface of the water. She wasn't a child at the beach with her father, she realized, opening her eyes in alarm. Where was she? Meera was once more bombarded with an explosion of indistinct light and color that her brain couldn't form into a single image. She struggled—striking out with her limbs—and the arm around her middle released her.

This time her kicking legs found the sandy bottom as did her hands, and she grounded herself on all fours in the shallows, breathing hard. The strong hands returned, grabbing her under her armpits and hauling her to her feet. She swayed, but the hands held her steady. She brought her palms to her face to block out some of the sight overwhelming her.

"Meera?" said a voice so loud and jarring that she flinched violently and slammed her hands over her ears. Her head rang from the impact, and her eyes were once more flooded with light and images. But this time they managed to focus on something—someone: Shael stood before her, dripping and looking into her face with concern. Meera's gaze was caught by his grey-green eyes; she stared at their outer, darker rim, then was sucked into their lighter depths. Her whole being zeroed in on a tiny gold fleck in his left eye that she had never noticed before.

Shael reached out, took her arm, and pulled her the last, stumbling few steps out of the water. Her visual concentration suddenly broke—the dry sand under her feet was like thousands of pecking birds supporting her weight, the air scraped its invisible teeth along her wet skin, and every hair on her body lifted and prickled in reaction. She stared uncomprehendingly down at her splayed toes and bare legs. What was this? She stared and stared and tried to process the torrent of information her body was sending her. Was she ... cold?

Once Meera made the connection between the sensations all over her flesh and the word for the feeling, she relaxed somewhat. She began to feel more normal—aware of the chill on her skin without needing to concentrate on every tingling pore of her body. She expelled a shuddering sigh in relief, but the sound of her exhale made her cringe and press her hands to her temples. Her focus shifted—honed in on the repetitive rushing of her lungs sucking air in and forcing it out. In and out, in and out, in and out. The sounds of her own body rattled her ears, and she tried to breathe slower—quieter—but it was no use—all she could hear, all she could think about was her breath. What was happening? Why wouldn't it stop?

As her panic rose once more, her heart thundered with it, and she was assailed by every squelchy, resounding thump of the muscle in her chest. She clawed at herself, willing her body to be quiet—to be still. Her head pounded with her heart's reverberations. Her ears ached. She just wanted quiet! Bending over, she braced her hands on her knees and stared and stared in bewilderment at her feet in the sand until her vision blurred from her shallow breathing.

"Meera? Are you okay?" Shael's insistent voice pierced through the noise of her body and snapped her out of her fixation.

She straightened up, glanced at him, and looked around, blinking and gasping. Her mind churned, slowly processing what she was seeing. She knew this place: she was at the Riders' Peninsula. She was standing next to the lake—had been pulled out of the lake. She wasn't at the beach by the Cerun Sea ... She wasn't a child. She was with Shael in Levisade, she remembered. Had she gone for a swim and nearly drowned?

"Are you okay?" Shael asked again, voice cracking. He reached out slowly and touched her cheek, drawing her attention.

Meera gaped at him. She wasn't sure if she was okay. She watched shiny droplets of water drip down the side of his angular face. His dark hair was slicked down from being wet, and his soaked clothes clung to the contours of his body. Then she looked down at herself and registered her nudity once more as well as her goosebumps. Wrapping her arms across her chest, she shivered, and Shael quickly removed his sopping shirt and draped it across her shoulders. The wet, heavy fabric clung to her skin, and she gripped it in front of her to hold it closed. The dark blue shirt covered her to her mid-thigh, and its empty sleeves hung uselessly on either side of her body like tired wings.

Meera looked again into Shael's eyes, but before she could say anything—before she could think of an answer to his question—more people appeared, running down the grassy slope to the beach, shouting her name and asking more questions. Isbaen and Hadjal arrived first. They stopped on the beach a little away from her, looking apprehensive. Their mouths moved, but Meera couldn't process what they were saying. She looked to Shael in confusion. What was happening? He was staring at her with a fixation so intense, she had to glance away. Then her father was there.

Orson Hailship reached the beach, hobbling and panting, and flung himself into Meera, nearly knocking her over. He held her to his chest, breaking away after several seconds to clutch her face in his hands and kiss her cheeks repeatedly. "Meera, are you okay? Are you alright?" he asked, just like Shael.

Meera's head spun, and she took a step back from her father. Her father! He was here! She had forgotten ... As she stared at him, her mind started to piece together flashes of memory. She remembered going on a journey to find her father. She hadn't found him ... but she had met a wild raek! With a rush of understanding, she whirled toward the lake to look at the cliff overhanging the far rock wall. However, the cloud-colored raek was no longer there; the cliff stood vacant and forlorn in the morning light.

Meera turned back to her father. "I'm alright. I must have hit my head on the water," she rasped, fingering her throbbing temples. She remembered climbing up to the raek. She must have fallen and smacked against the surface of the water. That explained why she felt so disoriented. Her shoulders loosened in relief, but when she looked at the faces around her, tension crept back into her muscles: Isbaen was frowning, her father seemed confused and unsure of what to say, and Hadjal was standing awfully far back from her, looking wary.

"What's going on?" she asked. She glanced at Shael and noticed the purple circles under his eyes and how thin he was with his shirt off. Before he could answer, there was a thump, and Cerun descended the slope, inserting his head between Shael and Isbaen. Meera looked into the bright blue, intelligent eyes of her raek friend.

"Do you not remember, Human Meera?" Cerun asked in her head, and strangely, Meera didn't feel the usual accompanying pressure.

She shook her head side to side in answer, clutching Shael's shirt tighter around her as she shivered once more. She saw Shael, Isbaen, and Hadjal exchange looks. "What's going on?" she asked them more forcefully, cringing at how loud her voice sounded.

Cerun stepped toward her and extended his shining, scaly snout until it bumped against her forehead. She froze expectantly, and images poured from him into her mind: she saw herself climb the far rock wall. She saw herself touch forehead to snout with the wild raek once, then again. She saw her body burst into pale flames, and she gasped and watched open-mouthed as, in her mind's eye, she fell to the lake's surface and lay still in a fiery cocoon.

For a moment, her mind was blank with awe and confusion, then she remembered. She remembered the wild raek showing her Aegwren, the first rider—a human rider. She remembered the raek offering her a bargain, and she remembered taking it. Meera broke away from Cerun and looked around her, absorbing how many details and colors she could see that she had never seen before. She clenched her hands under Shael's shirt and felt every muscle in them flex, responding with speed and ability. Her eyes widened as she came to understand that the wild raek had already changed her.

"I was on fire ..." she said disbelievingly.

"For three weeks," Shael replied, voice trembling. Meera stared at him once more. His high cheekbones protruded sharply from his face, and his ribs were visible above his abdominal muscles.

"Three weeks?" she repeated stupidly, glancing around to confirm. She couldn't believe she had missed so much time.

Cerun leaned forward and bumped his snout to her head again. Meera saw in flashes as on each new day, the sun rose and set over her burning, unmoving figure on the lake. She also saw Shael sitting on the rock protruding from the lake's surface, watching her and waiting for her ... day after day. Through her temporary mental connection to Cerun, she felt a sense of Shael's emotions lacing the memories, and she broke away, overcome.

She stared at her feet against the speckled, sandy ground, processing. Then her eyes filled until she couldn't make out her toes through the glistening barrier of her unshed tears. Shael had sat on that rock and waited for her for weeks. He had been there every day until she had needed him to help her from the water. Meera had been confused about his feelings toward her for so long ... But in that moment, her confusion melted away. She knew how he felt: he loved her.

Her chest squeezed and fluttered, and she swayed unsteadily on her changed feet. Then she looked at Shael who watched her along with everyone else. She was too moved to speak. Lifting one foot then the other, she slowly shuffled up to him and let her head fall forward onto his chest just under his collarbone, resting that way. Her tears spilled over her cheeks onto his cool skin.

Meera stayed like that for a long moment, listening to Shael's body react to her in a way that she never could before. She became absorbed in the ragged sounds of his breathing and his thumping heart as it beat faster and faster next to her face. She felt his muscles tense and awaken at her nearness and saw the skin of his chest pebble where her breath brushed it. She couldn't resist poking one of her hands out from under her makeshift shawl and running her fingertips lightly over his stomach. The waves of muscles under her touch tightened before she felt a shudder through his entire body.

"Thank you," she whispered. It was all she could think to say.

Shael wrapped his arms around her back and crushed her to him, quaking with suppressed emotion. Meera's arms were pinned between them under the barrier of his soaked shirt, and she pushed gently at him until he loosened his grip. Circling her hands around his back, she let the shirt across her shoulders hang open, so when she hugged him back, her bare chest squished between them. She was too overwhelmed to feel embarrassed. Her mind turned again and again, and she began to shake with the knowledge that she was a rider, that her body was changed, and that Shael loved her. He hugged her tighter, and another tear trickled from her skin to his.

Then a new voice snapped them back to the present: "Meera! Is she okay? Is she hurt?"

Shael broke away from her, and Meera quickly pulled the dripping shirt back over her exposed front. Soleille was running down the slope, shouting, followed by Katrea, Sodhu, and Florean. Meera smiled at the sight of everyone. Her brain seemed to be acclimating to her new, heightened senses. She was briefly distracted by the thrumming wings of a dragonfly and flinched when it veered toward her before realizing it was at least fifteen feet away. Then she blinked and refocused on the people gathered around her. They were all studying her like a peculiar new animal.

Soleille took a tentative step forward. "I am going to scan your body," she said.

Scan her? "No!" Meera shouted suddenly, stumbling backward. She hadn't meant to shout and felt blood rush to her cheeks as everyone surveyed her. "I'm fine," she said in a quieter voice.

She wasn't sure why, but she wasn't ready for them to know. She wasn't ready to tell them everything yet—she was still trying to process it all for herself.

Soleille frowned at her, but Meera shook her head insistently.

"Meera, please," Shael implored, touching her arm through his shirt.

She gazed at him, again registering how exhausted and thin he looked. Knowing he had sat on that rock waiting for her day after day made her heart crack wide open. She didn't want him to worry about her any more than he already had, and yet ... She didn't want to tell him everything—not yet. Part of her glowed with the hope that having a knell lifespan would mean she and Shael could be together—that only their different races had stood in the way of their love—but she didn't actually know what had stood in the way of Shael's love for her.

She now felt certain that he did love her, but he had been resisting it; he had been letting something keep them apart when she had not. She had been willing to be with him despite their differences, and he hadn't. Meera still wanted Shael to choose her for her—regardless of how long she would live or how fast she could run—and he could only do that if he didn't know. "I'm fine, really," she said, looking into his eyes. Seeing him so thin and ragged brought her back to when he was her prisoner, and she knew, suddenly, that she had failed him; he had sat on a rock and waited for her every day when she was unconscious, and she had left him in that dungeon cell by himself—freezing, hurt, and alone. Shame roiled in her gut.

"Meera, you should really let Soleille scan you," Hadjal said, but Meera wasn't listening.

"I'm sorry," she said to Shael, trembling with cold and remembrance. "I didn't even bring you socks. I should have stayed down there with you. I shouldn't have left you." She stared up at him, willing him to know how sorry she was. She should have done more—she should have been there for him like he had been for her.

"Meera, what are you talking about?" her father asked. "I don't think she's well," he said in a stage whisper to the others.

Meera could see that Shael knew what she was talking about, and he shook his head infinitesimally at her.

"Meera, we need you to tell us what the wild raek did to you," Isbaen said, trying to catch her eye.

She glanced at him, briefly, before returning her focus to Shael. "Shael looks like he hasn't eaten in three weeks," she replied. "Let's eat. Then I'll explain everything."

Shael nodded at her ever so slightly.

"Thank you," she said, holding his gaze. She wanted to go to him—to hug him once more—but she held back.

Shael nodded again and swallowed visibly.

Finally, Meera forced her eyes from him, glanced at the others around her, and said, "I'm going to get some clothes," before stepping forward awkwardly and starting to climb the slope up toward Hadjal's house and the cabin where she and her father had been staying. At first, her muscles jolted clumsily, unaccustomed to their new strength. But with each step, she acclimated to the feel of her new body—with every stride, she became more sure of her movements. She wanted to run—to test herself—but she held back.

2

SHAEL

Shael watched Meera go and had to stop himself from running after her. She really did seem fine—seem herself. He was so relieved, yet he stood rigid, repressing the emotion that wanted to gush out of him—tempering the sobs that threatened to wrack his body. Meera was awake. Meera was alive. Meera had touched and hugged him in ways that had brought unbidden thoughts to his mind, and he all but shook with the effort of quashing his feelings. They could only be friends, he reminded himself.

"She appeared normal," Sodhu said in a quiet, hopeful voice.

"Then why would she not let me scan her?" Soleille asked, looking put-out. She shot Meera a suspicious look up the slope.

"I agree," said Isbaen. "That raek fire must have done something to her. Otherwise, why would the wild raek have used so much energy to sustain it?" Shael had the same suspicion as his mentor, but he was still so relieved that Meera was awake and herself that he could not find it in himself to be overly concerned.

"What was she babbling about, Shael?" Katrea asked, and

everyone looked at him. "She sounded like her brain may have fried in that fire."

Shael shook his head. "She was of sound mind," he responded vaguely. Meera had been thinking of him in the dungeon of the Altus Palace. He hated to be thought of that way—weak and frail —but looking down at his torso, he saw how emaciated he had become; it was no wonder she had connected his appearance now with their time in Terratelle together. As far as Shael could tell, Meera had been confused at first but had remembered everything after a minute or two. He knew Cerun had shown her the three weeks that had passed and felt embarrassed that she had seen his obsessive waiting and watching on his boulder.

"Meera said she would explain, so we will just have to wait and let her tell us when she is ready," Hadjal said with an even voice that was at odds with the worry flickering in her gold-hued eyes. Sodhu placed a comforting hand on her partner's back, and Shael noted the gesture with envy; all he wanted was that easy comfort with someone, but it would never be easy for him.

"Who will help me prepare a large lunch?" Sodhu asked, and the other riders began to turn and migrate back up the slope toward Hadjal's.

Shael did not move with them. He felt stuck—rooted in place —still resisting the urge to run after Meera. He knew he should give her space and wait for her to explain with the others. But he was so used to centering himself around her—to watching her form all day—that he felt untethered. He was adrift and unsure of how to focus his energy now that his concentration need not burn with the pale raek fire that had encased Meera for so long. Then a breeze chilled his damp skin, and he thought he ought to start by finding dry clothes.

He was about to follow the others up the slope, but he turned toward the lake one last time and found Meera's father standing by the water, observing him. Shael started; he had not realized Orson was still there. Meera's father was wearing a simple knell-style outfit in a beige somewhat lighter than the man's golden-brown skin. He wore his wire-framed glasses over his eyes—eyes that were almond-shaped like his daughter's—and Shael could still see the glistening trails left from Orson's tears at finding Meera awake and well.

Orson smiled at him—a smile that crinkled the edges of his eyes and spread his nose wide on his face. Shael attempted to smile in return and managed to lift one side of his mouth fleetingly. He should be able to smile, he thought; he should be able to grin and laugh and dance now that Meera was awake. But he still felt so uncertain and unsettled. "She seems okay," he said, unsure of what else to say to the man he had rescued not long ago but had hardly spoken to since.

Orson nodded his head. Then he removed his glasses, wiped the lingering tears from his eyes, and proceeded to rub his glasses clean on the bottom of his shirt. "You know, I don't see very well," he said to Shael, who furrowed his brows, unsure of how to reply to the older man. Meera had always said that her father was intelligent and witty, but he had returned from the war altered—a shell of his former self. Shael was not sure the man was all the way present in his mind.

After an overlong pause, Orson continued, "I don't see very well, but I'm not blind." He replaced his glasses on his nose and looked at Shael with enough intensity to make him shift on his feet. "I'm glad my daughter has you looking out for her. It eases my mind that she will be in good hands when I'm gone." It was not the first time Shael had heard Orson speak like he was about to die. Although, he supposed that compared to knell, humans were always about to die. He thought of Meera, and his stomach turned.

"I will always take care of her," he told Orson, hoping to comfort the man. It was true, too. Shael might not be able to be with Meera, but he could not imagine living without her; he was doomed to watch her grow old and do everything he could to help preserve and protect her short, human life.

"Good," Orson replied with another smile. Reaching into the neck of his shirt, he added, "I have something for you." He pulled a chain over his head, on which were two rings: a simple, silver ring and a gold ring with small white pearls surrounding a blue center stone. The decorative ring matched the earrings that had belonged to Meera's mother. To Shael's utter amazement, Orson fumbled with the clasp of the chain, slid off the finer of the two rings, and held it out to him.

Shael stared at the offering and slowly shook his head, beyond words.

Orson emphatically pressed his hand out further. "Take it, Shael," he insisted.

Shael just kept shaking his head. He looked with bewilderment from the ring to Orson's almond-shaped eyes and beheld the twinkle of laughter in their brown depths. "I ..." he started to say and trailed off. "No, Orson, I ... we are not the same—Meera and I. I am half-knell—"

Orson laughed heartily. His thin frame shook with his laughter until he coughed a few times and regained control of himself. "Meera's mother and I were not the same, you know," he said. "Carmella came from a wealthy family. She was a lady, and I was a poor nobody. I was my parent's only child, you see, and after they died, I used every last bit of their inheritance to pay for school. I wanted to learn everything there was to know. I thought there was no greater use for money than knowledge—and no greater purpose. I was wrong, of course!"

He chuckled again, before continuing: "When I met

Carmella, I learned just how little I knew. It's love! Love is the most important thing. We loved each other, but her parents wouldn't see her wed to someone like me—a poor scholar. We ran away together and got married anyway because, different though we were, we were the same. I couldn't even buy her a ring. She wore this one, which she had brought with her." He paused and cleared his throat. "Here I am again, just a poor scholar, but I have this ring, at least, for Meera to wear," he finished. He tossed the ring in the air, and Shael caught it reflexively.

"No, Orson. I cannot," Shael started to say, holding the ring back out toward Meera's father.

"Even after Meera was born, Carmella's family wouldn't accept our marriage. They never wrote back to her, never inquired after the baby. Meera doesn't know, you know. I let her think all of her grandparents were dead. I didn't want her to think she wasn't worth knowing when it was they who were unworthy of her," Orson said. Then he looked very serious and regarded Shael with clear, sober eyes.

"My Meera has chosen you. I will not make the same mistake as her grandparents and try to turn you away, but I do expect you to make her happy," he said. With that, some of the clouded sadness returned to his eyes, and he turned away, meandering toward Florean who fished on the bank of the lake some ways away.

Shael stood absolutely dumbstruck, staring at the ring in his hand. Meera's father had just tasked him with the job of making Meera happy, something Shael wanted to do but didn't think he was capable of. He had left Meera in Sangea with his parents, hoping a quiet life among humans—possibly with a husband and children—would make her happy, and she had left that life through the Forest of Shayan. Shael shuddered at the thought.

Could he make Meera happy? He supposed it was possible, and yet, he could not give her a child like Orson had given Carmella.

Tucking the ring into the small leather pouch he wore at his hip, Shael told himself he would find another time to return it to Orson with his apologies. Still, he could not help but picture himself down on one knee, proposing to Meera in the human style before lifting her off her feet and kissing her. No, he thought; he could not do that. It was not what was best for her. He could not burden her with himself ... But he could go and see how she was doing. He could make sure she got warm and had plenty to eat after her three-week fast.

Shael walked up the slope toward Hadjal's table, where Isbaen, Soleille, and Katrea were deep in conversation, probably discussing Meera's sudden awakening. He could hear Hadjal and Sodhu inside the house preparing food. He skirted the table to go around to the cabin where Orson and Meera had been staying. Isbaen tried to catch his eye, but Shael ignored his mentor, suddenly desperate to see Meera again and to assure himself that she was still alive and well.

3

MEERA

Meera entered the small cabin she shared with her father, chilled and longing for dry clothes. Even so, she took a moment to stand in front of their small mirror and study herself. She didn't look different—her new, sharper vision let her see herself with more clarity and range of colors than ever before, but she was still the same round-faced woman as always. The wild raek had given her a knell body in practice but not in appearance. Meera wasn't disappointed; if anything, she was relieved to still look and feel like herself. The knowledge that she could now live for a thousand years was enough change for her to contend with.

Pulling Shael's shirt off of her shoulders, she reached out to drape it over the solitary, wooden chair in the small cabin, but she hesitated and brought the shirt instead up to her face, breathing in Shael's familiar scent. She still couldn't believe how awful he had looked and felt guilty for causing him unnecessary grief and worry. Then she remembered the emotion she had felt lacing

Cerun's memories and thought of how Shael had clutched her to himself so tightly, and her stomach fluttered with more than her pressing hunger.

Meera threw the shirt over the chair and chose one of her knell-style pant and shirt sets. She dressed quickly, eager to see Shael again—she always was, but this felt different, hopeful. She willed him to share his feelings with her, and she hoped he would do so soon—before she shared her news with everyone. She was about to run out the door, but she glanced in the mirror again and decided to take the time to comb her damp hair.

It took her a while to work through all of her snarls. She started at the bottom of her strands and impatiently moved her comb ever higher until she reached her roots. Once detangled, she dropped some lavender oil into her palms and ran them over the length of her curls. Her hair was getting quite long; it reached to her mid-back when wet—though as it dried, it would shrink up to around the bottom of her shoulder blades. Meera took the curls in front of her ears, twisted them back, and tied them together. Then she grabbed Shael's shirt and left the tiny cabin with a feeling of heady expectation.

She took only one step out the door, however, and stopped. There, standing twenty feet in front of her, was Shael. He was still damp and still shirtless, and he appeared to be standing and watching the cabin, waiting for her. Meera couldn't help but smile, then she rolled her eyes at him. He gave her a small smile in return but didn't make any move to approach her or to speak. Typical Shael, she thought.

Meera was feeling more at home in her new body now that she had had some time to process it, and she walked toward him with confident, even steps. But despite her steady strides, her heart beat rapidly in her chest, giddy with nervous anticipation. She didn't know what to say or what to expect, but she stepped right up to Shael—slightly closer than she normally would—and she thrust his wet shirt at his chest before standing there, gazing up at him, waiting.

Even thin and tired, Shael was still absurdly beautiful. Dark lashes and brows accentuated his pale grey-green eyes, which Meera stared into with open abandon. His high cheekbones and beardless face always made her want to reach out and stroke his cheek, but she didn't. She waited. Every muscle in his chest, stomach, and arms was defined. He was slightly emaciated, but his shoulders were still broad and strong. She wanted to step into his embrace once more, but he didn't offer one.

Shael took his shirt and held it loosely in one hand. Otherwise, he just gazed back at her. Meera felt strong in her new body, and she felt bold with the knowledge Cerun had shared with her. She took one small step closer to him until their bodies were almost touching. Then she waited. Shael didn't move. He didn't speak. She could see his pulse racing in his throat and feel his heart thumping through the small gap of air between them. She even caught him look fleetingly at her lips, but still, he didn't budge. She continued to wait, but Shael was a statue.

Finally, Meera sighed in frustration, and with her eyes boring into him, she said, "You love me."

His eyes widened almost imperceptibly. His cheek twitched, but he didn't respond. He didn't confirm or deny her statement. He didn't move.

Meera didn't know what to do. Why wouldn't he tell her how he felt? She had confessed her love weeks ago ... She had had enough of this. Feeling immeasurably irritated, she leaned in even closer and whispered, "I love ... food!" Then she side-stepped and started to skirt around Shael toward Hadjal's house. But she didn't get far.

Shael dropped the shirt dangling from his hand and grabbed

Meera's waist, pulling her back to face him. Her lips parted in a gasp just before he bent down and claimed her mouth with his own. She stiffened at first, then melted into the warm pressure of his lips on hers. Shael kissed her hard and hungrily, crushing her body into his, and she kissed him back. Putting her hands on his bare chest, she felt her way down to his abs, running her fingers over all of the dips and grooves of his muscles. Then she grazed the skin of his stomach with her fingernails where she had touched him earlier that day and felt him shiver. Grinning against his lips, her joy threatened to bubble to the surface in a fit of giggles.

Shael pulled away just long and far enough to look into her eyes and cup her cheek with his hand. His other hand dropped down to her hip. He wasn't smiling, but Meera could see the light in his eyes before he tilted her chin up and reclaimed her mouth with even more ferocity, parting her lips and invading her with his tongue in a rhythmic push-pull that enlivened something deep in her core. She wasn't laughing now.

Wrapping one arm around his waist and the other around his neck, she pulled him to her. She wanted more—more of his mouth on hers, more of his hands on her body, more of her front pressed against him. Shael's hand on her hip held her at bay, keeping her at a distance even as he made her whole being tingle with the touch of his tongue.

Meera's hand wandered from his neck to his cheek, and suddenly, she remembered him pulling away from her in bed and stepping back from her in his parent's garden. Her chest constricted. Unable to bear the thought of him rejecting her again, she broke their connection, pulling her lips from his and opening her eyes. He was looking down at her, still holding her close, and she brushed a stray lock of dark hair behind one of his ears before removing her hands from his body and stepping out of his grasp.

Shael's eyebrows furrowed, and for once, his face wasn't stone; Meera could read the confusion and indecision in his features. She wouldn't speak this time, she decided; she would hold her silence and wait as long as it took him to tell her how he was feeling. She needed to know! She couldn't keep making proclamations for them both and living in an endless state of confusion between hasty kisses.

She waited, watching as agony spread across Shael's face. She felt her heartbeat accelerate and her stomach drop out from her body. Her eyes prickled and threatened tears, and she wondered how much longer she could wait before turning and fleeing. Why wouldn't he say something? Why did he make her feel so good and yet so bad? Why wasn't her new knell-quality heart made of something stronger than her old human one?

Finally, Shael crossed his arms over his bare chest in a gesture Meera could only read as barricading himself against her. She drew in a shaky breath and pressed her lips together tightly, willing herself to hold it together. He saw her distress, and—uncrossing his arms—he touched her shoulders, then her face—stroking her cheeks lightly with his fingertips. "Meera, I love you—of course, I love you, but I ... cannot," he said, shaking his head back and forth.

Meera reached up to her face and brushed away her tears before they could fall, knocking his hands aside at the same time. "Why?" she asked quietly, sounding surprisingly steady considering the herd of bison stomping her heart to pieces in her chest.

Shael shifted on his feet like he wanted to run, but he didn't run. He didn't look away from her face, either. "It would not be fair to you," he said. "Our lifespans are too different, and I ... would not give you children."

Meera gaped at him. She was so shocked, her urge to flee and cry disappeared completely. She had known their respective lifespans might be the issue—although it had been one she had always been willing to overlook in the name of short-term happiness—but Shael seemed to be thinking even longer into the future than she had. That knowledge bolstered her—made her think maybe he really did love her like she loved him. "*Would not?*" she asked in confusion. She had seen enough to know he wasn't impotent.

Shael sighed heavily and finally looked away from her before saying, "I made a vow to never make more partial-breeds like myself. I will never lie with a woman—not fully."

Meera continued to stare at him, her mouth slightly ajar. She almost couldn't process his words for a second; she never thought of him as being a half-breed. When Shael looked to her for a reply, she shut her mouth—she didn't know what to say. She thought it was ridiculous that he was using his vow as a reason not to be with her, and she felt hope that they could have a future together. Mostly, however, she felt sad for Shael.

"I wish you didn't think so little of yourself," she said quietly. She reached out and took one of his hands in both of hers, squeezing it to emphasize her words as she said, "Shael, you're not half-anything to me—you're everything." Her voice shook with emotion, and she saw tears in his eyes that nearly undid her composure. Swallowing, she made herself continue: "Living with you this summer was the happiest I've ever been. I'd rather be with you, for any amount of time ... in any capacity, than not be with you. I'm ... not concerned about children. I love you, and I would choose to be with you." She swallowed again and let go of his hand. "Now you have to choose."

Shael nodded with his lips pressed firmly together. There was only a foot of space between them, but Meera felt like she was reaching for him across a widening void. She didn't understand how they could be so close—so together—one moment and so distant the next. She waited for him to answer, but he didn't speak. She supposed he would answer her when he was ready. She wanted to reach out and touch him in some way—reassure herself that he was still there with her—but she felt frozen in place. Then her stomach growled, urging her to go, and she listened.

With a last look in Shael's pained eyes, Meera stepped around him and headed for Hadjal's table. She didn't cry or get upset; she felt vaguely empty. She had poured herself out to him, given herself over—again. Now it was up to him. She couldn't control him and refused to keep throwing herself in his path. Her hollow chest ached with need for an answer, but it was an ache she couldn't do anything about, so she walked away to focus on an ache she could address and patted her insistent stomach reassuringly. She really needed to eat something.

As Meera rounded to the front of Hadjal's house, she saw the other riders and her father sitting at the long wooden table and remembered that she had some explaining to do. She sighed, dreading it; she felt like she'd done enough talking and thinking for the day already. All she wanted now was to eat a large lunch and take a nap until dinner. Then, suppressing a groan, she realized that Shael hadn't made his choice yet, and he would soon know about her new lifespan. How would she feel if he wanted to be with her after the revelation but not before? Would that make him more practical than her, or would it mean he didn't love her as much as she loved him? She wasn't sure.

Her stomach turned over, and she considered going back to the cabin and feigning illness to get out of the coming meal. But the others had already seen her and looked expectant. Her father smiled at her, and his eyes even crinkled beneath their glasses. She smiled back, glad to see him doing so well, especially considering what her inexplicable burning had no doubt done to him these past weeks. Taking a deep breath, she resigned herself to whatever would happen.

4

MEERA

Meera walked to her usual seat, but on a whim, she took Shael's chair instead—a petty act of aggression toward the frustrating man she loved. Then she proceeded to avoid everyone's eyes and load her plate with heaping quantities of food. There was fruit, some sort of cold vegetable and chicken dish, and a seedy bread that always left bits stuck in her teeth. She thanked Sodhu for the food, but inwardly, she wished there was something heartier and cheesier to eat. A cake wouldn't go amiss by her either.

Once she started eating, so did the others. They clanked food onto their plates with silverware, crunched into the crusty, seedy bread, slurped juicy fruit, and mushed chicken salad in their mouths. Meera's entire body clenched from the racket of every-one's eating, and she felt her blood rushing in her veins as Florean smacked his lips loud enough to cause a stampede. She knew she was still adjusting to her new knell senses, but the knowledge didn't help to muffle the disturbing cacophony of sounds berating her ears. Leaning over her plate, she began shoveling her own food in her mouth in an effort to drown out the noises everyone else was making with her own hearty chewing.

"So, are we ever to learn what that raek fire was all about?" Florean asked, smacking his lips and picking a seed out of his teeth with a fingernail. Meera didn't look up at him; she thought if she did, her eyes might burn holes through his clothes, and she didn't want to see that. She felt suddenly hot all over like she was still trapped in her flaming coffin, and she took a deep breath and a long drink of water to cool herself.

Hadjal responded for her: "We will wait for Shael and let Meera eat something before we ask her our questions, Florean."

"Where is Shael?" Soleille asked.

"I last saw him looking for Meera," Isbaen replied, peering at Meera pointedly.

"If he's not fifteen feet away staring at me then something tragic must have happened to him," she said with a mouthful of food before clamping her lips shut. She hadn't actually meant to say that aloud. Apparently, her new body didn't give her any extra self-control, she thought.

Soleille laughed heartily. "I missed you, Meera," she said, and Meera couldn't help but smile at her despite her mood.

Isbaen didn't laugh, but he did look somewhat amused, she thought.

"Did your young Kallan upset you, Queen Thea?" her father asked, leaning toward her down the table.

Meera started. She knew the reference, of course; the rider, Kallan, rescuing the human Queen Thea from pirates was one of her favorite stories growing up. She had never thought of Shael as the Kallan to her Queen Thea, though, and she didn't exactly appreciate the comparison. "I'm not some pathetic damsel in need of rescuing," she snapped at her father, who held up his hands placatingly and continued to give her an annoyingly knowing smile. Meera stared fixedly at her plate. She supposed that even with one foot in the grave, she couldn't have expected her father to remain ignorant of the drama between her and Shael forever.

Everyone left her to her food after that—probably rightfully wary of being attacked. Meera couldn't blame them; she didn't like the way she was acting, but every sound grated at her nerves and the lights and colors before her eyes and sensations in her body all still felt so overwhelming. She continued to eat and didn't look up when, a few minutes later, Shael materialized and took the seat next to her—her usual seat.

Meera was beginning to feel full and realizing that she had piled far too much food on her plate. She pushed some vegetables around despondently with her fork. "Are you done eating?" Shael asked her.

Irrationally, she hunched over her plate and moved her right arm in defense of her food. Then she crammed in an unwanted bite and said, "Get your own food, Shael," around her mouthful. If she were any less irritable, she might have been embarrassed for behaving like a child. As it were, she could practically feel her mounting annoyance with everyone throbbing in her face. If quiet, peaceful Sodhu ate one more crunchy pomegranate seed, Meera thought she might hit her.

Shael ignored her obvious hostility and said, "You were right, Meera. It is time for me to choose, and I have made my decision."

Meera froze with half-chewed broccoli in her mouth, but she didn't move or look at him. She couldn't believe he was doing this now—in front of everyone and when she had food in her mouth! Was he about to reject her publicly? She wished her new body had claws with which to rip out his throat. Then she heard Shael move next to her, and there were several gasps around the table. Meera did look, then; she swung around in her chair to find Shael kneeling on the ground next to her, holding out her mother's ring. Her eyes widened at the ring, and she whipped her head around to glance at her smiling father before returning her focus to Shael. Kneeling. On the ground. With a ring.

Meera swallowed the lump of vegetables in her mouth with as much force as she could. Her chest reverberated with nerves. She hadn't expected this! Is this what Shael thought she had meant? Had she pressured him into proposing? She began to feel all kinds of doubt, but then she looked into Shael's eyes. They looked extra green against the grass behind him and the fresh green shirt he had put on, but mostly, they were steady. They caught Meera and held her with a look she could only call love.

"Meera Hailship, I love you. I would like to spend my life with you for as long as you will have me. Will you marry me?" he asked, his voice as steady as his gaze.

Meera, on the other hand, shook with emotion. Her jaw trembled, unsure if she should grin and laugh or cry tears of joy. She opened her mouth and wanted to scream "Yes!" but she knew there was still so much she hadn't told him. Her moment of confusion stretched until she could hear the uncomfortable movements of the other riders shifting in their seats behind her back. Shael's brows lowered over his eyes, and his pulse jittered visibly in his throat.

Panicking, Meera leaned forward and grabbed at his hands. "Get up! Get up!" she cried, pulling him up and shoving him into his seat. She suspected she had used more strength than she would have been capable of three weeks ago, but Shael didn't seem to notice. His eyes were darkening, and his shoulders were curling in protectively.

"No!" Meera cried, seeing the look of hurt on his face. "I mean

—*not* no!" She put her hands over her face; she was completely mucking this up. Taking a deep breath, she lowered her palms from her face and gripped Shael's hand in hers, which was still outstretched with her mother's ring in it. In a low, shaky voice, she said, "If you're asking me for forever, you ... should know that forever ... might be longer than you're imagining."

Shael's forehead scrunched in confusion. He had no idea what she was talking about. Meera thought maybe she should explain everything; she should explain and tell him to ask her again if he still wanted to. But explaining everything was a lot, and she squirmed in her seat, desperate to wipe the hurt look from his face. "I ... have a knell lifespan! I—I'm a raek rider! You should know that. Also, I have to end the war—or try, at least," she blurted.

She looked imploringly into Shael's face, willing him to understand her gibberish. His green eyes widened and mouth gaped slightly, and she gripped his hand harder, unintentionally grinding his bones together. He grunted in pain and looked down at his hand with an expression of dawning disbelief, and Meera quickly snatched her hands back into her lap. "Sorry!"

"Meera, maybe you need to explain what happened with the wild raek," Isbaen said softly from across the table.

Tearing her eyes from Shael, she found everyone staring at her with a mixture of apprehension and fascination. Her heart was bouncing off the walls of her chest in agitation, her head throbbed, and she felt like she would come undone from the pressure of everything. She looked back at Shael, who saw her distress. Putting her mother's ring down on the table in front of her, he took her hand in his, squeezing but not as hard as she had. Then he gave her a small smile and said, "Start at the beginning."

Meera nodded and calmed, staring into his eyes. She took a drink of water to douse some of the heat building in her body, and she explained: "I met the wild raek in the mountains. We sheltered under the same overhang during a storm, in which we were both injured. I helped her the next morning—I removed slivers of rock from her tongue and foot. She returned the favor by finding me later that day and giving me water. Then she sheltered me at night and helped me walk down the mountain."

"Wait," interjected Katrea. "A wild raek let you approach her when she was injured?" She sounded completely incredulous.

Meera shrugged. It was what had happened.

"Meera has a way with raeken," Shael said, giving her hand another squeeze. Meera squeezed back and felt bad for not sharing that part of the story with him when he had found her.

"Please continue, Meera," said Hadjal with a look to Katrea. Hadjal was sitting at the edge of her seat, clearly eager to hear the rest of the strange tale.

"Well," Meera continued, "the rest you saw ... sort of. The raek came here to see me. She showed me ... a lot of things. She showed me a feud that used to exist between raeken and humans. She showed me the first rider—the human, Aegwren—and his raek, Isabael."

At that, Florean snorted, "Aegwren was not a human, girl! What nonsense are you spewing?"

Meera looked around at the riders, most of whom looked like they agreed with Florean, though with less animosity. "No," she said, trying to remain calm. "Aegwren was a human. All of the earliest riders were because, once, there were only humans and no knell. The wild raek showed me how living close to raeken changed the humans over time, gave them magic and longer lives. Knell come from humans," she insisted. Looking to Shael, who appeared just as shocked and conflicted as everyone else, she wished she could show them what she had seen, but she couldn't. She didn't have any proof.

She wasn't sure if she should continue, at first, since she seemed to have lost her audience, but her father chirped, "What a fascinating bit of history! What else did the raek tell you?"

Meera took another drink of water. "She told me that the wild raeken have been struggling to breed. They normally migrate to the mountains north of Terratelle, but they haven't been able to since the war broke out and Terratellen soldiers started persecuting raeken." She paused, but no one looked ready to question this bit of information, so she continued, hesitantly:

"She ... said she had never considered taking a rider before, but she felt she needed one to help her end the war for the sake of all wild raeken. She asked me to be her rider and offered me the lifespan and physical abilities of the knell in exchange ..." Meera trailed off and looked around her at the disbelief on everyone's faces. Then she felt the need to add, "That's why I was in the fire. I was ... changing."

She looked at Shael with her heart in her throat. Shael lifted her hand between them and positioned both of their hands, so they were sitting with their palms together. Then he pushed against her palm, first lightly, then with increasing strength. Catching on to his test, Meera grinned and started to push back, glad to finally flex her new knell muscles. It wasn't just her arm that felt the strain as she and Shael went hand-to-hand; every muscle in her body tensed to keep her in her seated position.

"Do not break my chairs," Hadjal warned them as they both started to tremble.

Meera laughed and pulled her hand away, "I give!"

Shael smiled, but there was something sad in his smile. "You will be stronger than me with training."

Meera smiled back but didn't know what to say.

Soleille saved her from responding: "Can I scan you?" she asked. This time, Meera agreed, and she stayed still while Soleille held out her hands in a circle and peered through them at her body. "She looks human but feels knell," Soleille concluded, looking amazed.

Isbaen leaned forward with intrigue and proceeded to ask her a lot of questions about her senses, which Meera answered as best she could. Then Sodhu wanted to hear more about the scenes the wild raek—her raek—had shown her. Even Florean wanted a physical description of Aegwren and Isabael. The riders couldn't argue with Meera's changed body and seemed to accept it as proof of all her claims. She tried to be patient with their curiosity, but she kept noticing her mother's ring on the table in front of her. All she really cared about in that moment was what Shael thought and whether he still wanted to marry her.

Meera made eye contact with her father, and it occurred to her to wonder what he would think of her hasty life-choice. She grimaced at him, but he smiled in return. "It will be a gift to me to never have to watch my daughter grow old," Orson said quietly. "And I am glad to know you will always have the riders as your family."

Meera nodded at her father, but her throat constricted, knowing that she would still have to watch him grow old and die.

"New riders must be approved by Darreal and her council," Florean reminded them. "They barely accepted Shael, so I cannot imagine they will accept a human as one of the Riders of Levisade." Meera might have been offended, except Florean sounded more matter-of-fact than scathing.

"Riders are also usually presented to the council with their raeken," added Soleille, pointing out that Meera's supposed raek hadn't been seen in three weeks.

Meera shrugged; they were all getting ahead of her. What did she care what Darreal's council might think of her? Shael had proposed! Finally, she couldn't wait any longer. She picked up the ring and turned toward Shael, holding it out in front of her. "Do you still want to marry me or not?" she asked, more aggressively than she meant to.

"Was that a proposal?" Shael asked with a twitch of his lips. "Because mine was better."

Meera laughed. "Was it? I had a mouthful of food!"

Shael took the ring from her and knelt back down on the ground with a smile. Clearing his throat with playful drama that was rather unlike him, he said, "Rider Meera, I have taken your new lifespan into consideration and would still like to spend my life with you. Will you marry me?"

Blood rushed to Meera's face when she said, "Yes!" and let Shael slip the ring onto her finger. Then he stood up enough to cup one of her flaming cheeks and kiss her in front of everyone. His kiss was soft and gentle and lasted a moment longer than she might have thought was appropriate considering their audience, but everyone at the table clapped and congratulated them, even Florean.

Isbaen looked especially joyful and came around the table to hug Shael. Meera was extremely happy but also embarrassed, and she grinned and averted her eyes through most of the congratulating. Then her father rose and hugged her and Shael in one embrace, which made her laugh. And when she saw that her father had tears in his crinkly eyes, she felt her own eyes sting.

Sodhu went into the house and returned with bottles of fruity knell wine and chocolates for them to celebrate. Meera avoided the knell wine which—judging from her father's reaction—was stronger than human wine, but she was glad to indulge in some sweets after going so long without any. The whole time they ate and laughed, she kept gazing at Shael and down at the ring on her hand. She felt like everything in her life was falling into place at once; she had her father back, she was a rider with a new purpose, and she was going to marry the man she loved.

Glancing at Linus's bracelet on her wrist, she stroked the cool purple beads. She wasn't sure she had any right to be so happy. Shael caught the gesture and took her hand in his. Meera loved the feeling of his large, strong hand around hers, right there in the open in front of everyone. She intertwined her fingers with his and felt a jolt in her stomach when he rubbed his thumb along the sensitive skin between her thumb and pointer finger.

As they all celebrated, their late lunch morphed into an early dinner, and Meera was surprised when the sun began to lower in the sky. "Will you move back in with me?" Shael asked her.

"Well, sure. That's part of being married," she said, but she immediately regretted her words—Shael had already shared one aspect of marriage he would not partake in.

"Yes," he replied patiently, "But will you move back in with me now? Tonight?"

"Oh!" Meera exclaimed, shocked. She knew everyone was listening to them, and she glanced at her father with uncertainty, wondering how much knell culture he could handle and whether he would feel abandoned if she left their cabin so suddenly.

Orson had his arm around Florean's shoulder and was telling him about the organizational system in the Altus Grand Library in slurred words. Florean actually looked amused. Her father didn't appear to have heard Shael's question, so Meera called, "Father, is it alright with you if I move back in with Shael?"

Orson squinted at her down the table, swayed, hiccupped loudly, then yelled, "Don't waste any time! Go! Love is precious!" The word "precious" came out slurred and prolonged.

Meera stifled a laugh. Then she turned back to Shael, who had had half a glass of knell wine and looked more relaxed and rosy-cheeked than usual. "I'll ... go and pack," she said, and she rose from the table. She trailed her hand across his shoulders as she walked behind him and headed for the cabin to retrieve her few possessions. This was happening, she thought; she was a rider, and she was going to marry Shael. She practically skipped once she was out of sight of the others.

5

SHAEL

Shael felt like he was glowing from the inside out. After he had kissed Meera outside the cabin, and she had told him to make his choice, he had finally felt free to do what he wanted and not worry about doing what was best for others. He had finally realized that Meera's choice was her own, and if she was willing to live with their differences and his vow, then he could choose to do the same. And he had; he had sprinted home to change his clothes, repeatedly fingering the ring in the pouch at his waist. If Meera wanted it and Meera's father wanted it, then who was he to say *no* to his own happiness?

Shael had not hesitated to drop to his knee and profess his feelings for Meera in front of everyone. The riders were his family. For several long moments of painful doubt, he had not been sure she would say *yes*. He had thought maybe he had gone a step too far—that maybe she had wanted to be with him in more of a casual knell sense than a permanent human one.

Learning that she was a raek rider and now had the body and lifespan of a knell had far surpassed anything Shael had imagined when trying to puzzle out the pale flames encasing her the past three weeks. A small, bitter part of him did not like that she could be stronger than him—that she now had the body of a full-knell. But mostly, Shael rejoiced knowing that he would not have to watch Meera grow old and die far too soon. They could spend their long lives on the peninsula —together.

He smiled to himself and took another sip of the strong citrus wine that Sodhu had made. He did not usually allow himself to drink alcohol, but he was feeling especially light and free that day. Meera was alive, awake, and packing her belongings to move in with him. Realizing he was taking her back to his house and probably his bed, Shael pushed his glass away, resolved to keep his wits about him.

Isbaen came around the table and ushered him out into the field with him. He put an arm around Shael's shoulder, and Shael suspected his mentor had been enjoying Sodhu's wine more than usual as well. "I am so happy for you, Shael," he said, turning to him and kissing him on the cheek. It was more affection than Shael was comfortable with, but he managed not to cringe away and thanked his mentor and friend.

"How astounding is it—what Meera said? We are all descended from the same people, humans and knell alike. I imagine the knowledge brings you comfort now that you have put your vow aside," Isbaen said. Shael looked down uncomfortably, but even in his inebriated state, his mentor did not miss his look. "Have you not put your vow aside? You asked the woman to marry you—"

"I told her of my vow, Isbaen. She knows," Shael assured him, hoping they could never discuss the subject again.

Isbaen's joyful expression evaporated from his handsome face. "You know, Meera is also something between human and knell now. You two are the same in that way, as your children would be," he said in an even voice.

Shael sighed in exasperation. He did not want to talk about his future children with Meera because they would not have future children. "Meera is as good as full-knell, and I am still a half-breed. That will never change," he answered with finality.

Isbaen nodded sadly and gestured behind Shael where Meera was approaching them across the field. "I wish you both every happiness," he said before drifting away toward the lake. Shael looked after his mentor, wondering if Isbaen—in part—resented Shael's happiness because of his inability to find his own. Then he dismissed the thought; Isbaen was not nearly as weak-minded as he was.

Shael walked toward Meera just as the golden light of the setting sun spilled over the grassy field. Her bag was slung across her body, and her hair had dried and was bouncing wildly around her shoulders. The gold sunlight brought even more warmth to her glowing skin and rich, brown eyes. She was so beautiful.

The wine in Shael's stomach was souring after his talk with Isbaen. Was he condemning Meera by marrying her? Did she deserve more than him—more than half-a-man, one way or the other? He reminded himself that he was her choice, and she had a right to choose her own path in life. He should be grateful, he told himself. Still, Meera met him with a wide smile he found he could not return. Reaching out, he took her bag from her. She was strong now, but he would still carry her bags; he was still that much of a man.

"Do you want to walk or fly?" he asked. He wondered whether it would be appropriate for her to fly on Cerun's back with him since she—ostensibly—had a raek of her own to ride.

"Let's walk," she replied.

As one, they turned toward the path leading to Shael's house in familiar habit, and Shael could not help but wonder if he was leading Meera to a doomed future. He felt certain of his feelings. He even believed that she loved him—but how much? She had only known him for a matter of months and was pledging herself to him for hundreds of years. He would not make her stay, of course, if she were ever unhappy, but humans committed to marriage forever ... What if she felt obligated to stay? What if she grew to want children and resented him? What if she did not want to be a thousand-year-old virgin and hated him for his vow?

They walked the path in silence. While plenty of light filtered in through the leaves above from the setting sun, Shael felt like a dark mass was pressing down on him from above. He bent his head under its weight and could only focus on the dirt in front of his feet. He saw Meera watching him in his peripheral vision and knew he should say something—should snap himself out of his spiraling mood—but he could not.

Finally, she grabbed his arm and forced him to stop with more strength than she probably meant to use. "What's wrong?" she asked, putting her hands on either side of his face and gazing up at him. She made him look at her, and the warmth and love in her brown eyes steadied him. Still, he did not answer. "Shael, talk to me. What's going on? Do you feel okay?"

Her hands on his face were so soft, and her voice so full of concern and love. Shael inhaled a deep, shuddering breath. He could smell her lavender hair oil and the chocolate she had eaten. He dropped her bag on the path beside him and reached out and touched one of her curls, letting it coil around his finger. "I want you to be happy," he said. "I do not want to mess this up."

Meera raised her eyebrows and gave him a look reminiscent of one of her eye rolls without actually rolling her eyes. He quirked a smile at her poor attempt at restraint. "I *am* happy. Why don't you try looking less like you're walking to your doom? Aren't ... *you* happy?" she asked, suddenly looking uncertain. Her hands dropped from his face.

"I am only happy when I am with you," Shael answered with feeling, which only made Meera scrunch her eyebrows, looking more concerned.

"Then what's wrong?" she asked, her voice raising.

"I want you to be happy," Shael tried to explain again. "I do not want to ruin your life."

"Okay ..." Meera bit her bottom lip, which succeeded in drawing all of Shael's focus to that spot and making him want to bite that lip. He scrubbed a hand across his face. He should not have had any wine; he needed to get control of himself.

"Why do you think you're going to ruin my life? You asked me to marry you, and I said yes and now ... You're the one who seems unhappy," she said. She crossed her arms over her chest and took a very slight step backward, drawing away from him. Her eyes had a tell-tale sheen like she was holding back tears.

Shael hated that he did this to her—made her question his feelings with his erratic behavior. He needed to do better—to be better. He needed to communicate more and express himself more. He needed to open his damn mouth before Meera turned and ran back to the peninsula. "I'm—I am worried that you will resent me for my vow," he said at last, breathing like the admission had overtaken him in a race.

"Oh ..." she replied, dropping her arms to her side.

"I still plan to uphold my vow if we get married," he explained.

"*When* we get married," she corrected, which made him smile.

"When we get married," he amended.

"Shael, can you just assume I'm happy unless I say otherwise?" she asked, stepping toward him and putting her hands on his waist.

"I will try," he told her, placing his hands on her upper arms and releasing a breath along with some of his pent tension.

"Okay ... so, do you want me to stay in my old room?" she asked in a small voice, looking up at him with big, round eyes that made the muscles in his chest tighten painfully.

"No," he whispered in a puff of air against her lips as he bent down and kissed her, slowly and gently. He took his time, just enjoying the feel of her soft lips against his. Meera wrapped her slim hands behind his back and trailed her fingers along his spine —making him tingle and shiver—and he ran his own hands up and down the side of her neck, feeling her swirling scar under his left fingertips. He traced the swirls to where they disappeared under her shirt. Then he pulled away from their kiss and hugged her to his chest. He did not want to rush her into anything. If they were to have a lifetime together, they had plenty of time.

Meera hugged around his middle and pressed her face into his sternum. Shael kissed the top of her head and breathed in her lavender scent. "So ... where is the line?" she asked in a voice muffled by his shirt.

"The line?" he asked. He tried to look down at her, but she kept her face obstinately pressed into his chest. He was not sure what she was asking.

"You want me in your bed, and you don't want to break your vow. I ... don't want to do something wrong," she said into his shirt.

Shael could feel her heartbeat accelerating as she spoke. He froze for a second—processing—then he clutched her tighter to him. He had shared his fears about his vow, and now she was sharing hers. "There are still plenty of things we can do without ... the full act," he assured her, "And you could not do anything wrong." He had the disconcerting feeling Meera was burrowing into his abdomen, she held onto him so tightly.

"You sure?" She asked in a quiet, muffled voice.

"Yes," he replied with a laugh. "But you do need to learn your new strength," he said, gently loosening her arms around his middle.

Meera popped away from him. "Oops!" she said. It was starting to get dark, but he could still see the color flushing her cheeks.

Knowing that Meera was imagining them returning to his bed was enough for Shael to want to give her a demonstration. He had been admiring her curves for months and wondering what they would feel like. Putting both of his hands low on her hips, he pulled her toward him. Then he bent and took her full lower lip between his, sucking it and nibbling it where he had seen her bite earlier. Meera responded instantly with her hands on his chest, gripping his shirt where her face had been. She opened her mouth to him and met his tongue with her own, flooding him with desire.

Pushing one hand under her shirt and up her back, Shael ran his fingers along her spine until she shivered as she had done to him. Then his other hand roamed from her hip down over the curve of her butt cheek and grasped it firmly, pulling her against him, thigh-to-thigh. Meera made a small sound at his touch and put one of her hands in his hair, keeping his face down where she could reach him and kissing him with passionate abandon.

Her other hand remained on his chest over his heart, no doubt feeling it thump ever harder at her touch. Shael was losing himself to sensation. His eyes were closed, and all he knew was Meera. The forest around them disappeared, and all that mattered in the whole world was the woman pressed against him. He wanted to tell her he loved her, but his lips moved of their own accord—kissing and tasting.

Suddenly, he felt intense heat against his chest and flinched back, reflexively snatching Meera's wrist with his hand. He opened his eyes just in time to see pale flames dancing along the length of her palm. His gaze rose to find fear and horror in her eyes. "Wha—are you okay?" she stammered, stepping back from him.

Shael released his grip on her wrist. Looking down at his chest, he found a hand-shaped singe mark on his shirt. He pushed open the front of his shirt and saw a red handprint on his chest. He was only very slightly burned. "I'm okay," he said, shaken. He could not help but stare at Meera's offensive hand.

"Wha—what was that?" she asked, starting to tremble and looking heartbreakingly innocent with her big, brown eyes stretched wide.

"Shhh, it is okay," Shael said, rubbing his hands along her upper arms. "You ... have fire magic, Meera." He only registered the fact as he said it. For a moment, he had to look away from her to hide his jealousy—his weakness. Meera would become stronger than him with training, and she would be able to shape fire, a rare gift. Then he hugged her to his chest and stroked her back comfortingly.

Meera did not hug him in return; she kept her hands clenched in fists out to the sides like they might explode. Choking out a small laugh, she looked up at him. "And you said I couldn't do anything wrong," she said with a wry smile.

6

MEERA

Meera tried to laugh off this latest development, but fire coming out of her body felt like more than she could handle. Breaking away from Shael, she stared at his chest where she had burned him. "I thought knell shaped what already existed. Why is the fire coming out of me?" she asked in confusion. She was starting to shake—overwhelmed by all the changes in her life that day—and she realized, completely exhausted.

"I suppose you ignited the air along your hand," Shael replied, bending down to retrieve her bag from the path. "Come on," he said, beckoning her. "You need some sleep." He put a gentle hand on her back and propelled her forward down the quickly darkening path.

Meera continued to shake and fret about her new ability. She wanted to ask Shael more about shaping, but he didn't seem inclined to talk about it. She knew he resented his inability to shape like the other riders, and she didn't want to make him uncomfortable by asking him questions he couldn't answer. So, they walked in silence while her mind reeled—trying to digest that she could do magic.

She could shape! Somehow, Meera had readily accepted that she would be faster and stronger and live longer but had not considered that she might actually be able to shape. She wondered what she would be able to do with some training and hoped she would be able to do something other than make fire. Why fire? She would gladly have a water ability like Hadjal or be able to heal people like Soleille. Why did she have to have fire abilities? Fire was so destructive ... She tried to reassure herself; she told herself that a fire ability would have kept her warm in the Forest of Shayan. But she knew that if she couldn't control it properly, she could raze a forest to the ground or hurt someone.

Meera glanced at Shael, whose face was stony with thought. "I'm sorry, Shael," she said quietly. Great, she thought; now she was the one making vague apologies. She wasn't even sure why she was apologizing—for hurting him, sure, but really, she felt like she was apologizing for more than that. She would gladly give him her fire shaping ability if she could; she certainly didn't want it.

Shael didn't say anything, but he reached out and rubbed his large, comforting hand across her back once more. Then he leaned toward her and kissed her temple, and she couldn't help but smile up at him. When they reached the house, Meera felt like she was returning home. She had missed the familiar pine scent of the floorboards, and the kitchen and reading nook looked the same as when she had last seen them. Exhaling, she released some of her anxiety, but when she returned her gaze to Shael, she tensed once more.

He was standing in the middle of the floor between their bedrooms, holding her bag and looking questioningly at her. She glanced toward his room, but then she looked down at her hands, one of which bore her mother's ring. She stared at the ring; it gave her butterflies just looking at it on her finger and knowing that Shael wanted to be with her. She wanted to be with him, too—she wanted to follow him into his bedroom and never sleep anywhere else, but ... She didn't want to hurt him again. Meera didn't understand what had happened when her hand had flared and felt too tired and overwhelmed to trust herself. The next day, the other riders could help her learn to control her abilities. Then she would be safe to be around. Until then ...

"I think I should stay in my old room—for tonight," she said, looking sheepish.

He nodded, walked over to her, and held out her bag. She took it, but she didn't move away; she just stared down at her bag, incapable of dragging herself away from Shael. She felt unsettled like there was something unspoken between them, but she wasn't sure what it was. "I just don't want to hurt you," she whispered, peering into his face for understanding and reassurance.

"I know," he said, giving her a small smile that didn't reach his eyes.

"Okay ... goodnight, then," she said, shifting on her feet but still not moving away. Twiddling her mother's ring with her thumb, she wished Shael would at least ask her to stay with him. Then she wondered if he was glad to have his bed to himself. Maybe he was just tired from three weeks of waiting for her to wake up, she thought; he did look tired. Or maybe he didn't want to be burned alive in his sleep, she considered, grimacing inwardly.

Meera finally moved, but instead of going to her room, she stepped forward until her head rested against Shael's collarbone. She pressed a kiss to the base of his neck, careful not to put her hands near him, and she turned and walked into her old room. If he said goodnight, she didn't hear him. After placing her mother's ring reverently on her dresser, she took her time undressing, bathing, and putting her nightgown on. She was exhausted but also jittery, and she hoped the routine would calm her enough to sleep.

However, when she finally turned out the light and crawled into bed, she just lay there, thoughts spinning and new knell muscles screaming for movement. She tossed back and forth and adjusted her pillows repeatedly, but nothing made her comfortable—nothing eased the strain in her mind. Finally, she couldn't stand it anymore; she got out of bed, left her room, and padded noiselessly across the house to Shael's door. It was slightly ajar, and light spilled through the crack. Meera leaned her head against the doorframe and peeked inside to see Shael sitting up in bed with a book in his lap.

"Are you really reading, or are you just pretending?" she asked quietly, knowing he could hear her with his knell senses.

"Pretending," he said, quirking a smile at her over his book.

"Well, you're doing a good job. It's right side up and everything," she replied, glancing at the cover of the book he held.

He closed it and put it down on the table next to him. "Are you coming in?" he asked.

Meera loitered on the dark side of the doorframe, suddenly aware that she wasn't wearing much of anything. She tried not to dwell on the fact that she had been naked in her flaming cocoon for three weeks as well as when Shael had pulled her from the lake that morning. But she wasn't overly self-conscious, all bodies had their flaws and peculiarities—human bodies especially.

After a moment, she said, "I don't know ... Do you have water buckets and sandbags just in case?" continuing to lean against the doorframe and drumming her fingers on the solid wood. She knew she probably shouldn't go in, but she also knew she wouldn't sleep otherwise.

"No," Shael replied, "But I have a friend who is a good healer." He reached across the bed and flipped up the covers to his right in invitation. His torso was bare, and she could still see the red hand-print on his chest—a glaring sign that she should go back to her own room. When he moved, she also saw that he was wearing pants, which must be for her since he normally slept naked. His dark hair was loose on his shoulders and fell just past his collar-bones. Meera ignored the sign.

She pushed open the door timidly. Her own hair was loose and fell over the front of her nightgown, giving her some sense of modesty. Walking into the room, she stepped around to what was apparently her side of the bed. Shael's bed was plenty big enough for both of them, at least twice as wide as the small one in her room. He watched her with a predatory gaze as she circled and climbed onto it. Then she sat against the pillows and faced him, wishing he would stop staring at her or turn out his lamp. However, in true Shael fashion, he remained stone-still and silent.

"I couldn't sleep in the other room," she said, breaking the silence.

"If you came here to sleep, you should cover up," he said quietly, his eyes roving over her. "That is my favorite nightgown."

Blood rushed to Meera's cheeks, and she squirmed, resisting the urge to pull the covers over herself. "This is my only night-gown," she said with a nervous laugh.

"I have fond memories of it," he replied with molten desire in his eyes.

Meera swallowed. She remembered the last time she was in Shael's bed in her nightgown as well, but she didn't remember that night with much fondness. She remembered him looking up at her and pulling away. Her thoughts must have shown on her face because he reached out and smoothed a finger down her cheek, frowning. "I love you, Meera," he said.

She nodded in a combination of agreement and acceptance.

"Do you want to sleep?" he asked.

She shrugged then shook her head. The movements made her full, unbound breasts sway under the thin fabric of her gown, and she saw Shael's eyes flicker down to them. Then she scooted closer to him on the bed until their legs touched under the covers. "My hands aren't safe," she whispered, feeling her heart flutter in anticipation. He shrugged, making the muscles of his chest and shoulders flex. The red handprint stared at Meera in warning, but she ignored it.

Tucking her hands behind her back, she smiled up at Shael expectantly. He leaned toward her and kissed her softly, his hair tickling her cheeks. Meera wanted to reach out and run her fingers through it, but she couldn't. So, instead, she nudged open his lips and slipped her tongue in his mouth, reaching out to him another way. Shael responded with vigor, kissing her until she gasped for breath and running his hands up and down the sides of her body.

When his hands landed on her hips, he gripped them hard and tugged, jerking Meera's butt out from under her, so she rolled onto her back. Squealing and laughing, she flopped back on the soft bed. But she quickly stopped laughing when Shael hovered the length of his body over her, bracing his weight on his forearms. His dark hair fell forward like curtains on either side of her face, and Meera looked up into his eyes. They were grey in the light, and she felt like she could lie there forever staring into them.

Shael was still for several long moments, just gazing at her with a mix of hunger and love. Then he reached one hand out of sight and gently encircled her wrist, dragging her hand up over her head and holding it there. Meera smiled and lay perfectly still while his other hand retrieved her free wrist and dragged that one above her head as well. She still longed to touch him, but she wanted him to be safe and was enjoying letting him be in control.

Shael leaned his head down and kissed her with the tantalizing push and pull that made her want more. His tongue darted in and out of her mouth, making her squirm, but her wrists were trapped in his gentle grip. Finally, he gave her the contact she desired, lowering the weight of his body down onto her. His legs rested between hers, and she felt his erection press against her through their thin layers of clothing. Drawing in her feet, she lifted her hips and angled her sensitive crux into his hardness. Then she moaned as he started to rock up and down her body with the rhythm of his kisses.

Meera was a tangle of sensation; she writhed against Shael's body, sure he could feel her wetness through their clothes. Arching her back, she pressed her breasts to his chest and delighted at the feeling of his muscled body brushing her nipples through her gown. She didn't think she would ever get enough of his mouth on hers and kissed him with a frenzied passion that would leave her swollen later. Her heart pumped burning heat through her veins, and all she could think was that she wanted more.

Shael shifted his position, putting both of her wrists in one of his hands. He traced his other hand down her arm and along the side of her body. Knowing where he was going, she shuddered in anticipation, and as his hand skimmed her hip, she suddenly felt hot—too hot. Meera jerked against Shael's hands and cried incoherently into his lips, but she was too late—she burst into pale flame on her abdomen. Shael was quick to snatch his hand away from the fire but not quite as fast to remove his body from on top of hers.

He wrenched away from her with a strangled cry and tumbled across the bed onto the floor a moment before Meera leapt to her feet and away from the flammable materials of the bed. Standing in the center of the room, she gaped down at herself as her night-gown was quickly devoured and only bluish white flames were left dancing in its place. Even though she couldn't feel the heat of flames, seeing her body encased in fire made her heart leap and panic set in. She let out a low keening cry, and her fire spread further down her limbs.

Linus's bracelet was in its usual place on her left wrist, and its leather strap snapped the second the fire touched it, spraying tinkling glass beads across the pine floorboards. Meera looked at the floor and breathed faster and faster, knowing the fire was spreading down her legs and would soon touch the wood beneath her, igniting the house. Shael was standing in front of her, staring with wide eyes that reflected the bright, flickering flames. "Meera, slow your breathing!" he shouted. "You're okay! You just need to calm down. Breathe! In-two-three, Out-two-three."

She listened and closed her eyes to block out the fire encasing her, breathing and counting out each breath until she reached seven seconds of exhale.

"It's okay," Shael said quietly. "The fire is gone."

Meera opened her eyes and blinked, trying to disperse the streaks left on her vision from staring at the flames. Looking down at her naked body, she sighed to see that she was unharmed. But she shook all over with emotion and exhaustion, and when she looked at Shael, a sob rose in her throat; his bare abdomen was marred by an angry red burn that had melted some of the flesh of his stomach. She gaped at what she had done and shook her head back and forth, choking on her heaving breaths.

She had hurt Shael. Once again, she had wrought pain and destruction with her selfish stupidity. Meera grabbed reflexively for her bracelet, thinking of Linus, and finding her wrist bare of her friend's beads, she whimpered, her tears starting to flow. She destroyed everything! She ruined everything! Even with a strong knell body, she was completely, utterly useless. Her legs gave under her, and she crumpled to the floor, clutching her shins and hiding her face in her knees. Holding her wrists with an iron grip, she contained her demonic body in a small cell.

"Meera," Shael said, walking toward her and putting his hand on her shoulder.

"Don't touch me!" She cried, jerking away from him.

"Everything is okay," he said. She thought it was one of his more blatant lies.

Then, realizing that Shael was hurt, and she was the one crying on the floor, she begrudgingly released her wrists and stood on wobbling legs, too exhausted to care that she was completely naked. "I'll get Soleille," she said, glancing at Shael's burn and moving toward the door.

7

SHAEL

Shael stepped in front of Meera and blocked her path, holding up his hands. She looked like she was going to collapse—like an errant breeze might overwhelm her trembling limbs and entirely uproot her. The burn on his stomach stretched and seared with his movements, but he had experienced pain before; he could live with this pain until morning.

"No, Meera," he said softly. "It can wait. You need rest." He wanted to scoop her into his arms and place her back in the bed, but he feared touching her—he worried it might upset her enough for her to flare up again. A bead of sweat trickled down his forehead from the heat left over from her flames.

"I—no, but I ..." Meera stammered and swayed. Shael took a step closer in case he needed to catch her. "What's wrong with me?" she asked in a high-pitched voice he had never heard from her before.

His chest ached to see her so upset. He wished he could hold her or knew what to say to comfort her. "Nothing. You need rest," he said. "Come to bed." Stepping toward the bed, he beckoned her over.

Meera shook her head but followed even as she resisted, and Shael waited for her to climb up and covered her in blankets before lying down beside her—on top of the covers. He felt hot and clammy, either from the now extinguished fire or from his injury. Rolling slowly onto his side—careful not to brush his burn against anything—he very gently stroked her hair. Meera continued to shake, but it was not long before her breathing slowed, and she fell into a deep sleep.

Shael took longer to fall asleep; his burn nagged at him, but louder still, was the voice in his head saying that this was not working—that every time he got near Meera, he caused her pain. He wanted her to be happy, but he could not give her a full marriage, nor could he defend himself against her shaping.

Cerun was quietly monitoring his mind. At Shael's initial burst of pain and panic—when Meera had ignited beneath him—his raek had all but ripped open the side of the house to save him from an unknown attacker. Shael had shown Cerun what was happening and assured him that it was only Meera, but the raek was only partially mollified. "Human Meera may not wish to cause you harm, but that does not make her any less dangerous," he said, distracting Shael from his worries.

"She is asleep now," he assured his friend in irritation. "She will not create fire in her sleep." Even as Shael doubted their relationship in his head, he felt the need to defend it outwardly.

"You do not know that," Cerun chided, raising Shael's temper.

"Must you remind me of my inadequacies?" Shael pressed back. He already knew that he could not shape and would never truly understand magic without Cerun reminding him.

"I will continue to remind you if it is necessary to keep you safe," his raek retorted, fighting back against Shael's anger more than usual.

Shael could sense a swirling kernel of uneasiness in Cerun's mind that did not usually exist. "What's wrong?" he asked, startled and forgetting to modify his human speech tendencies.

His raek grumbled mentally and gave Shael a nudge away from the kernel of thought, clearly trying to hide something from him. This completely unnerved Shael. "What?" he asked more forcefully, threatening with a flash of images to go outside and make Cerun tell him.

"You know I wanted you and Human Meera to be mates. I thought it would be good for you ..." Cerun started, making Shael dread where he was heading.

"But?" he asked, reluctantly.

"I think this will only hurt you," Cerun admitted.

"Meera will learn to control her shaping," Shael replied.

"That is not what I mean, and you know it."

Shael's temper rose again. "You are only jealous because I have someone new in my life! Do not forget, I once had to share you with Meera, so you have no right to feel slighted," he said angrily. He knew that was not how Cerun was feeling—he was in his raek's mind, after all—but he did not wish to acknowledge Cerun's actual concerns in case there was any truth in them.

Cerun did not bother to respond; he knew Shael was too upset to be reasoned with and would only continue lashing out. Shael sensed his raek's resignation and felt embarrassed by his own shortcomings. Then Cerun soothed Shael's mind until he fell into a shallow sleep that was disrupted whenever he forgot his injury and moved, causing his burn to scream and sear. In those moments, he took comfort in Meera's warm shape next to him and in her even breathing.

THE NEXT MORNING, Shael awoke to Meera jerking bolt upright in
bed. "Are you okay?" she asked. She had apparently received the
rest she needed and remembered the events of the previous night.

"Yes," he said, rubbing his eyes before regarding her. She sat in
the bed next to him with the covers pulled up to her neck like he
had not already seen her naked breasts many times, and he slowly
raised to a seat, careful not to grunt or grimace with her watching.

"It's really bad!" she exclaimed, staring at him with round eyes.
"We should go to Soleille! I'll get dressed." With that, she rose
from the bed and scampered toward the door, clearly trying to
pretend her nudity didn't bother her.

Shael smirked as he watched her go. Then he grimaced with
pain as he swung his legs down from the bed and stood. He went
to the washroom before putting on fresh pants, but he held the
accompanying shirt in his hand, unwilling to let the fabric rub
against his burn. He waited in the small kitchen.

Meera appeared shortly thereafter, clothed with her hair
thrown in a messy bun on top of her head. Shael's eyes trailed
lovingly over her, wondering if she would let him touch her on
this new day. Then his gaze snagged on her bare left hand.
"Where is your ring?" he asked, already thinking the worst—that
one night with him had been enough for her.

She touched her naked finger. "Oh, well I don't want to … melt
it or anything. It's too important," she replied.

"Right," Shael said, nodding his understanding. Meera kept
looking at his stomach, and he was doing his best to act like it did
not hurt. It did.

"Walk or fly?" she asked, already moving toward the door,
looking anxious.

"Walk," he replied. He did not think walking would hurt as

much as climbing onto Cerun's back, and he was still trying hard to ignore his raek's concerns from the previous night—his own concerns as well.

Together, they left the house and started down the path toward the peninsula. Meera walked furiously, clearly desperate to get to Soleille even though a few extra minutes would not cause Shael any further damage. He reached out and took her hand to slow her down, but she yanked it out of his grasp like she was the one burned. "Sorry," she said, slowing and looking into his face. "I just don't want to hurt you ... any more than I already have, that is."

"I will be fine, Meera. Slow down. I want to have a nice walk with my betrothed," he said.

She smiled at that, and some of the darkness cleared from her troubled eyes. But even as Shael smiled down at her, the darkness returned, creasing her brows and gnawing her lip. "I didn't ... pressure you into that, did I?" she asked. "I didn't mean ... I mean, when I told you it was your choice, I didn't mean that you had to propose."

Shael looked into Meera's troubled face and wondered if he had somehow pressured her into agreeing to marry him. Was she trying to get out of it? Already? She had seemed willing enough, but ... maybe she wanted a relationship but not a promise for forever. Had he pushed her by asking her in front of everyone? "I want to marry you, Meera, but if it is not what you want—" he started to say, the words hurting more than his burn.

"I do! I do want to marry you! You just seemed so uncertain one second and were down on one knee the next ... When did you ask my father for the ring, anyway?" she asked.

Shael ducked his head. He did not wish to tell her that he had not gone to her father for the ring, but he did not want to lie to her either. He was silent for several long moments.

"Wait ..." she said, "When *did* you ask my father for the ring? He was at the table when I arrived, and you showed up with the ring a little while later. But if you had known you wanted to marry me, why were you so undecided outside the cabin?" Meera stopped in the path and turned to him, confusion written in the soft curves of her face.

Shael did not want to answer; he did not want to hurt her and cause her to doubt his feelings for her. He had done that enough already. Instead, he leaned down and kissed her frowning mouth, ignoring the pain the movement caused his burn. It was a light, chaste kiss. He did not wish to inflame Meera in the literal sense. She kissed him back, then pulled a breath away. "Shael, you need to start using your words, not just your lips."

"Are you sure?" he asked with a devilish smile, and he dared to kiss her again, deeper this time.

Meera groaned against his lips before breaking away, laughing. "Yes, I'm sure," she said with an eye roll. Then she waited for him to answer her question.

He looked away from her eyes and studied the silver scar swirling up her neck. No matter how many times he looked at it, he could never quite memorize every groove and curve of the raek fire scar left on her from Cerun's flames. "Your father gave me the ring after you woke up yesterday—after we emerged from the lake," he said evenly, watching her process the information.

Her face and eyes went uncharacteristically blank. "Oh," she said. "He just ... gave it to you?"

"He said he could see that we love each other and gave it to me so that I could take care of you and make you happy. That is all I want," Shael replied, reaching out a finger and stroking her still cheek. She smiled at him, but a crease formed between her eyes in the same instant. He sighed. He did not know how to prove his love to Meera; he seemed to always hurt her.

"Let's go," she said, reaching out and squeezing his hand before remembering herself and pulling away.

They walked in silence, and when they arrived at the peninsula, Hadjal, Sodhu, and Isbaen were having breakfast. As they approached the table, all three of them looked up with smiles that quickly evaporated. "Shael, what happened?" Isbaen asked, standing from his chair and stepping toward him to inspect his wound.

"It was me!" Meera declared before Shael could respond. Her statement halted Isbaen in his tracks, who looked uncharacteristically startled. His widened eyes somehow made him look younger and even more handsome.

"What do you mean?" Hadjal asked, getting up and taking control of the situation.

"Where does Soleille live?" Meera asked, ignoring the question. She was looking around anxiously.

Shael put a hand on her shoulder to calm her and to signal to the circling riders that Meera had not actually harmed him on purpose. "She will be here soon," he assured her. "I can wait."

She gave him a piercing look of annoyance. "You've waited all night, Shael! You've waited long enough. Where does she live?" she asked more forcefully.

"This happened last night?" Hadjal asked. "How?"

"I did it! It was me! Where does Soleille live?" Meera practically shouted at Hadjal, who looked affronted.

"Uh oh!" Came Soleille's voice from around the house. "Meera does not sound happy, Shael. You know, if you ever need advice about the female body—" she cut off when she saw Shael's stomach, ignoring the glaring look on his face. "What happened?" she asked. She and Katrea arrived together, both sweaty like they had gone for a run. Katrea barely regarded Shael before sitting down, picking up a roll, and biting into it. Soleille walked over to him but seemed to expect an explanation before she actually healed him.

"It—" he started to say, but Meera cut him off.

"It was me! Please heal him—he's been hurt all night," she pleaded.

Soleille looked startled, but she held her ground. "What do you mean it was you? Did you push him into a fire? Wait, was this kinky or something? I want details!" she cried. She was not only not in a hurry to heal Shael, but she sounded delighted at the prospect of new gossip.

Blood rushed to Meera's cheeks, and Shael managed to break his silence and go to her rescue for once. "It was an accident," he explained. "Meera can shape fire." At that, everyone looked shocked.

"Really?" Isbaen asked. "I did wonder if you would have shaping abilities."

"Did you get really angry while you were sitting next to a fire or something?" Soleille asked, still keen for details.

"Uh ... no," Meera replied.

Shael wondered when Soleille was actually going to heal him.

"Really?" Soleille asked. "It was anger for me the first time. I was outside hiding from my grandmother, and a bug kept buzzing in my ear and bothering me. I made it explode. It took me months to manage to shape at all afterward and years before I could consciously shape living things, but often our first bursts of magic come with strong emotions." Katrea nodded her head like she, too, had first shaped when she was angry.

"Fire is a rare ability," Isbaen told Meera. "With practice, you should be able to do some other shaping as well, of course."

Shael cleared his throat but was ignored.

"So, let me guess," Soleille said. "You lit some romantic

candles and got really nervous. Was that it? Humans always strike me as such nervous creatures."

Meera looked angry at that, and Shael thought if strong emotion could cause shaping outbursts then Soleille was asking for it. "Any chance you can heal me, Sol?" he asked, getting annoyed himself.

"Once you tell me exactly what happened," Soleille said with a smirk. "I need to know the details of the wound I am healing." She did not need to know the details, and they all knew it.

Shael glared at her. She was not looking at his face, though; rather, she was staring at his bare chest, and her lips parted suddenly. "Is that a handprint?" she asked, reaching out and touching Shael where a red hand-shaped mark still stood from Meera's first accidental shaping. Hadjal and Isbaen both stepped closer to see.

Meera looked so uncomfortable, Shael thought she might actually run away. Then, very quietly, she said, "First, we were kissing, and my hand burst into flame." She gestured at Shael's exposed chest. "Then ... later ... my stomach spouted flames, and they spread over most of my body." She looked embarrassed but also scared, he thought. "There was no fire—no candles or anything, I mean," she explained.

Shael realized then—as Meera clearly already had—that Soleille had expected there to be a source of fire for her to shape. He looked around at his fellow riders and saw confusion on their faces. "You made the fire?" Hadjal asked, sounding fascinated.

"I guess," Meera replied.

Hadjal merely hummed a note of intrigue in response.

Shael cleared his throat again.

"Sorry, Shael," Soleille said before placing a hand on his chest to shape him. He gritted his teeth through the usual itching, burning sensation of his skin healing and knitting back together.

Then Soleille dropped her hand to her side and looked down at his abdomen long enough to make him uncomfortable. He glanced down at himself, expecting to see smooth, unmarred skin. The handprint was gone from his chest, but the burn on his stomach had healed in a swath of silver swirls like the scar on Meera's neck.

8

MEERA

"No!" Meera gasped. "No! Please, Soleille! Please, you have to make it go away!" She stared at the scar on Shael's stomach and brought her hands to the sides of her head. She couldn't breathe. She couldn't stand to look at what she'd done, but she couldn't look away either; she had left a permanent mark of pain and violence on Shael—Shael, who she loved, who had already been through too much. The torture he had suffered had been wiped away with magic, but she could not be—her mark stuck. He would live with her scar forever—for hundreds and hundreds of years, he would look down and know she had hurt him.

Her vision blurred, and she swayed. Was she breathing? She didn't think she was breathing. Forcing in a ragged gasp of air, she tried not to immediately sob it back out. Then she became aware of the other riders staring at her, and she tried to regain control of herself. But were they looking at her with concern or fear? She clutched a hand to her chest and doubled over. Shael stepped toward her and reached out.

"No, Shael!" said Hadjal, sharply. "Do not touch her when her emotions are high."

She was a monster, Meera thought. She was a monster who wrought pain and destruction, and now they all knew it. Shael hesitated, unsure.

"Raek fire?" Soleille asked, "How can that be?"

"There appears to be much we do not understand about raek magic," Isbaen said calmly.

"Meera," Shael said, trying to get her to look at him. She managed to straighten up and look at his face. "It is just a scar. It does not look as good as yours, but I will live," he said with a smile.

Meera just shook her head and pressed her lips together, so they wouldn't tremble. Shael stepped forward, took her shaking head in his hands, and kissed her forehead. She stared down at the scar in front of her and reached out a hand to touch it. It looked and felt like hers. She took a breath. He was right, she told herself; it was just a scar. She hated that she had done it to him, but she had forgiven Cerun for her burn; she supposed she owed herself the same forgiveness. This time, she told herself, but now that she knew she was dangerous, she could never hurt anyone again.

She stepped back from Shael. "Hadjal's right," she said. "You should stay away from me."

Shael's reassuring smile faded, and his face turned to stone.

"Sit and eat, everyone," Sodhu said, trying to dispel the tension. She never seemed to handle high emotions well. Still, Meera was grateful to have everyone's eyes off of her for a moment while they took their seats and piled food on their plates. She ate ravenously, and for several minutes, they all put aside the topic of her apparent raek fire abilities.

"You know," she said, finally, breaking the silence, "Knell sleep is different from human sleep."

"Is it?" Isbaen asked with obvious interest.

"It felt much deeper and heavier," she explained.

Isbaen nodded like what she said made sense, but before he could answer, Florean and her father arrived from the lake, fishing rods in hands. "No bites," Florean lamented. Meera was glad; she didn't have much taste for fish.

"How are our lovebirds this morning?" Orson asked, making Meera cringe. "Why aren't you wearing your mother's ring? You know, she wore it every day."

Once again, all eyes were on Meera, and she sunk lower into her chair. "Father, I ... seem to have raek fire magic. I accidentally burned Shael last night," she confessed.

"Oh?" Orson replied, looking only vaguely startled and continuing to butter a piece of bread. Meera didn't want to alarm her father, but she was also bothered by how little interest he seemed to show in her lately. She felt like even when he smiled the right smile and said the right things, he wasn't all the way present. He still hadn't fully returned from his ordeal in the war. It was like his emotions and interactions were dulled, and she was only getting a shadow of her former father.

"All will be well," Isbaen assured them both. "Meera will need to train her new abilities to gain control over them."

"Yes, of course," her father replied. "Which has me thinking, Meera. Since you'll be so busy with your training, I—I thought I'd go do research at the Levisade Estate. You know, when you were ... unwell, the queen told me I was welcome to make use of their old manuscripts." Meera stared at her father, a gaping wound opening in her chest as he spoke. "I'd like to see what I can make of knell history. Especially after what you said about a possible human origin. How fascinating!" he added, unaware of her feelings.

Meera supposed she should answer—should be happy that her father was finding some of his old interest in work again, but she felt only hurt. First, he had given Shael her mother's ring and tasked him with caring for her, and now he was leaving. She felt like he'd had enough of her. She had only just gotten him back, and he was doing everything in his power to get away from her—to relinquish any and all responsibility as her father.

Shael took her hand under the table, sensing some of her emotion, but she yanked it away. She wasn't safe to touch, to sit next to, even. She rose suddenly from the table. "I'm going for a run," she announced, already turning away.

"Have fun!" Her father chirped, completely unaware of her distress. He munched on his buttered roll with a look of far-off wonder on his face.

Meera almost stormed away, but she caught herself. "You should go to the estate," she told her father. He hadn't asked to be in Levisade like he hadn't asked to be conscripted to fight Terratelle's war. She knew she should set him free to live his life. Besides, she thought; he would be safer away from her. Then she turned and ran. She ran around the lake not once, but twice, pushing her new muscles to their limits, testing her speed and endurance. The exertion still felt hard—she still had to work—but her new body raised all of her base levels, so she could go twice as far as before at twice the speed.

Finally, she came to a halt on the beach where Isbaen and Shael were sitting together. Panting, she looked out at the water, and as she stared at the opposite cliff, she wondered where the wild raek—her raek—was. The raek had asked Meera to be her rider, changed her, and disappeared. Meera stared hard at the spot like she could will the raek into existence.

"Can you feel her in your mind?" Shael asked, clearly discerning what she was thinking about.

"Should I?" she asked, turning to him and wiping a bead of sweat from her forehead.

"It may come with familiarity," he replied. "I do not remember."

Meera turned back toward the still water and wondered how she was supposed to become familiar with the raek if she wasn't around.

"Meera, I have volunteered to begin your training. Your rider training will have to wait until the council approves of you, but we all agree that your shaping training must begin immediately," Isbaen said in an even voice.

Meera nodded. She wasn't safe to be around until she could control her fire—her inexplicable raek fire. Again, she wondered why it had to be fire. Then she looked down at the sandy beach and touched her wrist, thinking of Linus. Was the universe punishing her for her mistakes, or was the violence ingrained in her somehow? "I'm ready now," she said. The sooner she could control herself the better.

"Good. Come and sit," Isbaen replied.

She walked over and sat in the sand, glancing at Shael, who showed no inclination toward leaving. "You don't have to watch me all day," she told him, but it sounded sharper than she meant it. She just wanted him to go and live his life—take care of himself after three weeks of worrying about her obsessively. He couldn't help with her shaping, after all.

Shael's face turned to stone.

"I mean, you should go and run or read or train—do something for yourself," Meera explained. He stood stiffly, and she stared at his stomach, glad she couldn't see his new scar through his shirt. Extending a hand, she touched his knee, unable to stop herself from constantly reaching out to comfort him even though she knew she wasn't safe to touch. "I'll see you later," she said feebly, knowing from the look on his face that he had withdrawn far away.

Shael nodded but didn't reply, and he walked away.

Meera sighed out a great puff of air.

"You will need to let all of that go for the moment in order to shape," Isbaen said quietly.

Meera barked a laugh. If that was the case, she felt doomed from the start. Her head swirled constantly with her concerns. "I'll try," she promised.

"Sit comfortably, close your eyes, and clear your mind," Isbaen told her. He watched while she settled into a cross-legged position and closed her eyes. But the strain on her face must have betrayed how muddled her mind was because he soon said, "Try opening your eyes and focusing on the still water. Endeavor to make your mind just as still and smooth. If a thought ripples the surface, acknowledge it briefly then push it away."

Meera did as she was told; she stared at the calm blue lake and imagined that her mind was as clear and still. She thought about Shael's look when she had encouraged him to go, and she pushed the thought away; she could talk to him later. She thought about her father's decision to leave, and she pushed the thought away. She thought about her breast wrap digging into her ribs, and she pushed the thought away. She breathed slowly and evenly and stared fixedly at the lake.

She felt like it was working; she felt calm and steady. Then she realized that by thinking about what she was doing, she was thinking, and she tried to push the thought away. Inhale—still water. Exhale—still water. Suddenly, Meera's eyes flashed to the rock protruding from the water near the rock wall. She thought of Shael sitting on that rock every day. She thought of how tired and ragged he had looked. She thought of him in the dungeon. She thought of herself shutting the dungeon door behind her and walking away time and again. She thought of his bare feet when he had run for Cerun on the beach because she had never remembered to bring him socks.

Meera's whole body tensed with her emotion. She thought of the words that had scarred Shael's chest and stomach and the silver swirls left behind by her fire. Her fists clenched. Still water, she told herself. Still water. She tried to regain her focus, but her thoughts continued to spiral. She pictured Shael's dark eyes when he had told her she had magic. She pictured his hands and his body on hers in his bed. She heard Linus's beads clatter to the floorboards.

Squirming in her seat, she clenched her eyes shut and opened them again, trying for a fresh start. Her eyes landed on the cliff across the water, and she wondered, once more, where her raek was. "I can't do this!" she cried in frustration, turning to Isbaen.

Isbaen had not so much as moved; he still sat calm and still, regarding her. His hair was woven back in a new and intricate combination of braids, and not a single line or shadow marred his striking, angular face. "You must be able to clear your mind to access the magic within you," he said. "We can talk through your troubles if you think it will help."

Meera pouted and shook her head. She didn't really feel like unburdening herself to Isbaen; she would feel weird discussing Shael with his mentor. Closing her eyes, she deepened her breathing and tried again. And again. And again. Eventually, Isbaen left her on the beach to continue on her own, and once alone, Meera took a minute to rage at the foolish activity. She felt like it was getting harder and harder as she sat there, not easier. But then she took a breath, closed her eyes, opened them, and tried again. And again.

Meera sat on the beach all day trying to clear her thoughts with little success, and finally, her stomach growled loudly enough that she gave up. She could hear the others gathering at Hadjal's table for dinner, so she rose stiffly and rubbed her arms with her hands; she had a chill from sitting still for so long after sweating even though it really wasn't cold out. Stretching her legs, she plodded up the hill toward food and a welcome distraction from her struggles.

"Meera!" Soleille called as she approached. "How is your training going? I did not see any fire from up here."

Meera couldn't tell if Soleille was genuinely interested or just mocking her. "I'm not very good at sitting still and not thinking," she admitted.

"Who is?" Soleille asked, and Meera smiled at her, taking her seat next to Shael. She tried to catch his eye, but he didn't look up at her.

"I think Isbaen is going about this the wrong way," Soleille announced loudly. Isbaen gave her a look but didn't interrupt. "Meera just needs to feel something strong enough to trigger her shaping. After a few times, she will get a feel for where her magic lives in her body and be able to shape at will."

"Should we scare it out of her?" Katrea asked with a glint in her eyes. Meera glared at the red-headed knell woman even though Katrea could probably crush her head with just two of her muscled fingers.

"That is a terrible idea," Hadjal said dismissively.

"She must learn to control her thoughts and emotions before she can control her shaping," Isbaen added.

"What if I don't want to control it?" Meera asked. "What if I just want to repress it? I never want to use raek fire anyway." She pictured Linus's burnt hand and Shael's scar.

"If you live in fear of your ability then it will control you, not the other way around," Florean said wisely. Meera just gaped at the older man. She was surprised he hadn't said something snarky about humans being unable to control themselves and wondered whether Florean's friendship with her father was changing the older knell's mind about humans. Then she thought about what he had said: she *was* afraid of her ability.

"How can I not be afraid of something that lives inside me and might hurt the people I care about?" she asked earnestly. She wished Shael would take her hand, but he sat rigidly next to her, barely touching his food.

"It is not a matter of not being afraid," Isbaen explained. "You must sit with your feelings and learn to live with them in peace before you can expect to harness the magic in your body. You see, our emotions and past traumas live within us and can block our ability to shape. Likewise, those emotions can shift and release our abilities when we do not intend to. You must become familiar with your emotions and where they live in your body, and you must learn to find peace in your mind in order to shape."

Meera just stared at Isbaen. Was that what she was supposed to have been doing all day? She didn't feel like she'd accomplished anything. She also had no idea how she was supposed to sit with her feelings when they might inadvertently release an inferno from her body. Pushing her fork into her open mouth, she chewed in lieu of responding.

"There are different methods," Sodhu added. "I admit, I can hardly remember how I first came to understand and control my shaping. Then again, moving objects around by sight is not nearly as noteworthy as creating raek fire," she added with a smile at Meera. Meera suspected it was meant to be a compliment, but she just wished everyone would turn their attention elsewhere for once.

"I do not know ..." said Soleille, tapping her knuckles sharply on the table. "Isbaen's method may be best for those with endless amounts of time, but Meera's ability is dangerous. I think it warrants an expedited approach." Meera wasn't sure she liked the look in Soleille's summer blue eyes.

Neither did Hadjal: "Soleille, leave Meera's training to Isbaen. He volunteered for the task and is probably the best person for the job."

Meera cringed, knowing Soleille would not like to be pushed aside.

"Fine," said Soleille. "I will leave it to Isbaen and be waiting in the wings to heal his burns. That is fine with me. I would rather not be covered in raek fire scars, anyway." Meera's stomach dropped; she certainly hoped she wouldn't hurt Isbaen during their training. When no one responded to Soleille, she kept talking: "After all, we have all met Meera ... Her training will be some big drama, I am sure. I would go on an extended trip to miss it, except that I will be needed to heal everyone."

She turned to Meera, then. "You have had the body of a knell for ... one day? And you have burned Shael twice in that time. Let us see," she said, pretending to tally on her fingers, "How many burns do you think I will have healed after a week? A month? What? Not sure? What about after a year? Most knell do not learn to control their abilities in less time than a year."

Meera was getting the distinct impression that Soleille was baiting her, trying to upset her to draw out her fire and prove some sort of point about methodology. She wouldn't react, she told herself; she didn't care what Soleille said about her.

"That is enough, Sol," Isbaen warned.

Soleille ignored him. "You are being awfully quiet," she said, turning to Shael. He looked up but didn't answer. "Yesterday you were on one knee practically gushing your love to Meera and, what? You had one night together and are over it? So much for marriage!"

Meera's cheeks felt hot, and her earlier chill was forgotten as her muscles tensed at Soleille's words. Breathe, she told herself. She knew Soleille was trying to get to her. Admittedly, it was Shael's silence that was nagging at her. Why was he being so quiet and stony?

"Shael, did you tell Meera's father about your vow when you asked for the ring?" Soleille asked with the silky voice of intrigue.

"Just leave him alone," Meera said, keeping her voice low and even.

"Why? Is that a touchy subject? Which? The vow or the ring?" Soleille asked.

Katrea chuckled quietly. Meera's heart thudded in her chest, and she touched a hand to her temple where she felt a headache forming after a long, frustrating day. She thought maybe she should get up and walk away, but she didn't want to be as dramatic as Soleille was accusing her of being. Looking down at her plate, she tried to clear her mind. She thought of the still lake and pushed beans around with her fork.

"Shael was a little reluctant to take the ring," her father chirped from down the table. "He tried to give it back, but I have an eye for these things. He couldn't fool me!"

Meera's hand trembled in her lap. Why was her father so desperate to pass her off to Shael? Why did Shael propose if he was uncertain? Why did everyone always have to be looking at her and talking about her? Why was Shael being so damned quiet?

Everyone was silent after Orson's statement, but her father was oblivious; he was eating and reading from a large volume at the same time and didn't seem to remember that he had spoken moments ago. Meera was so tense, she could hear blood rushing in her ears. She had just swallowed and could swear her food was stuck halfway down her throat from her muscles clenching so hard. Still, there were no flames. She felt a jumbled mixture of sadness, anger, and embarrassment, but she had not created any fire.

She took a breath. Maybe everything would be okay, she thought; maybe she had just been too exhausted the night before. Exhaling, she felt her shoulders drop and her neck relax. Then she looked down at her hands, which were flame-free, and she smiled. "Look at that, Soleille," she said, holding up her hands, "You did your worst but no fire!" She felt like a load had been lifted from her.

"Please! That was not my worst," Soleille said, smiling.

Meera threw back her head and laughed as she lowered her hands to the table in front of her. They burst into flames.

9

SHAEL

Shael was looking at Meera when it happened, and he quickly leapt to his feet and backed away from the fire. The other riders responded just as rapidly, vacating their chairs and preparing themselves to act. Orson moved slower but also rose from his seat and stepped back. Meera stood staring at her fiery hands—holding them out away from her and everyone around her—but it was too late; the old wooden table had ignited under her palms, and the raek fire was spreading, eating through the knotted planks of ancient oak.

"No!" Hadjal yelled throatily. She reached toward the table where it burned, but Sodhu held her back. Shael knew the old table was important to Hadjal; he had seen her oil it with loving care and suspected it was as old as her ancient house and had probably borne witness to countless rider meals.

"Meera, you have to stop feeding it energy!" Hadjal shouted desperately. "Put it out! Put it out!" She broke free from Sodhu's grasp and paced back and forth, watching helplessly with everyone else as the pale fire quickly spread.

Meera stepped back further from the table, still holding her flickering hands before her body. "I can't! I can't!" she choked. Her face was agony, and Shael's stomach clenched at the site. He stepped toward her but was not sure if he should touch her or not. Hadjal fell to the ground and wailed in a horrible, drawn-out cry, and Meera's fire rose with the sound, devouring the table and leaping to the chairs. She put her flaming hands over her ears and buckled to her knees.

They all watched as the ancient table and chairs disappeared in the eerie pale flames that continued to dance and swirl even without fuel left to consume. Shael was worried the grass would ignite, but the area around the table was bare, trampled dirt, which, thankfully, did not catch fire. Several moments after the table was gone, the fire finally went out, and Shael was left staring at the dirt and ashes with the flickering shadows of flames burned into both eyes.

Hadjal continued to cry, and Sodhu led her away into the house. Everyone else looked astonished—frightened, even. Meera was crumpled on the ground, staring straight ahead, and Shael crouched in front of her. Some soot had blown onto her face, and her tears left tracks through the black dust. "I'm sorry," she said, not looking at him particularly. "I'm so sorry. I don't know what happened."

"Everything is okay," he said. "No one is hurt." He wanted to pull her into his arms and hold her, but he did not.

"Hadjal," Meera said in a whimper.

"Hadjal will be okay," he assured her. He reached out and wiped at the tears on her face but only managed to smear them in the soot caking her cheeks. "I think you have had enough for today. We should go home."

"Home?" she asked despondently.

"Meera, I would like to ask you some questions before you go anywhere," Isbaen said, standing beside Shael.

"I'm not going home with you!" she cried, looking at Shael with an expression like he had suggested she eat raek droppings. Shael's heart stopped in his chest for a moment as his whole body paused in anticipation. Was this the rejection he had been waiting for? Was Meera finally going to turn him away?

Rubbing at her eyes, she looked at him and must have seen something of his thoughts on his face because she reached for him, hesitated, then put her hand on his arm. "I'm not safe, Shael. I'm not going to sleep in your wooden house with you in it." She squeezed his arm once and withdrew her hand quickly.

Shael nodded his understanding and stood. Meera also rose to her feet, looking exhausted and defeated. Most of the other riders still lingered, staring at her with curiosity and trepidation, but Isbaen looked unruffled as usual. "Meera, as I said earlier, our shaping is often affected by our emotions before we learn to be present in our bodies and control our magical energy. For now, you should be able to avoid outbursts of raek fire if you can avoid the feeling triggering your shaping," he explained.

Meera nodded her understanding, and Shael crossed his arms in front of his chest, useless in a discussion of magic.

"So, what were you feeling the three times you exploded?" Soleille asked. "Because making you mad did not seem to work." Her pink lips twisted in a grimace. Even though she had not directly caused Meera's flames, she seemed to regret her attempts. Raek fire was not something to play around with. The riders could have done something if it had been regular fire, but there was nothing to be done about raek fire except avoid it.

"I could have swallowed it," Cerun lamented in Shael's mind. "If I had been there, I could have bitten the table before the raek fire could spread." Cerun was hunting with some of the other raeken. Shael mentally waved away his raek's regrets. The table would have been ruined regardless.

"I ... don't know," Meera said in answer to Soleille's question. She was staring at the dirt ground where the table had been. They were all still circled around the spot, unsure of where to put themselves without their usual seats. Only a few flecks of grey ashes swirled through the air.

"You need to try," Isbaen told her. Meera crossed her arms before her chest defensively and did not respond.

"She does not need to share her feelings with everyone," Shael said, sensing her discomfort with the conversation.

"She does," Isbaen replied. "It is a matter of safety. We cannot help her if we do not understand what is triggering her." His mentor's deep blue eyes were focused only on Meera, patiently waiting for her to share.

Sighing, Meera kicked at the dirt. "I was ... with Shael the first two times," she reminded them all with obvious embarrassment. Shael shifted on his own feet, suddenly very aware of Orson's presence, although he was sitting on the ground bent over a book and hardly seemed to notice that there were other people around him.

"Yes, but what were you feeling?" Isbaen prompted.

"I ... just ..." Meera glanced at Shael, and he wondered if she did not wish to share in front of him.

"I can leave if you want," he offered.

"What?" she looked baffled by the suggestion.

Isbaen gave Shael a look that clearly told him to stop distracting Meera.

"She was happy and laughing when she burned the table, and she was probably happy with Shael," Soleille supplied. "Maybe joy is her trigger."

"What did you feel at the table tonight?" Isbaen asked, still focused on Meera even though she stood hunched and holding her arms like she was trying to shrink out of sight.

"Relief? I ... felt relieved that I hadn't flared up when Soleille upset me. I thought maybe last night was an anomaly, and I was safe," she said, her voice cracking.

Isbaen looked like he was thinking.

"You let down your guard," Katrea suggested.

Meera nodded. "I guess, with Shael I ... felt free ... from my worries," she glanced at him again, and her warm eyes melted some of the frost around Shael's cold edges. He had assumed Meera had felt desire when she was with him, but it was nice to know it was more than that. He was glad his presence lightened the burdens on her as her presence did for him.

"Hmmmm," Isbaen hummed ponderously.

Meera huffed a laugh. "You sound like Carabaen," she remarked. Shael saw Isbaen flinch at the comparison, but he quickly smiled at Meera, recognizing that she did not mean him offense.

"I have a theory," Florean announced.

Shael turned to look at the older knell man, daring him to say something harsh to Meera—something about humans; Shael would relish an excuse to go after Florean in that moment. He felt he had some pent emotions of his own that could use venting, and he didn't have raek fire to call upon to burn the world around him.

"I believe there are those of us who repress our emotions and traumas, barricading them within ourselves to pretend they do not exist. In which case, letting them out—such as outbursts of anger—" he clarified, looking at Soleille, "also expels magical energy. However, I believe there are others who live with their emotions and traumas on the surface, who are prone to outbursts of energy when they let go of their feelings. Meera seems to be the latter, at least in this instance. When she relaxes and lets her feelings drop away, she also releases a torrent of raek fire."

Shael stared at Florean. It was possibly the most he had ever heard the man say at once, and it was actually helpful.

Isbaen looked delighted. "Very astute, Florean! I do think your theory has merit. It certainly explains Meera's outbursts. Does it make sense to you, Meera?" he asked.

"It does," she said quietly. "But I ... how can I live and never relax or let my guard down?"

Shael wondered which kind of person he was. He was not sure. He certainly repressed his reactions, but did he repress his emotions or torture himself with them? He felt like he did a combination of both; he supposed everyone probably did. Besides, he thought; it did not matter for him because he would not be expelling magical energy either way. "Now that you understand what is triggering Meera's outbursts, you can help her control them, right?" he asked.

"Meera's progress is really up to her," Isbaen replied calmly. "Self-understanding can be a long journey."

Shael stared blankly at his mentor. That was it? That was all the reassurance Isbaen could offer? Shael thought it was no wonder Meera had arrived for dinner after her training looking extremely irritated. He glanced at her now, and she looked downright hopeless, still staring at the dirt. "Walk with me?" he asked her, ready to be away from the burn site.

Meera nodded, but instead of turning toward the forest and his house, she turned toward the lake. He followed. "It may take time for you to control your shaping, but you have time," he reminded her. If the wild raek was to be trusted, Meera had hundreds of years to train and live.

"Will you wait for me?" she asked quietly.

"Of course," he said, reaching out and wrapping his arm

around her shoulders.

She sighed at the touch but then quickly shrugged out of his embrace, putting more distance between them. "Please, stop touching me, Shael. I can't hurt you again!" her voice rose and wavered.

He was not sure he could promise that. "It is worth the risk," he said.

"Not to me!" she replied.

Shael felt stung even though he knew Meera just did not want to hurt him. Her words hurt, he thought, more than her fire. Just then, he felt Cerun touch down in the field, ready to fly him home. Shael considered inviting Meera to fly with him, but he knew how free she felt when she flew, and he knew it was not safe for her to feel that way. Shael ground his teeth in frustration; he wanted to make Meera happy and help her forget her past, but he could not do either without risking her fire.

"I'm going to sleep on the beach," she announced, pulling him from his thoughts.

"Do you need anything from home?" Shael asked, refusing to acknowledge that his home may not be her home.

"No," she said softly, looking out over the water. "Shael, I—I think I need to stay away from you ... until I'm safe to be around. I'm sorry, I don't want to, but I couldn't live with myself if I hurt you again," she said, looking up into his eyes.

Shael wanted to argue, but he did not. He wanted to say he was not sure how long he could live without her, but he did not. He did not say anything.

"I want to waltz at our wedding and know that I won't incinerate you," Meera added with tears in her eyes.

Shael smiled at that even though the small amount of hope he had for their future did not still his churning gut. Then he bent forward and kissed her lightly. She kissed him back before pulling away and rolling her eyes at him. "I will not touch you starting now," he promised. "I will give you space to train."

"I'll train as hard and as fast as I can," she promised in return, but her eyes betrayed her doubt.

10

MEERA

Meera retrieved bedding from her father's cabin and lay down on the beach, hoping the sand and water were impervious enough to raek fire to prevent her from destroying anything if she burst into flames in her sleep. How was she even supposed to sleep if relaxing was dangerous? How was she supposed to live her life at all if forgetting her past and her emotions could burn everything around her?

She wondered if she had made a mistake—if she had agreed to the raek's bargain too quickly, with too little thought. She had never even considered that she would have magic, which she should have realized was a possibility. Then again, if she had considered it, she still would have wanted to go through the change. She couldn't have known that she would have raek fire when no one else seemed to. Her father had mentioned Darreal visiting when she was encased in fire, and Meera wondered how long it would be until the queen showed up to gawk at the new spectacle she had become.

Sighing, she released some of the tension building in her

body. Then she remembered herself and quickly clenched her muscles, trying to keep her magical energy shut up inside her. She needed to train to control herself, but how could she train if she wasn't safe to be around? All of the hope and certainty she had felt the day before about her future was rapidly fading. She wouldn't be able to marry Shael or help end the war if she spent the rest of her long life trying to conquer her new ability.

Shael had said he would wait for her, but how long would he wait when he had been uncertain to begin with? Her father had—apparently—forced him to take her mother's ring. Meera's cheeks flamed at the thought, but luckily, no actual flames appeared. She felt like a monster and a burden. She had traded her human body for a knell one and felt just as painfully useless as ever before. She had wanted to take control of her life, and now she couldn't even control herself.

Lying awake for a long time, she stared up at the stars and wondering what she should do. She knew she should probably leave—go somewhere she could train and not hurt anyone, some-where far away from Hadjal's wooden house. But where? Where could she go? She had survived the Forest of Shayan but barely, and she had needed Shael to rescue her from the mountains. How could she live by herself?

Meera wished she could sit with Shael, talk to him, and feel his reassuring arm around her shoulders. Somehow, they were engaged to be married, and she felt more distant from him than ever. She continued to be confused by his behavior, and now she was afraid to be near him. She missed Cerun, too, but she had been missing him since Terratelle; their relationship was forever altered by Shael's presence.

She supposedly had her own raek, she thought bitterly, but she had no idea where the wild raek might be or whether she would return any time soon. Ruminating on what Shael had said about feeling Cerun in his mind, Meera shut her eyes and tried to feel the wild raek, but she couldn't. She didn't even know what the raek would feel like. Then she thought back to when Carabaen had located her father by following her invisible tether to him, and as she had done with her father, she pictured the wild raek.

She imagined what the cloud-colored raek looked like, how her feathers and scales glistened and reflected blues and greys from the sky and stones. She remembered first meeting the raek after the storm and how she had returned to her with water and assistance. She thought of them both standing on the cliff over the lake and the feeling of the raek pressing into her mind to speak to her and show her memories. She pictured the raek's eerie, pale eyes that felt fathomless like looking into infinite air.

Meera spent a long time trying to connect with her raek and feel her inside her mind. She couldn't actually sense the wild raek's location or see their invisible tether like Carabaen could, but she felt more and more sure that the raek would return for her. She always had before, after all, and with that thought, she was finally able to drift into a deep sleep.

The next morning, she awoke as the sun broke over the horizon and light penetrated her eyelids with a reddish glow. Sitting up, she opened her eyes, looking around in confusion at first until she remembered that she had slept on the beach. Then she sighed heavily, knowing that up the slope behind her was an empty patch of dirt where Hadjal's table should be, and before her awaited a monumental task. It was time for her to train—all day every day—until she could control her abilities. Unwilling to face the day, she clutched her blankets to her and slumped back onto her bedroll.

Meera shut her eyes for a few more minutes of rest and denial; the day could wait a few minutes—training could wait a few minutes. She pulled her blankets up to her neck and rolled onto her side, snuggling into the pliable sand beneath her bedding, but something felt different—not in her body, but in her mind. She felt a little niggling sensation in a corner of her consciousness. At first, she opened her eyes—startled—but then she shut them again and tried to concentrate on the sensation.

It was the raek, she realized. She didn't understand how she knew it, but she felt the cloud-colored raek coming toward her across a great distance. The small niggling feeling in her mind was slowly building and growing. Meera sat bolt upright in the sand and squinted around at the sky even though she knew instinctively that the raek wasn't that close. Still, she rose hastily, bunched up her bedding, and carried it to her father's cabin where she left it outside the door so as not to disturb his sleep.

As she walked away, she wondered if she really hadn't wanted to disturb her father, or if she just hadn't wanted to see him. She was still trying to reconcile herself to this new version of her father and their new relationship. Then again, she supposed she was also a new version of herself and considered that her father might not know how to behave around her either. She wanted to remedy that—to try harder to reconnect with him—but she couldn't do that until she was safe to be around. Marching with purpose through the woods, Meera eventually spurred her legs into a run and sprinted for Shael's house.

When she reached the small, wooden house, she stood at the door feeling uncertain. Should she knock? Should she walk in? Was this her house too? She wasn't sure. She could hear Cerun's snoring around back and thought Shael might still be sleeping too. She didn't want to wake them, so she quietly turned the door-knob and entered. The familiar smell of pine floors gave her a pang of yearning. She wished she could stay, but she knew she couldn't.

She went into her bedroom and began gathering her clothes.

She had her back turned to the door and was shoving them into her bag when the hairs on the back of her neck prickled. Spinning around, she found Shael in the doorway, dressed but looking groggy. "You're quiet!" she said in surprise, unsure how he had managed to sneak up on her with her new knell hearing.

"You are not," he replied with a small smile. He leaned against her doorway, looking pleased to see her until his eyes wandered to the bag in her hand, and his eyebrows drew down. "You are packing," he said.

Meera finished shoving her clothes in the bag and dropped it on the bed beside her. "I need to go somewhere on my own— somewhere I can train without hurting people," she said, imploring him to understand with her eyes.

"Where?" he asked simply.

"I don't know, but my raek is coming for me," she replied, feeling a certainty in the words as they came out of her mouth. The presence in her mind was growing—nearing. She knew the raek—her raek—was coming to get her.

Shael nodded, but his expression looked pained.

Meera didn't want to leave with things between them feeling so strained and uncertain. She averted her eyes to her dresser and her few remaining possessions, and there sat her mother's ring, her mother's earrings, and Linus's purple beaded bracelet. "You fixed it," she said, reaching out and fingering the cool glass beads on their new leather strap.

Shael didn't answer.

"Thank you," she added, holding the bracelet lovingly for a moment before placing it back on the dresser. She also touched the ring and ran her finger along the circle of pearls embracing the blue center stone. Then she turned and faced Shael, who stood silently watching her. "Can I leave these here until I get back?" she asked.

He nodded stiffly like the movement was a great effort for him.

Meera's heart ached, and she stepped forward. Deciding that she was so overwhelmed with emotions that she wasn't in any danger of releasing raek fire, she wrapped her arms around Shael's middle and leaned her face into his chest. It took him a moment to return the hug, but when he did, he held her like he'd never let go. She felt tears form in her eyes, and she swallowed, trying to hold them back. "I'll miss you," she said into his shirt.

"You can stay here and train," Shael said. "You belong here." Meera wasn't sure if he meant she belonged with him or that she belonged at the peninsula as a rider.

Either way, the sentiment was moot; she needed to leave. She felt absolutely certain that she needed to leave in order to train, but she didn't bother saying so—she didn't want to argue. "As soon as I'm safe, I'll come back," she promised, looking up into his grey eyes.

Shael's face was blank and closed-off, and Meera put her hands on either side of his waist and shook him, trying to crack his exterior shell. She needed him to say he would miss her but that it was okay for her to go—that he would wait for her. She needed him to say that he loved her and would still love her when she returned. He was silent. She extended a tentative hand and touched his stony face, then lifted onto her toes to kiss him. It was like kissing a statue. "I love you," she told him.

Shael didn't move or speak.

Meera felt like birds were freefalling in her stomach. She took in a shuddering breath and turned away from him to retrieve her bag. "Goodbye," she said as she squeezed past him in the doorway.

"Wait!" he called when she was almost at the front door. Meera turned with tears sliding down her face, hoping for a hug and words of reassurance, but instead, Shael disengaged from the doorframe and disappeared briefly into his room. Moments later, he reappeared holding a black leather jacket. "It is a riding jacket," he said, handing it to her. "You might need it for colder weather."

Meera grasped the jacket and nodded, grateful but also disappointed. She might need the jacket, but she definitely needed Shael, and he wasn't there with her—not really. "Thank you," she managed to whisper, swallowing the ache in her throat. Then she turned and left, closing the door behind her.

Cerun was in front of the house, waiting for her. Meera approached the raek, put her hand briefly against his snout, and took the leftmost forest path toward the peninsula. She didn't say anything to Cerun, and he didn't say anything to her.

As she walked the familiar path, she shut her eyes briefly and concentrated on the separate consciousness lurking in the back of her mind. Her raek was still there within her and was growing larger. She hurried toward the peninsula, sure the cloud-colored raek would look for her there, and when she emerged from the woods and walked down the slope toward Hadjal's house, there was only a lone figure outside where everyone normally ate breakfast. Isbaen sat in the middle of the worn dirt patch with a mug of tea in his hands and a plate of food on the ground before him. He looked entirely at peace like he was exactly where he belonged.

"Good morning," she said as she approached.

"Is it?" Isbaen asked, eyeing Meera's face and bag.

"I'm leaving," she said without preamble.

Isbaen nodded, unsurprised.

"My raek is coming for me. Will you tell Hillgari?" she asked. She didn't want the other raeken to react aggressively when the wild raek appeared.

Isbaen nodded once more and sipped his tea.

Meera's temper rose; would no one say goodbye to her? Wish

her well? "Is Hadjal awake?" she asked. She wanted to apologize before she left.

"Hadjal and Sodhu left early this morning to visit friends," Isbaen replied.

"Oh." Meera looked around, unsure of what to do with herself. Her stomach growled hungrily, but she didn't feel comfortable going into Hadjal and Sodhu's house for food, knowing they had left because of her. She wondered where the others were. She wanted to say goodbye to everyone.

"Your father and Florean went fishing, and Soleille and Katrea went for a run," Isbaen said, sensing her thoughts.

Meera bit her lip with uncertainty. Looking up into the sky, she expected the wild raek at any moment. "Isbaen, will you tell them all that I left and will be back when I'm safe?" she asked lamely, wondering if she should write her farewells down on a piece of paper. She dismissed the idea; she wouldn't have anything better to write than that.

"I will. Be well, Meera." He said it with enough finality that Meera backed away, turned, and headed for the beach for lack of any better ideas. She was hungry, but she had no house and no food of her own. She was a useless beggar who didn't feel like she deserved any charitable food at the moment, and with no idea where she would go or what she would eat while she trained, she waited for her raek.

She stood on the beach and watched the sky for what felt like a long time, keeping her bag on her shoulder and Shael's jacket in her hand, ready to go. Eventually, an enormous shape detached itself from the clouds above and circled above her once, twice, three times, before deciding it was safe to land. The wild raek lowered onto the grassy slope, buffeting Meera with bursts of wind.

Meera looked around to see that Hillgari and Cerun were both further up the slope, but neither raek moved toward the intruder. Isbaen, Soleille, Katrea, and Shael stood outside of Hadjal's house, watching. The wild raek observed the other riders and raeken with obvious trepidation, and she kept her wings folded loosely, ready to fly. Her long, tufted tail switched back and forth in agitation. The raek's reflective feathers and scales took on a greenish tint as she stood in the grass, and Meera wondered whether she was truly white and not bluish grey.

She approached the raek—her raek, she reminded herself yet again—stopping ten feet from the raek's large, swirling eye. For several long moments, they stared at one another. Meera didn't know what to say, and she shifted on her feet. Her new knell muscles felt spring-loaded and ready for action, but her chest ached at the thought of leaving, and her stomach rumbled as a reminder that she had no idea how to take care of herself.

"Hello," she said finally, unsure of how to communicate with the raek in her mind. The raek didn't move or answer, and Meera wondered if everyone was determined to ignore her that day. "I'm glad you're back," she added.

The raek pressed into Meera's mind to reply, but there was no agonizing pressure like before. She supposed her new body was better equipped to receive raek messages. "You called me here," the raek's disembodied voice rang in her head. "Why?"

Meera gaped. She must have called the raek to her when she focused on their connection the night before. "You changed me and left me here," she replied defensively. "We're supposed to be partners."

The raek shifted and swung her head around to peer at Meera through both of her unnerving eyes. Meera had to resist the urge to step back. She was feeling less and less sure that this raek would take her anywhere. "I retreated to the safety of my nest and used all of my energy to change you for what you would call three weeks. Then I arose and needed to hunt," the raek responded tonelessly.

Meera didn't know what to say to that; she hadn't considered how much of the raek's energy it would take to change her. She nodded stupidly, unsure if the raek even understood nodding or not. "Are you fed and rested?" she asked, attempting to be polite.

"My claws and teeth are sharp, my magical energy is replenished, and my wingspan is among the largest in the sky," the raek responded, accompanying her words with a low hum.

Meera swallowed and nodded once more, wondering if she and this old, wild creature were really capable of understanding one another.

"I find your human speech tedious," the raek said. "I sense you need something. What is it?" The raeken higher up the slope shifted, clearly unhappy that the larger raek had not flown away yet, and the wild raek swiveled her head toward them and screeched a warning.

"Stop!" Meera said. "They're friends."

"They are pitiful excuses for raeken with much too flashy feathers," the raek replied with disgust that Meera could feel inside her head.

Closing her eyes, she mentally reached for the wild raek's emotion, trying to get a feel for their connection. Then, in her mind, she replied, "They are raeken with riders, and now you are one of them." Meera knew the raek heard because she bristled mentally and visibly at her words, puffing up the feathers around her shoulders in indignation.

"I took a rider to save my species," she replied. "I do not intend to spend my life preening on this small piece of land." Her tail swished again, and she looked ready to leave already.

"What is your plan?" Meera asked aloud, finding their mental link slippery and difficult to pin down.

The wild raek was also losing patience with their communication and projected a series of images into Meera's mind rather than answering with speech. Meera saw herself looking like a warrior on top of the raek's back while she flew overhead of Terratellen troops and scorched them with her raek fire.

Cringing, she pulled away from the images; she had agreed to help end the war, but that wasn't exactly what she had had in mind. "Right ..." she said. "Well, my body is different, but I'm not a warrior yet. I have magic—raek fire, actually ..." She eyed the raek, wondering if she knew that already, if she had planted it into her somehow. The raek didn't react physically or mentally. "I need somewhere to train—somewhere my raek fire won't hurt people or burn down a forest. Is there somewhere we can go?"

The raek flashed an image of the first rider, Aegwren, into Meera's mind and what looked like a rock wall.

"Is that a yes?" Meera asked.

"Yes," the raek replied.

Meera gave the raek a small smile. Her hope was returning. Her raek had somewhere for them to go. "Do you have a name?" she asked.

"Raeken communicate with mental images, not speech," the raek replied. Meera took that as a no.

"Can I ... give you a name?" she asked uncertainly, not wanting to offend her new partner.

The raek huffed a puff of air in what Meera assumed was the raek equivalent of a shrug, so she tried to think of a suitable name. She didn't want to choose something Terratellen, but she didn't know many knell names. She stared into the wild raek's pale eyes while she thought. They always reminded her vaguely of the Forest of Shayan—like they were born from the same ancient magical source. "How about Shaya?" she asked, thinking the variation on Shayan felt appropriate to her.

The raek huffed again.

"Okay ... Shaya ... where are we going?" she asked.

The raek once more projected images of Aegwren, the first rider, and what looked like a rocky mountainside.

Meera sighed. She supposed she would need to get used to Shaya answering in her own language. She pushed toward the raek's consciousness in her mind and imagined herself climbing onto her back, trying to convey the image as a question.

Shaya's eyes had been wandering around the peninsula, but at the suggested image, she fixed her cat-like pupils back on Meera. Meera flinched, but the raek hummed a soothing note like a purr and projected the feeling of approval; she seemed glad that Meera was learning to communicate in what she clearly thought was the best way. Meera thought image communication left something to be desired, but she proceeded to step toward Shaya and ask the mental question again, picturing herself climbing onto the raek's back.

Shaya lowered her head in what Meera took as acquiescence, and she approached the raek's side, glancing one last time toward Hadjal's house where some of the others were still watching her. Shael stood next to Isbaen, looking tense, and Meera lifted her hand and waved to him, hoping he understood why she had to go. Shael raised his hand in reply, but his expression remained the same. Looking away from him, Meera focused instead on the raek before her—her new partner.

She hoped they would be partners, too; she hoped they would be close like Shael and Cerun. However, despite Meera's obvious emotion, Shaya said nothing and offered her no comfort. Meera placed her shaking hand against the large raek's neck and leapt onto her shoulders, accustomed to mounting Cerun and finding the motion even easier with her knell body. Then she slung her bag across her torso, looped Shael's jacket through its strap, and leaned forward to grip Shaya's feathers with both hands.

When she looked back at the other riders, she couldn't help but grin; she was a rider too now, sitting on top of her raek. Her stomach barely had a chance to flutter with nerves when Shaya launched aggressively into the air, nearly unseating her. Meera clutched the feathers before her and leaned forward with every newly activated muscle in her body, just barely preventing herself from sliding back from the force of the raek's leap.

After several mighty flaps of her wings to raise them into the clouds, Shaya evened out, and Meera was able to sigh a breath of relief. "That was too fast!" she yelled over the wind. "You have to remember that I'm back here!"

The raek hummed her derision before folding in her wings and leaning forward. With a yelp, Meera clutched Shaya's feathers once more in an effort not to be thrown from the raek's back as they nose-dived through the air toward the lake below. Her eyes watered, watching the lake grow larger beneath them. Panic rose in her chest, and she was considering leaping from the raek's back and taking her chances falling into the water, when Shaya pulled up suddenly and swept along the lake's surface, opening her mouth to drink.

Meera sat back and unclenched her muscles, but she kept a firm grip on Shaya's feathers; she didn't trust her to make any effort to keep her in her seat.

"My job is to fly. Your job is to hold on," Shaya said in response to Meera's thoughts.

Meera reached out mentally to touch the source of the words and tried to project her own voice down their tether of connection. "We're partners, Shaya! We're supposed to work together," she said.

Shaya huffed a puff of smoke in reply, but when she pulled

back up into the air, she did so more gradually. Then she sent images into Meera's mind of Meera yanking out her feathers and her retaliating by pulling out Meera's hair.

Meera laughed and loosened her grip on the raek's sleek neck feathers. And as they soared through the air, she settled into her seat and herself. Wind whipped at her skin and clothes, but she felt like she could breathe freely for the first time in a long time. The sky reached out around her with endless possibility, and her burdens were left far beneath her. Suddenly, Meera's hands flared with pale fire. She jumped and removed them from Shaya's neck, but she couldn't hurt Shaya with raek fire. Laughing again, Meera spread her arms wide and let the fire from her palms trail through the open air behind her like flaming wings.

She felt Shaya's curiosity before her presence intensified as she looked through Meera's eyes at her raek fire. Shaya hummed her approval. "You will be a strong warrior," she said.

Meera's hands flickered out as some of her worldly burdens settled back onto her shoulders. Then she experimented, closing her eyes and pressing her mental self closer to her raek's. Suddenly, she was sucked into Shaya's overwhelming conscious- ness like a leaf in a whirlpool. She felt the raek's thrumming power like it was her own and looked out over the landscape with eyes that caught every minute movement if not every color.

Shaya's body was a mighty force of muscle and swirling magical energy, but her mind was a dark and ancient labyrinth. Meera had the eerie feeling of being back in the Forest of Shayan, surrounded by tall and menacing trees that she couldn't see. Shaya's enormous heart pounded in her chest in a rhythm different from the one Meera was used to. It was a disconcerting feeling, and she tried to pull away—to separate from Shaya's consciousness.

For a moment of panic, Meera felt lost, unsure of how to

return to her own body. Then Shaya gave her a mental shove, and she tumbled back into herself, heart thumping wildly and head spinning. Gasping in breath, she looked with relief out of her own eyes. Gazing around them, she could tell that they were heading toward the mountains, the same mountains where she and Shaya had met—the mountains that had almost killed her. Meera gritted her teeth. She didn't know how she would do it, but she was determined to take care of herself—to survive and train on her own and eventually forge her own path in the world.

11

MEERA

Meera's determination turned to trepidation with every insistent grumble of her stomach. She and Shaya had been flying for several hours, and all she could think about was food. Why hadn't she eaten anything that morning? Why hadn't she packed food? Why did she continue to make impulsive decisions? She was tired of the misty wind buffeting her and longed to land; she had a chill from the dampness, and her lips were getting chapped.

Remembering Shael's jacket, Meera pulled it on and was struck immediately by his familiar smell. She felt an overwhelming desire to turn around and go back to him, but she fought the impulse by thinking of his new swirling scar—the scar she had given him. She couldn't return to Shael until she was safe, she told herself. Something hard hit her hip from inside his jacket, and she reached into its pocket to find Shael's little jar of lip balm. She smiled, knowing he had tucked it in there for her, and she smeared some on with relief.

Meera felt a growing anticipation in Shaya and assumed it

meant they had almost reached their destination. They were flying over the mountains and had been for some time. She was glad that she would be far from people and forests for her training, but she had no idea how she was going to survive so far from civilization—not that she had much money left for surviving in civilization, she reminded herself.

Shaya swerved back and forth several times and seemed to be scanning for a particular place before she finally found it and dove for a small valley between two peaks. They landed with a thump, and Meera looked around anxiously. They were in a desolate little valley with a creek running through it. Rock rose up on either side of them, shielding them from the wind that usually whipped the mountains so high up, but there did not, at first glance, appear to be shelter of any kind.

Fresh water was good, Meera told herself, even though she was starving and still had no notion whatsoever of what she would be eating in the coming days. Maybe there were fish in the creek ... not that she liked to eat fish or knew how to catch them. Swinging a leg over Shaya's neck, she slid down, jarring her stiff limbs against the hard ground. For a moment, she almost scrambled back onto Shaya's back; she felt unbelievably vulnerable being back in the mountains again without food.

Shaya didn't offer her any comforting words or images, but the raek did walk toward what appeared to be a crack in the rock wall, and she gestured to it with her scaly head. Meera stepped around Shaya and peeked inside the crevice, but it was too dark for her to see anything. She hesitated, not sure if she trusted Shaya enough to go inside, and Shaya just stood and waited, her fathomless eyes fixed on Meera.

Meera took a deep breath. Shaya had chosen her because she had the heart of a warrior, she reminded herself. However, rather than bolster her confidence, the reminder only made her question the raek's judgment. Shoving her doubts aside, she propelled herself forward, taking one step into the dark space and another, her hands outstretched before her. Then she waited for her knell eyes to adjust to the darkness. After a few moments, she could tell the space was relatively large and had some objects in it, but that was all she could see.

Meera turned back toward Shaya to ask what they were doing there, and it was then that she noticed the oil lamp hanging from the stone wall near the entrance. Inspecting it, she found that it was full and appeared to be working, but the unlit wick stared back at her tauntingly. Glancing at her palms, she didn't think she could conjure her raek fire on command. And she was afraid, she admitted to herself alone in the dark; she was afraid to destroy whatever was in the cave. She was afraid Shaya would deem her useless and leave her in the mountains alone.

Meera patted Shael's jackets and put her hands in the pockets, wondering if he could have possibly foreseen her need for fire. To her absolute delight, she pulled out a small bundle of matches tied together with string. Something small and white fell out of the pocket when she withdrew the matches, and she bent to find a piece of folded paper.

Her heart raced at the site of the small scrap of paper, knowing Shael had left her some sort of message. Fumbling with the matches, it took her shaking hands several tries to light the oil lamp. Once it was lit, she didn't look around; she unfolded her scrap of paper, desperate to know Shael's parting words to her after his silence earlier that morning. There was one sentence scrawled across it: *Come home to me.*

Meera's lip trembled as she struggled to hold in her emotion. She wanted to go home to Shael's house—to Shael. She already missed him terribly and craved his companionship, but she couldn't. Swallowing her feelings, she tucked the paper back into the jacket. She had work to do. She had left the peninsula to protect the other riders from her fire but also to have the time and space she needed to focus on herself. Isbaen had said she needed to connect with herself and her emotions in order to control her shaping, and that's what she intended to do.

Meera turned around to take in her surroundings and found herself in a dimly lit cave that was slightly larger than her father's cabin. It was a single room containing a bed, a chest, a fireplace, a shelf covered in what she hoped was food, and other various objects strewn around. Lighting the other oil lamps on the walls, she took a closer look at everything.

There was bedding on the bed that looked strangely clean, if rumpled like someone had just arisen from it. Opening the chest at the foot of the bed, she expected to find clothes but found, instead, a set of armor and a sword with a large opal set in its hilt. She shut the chest in confusion. Who lived here? Shaya had shown her images of Aegwren, the first rider, but this cave looked well-kept and clean. She walked over and inspected the stores of jarred food and bags of grain. They all appeared to be fresh.

"Shaya, who lives here?" she asked as she exited the cave, feeling like she was intruding on someone's private space.

"Aegwren, the first rider, used this cave long ago as a private refuge," Shaya replied.

"But who lives here now?" Meera asked.

"No one. The cave is preserved by Isabael's magic. It is yours to use since you are tasked with ending the persecution of raeken as Aegwren once was."

Meera was dumbstruck. This cave had been untouched for thousands of years? She thought hungrily of the food stores and wondered how old was too old when it came to magically preserved food. Everything had looked clean and unspoiled ... She suspected if she got in the bed, it might even smell like its previous occupant from many thousands of years ago. The thought made her shiver.

As she was processing the new information, Shaya bent her neck to drink from the creek, then extended her wings like she meant to fly away. Panicking, Meera shouted, "Wait! Where are you going? Will you be back?"

The raek regarded her with her strange, expressionless eyes. "We will both live here while you train. You will need Aegwren's memories to become a warrior. For now, I go to hunt." And with that, she launched herself into the air and flew away.

Meera was reassured by the fact that she could still feel her tether to Shaya after she left, but she still felt very alone and abandoned. For several moments, she stood unsure of what to do until her stomach growled pitifully and reminded her of her most pressing concern. She reentered the cave—her new home, she told herself. Removing Shael's jacket, she put down her bag and got to work lighting a fire in the fireplace and cooking a pot of grain to eat. When she found a jar of honey with which to sweeten her grain mush, she smiled and decided that living in the cave wouldn't be so bad.

After her stomach was full, Meera washed her dishes in the creek and took a walk around the area to familiarize herself with her new home. There were some small ferns and shrubs growing out of the ground in the valley, but mostly, there were rocks— plenty of lumpy bumpy grey rocks and not much else. She climbed the steep slope above the cave and found herself on a windy mountain peak, looking out over the range on all sides.

Marveling at the beauty of being so high up, Meera enjoyed the sensation of feeling small and unimportant. However, she kept checking the clouds distrustfully, remembering the storm that had once threatened her life on that same mountain range, and when goosebumps rose along her arms, she descended the slope and returned to her valley. She supposed she should start training but wasn't entirely sure where to start.

Finding a relatively flat and level area next to the creek, she sat down cross-legged like Isbaen always did. Then she stared at the moving water in front of her and tried to remember all that he had told her about shaping. He had said that she needed to come to terms with herself and her emotions in order to control her flow of magic, and Florean had suggested that her magic rushed out of her when she cleared her mind of her feelings and worries, which seemed to be the case.

Meera supposed the first step in the process was for her to process all of her feelings and learn to coexist with them without letting them control her. Suspecting that was much easier said than done, she squirmed in her seat, already uncomfortable with the idea. Florean had been right that her emotions were always close to the surface—she flitted from joy to anguish and guilt at the sight of anything that reminded her of Linus or the duke.

She should start there, she knew; she had been distracting herself from her past since she had arrived in Aegorn—since before then, even. Meera took a deep breath, and for once, she invited in all of her feelings of grief and guilt and anger toward herself for the decisions she had made and their unintended consequences. She pictured her friend, Linus, and his horrible burn. She imagined the burial his mother may have had for him. She pictured Duke Ned Harrington's kind face and loving wife. She imagined the daughter he had left at home waiting for him, who would never see her father again because of what she had done. As she let her guilt build within her, she also saw Shael's scar and his bare feet running for Cerun at the palace.

Meera let herself feel all of the emotions she had been both holding onto and holding at bay. She let her breathing become rapid and her face scrunch and her tears flow. She welcomed the nausea that made her crumple over. She buried her face in her hands and sobbed and choked on her sobs and dripped a steady stream of drool and snot onto her brown leather boots. She quaked and trembled and rocked back and forth, clutching her throbbing head. After a retching heave of her gut, she threw herself forward in time to puke the contents of her stomach into the creek, which merrily ferreted them away from her. Then she lay back across the hard ground and continued to shake and allow tears to spill from her eyes for a long, long time.

Eventually, she lay still and drew in deep, even breaths. Her head rested on the hard rock, and her limbs were strewn around her. She was emotionally drained—she had felt and processed all the anguish her body could handle that day. She felt lighter, freer. Her mind was strangely and eerily blank. What thoughts she had moved as slowly as the sluggish clouds above her, and she was able to dismiss them each with an exhale. Staring up at the endless sky, she vaguely registered that her palms were on fire.

Meera felt the gentle warmth and tickle of her raek fire through whatever magic protected her from it and raised one hand above her face to look at it. She observed the pale flames dancing on her skin but did not judge them or fear them. Curiously, she sat up and dipped her flaming palm into the creek, watching as her hand went into the water, and raek fire continued to rise and swirl from her skin. It heated the water, causing it to steam and hiss and spit. Hot water splattered her cheek, and she flinched back, pulling her hand from the creek. In her distraction, her fire went out.

Utterly exhausted, she dragged herself to her feet and went in search of more food. She ate some preserved fruit straight from the jar and curled up on the bed in the cave. No longer caring if it smelled like Aegwren from thousands of years before, she lay her aching head on his pillow and burrowed under his blankets, sighing from the simple pleasure of a comfortable bed.

Sometime later, she awoke to the sound of Shaya thumping down outside. Rising and exiting the cave, she rubbed her eyes blearily to find that it was still daylight. Shaya didn't greet her in any way; she simply dropped a piece of mangled flesh at Meera's feet and proceeded to curl up in a sunny patch and preen her feathers. Meera stared blankly at the bloody thing in front of her before her tired mind processed that it was the leg of a mountain goat. She supposed it was nice of Shaya to bring her something to eat.

Gingerly, she lifted the goat leg between her fingers and carried it into her cave to make it into a stew. Food preparation used up the remainder of the day's light. After she was done eating, she carried her leftovers outside to offer them to Shaya. The raek looked disdainfully at the unfamiliar food at first before craning her neck to sniff it. She then stuck her large tongue in the pot and lapped up the contents with two swipes, humming in pleasure. "I will bring you the entire goat next time," she said.

Meera assumed it was a compliment to her cooking, and she laughed. "I'm here for a reason, and it isn't cooking," she told the raek.

"Tomorrow, we will start with Aegwren's memories," Shaya replied.

Meera had forgotten that Shaya had told her they would train with Aegwren's memories. She almost asked what that meant but supposed she would find out the next day. She would also continue to sit with her emotions, she decided. It hadn't been pleasant, but it had helped her clear a path to her magic. She felt better, having given her feelings the time and consideration they needed. They were still there, but they didn't press at her as urgently as before; they lay curled and sleeping in her gut instead of pacing restlessly under the surface of her skin.

Meera slept soundly that night and awoke with a fresh determination. She started her day by training her muscles, carrying large rocks under each arm and climbing up and down the steep slope to the overlook above. First, she walked, then ran with her load, and afterward, she returned to the valley, sweating and panting, with dust and dirt coating her shirt. Shaya stood licking her claws after an early morning hunt. Meera approached her raek and attempted to pat her shoulder affectionately, but Shaya shifted her bulk away from her hand.

"Good morning," Meera said aloud.

"Is it? Why?" Shaya asked.

"It's just a greeting," Meera explained.

"Frivolous human nonsense," Shaya replied before hefting her weight to the edge of the creek and bending to drink.

Meera rubbed her arms; she was getting a chill from sweating and standing still. Anxiously, she looked around the mountainside and wondered how cold the winter would get.

Shaya turned and snorted in Meera's direction, spraying her with droplets of water. "You have raek fire—my raek fire. Why worry about the cold?" she asked, sounding more contemptuous than curious.

Meera felt irritated that Shaya seemed to be monitoring her thoughts, and she couldn't even tell. She didn't bother answering her raek; they both knew she couldn't control her raek fire yet. She turned to retrieve her quilted jacket from the cave, but Shaya demanded her attention with a hum. "It is time to start your training," the raek said in her mind.

Then—without warning or explanation—Meera was suddenly pushed into a memory. She was both standing in her valley and standing in a forest clearing beneath trees with green foliage. Looking down, she saw her orange outfit, but when she blinked her eyes, she was looking down at a plain white linen shirt and brown trousers over a body that was not her own. Disoriented, she stumbled back and fell on her butt, wincing as the hard ground jarred her spine.

A gruff voice said, "Today, we start your training." The voice came from right in front of her, but no one was there. Meera clutched her head in her hands, confused. Who was talking to her?

"It is about time, Uncle," she felt herself say in a voice lower than her own. "I am practically grown." Meera felt herself stand straight and tall and puff out her chest even though she was doing no such thing; she was crumpled and hunched on the ground. Shaking her head, she tried to rid herself of whatever Shaya was doing to her.

"Close your eyes," the raek told her in her mind. "It will make it easier."

Meera obeyed, shutting her eyes. She was standing in a forest full of soft green light. There was an older man in front of her with olive skin and a salt and pepper beard. She jittered with excitement and anticipation—except she didn't jitter. Whose body was this? The man stepped toward her. She felt anxiety, but she also felt her other body's familiarity with the man.

"Aegwren, you are far from grown, but it is best we start now. These are uncertain times, and you must learn to fight and use a sword. I wanted to start your training sooner, but ... your father would not hear of it," the man said, his eyes darkening under his thick eyebrows.

She was in Aegwren's body! Meera felt his chest constrict at the mention of his father, and she knew from his emotion that his father had died. She felt the loss of her own father with Aegwren.

Even though he was alive and well on the peninsula, she still felt as if she had lost the father she had known.

"Stand before me," Aegwren's uncle said. "Feet hip's width apart. Bend your knees. Tighten your core. Turn to the side. Bring your arms up."

As Aegwren obeyed his uncle's instructions, Meera scrabbled off the stone ground of her valley, keeping her eyes shut and doing her best to mimic Aegwren's movements. She could feel both her body and his layered on top of one another. She felt her trusty and well-worn leather boots as well as the soft grass under Aegwren's bare feet. She felt a breeze tickle her exposed, sweaty neck as well as the silky brush of his straight brown hair. She felt the weight of her breasts in her breast wrap as well as the pendulum swing of his dangling man-parts in his trousers—an especially strange feeling.

Aegwren's uncle proceeded to lead them through some basic stances and maneuvers, many of which Meera had already learned from Shael. She stumbled several times—dizzy with the feelings of two bodies in different places—but after a while, she found that focusing on Aegwren's body and mind helped her keep her balance. Her own body mimicked his movements, believing them to be her own, without her conscious effort. It was a bizarre sensation—giving herself over to the thoughts and actions of another person.

Aegwren was young and enthusiastic. His movements were fast and graceful—for a human—and he committed himself fully to every new exercise. Meera felt the deep respect he had for his Uncle Fendwren, intermingled with complex feelings about his father. Aegwren was also hard on himself; when he tripped and fell, he arose with a flared temper and new determination when Meera might have laughed. When his uncle chastised and berated him, Aegwren worked harder and did better when Meera would have grown angry and despondent. Still, she found that she liked the young man and didn't mind joining him in his memory.

Meera's chill was quickly forgotten as she worked and moved with Aegwren, refreshing what she already knew about hand-to-hand combat and learning new movements as well. Sweat dripped down her forehead, and her stomach growled, but she kept going. Occasionally, she slammed her toes into a rock or stepped into the creek and had to open her eyes to her valley and reposition herself back into the center of the open space. Sometimes she scraped her skin against the stone ground when Aegwren and his uncle sparred, and she fell repeatedly on her butt when Aegwren moved in ways she could not quite replicate. Body-sharing was not easy.

Just when Meera was starting to feel a sense of connection and oneness with Aegwren and rolled her shoulders back with him in preparation for another sparring match, her surroundings shifted and changed. Suddenly, it was drizzling in the clearing, and she was facing a different direction—Aegwren was facing a different direction, that is. His uncle was wearing a new shirt and was explaining something about breaking an opponent's grasp.

Meera opened her eyes, briefly, confused by the sudden change before realizing that Shaya must have switched to a different memory; her raek lay snoozing unconcernedly on the far side of the valley. Shutting her eyes, Meer focused on Aegwren again. His uncle seemed to be picking up where they had left off in the previous memory, so she assumed this was their next session. She continued to follow Aegwren's movements through that session and another and another; her knell body kept going despite her fatigue and hunger.

Hours later, her surroundings blurred and disappeared, and she was left in the dark for a moment—confused—before she remembered that her eyes were closed and opened them, blinking into the true day around her. Shaya was rising onto her feet and stretching. She didn't say anything before launching into the sky and flying away. Meera looked down at herself, readjusting to being in her own body. Her knell body felt stronger and faster than Aegwren's, but her soft feminine curves also impeded her movements in ways that the lean, young man didn't experience. Relieved to have a chance to rest, she drank deeply from the creek and went into the cave to get something to eat.

After a break, she decided that there was still plenty of time in the day, and she plopped down by the water to resume her shaping training and sit with more of her feelings. She let her thoughts stray, and they stuck once more on the scar she had given Shael. Then Hadjal keening beside her burning table rose to her mind. Meera let herself flood with her emotions, feeling both worthless and dangerous. Then she thought of her father and how he seemed to want to get away from her and pass her off to Shael. She thought about the other riders—how desperately she wanted them to accept her and how distant she felt from them at times.

Meera sat and felt and cried until her energy waned and her mind cleared, and as had happened the day before, working through some of her emotions allowed her raek fire to emerge from wherever it lay dormant within her; her palms alit with pale flames, and she stared at them, trying to manipulate them in some way. She willed the fire on her right palm to grow higher and watched with delight as it did, swirling several inches into the space above her skin. She smiled at her success, but as she did, her fire flared and licked her sleeve. Her shirt quickly ignited.

By reflex, she gripped her flaming sleeve and tore it off, throwing it to the ground. Before it hit the stone, the fire was already out, and Meera sighed in relief and looked down at herself. After one day of training, her clothes were covered in grey dirt, there were rips in her shirt where she had rested rocks against her body while running, and she had only one sleeve left. She glanced at her old brown boots, which were also beaten and worn; the left boot especially was still stretched and misshapen from when she had broken her ankle. But Meera supposed her ragged appearance didn't matter much since there wasn't anyone around to see her.

Leaning over the creek, she splashed her face with the cold mountain water. She knew her training would be a long, arduous process, but she felt hopeful. It had only been one day, and she was already seeing progress. When Shaya returned with another piece of goat, she cooked it and ate hungrily, and the second she lay down on her bed and closed her eyes, she fell asleep. The next morning, she awoke ready to start all over again.

12

MEERA

After several weeks, Meera felt stronger and more capable. She could run up the mountain's slope faster while carrying more weight, and she had progressed far enough into Aegwren's training that she felt she could actually hold her own in a hand-to-hand fight against an attacker. Sitting with her emotions was still a daily part of her routine; she would never be rid of her regrets and traumas entirely and also had to cope with the new rising feelings of loneliness and isolation that threatened to overwhelm her living in the mountains alone.

Shaya was there with her most days, but the raek refused to offer Meera any amount of comfort or companionship. Meera was beginning to wonder if Shaya would ever attempt to bond with her in any way, or if their relationship was purely transactional. She let herself feel that disappointment and doubt and more until she was able to produce her raek fire at will, but while she could conjure pale flames to her palms with little effort now, she still could not entirely control the fire. After just a few weeks, she had lost the sleeves of every shirt she owned and a few of her pant legs as well.

During one particularly disastrous attempt to control her fire, Meera's entire body had gone up in flames, disintegrating her clothes and melting the pins in her hair before she could douse herself. She had spent most of the remaining day disentangling and ripping her melted pins from her hair, and after that, she had taken to twisting back the curls in front of her ears and tying them together behind her head to keep them out of her face. She didn't have any extra hair pins or leather straps. She didn't have much, but she was surviving, and she was progressing.

A LITTLE OVER a month into her training, Meera began to feel like Aegwren was a part of her—or at least a good friend. She looked forward to resuming his journey with him through the memories Shaya projected into her mind, and she enjoyed the company of his stern but loving Uncle Fendwren. They were her only source of company and comfort on the mountainside even though they didn't know she was there and never would.

One day, she sat cross-legged in the forest clearing with Aegwren, awaiting his uncle with him. Aegwren's irritation—and Meera's along with it—mounted the longer they waited. Uncle Fendi was never late, Aegwren thought. He shifted in his seat and started to worry. His anger had almost fully morphed into fear when Fendwren finally came down the path carrying a long bundle in his arms.

"What do you have?" Aegwren asked his uncle. Leaping up with curiosity, his former feelings were forgotten.

Meera felt jarred by his sudden shift in attention—she was not quite as easily distracted. She sometimes felt odd in Aegwren's body; they were not entirely dissimilar people, but they were not the same, either. That said, she was mostly used to his thought patterns and moods. From what she could tell, she had already experienced about a year of his training. She could feel and see his body changing, filling out with muscle and developing the broad shoulders of a man. His cheeks itched where his beard started to grow in.

"Well," Uncle Fendwren replied, "I think it is time for us to start your sword training."

Aegwren's whole being was flooded with joy and anticipation, momentarily overwhelming Meera enough to block out her own concerns. She craned her neck with him as his uncle unwrapped the blanket bundle he carried and revealed two gleaming swords. Aegwren reached out to touch the swords reverently, but Meera wondered what she would do with a sword and whether these memories would have any use for her.

"Human warriors need weapons," Shaya told her with exasperation. "Your bodies are too blunt and useless otherwise."

Meera bristled slightly. For once in her life, she didn't feel useless; she was beginning to feel strong and competent. She hadn't actually sparred with another person in her own body, but she knew the movements and had the muscles to back them. She had been working extremely hard to become someone who could take care of herself.

Meera had gladly learned hand-to-hand combat as an extension of the self-defense training Shael had started teaching her, but she wasn't sure she wanted to know how to use a weapon. She didn't want to hurt people; she was in that valley learning how to control her shaping so that she *wouldn't* hurt people. The thought of stabbing someone with a sword made her stomach lurch.

Maybe she should spend more time shaping and less time in Aegwren's memories, she thought.

"No," Shaya said adamantly, pausing the memory Meera was in so that Aegwren's thoughts could not distract her. Uncle Fendwren stood unnaturally still with the swords in his arms. "You need to be able to fight if necessary—to at least defend yourself. If you face an opponent, they will have a weapon. Your raek fire may be a suitable weapon when you have mastered it, but until then, you must train with a sword." Shaya didn't leave any room for doubt or dissent.

Meera supposed she was right; it wouldn't hurt to be able to defend herself and use a sword if she had to. She even felt a little thrill at the thought of twirling and slashing with the other riders in the sparring dances she had seen them perform with their swords. Opening her eyes to disengage from the memory, she walked into the cave. There, she tugged open the trunk at the foot of the bed and pulled out the sword that rested within. She didn't know anything about swords, but she could tell it was a fine one—the large opal in the hilt was a clue. It was a light-colored opal with glistening hints of blues, greens, and the palest pinks.

Touching the carved hilt, she wrapped her slender hand around it and lifted the sword from the chest. Then she gripped the leather sheath around the blade and slid it off to examine the steel beneath. The metal was untarnished despite being in the cave for so long and still looked remarkably sharp. Meera didn't dare touch its razor thin edge. Instead, she resheathed the sword to practice with it. But she hesitated for a moment, wondering if she had any right to this historical treasure.

Meera only knew teenaged Aegwren—not Aegwren, the first raek rider, who had ended the long war between humans and raeken. However, she felt pretty sure he wouldn't mind her using his sword. After all, she also sought to end a war to the benefit of raeken. Closing the chest, she left the cave with her new blade, eager to train and learn. Shaya looked at her lazily when she approached the center of the valley and resumed Aegwren's memory.

"These are not sharp for training purposes," Uncle Fendwren explained, handing Aegwren one of the swords—neither of which was the opal-hilted sword that Meera now held.

Aegwren took his sword and immediately started waving it through the air, jabbing at mock opponents. "Enough of that," Fendwren chastised. "Listen to me." Aegwren stilled and offered his uncle his full attention, as did Meera.

"Sword fighting is nothing like hand-to-hand combat," he began. "When fighting with our hands, it takes deliberation and strength to injure an opponent. However, with a blade, injury— death even—can be a matter of accident. A slash in the right place can block a blow. An inch too low, and your throat could be slit. An inch too high, and you may meet flesh instead of steel. With a sword, comes responsibility. It is a responsibility for which I believe you are ready," he said, placing an affectionate hand on Aegwren's head.

Meera's own throat constricted from the touch; she was sorely missing the touch and companionship of other people in her mountain valley. Even so, she felt a new strength at being alone— mostly alone, anyway. She had forced herself to feel her emotions and live with only her own company and felt she was making great strides on her journey of self-understanding and control. She felt pride in herself, just as Aegwren felt the pride of his uncle's belief in him.

"Now, I know what you are going to ask," Fendwren continued. "Many use spears these days because they have better reach when fighting raeken and because they can be thrown a great distance

—" Meera started. She had not realized Aegwren was training to fight raeken. "However, spears are fragile, easily broken, and easily lost when thrown. Even if you choose to use a spear, it is always best to also have a weapon that you can wear on your body and use in close-combat. If your father had had his sword ... Well, things may have ended differently," he finished with a weary sigh.

Meera felt Aegwren's grief for his father swirl in his gut, but she also felt his frustration that his father had not had his sword and anger that he had left Aegwren and his mother to go raek hunting to begin with. Aegwren's emotional output was so strong, it momentarily distracted Meera from her own disbelief and disgust that Uncle Fendwren was preparing his nephew to face raeken as well as human attackers. Meera couldn't tell what Aegwren thought about raeken; she could only experience what he was experiencing and thinking at the time of the memory, and from what she could tell, he didn't think of them at all.

"Let us get started," Fendwren said, grasping the hilt of his own sword.

Meera rolled her shoulders back with Aegwren in readiness. It was his habit before fights, and one that she was quickly picking up. They started with basic postures, and Meera held and moved her opal-hilted sword in time with Aegwren's movements. Despite her knell muscles, her arm and wrist were quickly fatigued from the effort of swinging the heavy sword. She suspected that the blade was slightly long for her since she wasn't as tall as Aegwren. Her thrusts and swipes were extremely clumsy, and she accidentally struck her long, sheathed sword against the rocky ground several times.

As Shaya continued to show her subsequent memories without allowing Meera time to rest her aching wrist and forearm, she had to resort to holding her sword with both hands and modifying Aegwren's movements accordingly. She had an easier time holding and swinging the sword in a two-handed grasp, and the sword's hilt was plenty long enough for both of her slender hands. Swinging a sword with her eyes shut, however, proved to be a much greater challenge than practicing hand-to-hand combat moves.

Meera slammed the sheathed sword into rock walls and against the hard ground over and over again, jarring her arms, rattling her teeth, and distracting her from Fendwren's lessons. For several frustrating days, she had to repeatedly open her eyes and reset her position in the valley. Shaya also grew annoyed since she often asked the raek to pause the memory or go back, fearing she would miss something.

Then, one day, something changed. Meera shut her eyes and rolled her shoulders back with Aegwren, preparing to face his uncle. They both held their swords at their side since Fendwren never allowed Aegwren to start a match ready to fight. Then Fendwren attacked with a step and a strike. Meera was about to step and parry with Aegwren when her foot halted in mid-air. She could sense that she was about to step on a large rock and stopped herself before she could trip and fall. Confused by what she was sensing and by Aegwren moving on without her, she opened her eyes.

There, before her and under her raised foot was—in fact—a large rock. Meera stared at it. She didn't know how, but she had somehow known it was there with her eyes shut. Shaya stopped the memory, sensing her distraction. "What is it?" the raek asked impatiently.

"I sensed that this rock was here with my eyes shut," Meera said disbelievingly.

From what she understood, basic shaping usually involved sensing that which one was experiencing with one of their five senses. Specialty abilities circumvented the need to see, hear, touch, smell, or taste whatever one was shaping, but Meera had raek fire abilities ... Why could she sense a rock? Perhaps her subconscious just knew it was there from her familiarity with the valley. She had never heard of a knell having more than one elemental ability.

"Close your eyes," Shaya instructed.

Meera obeyed reflexively, expecting to enter another memory, but instead, a rock pummeled her in the gut. She grunted, bent forward, and opened her eyes in alarm. Shaya was facing her with another rock grasped between her teeth. "What's wrong with you?" Meera raged, rubbing at her abdomen where the rock had hit her just an inch under her lowest rib. She knew how much a broken rib hurt, and she couldn't train in the mountains alone if she got injured.

Shaya sent a thin wisp of remorse to her through their mental connection.

Meera scowled at her and decided she was done training with Shaya for the day. She turned away to practice shaping by the creek. First, she removed her clothes. The season was growing steadily colder, but she didn't have many clothes left and needed to preserve some for the coldest part of winter. Standing naked in her usual place, she conjured her fire to her palms with relative ease.

Meera could now reliably summon and extinguish her raek fire. Part of her wondered whether she should return to the riders, having accomplished her initial goal, but she knew she still had so much more to learn. She missed Shael and the others desperately, but she felt like she had only just gotten into a rhythm living in the valley and was still finding herself. She was sick to death of eating mountain goat almost every day, but she was getting progressively stronger and better at shaping.

For a time, she practiced raising and lowering the flame on her palm. Then, curiously, she shut her eyes to experience sensing and shaping her flames without sight. She was still aware of the location of her fire and could still expand and contract the flames at will. About to open her eyes, she sensed something whirring toward her back, and instinctively, she spun around and held out her still flaming palms to block the object. Whatever it was hit her hands lightly and burst into flame.

Meera opened her eyes—startled and blinking—and found her precious quilted jacket in a flaming heap at her feet. It was the jacket Darreal had given her to find her father, the one she had worn previously in the mountains that still bore a blood stain from her fall in the storm. It was also the warmest layer she had beside Shael's riding jacket. Meera extinguished the fire quickly, but it was too late to save the pitiful scraps of fabric on the rock.

She glared at Shaya, who had clearly retrieved her jacket from the ground and thrown it at her. "Humans need clothes," she told Shaya in the same level tone the raek always used when berating her. "We are useless and featherless, remember?"

Shaya huffed a puff of smoke. Then she showed Meera the image of her blocking the jacket with her eyes closed. Meera stood with her mouth slightly open in amazement at what she had done, and Shaya curled up on the ground with a self-satisfied hum.

"How did I do that?" Meera wondered aloud. She had sensed the jacket flying through the air, and she had sensed a rock on the ground before her. She had a strong suspicion that spending so much time with her eyes closed had awakened some new magical ability, but she wasn't sure what it was. What was she sensing? The air?

Meera tried for the rest of the day to understand her new ability without success, and Shaya continued to toss things at her when she wasn't looking, resulting in several large bruises and a scrape on her head. Meera couldn't tell if Shaya was actually trying to help or just found the game amusing, but she was not amused. Crawling into bed that night, she felt especially worn-out and lonely. She held Shael's jacket bunched up against her chest and pulled out his note, staring at the words: *Come home to me.*

In that moment, Meera considered leaving. She imagined getting up early and flying back to the peninsula in time to surprise everyone at breakfast. She pictured the smile on Shael's face when she ran into his arms and kissed him—because she wanted to but also because she could without burning him. She felt confident that she could control her raek fire enough not to hurt Shael even if she couldn't actually use it for anything.

Eyes closed, she imagined their reunion over and over again until her mind strayed to falling into Shael's bed with him. She remembered his kisses and the weight of his body on top of her, and she began to move and squirm under her blankets. She trailed her hand down to where his had never reached, feeling the hot wetness between her legs. This was something she'd never done before, and she thought of Shael while she touched and explored herself.

"Is this human mating?" Shaya asked suddenly in her mind.

Meera jumped, removed her hand from her body, and pulled her blankets up over her head even though her raek couldn't see her. "Get out of my head!" she shouted mentally, enraged by her lack of privacy and inability to tell when Shaya lurked inside her.

The raek didn't answer, and Meera could only assume that she had gone. It took her a long time after that to settle her heart rate, but she eventually fell into a deep sleep. Sleeping since her change felt heavier and denser than it had before. Meera also found that she was hungry all the time, either from her training or because her new knell body needed more fuel.

She was quickly working through the stores of food in the cave and relying more and more on the meat Shaya brought her. However, despite her dwindling food stores and thoughts of leaving, she awoke the next morning and resumed her training. And she did the same the day after that, and the day after that, and so on, until the full force of winter was upon her.

13

MEERA

By the time freezing temperatures reached her valley in the mountain, Meera was able to control her raek fire well enough to keep several fires burning around her while she trained. It was all she had to keep herself warm in the low temperatures and often whipping winds. The few scraps of clothing she had left provided little coverage for the winter weather.

The more she needed to use her raek fire, the more adept Meera became at controlling it. She also continued to develop a sense of her surroundings with her eyes shut. When she and Aegwren swung their swords in unison, she could sense every snowflake fluttering around her. She practiced with her sword unsheathed now that she was competent enough not to hit the ground or herself with the blade, and she took great pleasure in slicing it through the air and cutting into the swirling flakes of snow around her.

"Good!" Fendwren said to Aegwren after a sparring match.

Meera paused with Aegwren to listen to what his uncle had to say. Her hot breath fogged the air before her as she panted. Since Fendwren couldn't actually see her, she took the opportunity to stretch her limbs while he spoke.

"Your technique is getting very good," he told Aegwren. "But you are too predictable. If you let yourself fall into a rhythm, your opponent will be able to anticipate your moves." He proceeded to point out that Aegwren always blocked certain maneuvers the same way and favored attacking whenever Fendwren's sword was on his left.

Meera listened, but she had noticed the same patterns in Aegwren's fighting and wished she could actually spar for herself and learn what her own tendencies were. She still enjoyed Aegwren's memories, but she was growing a little weary of always training as someone else. When Shaya released her from the memory, she got up to stretch and go hunting, so Meera sat down next to the creek, relieved to spend some time in her own skin.

With her eyes closed, she attempted to manipulate the air. It was the air she was sensing, she had decided, though she hadn't yet managed to shape it. Sensing the air gave her a full picture of the world with her eyes shut because everything that wasn't air was outlined, and she was getting good at distinguishing what the outlined shapes were. Eyes still shut, she sensed the snowflakes falling around her and marveled at all of their detailed splendor. She tried to shift the air currents to push them, but nothing happened.

Meera was so focused on her immediate vicinity, she didn't notice Shaya circling above. Suddenly, she sensed a mass hurtling down toward her. She dove to the side, but in the same instant, she gave the mass a mental shove away from her. A rock the size of her head cracked into the ground ten feet away and tumbled even further from the momentum of her shove. Her eyes flew open, and for a moment, she stared stupidly at the rock.

Then she looked up and around wildly and saw Shaya above her in the same instant that she sensed her raek's triumph. Meera's rage with the raek broke forth like never before; she stomped over to the large rock, picked it up, and hurtled it up at Shaya with all of her strength. Even with her knell muscles, the attempt should have been futile, but Meera put everything she had behind the throw and stared at Shaya's flying shape like she could hit the raek with sheer willpower.

To her utter disbelief, she did hit Shaya. The rock soared up and up, much higher than she could have thrown it. Then, rather than reach its peak and arc back toward the mountainside, it kept moving and slammed into Shaya's underside, knocking her off course. Meera felt her raek's alarm and confusion, and it mingled with her own. Had she just shaped a rock through the air? Shaya's alarm quickly turned to admiration when she grasped what had happened. She landed back in the valley with a resounding thump and appraised Meera with both of her pale, unnerving eyes. "I chose well," she said. Meera wasn't sure if Shaya was complimenting her or herself.

"I'm sorry," she said. "Are you okay?" She had been angry, but she would never really want to hurt Shaya—or anyone for that matter.

Shaya didn't seem upset. On the contrary, Meera felt her raek's delight and sensed that she was deliberating something. Meera was about to ask what she was thinking, not having mastered the art of entering her raek's mind, when she felt Shaya's click of decision, and a moment later, Shaya lunged for Meera with a swirling orb of raek fire in her open mouth. Startled, Meera backed away and started to ask what the raek was doing, but Shaya came at her at full speed. The raek fire was almost upon Meera, and for a split second, she felt panic and recalled her pain when Cerun had burned her. Then, she threw up her hands instinctively and blocked the onslaught, directing the raek fire harmlessly around her body.

She sweated from the heat of the fire but was otherwise unharmed. Shaya retreated with what Meera could only describe as a devilish grin before lunging back toward her with more raek fire, this time slashing a massive, clawed foot down at her as well. Meera ducked and dove and redirected Shaya's flames over and over again, giving up on trying to understand what her raek was doing and focusing all of her energy on surviving the relentless attack.

Shaya's onslaught was merciless and continuous, and eventually, she started throwing rocks as well, which Meera either dodged or deflected with magic, completely unsure if she was shaping the air or the rocks themselves. She panted as she moved, and her chest ached with strain as she gulped in air that was stiflingly hot from all the raek fire. Finally, exhaustion got the better of her, and a rock clipped her jaw, jarring her teeth together and knocking her to the side.

Shaya immediately stopped; she went from full raging raek mode to sitting perfectly still in just a fraction of a moment. Meera was left shaking and disoriented. She rubbed her sore jaw and stared at her raek distrustfully. She knew Shaya was trying to help her train—she could sense the raek's intent. She also knew it had worked—she had shaped like never before and on pure instinct. However, training wasn't everything, and Meera resented Shaya's lack of decency toward her. "Do you even care about me? Or are you just trying to use me to end the war?" she asked, her voice trembling as much as her exhausted limbs.

"Care about you?" Shaya asked like it was a strange idea she had never considered before.

"Is friendship and love a human thing?" Meera asked, suddenly feeling immensely foolish and wondering if she had expected entirely too much from this wild animal. But how could that be right? Cerun loved ...

"I am acting out of love for my kin," Shaya responded after a moment of consideration.

"We're supposed to be kin, too!" Meera shouted.

Shaya just stared at her with her fathomless, unblinking eyes, and Meera opened her mouth and huffed a puff of smoke at her in true raek fashion—something she didn't know she could do until she did it. Then she turned and went inside the cave.

DESPITE MEERA'S PROTESTS, Shaya continued to attack her when she least expected it. It upset Meera and angered her, but it also helped her finely hone her raek fire abilities and get a better feel for shaping the air. While she seemed to be able to shape both wind and rocks, it was the wind she shaped the most out of instinct. She succeeded in occasionally sensing and shaping the rocks Shaya threw at her, but mostly, she knocked them aside with gusts of air.

Occasionally, Meera stopped to wonder how it was that she could shape three different elements, but all she could do was shrug and assume it was due to Shaya's infusion of magic. Despite her special abilities, she didn't seem capable of the standard shaping that most knell learned; she could not move objects around the cave no matter how hard she stared at them. Even so, as the winter went on, she grew stronger and more capable. Her shaping and fighting progressed rapidly, and yet, she didn't return to the peninsula. She craved more—she wanted to be stronger.

One especially blustery winter's day, Meera got up and suggested to Shaya that they practice flying. She sent images of her suggestion to her raek through the tether in their minds.

"I know how to fly," Shaya replied predictably. "What is there to practice?"

Meera rolled her eyes at the raek's arrogance. "The other riders practice flying drills with their raeken," she explained. "We need to get used to the feel of one another. We need to be able to fly and fight as a team."

Meera believed what she was saying, but she also wondered if this was the worst idea she had ever had. She hadn't ridden Shaya since their flight to the valley; she had barely managed to stay on the raek then, and Shaya was certainly not being any gentler with her lately. The raek cocked her head in consideration, then hummed her agreement, and Meera's breakfast flipped in her stomach with anxiety.

Trudging back into the cave, she put on all the clothes she had as well as Shael's leather jacket. Then, on a whim, she strapped her sword to her waist to get a feel for wearing it. Meera could barely walk with the long sword dangling off her hip, and when she crouched to jump onto Shaya's back, the point of the scabbard slammed against the hard ground, knocking her off balance. "This isn't going to work," she muttered to herself. She was getting more and more in the habit of talking to herself since hers was the only voice in the valley.

Removing the sword from her hip, she slung the belt across her body, wearing the long sword on her back instead. She took a few experimental steps around and practiced removing it quickly to unsheathe her sword several times to make sure the position would work. When she felt satisfied, she leapt adeptly onto Shaya's back, settling herself at the base of the raek's neck. Then she bent and held tightly to the iridescent feathers before her. The second Meera stopped moving, Shaya vaulted into the air, forcing her to clench her thighs and cling to the raek with all of her strength. Meera sent a wave of displeasure through her mental tether to Shaya, but the raek ignored her.

Shaya propelled herself through the air at a speed Meera hadn't known raeken were capable of. Then she stopped short, dove, swept back into the air just before hitting the mountainside, and flipped herself upside down. Meera, meanwhile, kept her mouth clamped as tightly as her thighs in an effort not to spew her breakfast everywhere. But when Shaya finally stilled enough for her to think, Meera wished she *had* puked all over the raek just to annoy her. She had barely managed to stay on Shaya's back, and after only minutes, she was already trembling and stiff from the cold. "I know you can fly!" she shouted over the biting wind. "That's not the point!"

"I am flying, and you are practicing holding on," Shaya replied obstinately.

Meera leaned forward to shout her response, feeling like the raek ignored her less when she spoke aloud. Her grip loosened as she opened her mouth to speak, and in the same instant, Shaya rolled sideways in a series of barrel rolls. Meera managed to cling to her through her first airborne tumble, but by the second, her cold hands reached the ends of the glossy feathers in her grasp, and she fell.

Plummeting through the air, she tumbled over herself again and again. Her heart and stomach clogged her throat, and she flailed, completely helpless. Bursting through a freezing layer of cloud to see the ground quickly approaching below, she couldn't think; her mind was as blank as the space between her and the rocky mountainside. She didn't know what to do or how to save herself and sent a mental plea to Shaya. A second later, her raek was beneath her.

Meera crashed into Shaya's back with enough force to knock the breath from both of their lungs. Shaya, at least, continued to fly, while Meera lay prone and gasping across her expansive back. Her legs sprawled across one of the raek's wings and lifted and fell with her flapping. After a moment, she dragged her body along Shaya's and repositioned herself on the raek's shoulders. She was relieved to be alive but also bitterly cold and scathingly angry.

Before Meera could express her feelings, however, Shaya said mentally, "That was poorly done. You should have been able to catch yourself."

"Catch myself?!" Meera shouted, barely audible over the gusting wind. "You're supposed to be the one that flies, remember?" She was shaking from her fall and the biting winter air. Out of the valley and away from her fires, the wind and cold froze the flesh of her body, leaving her stiff and numb. Her cheeks and ears screamed from the constant lashes of wintry air, her hair tangled around the sword on her back, and her fingers felt too frozen to grip Shaya's feathers.

"Take me down," Meera told her raek mentally.

Shaya ignored her.

"Take me down!" Meera screamed in her mind. All she could think was that she was cold—too cold to hang on. She didn't trust Shaya to carry her safely, and she didn't know at what point her body would stop functioning. She already felt a soothing numbness spreading through her arms that worried her.

"You have magic," Shaya reminded her, nonplussed by her fear.

Tears crusted on Meera's lower lashes, freezing the instant they met the wind. The air bellowed in her ears so loudly she wanted to clamp her hands over them, but her hands were stiff and immovable in their curled fists. Suddenly, all she wanted was some quiet. She couldn't stand the howl of the wind anymore and clenched her stinging eyes shut. She couldn't think. She couldn't move. She wanted it to stop!

The next instant, the wind pummeling Meera's body stopped. The air around her grew eerily still and quiet. Opening her eyes, she released a sigh of relief; she had shaped the air to stillness. She could shape air, she reminded herself, feeling stupid. Her dry, chapped lips cracked into a smile, and she put her numb fingers under her armpits, feeling like she could move and think again. Shaya continued to flap and soar beneath her, relatively steady against the gusts that continued to push and pull her large body.

"I still need to get down," Meera told her raek mentally as her teeth chattered.

"Then get down," Shaya said before once more tucking in her wings and rolling onto her side then back.

Meera lunged forward and clung on, but Shaya remained upside down, slowly curving downward toward the mountainside beneath them. Meera gripped the raek's feathers hard and craned her neck to look where they were headed. Her knell eyes could see that they were directly over their small valley between two peaks and looking up to look down felt unspeakably wrong.

Mentally, Shaya was showing Meera that she should let go and catch herself with her air shaping, but Meera didn't trust that she was capable of such a thing. Suddenly, she could make out the rocky details of their valley—complete with its few hearty shrubs —and fear crept up her spine. Her rapid breaths and pounding heart rattled in her cold chest. "You're going to pull up, right?" she asked her raek.

Shaya didn't answer.

"Pull up! Shaya, stop!"

"You can catch both of us or only yourself. The choice is yours," Shaya replied calmly.

Meera screamed her frustration in a wordless torrent of sound. She knew Shaya wanted her to let go and fall. "This is not a choice!" she yelled, even as she let go and felt herself drift from her raek's back.

Shaya pulled up and away, righting herself and circling above the valley. Meera spread her arms and legs and stared at the rapidly approaching rock beneath her. She shut her eyes but could still sense the ground nearing, and she shaped a gush of air up toward herself. Her body slowed in its descent but continued to fall. She tried again, harder, but the push of air unbalanced her and flipped her on her back. For a moment, she struggled and flailed, opening her eyes in the process and becoming dizzy with the rushing colors all around her.

With a desperate flip, Meera managed to right herself. Once again she was spreadeagle and staring at the valley below, and she shaped another gust of air. This time she pushed it up at herself in a swirling motion. She slowed but didn't stop. She pushed harder, swirled the air faster. She dipped below the high peaks and was sandwiched between two rock walls with the valley spread out between them. She could no longer see the sky. Her wide eyes strained, fixed in horror on the approaching valley. Terror seized her already stiff flesh. The creek below grew steadily nearer; she could see every sheet of ice attempting to coat its rushing surface.

Meera was feet away from impact, still moving quickly. She wanted to shut her eyes and scream and be saved, but Shaya was far above her. There was no one else to save her; she had to save herself—save herself or die. With all of her mental energy, she pushed the ground away from her instinctively. Air rushed up under her and propelled her briefly upward before she flipped like a pancake and fell back down on her back. She hit the stone ground with a grunt of exhaled air, and her head cracked against a small patch of sandy dirt where some mountain ferns grew.

For an entire minute, Meera lay still like a squashed bug, staring at the sky above her where Shaya continued to circle. She heaved in a breath and choked out a sob of mingled relief and anger, but she didn't move—she was afraid to move because she was afraid to be hurt. If she was hurt, her training was over. She would have to return to the peninsula. A part of her wanted that —wanted to be around people who cared about her and eat something other than old jarred preserves and mountain goat, but she still wasn't ready.

When Shaya landed in the valley with a thump, Meera finally convinced herself to wiggle her fingers and toes and peel her aching body off the ground. Everything hurt—her head especially —but she stood and didn't think she was horribly injured in any way. Then she turned and slowly hobbled into the cave. She couldn't even look at Shaya, and she did her best to block the raek out mentally, though she was sure Shaya could overpower her mind if she wanted to. Meera withdrew to lick her wounds and seethe in what little privacy she could muster.

14

MEERA

For several days, Meera refused to look at Shaya, speak to her, or allow her to assist in her training. She focused, instead, on her shaping, and she practiced her sword technique on her own as much as she could. Her body remained sore and stiff from her fall, but mostly, it was her feelings that were hurt. Shaya had thrown her to the mercy of the elements and mountain and forced her into something she hadn't felt ready for. The raek's methods had worked ... But that was beside the point.

Meera continued to practice catching herself, jumping from a ledge in the rock wall along the valley where she risked a broken bone or two but not death. In those few days, she had a breakthrough and felt more capable of shaping the air at will—not just instinctively. She found shaping rocks to be more difficult, but she could move the small ones that littered the valley floor.

She continued to work on her raek fire abilities as well. One day, she stood on the edge of the creek and summoned her pale, swirling flames. For several minutes, she shifted them from hand to hand and morphed the fire into different shapes. Then she moved the raek fire from her hands to float in the air before her. She was staring into the large, spiraling white-blue orb of flames when a bird unexpectedly veered into her peripheral vision and careened toward her fire, propelled by the wind.

When Meera saw the bird, she froze. Rather than focusing her energy on her fire and putting it out, she just stared at the bird in horror and watched as it toppled into the swirling sphere of pale flames. Gasping, she managed to put out her fire at last, but it was too late. At least, it should have been too late, but the brown thrush landed on the ground before her, dazed but unharmed. Meera stood very still and observed the small bird, but when Shaya shifted her enormous weight to see what had caused her bout of emotion, the thrush quickly took flight and flapped away into the treacherous winter gales.

"No matter," Shaya told her despite Meera's best efforts at keeping a mental barrier between them. "It was hardly big enough for a snack." The raek seemed to think her jolt of feeling was at not successfully catching the small bird.

Meera wondered at what had just happened. How had the bird gone into her raek fire and emerged unharmed? She wasn't burned by her fire, but in her experience, everything else seemed to be. Conjuring her flames into her hand, she stared at them, thinking. Could she have given the bird the same protection she used unknowingly for herself? Glancing around, she found a stick on the ground and picked it up. Mentally, she willed the stick not to burn and held it over her flaming palm. It quickly burned to nothingness. Sighing, she tried again and again and quickly burned through every stray stick and leaf in the valley.

Shaya snorted, watching her. "Are you so angry with me that you would rather clean this stretch of mountainside than allow the memories stored within me to aid your training?" the raek asked.

Meera ignored her. After several sweeps around the barren valley for objects on which to test her new theory, she reluctantly went into her cave in search of something with which to practice. Eying the small space, she wondered what was least important and could be sacrificed to her fire. The few books? No—she might be a raek rider, but she would always be a scholar's daughter; she wouldn't burn books. She rifled around the shelves for a loose scrap of paper.

She had Shael's note in his jacket pocket, but that was too important to her. Meera paused and cringed at her next thought: maybe that was the point ... Maybe she needed to threaten something important in order to tap into her abilities. She hadn't actually been concerned about whether the bits of twigs and leaves she had held over her fire would burn or not. Maybe she needed to care.

Her heart thumped faster as she removed Shael's small, folded note from his leather jacket and walked into the open air with it. Opening the bit of paper, she read his words in case the worst happened: *Come home to me.* Her chest clenched. She wanted to; she wanted to go home to him and felt like learning to extend her protection to objects and people—learning to make her raek fire harmless—would be the final step in her shaping training. It would be the last log needed to dam her powerful, rushing magic and make her safe to be around.

Meera conjured fire to one of her palms once more, extending it away from her meager scraps of clothing. Then she held Shael's note in front of her and stared at it, willing it not to burn—trying to mentally extend her protection to the helpless scrap of paper. Shaya lifted her head from the ground and fixed her eerie gaze on Meera, sensing her emotion again. With a steadying breath, Meera slowly moved the note over the swirling flames in her palm and dropped it into the fire.

She held her breath and watched, waiting for the paper to quickly shrivel and be eaten, but it was not. It sat on her palm, engulfed in pale flames but unharmed. She could still read the words Shael had written to her. Grinning, she extinguished her fire and held the note triumphantly before her. "I did it!" she called to Shaya, momentarily forgetting to be angry with the raek.

Shaya discerned from the note in her hand and the memories in her head what it was she had done. "You see," the raek said smugly, "Sometimes you must be held over the fire to inspire your abilities." Meera knew she was referring to letting her fall and knew the raek felt entirely justified in her actions—even more so after watching Meera risk something important to her for the same reason.

Meera scowled at the raek but couldn't exactly argue with her; she did seem to progress in her shaping the fastest when she was under pressure. Even so, she turned away from Shaya and continued to practice her new ability on her own for the rest of that day and the two days following until she could extend her protection to anything with just a thought. After she successfully engulfed the entire cave with her fire and managed not to burn anything, she slumped onto the bed.

For the first time since she had burned Shael, Meera felt completely sure that she wouldn't accidentally hurt anyone. She felt more dangerous and more powerful than ever—but in control. She felt she could go home to Shael and love him and marry him and never leave another scar on his body. And yet, she didn't jump from the bed and run outside to Shaya; she sat and dawdled, wondering if her training was really over—if it was time for her to return to the peninsula.

The gleaming opal in her sword's hilt caught her eye. She had been itching to pick it up and resume her training with Aegwren, but she was still reluctant to interact with her raek. She had not entirely forgiven Shaya, though she didn't feel like ignoring the raek was teaching her anything. Swallowing her pride, Meera picked up her sword and stepped into the valley. "I'm ready to resume sword training," she told Shaya in a would-be-casual voice.

"Are you?" Shaya asked mockingly. "Are you ready to resume training with me as well?"

"What do you have in mind?" Meera asked, glowering at Shaya, who was sprawled out in a rare patch of direct sunlight. The light reflected off of her iridescent feathers, forcing Meera to squint.

"I will resume your memories with Aegwren, but I will also train you in whatever manner I deem necessary to make you a competent warrior," Shaya replied.

Meera rolled her eyes in a display of nonchalance she did not feel. She knew Shaya intended to drop her mid-air again— possibly worse—and she did not relish the prospect. "Fine," she agreed, biting her lip so she wouldn't take it back.

The next second, Meera was in Aegwren's memories, standing in the familiar forest clearing where they trained. She exhaled a sigh of relief to be back with her training partner. It was summer in this memory, and she enjoyed the warm breeze she felt on Aegwren's bare arms and the golden light dappling the grass at his feet. Holding her sword, she stood in quiet contemplation while they both awaited Fendwren's arrival. At this point, their training consisted almost entirely of sparring, and when Aegwren's uncle arrived, he always attacked without warning.

Meera and Aegwren waited together with joy and anticipation. Their minds both wandered occasionally down different paths before returning to the present and the hilts in their hands. Despite knowing they would be attacked, neither unsheathed their swords. Fendwren never allowed Aegwren to begin a sparring match ready to fight. At the very least, he was always made to hold his blade loosely at his side.

Meera jiggled on the balls of her feet, anxious to get started. Her mind roamed to the dwindling food stores in the cave and what she would eat that day, and just then, Uncle Fendwren emerged running from behind a large oak, brandishing his sword before him, gaze intent under his bushy brows. He immediately feigned an attack on their left side and drew back, bringing his sword down low instead. Meera and Aegwren unsheathed their blades and blocked Fendwren's upward slash with speed and skill.

They continued to spar and were at a level to be almost evenly matched with Fendwren's experience. However, Aegwren's uncle eventually landed a blow to his nephew's chest—one that Meera would have been quick enough to block with her knell speed— and Aegwren laughed and clapped his uncle on the back good-naturedly. "I will be able to best you soon, Uncle Fendi!" he said.

"You will, indeed," Fendwren replied with a fond smile.

The memory faded and was replaced with another memory from another warm summer's day, and Meera continued to spar with Aegwren for the rest of that day and the several weeks that followed. In that time, she also trained with Shaya, who took pleasure in bucking her off mid-air and forcing her to catch herself as well as attacking her at random. Meera became very good at catching herself from falling and even began to enjoy the heady freefalls through the air before the rising swirl of wind she shaped caught her.

On a particularly bitter, cold day, Meera stood in the center of the valley panting and sweating. She had spent the morning fighting Shaya, who had relentlessly attacked her with raek fire, stones, her snapping teeth, and her slashing claws. Meera was battered by the exchange but still standing. She had several fires blazing around her and was sparring in Aegwren's memories. At this point, Aegwren was able to best his uncle in two out of three fights.

Meera smiled with him when they brought their sword points to Fendwren's chest, winning another match. Fendwren put up his hands graciously and accepted his loss. "It would seem that our training is almost over," he said to his nephew sadly.

"Nonsense!" Aegwren replied. "We will both need to spar regularly to keep from getting out of shape."

Fendwren grinned and nodded, but his smile did not reach his solemn eyes. "May we spar long into our lives, then," he answered, slapping Aegwren lovingly on the back. Meera realized for the first time that, while Fendwren behaved like an elder, he really wasn't especially old. Regardless, there was a sadness in his eyes and a seriousness in his stern mouth that made it difficult to ever imagine him as young and spry as Aegwren.

The memory flickered and dimmed, and a new one took its place. Meera trained with Aegwren through several more memories until she could tell that the weather was turning to winter in his world as well; the trees around their clearing had few leaves left clinging to their branches, and she could feel the cold nip Aegwren's skin through his wool sweater. He won almost every match against his uncle now and had grown to be both taller and broader than Fendwren. His brown hair had grown long and swished across his shoulders as he and Meera swung their swords in unison.

After another fight in which Aegwren won, the memory flickered and changed once more. Meera was breathing hard and growing hungry. She considered calling it a day, but she felt she had one more spar in her tired muscles. However, when a new memory materialized around her, she sensed immediately that something was wrong. The scenery was the same—the same quiet and cold clearing met her eyes—but Aegwren was different.

Normally a jovial, peaceful spirit to share a body with, the young man writhed with anger and grief. Meera was pummeled with his strong emotion, even as she tried to block it out and keep her mind about her. What was happening? What was wrong? Aegwren lifted his sword, though no opponent stood before him, and proceeded to hack at the largest oak tree on the edge of the clearing, gouging ragged lines into its trunk. Then he fell to his knees and howled a sound of anguish that told Meera too plainly what had happened: death.

She didn't know who it was and couldn't decipher the tides of thought pushing and pulling in Aegwren's mind, but she knew someone he loved must be dead. Her chest ached for him, and her eyes filled with tears. She wished Fendwren would come and comfort his nephew—comfort them both with his steady voice and calm authority. It was then that Meera looked at the sword in Aegwren's hand and saw that it was not his, but his uncle's. Realization hit her like a sharp blade in a tree trunk, and she fell to her own knees, shaking from shock. What had happened? What had killed such a strong and competent man? Suddenly, the memory was gone, and she was alone with her grief in the middle of the mountainside valley—well, alone except Shaya.

"It would appear that your sword training is over," the raek said unperturbed.

Meera felt the cold air beginning to chill her sweat-dampened skin as she sat on the ground, but it was nothing compared to the coolness she felt toward Shaya in that moment. "What's wrong with you?" she asked. "Fendwren is dead! Don't you care?" She dropped her sword and clenched her fists to her stomach, feeling like she might be sick. Shaya didn't answer her, so Meera looked up into her raek's pale eyes.

It was then, staring into Shaya's fathomless gaze, that Meera realized how ridiculous she was being; of course, Fendwren was dead. Aegwren was also dead and had been for thousands of years. She sat with that thought, mulling it over in her mind for many long moments. Somehow, it didn't quite ease her grief. She still cared—she still mourned Aegwren's uncle like she had lost her own uncle. She mourned Aegwren as well—the young man who, presumably, would grow to be the first raek rider and end the war between humans and raeken. She felt like she knew them, like they were a part of her life—a part of her, even, and now they were both suddenly gone.

Shaya shifted uncomfortably nearby. Meera could sense her raek's creeping concern and could tell that Shaya was wondering whether she'd chosen a defective human to be her rider, considering she was on the ground weeping for two men who had been dead for thousands of years. The large raek stood and took several tentative steps toward her. Then she opened her jaws and exhaled a burst of steamy hot breath against Meera's cold skin.

Meera started. It wasn't much, but it was the most directly kind thing Shaya had done for her since they had joined as raek and rider. "Thank you," she said, touched by Shaya's attempt at comfort.

That seemed to be all the effort the raek was willing to put in, however, because she then leapt into the air and flew away to hunt, sending Meera images of mountain goats as she flapped into the distance. Meera dragged herself off the ground and began the tedious process of lugging water from the creek to the large basin in the cave so she could take a hot bath and warm her blood. As she lifted a full bucket with ease and carried it into the cave, she realized her training was over—her solo training, anyway. It was time for her to return to the peninsula and her life. She could control her shaping, she could fight, and she was ready.

Pouring the heavy bucket of water into her sloshing basin, she heated it with her raek fire. Then she undressed and stood in the cave looking down at herself. There wasn't a mirror in the cave, but she could still see that her body had changed; her muscles were visible beneath her light golden-brown skin, which held a number of bruises and scrapes from fighting with Shaya.

Even more than her physical strength, however, Meera felt a strength of spirit she hadn't had before. She felt comfortable and confident in her body and mind. She knew who she was, and she knew what she wanted. She ached and grieved for Aegwren and his uncle, but she knew her grief would not break her. She felt like a warrior. She felt like a rider.

15

SHAEL

When Meera took to the sky on the wild raek's back, Shael was left broken—broken but unsurprised. He had always known she would eventually leave him; it had been his primary reason for denying his feelings for her in the first place. He had not, however, imagined her leaving quite so soon. She had her reasons, of course—reasons that included caring enough for him to want to protect him from herself. However, understanding Meera's reasons did little to lessen Shael's pain.

At first, he hoped she would return quickly, but as the fall wore on, his hope decayed with the leaves on the forest floor. And when winter descended gradually and mildly on Levisade, Shael's pain froze and hardened into anger. It had been months, and Meera had not so much as sent word that she was safe. Surely, she was not so far away that she could not at least let him know she was alive.

A small part of him recognized that his anger was born from his love and fear for Meera, and yet, that did not stop him from lashing out at everyone and everything around him. He was boiling under the surface and barely keeping a lid on his emotions. Eventually, the other riders took to avoiding him completely. He could not blame them, but he was still angry; he was angry at Meera for leaving and angry at the other riders for not being able to help her and not trying to stop her from going.

One day, he finally had it out with Hadjal. They were all eating dinner at her new wooden table. Isbaen had made it for her, and every time Shael sat at the new table, he was reminded of the horrible day in which Meera had burned the old one and withdrawn from him completely. He could not help but hold some resentment toward Hadjal for how dramatically she had reacted to losing the table—it was just a table, after all; he had lost Meera.

The other riders were discussing the latest Champion's Challenge, which Darreal's blonde-haired champion had won, retaining his title. The knell man who had challenged him had reportedly been extremely physically fit and strong as well as a competent shaper, but he had not been very intelligent. Darreal's champion had outwitted him. Shael had not gone to witness the challenge, and he was having a difficult time paying attention to everyone else's discussion of what had happened. He did not care. He just stared at the knotted wood table before him, his emotions building beneath his calm facade.

"It was just a table!" he finally burst out, interrupting Katrea, who glared at him, the muscles in her neck flexing. Isbaen reached a placating hand out toward him like he was some sort of frightened animal, but Shael would not be silenced. "It was just a table, Hadjal! No one was hurt! If you had not overreacted, Meera would have stayed and trained here. Now she is probably dead somewhere!"

"Shael, we are all entitled to our emotions and reactions ... as you are exhibiting now," Hadjal replied, her golden eyes appearing older and wearier than usual. "But Meera left of her own free will, and I imagine with a raek that powerful as her ally, she will be perfectly safe."

"*Will* be?" Shael asked, leaning forward. "You don't think she'll return, do you?" he could feel the blood thrumming in his face—he could feel himself losing control, but he could not stop it. He was so tired, he realized. His nightmares had grown worse—more frequent—and he barely slept at all.

"Shael, I have made you a tea. It should help you sleep," Soleille said.

He stared at her blankly. He felt so deranged and paranoid that for a second he wondered if she had read his thoughts, but of course, she had not—of course, they could all see how worn and tired he was. Of course, his flaws were glaringly obvious to everyone.

"Calm yourself," Cerun said in his mind, but Shael ignored his raek.

"We are all concerned about you," Isbaen said. "We can tell you are not sleeping. We thought you would heal with time, but your condition is getting worse. It is time for you to let us help you."

"Help me?" Shael asked stiffly. They thought he was weak. They thought he was pathetic and useless and incapable of taking care of himself. They had gathered without him to discuss how to fix him—make him more like them—but he could not be more like them; he was a half-breed.

Shael's thoughts spiraled into the deepest core of his self-loathing, and he got up and left. He retreated to his house, and he did not leave for days. Eventually, he slept for a long time, awoke feeling more himself, and returned to his routine at the peninsula. The other riders had the grace not to mention his outburst or absence, but they continued to tip-toe around him. However, after

Shael had gone several days without another meltdown, Soleille once more offered him a tea, which he accepted with gratitude. Isbaen began leading him through a daily meditation, and Florean and Orson invited him to go fishing with them. Shael accepted, though he resented being the newest member of their sad men's club.

As the end of winter neared, Shael's birthday was soon upon him. Knell did not put much emphasis on birthdays, but regardless, he felt sulky that Meera did not return for his. He awoke in a foul mood and ran to the peninsula, wondering whether the other riders would even remember that he turned twenty-two that day.

His mother had sent him a package containing sweets and a vest that was far too gaudy for him. Shael supposed he ought to visit his parents since it was they who wanted to celebrate him. But his birthday always reminded him of his murky origins, and his parent's refusal to discuss his mysterious biological father made him feel unseen—even when they went through the trouble of preparing his favorite foods and making a show of celebrating him. Maybe next year he would return home for his birthday, he thought, but this year, he was in no mood.

Shael broke through the edge of the trees and slowed to a walk as he descended the grassy slope toward Hadjal's house and her new table. Through his bond with Cerun, he felt a thrill of excitement, but he ignored his raek, refusing to investigate the feeling; he was getting more and more into the habit of ignoring Cerun, who had thought it was for the best when Meera had left and refused to change his mind.

Shael stared obstinately at the ground as he approached his breakfast, bracing himself for the inevitable disappointment of being greeted as usual. He knew he was being childish and ridiculous. He supposed his expectations for his birthday came from his human upbringing, but he could not go back and change that even if he may want to. He wondered how long he would have to live in Levisade as a rider before he actually felt even half-knell, let alone truly knell.

"Not moping on your birthday, are you?" came a familiar—though long-unheard—voice. Shael's head whipped up in disbelief. There, rising from the table and walking toward him, was Kennick.

Speechless, Shael rushed forward and embraced his friend. Kennick squeezed him in return, and his long auburn hair stuck to Shael's sweaty face. After a moment, Shael broke the connection, having a lower threshold for displays of affection than Kennick. Then they just looked at one another. Shael could not believe how long it had been since they had seen each other—it was almost a year since he had been captured.

"It is so good to see you," Kennick said with enough feeling to make Shael look away. Kennick ignored Shael's discomfort and leaned down slightly to plant a kiss on his cheek, embarrassing him further.

"You as well," Shael mumbled. He met his friend's dark eyes once more and could see in them all of the things Kennick wanted to say about his capture. He shook his head slightly. "It was my own fault, and now I am back," he said dismissively before his friend could even broach the subject.

Kennick looked at him long and hard before silently acquiescing to dropping the matter. "I am also back," he replied, "Though I hear things are not as they once were. Is it true you are engaged?"

Shael looked aside again, and his jaw clenched. That was

another subject he did not wish to discuss. "She left," was all he said before skirting around Kennick toward the table.

The other riders greeted him and wished him a happy birthday, rising from their seats to hug him until Shael felt distinctly uncomfortable from all the attention. As they ate, they asked Kennick about his time with Aegorn's army, and Kennick regaled them all with his most entertaining stories and anecdotes. Shael could tell his friend was keeping the discussion light for his sake.

He also knew Kennick would ask him the hard questions once they were alone together, and despite anticipating seeing his best friend for almost a year, Shael dreaded explaining everything he had missed in his life. After they finished eating, Kennick invited Shael to spar with him by the lake, and Shael agreed, knowing they would not train. They walked silently to the beach together and both sat down immediately in the sand, not bothering with the pretense of sparring whatsoever.

"Are you back for good?" Shael asked, trying to head-off Kennick's questions.

Kennick sighed, which was so uncharacteristic that Shael immediately stopped fretting over his own life and turned to give his friend his full attention. "I was supposed to return months ago," he admitted. "Hadjal has been writing to me with increasing irritation, telling me that my training with the army was over, and I was to return for her to evaluate me and decide whether my training as a rider was complete." He paused, and Shael tried not to acknowledge the jealousy that brewed in his gut, hearing that Kennick was nearly a full-rider and not a rider-in-training. Isbaen had mentioned no such thing to him.

"I felt torn between my duties as a rider and my allegiance to the men at the border, but the soldiers needed me—really needed me, whereas Hadjal could wait," Kennick said. Shael could see how much leaving the army weighed on his friend; he looked more heavily burdened than the jovial, carefree version of himself Shael was accustomed to.

"A few weeks ago, Sodhu sent me a letter saying that you were not doing well," Kennick admitted. "At first, I thought Hadjal had put her up to it to entice me to return, but I had not heard from you at all ... It was time for me to come back and face some of the things I have been avoiding." He pierced Shael with his direct gaze.

"Shael, It was my fault—we both know that I was the one willing to disregard our orders and separate. If I had been with you ..." he trailed off, probably noting the look of irritation on Shael's face.

Shael tried to keep his expression blank, but Kennick could read him better than anyone else—even Meera.

"I wanted to find you," Kennick continued, "But breaking the rules was what had gotten you captured to begin with, and we had both agreed to uphold the code ..."

"I know," Shael told his friend. "I do not blame you." It was true; he did not blame Kennick for failing to rescue him from Terratelle. Shael had been captured due to his own ineptitude and would not have wanted Kennick to risk his life retrieving him —an incompetent rider. He supposed if he was still lying broken in the dungeon he might feel differently, but thanks to Meera, that was not the case. For several long moments, they were both silent.

"The others told me that a human woman rescued you," Kennick ventured.

"Meera," Shael supplied.

Kennick nodded. "So, this Meera rescued you, you brought her to Levisade, but she left?" he asked.

Shael wondered how much, exactly, the other riders had shared with Kennick. It did not seem to be much. "Something like that," he replied vaguely.

"You asked her to marry you?" Kennick persisted.

"I did."

"Hadjal said something about a wild raek changing her. She said you were hurt ...?"

"Barely," Shael replied taciturnly. He felt bad for not opening up to Kennick, but he just did not know how.

"Do you think she will return?" Kennick asked, sounding curious. Shael supposed Meera would be a curiosity to anyone who had not met her.

"She might."

"And if she does?" he asked doggedly.

Shael shrugged. He did not know. He loved Meera, but he also felt so angry with her for leaving and for being gone for so long. Besides, he thought, she would leave him again. She was always going to leave him, so maybe it was better that she had done so quickly.

"We should swim!" Kennick exclaimed, shaking off the serious tone of their conversation and giving Shael the broad smile he expected from his friend.

"It is winter," Shael replied, grinning. He knew Kennick would only take the dissent as a challenge.

His friend's dark eyes flashed, and by unspoken agreement, they both leapt from the sand, tore off their clothes, and flung their bodies into the cold water, racing for the far shore.

16

MEERA

"I t's time to leave," Meera told Shaya mentally as she tidied the cave and gathered her meager possessions. She was dressed in the best clothing scraps she had left—all of her outfits were ruined by a combination of raek fire, rock abrasion, and downright hard-wear. Her best remaining option was a pair of ripped and sagging brown pants and her original pale orange shirt from the Levisade Estate—or what was left of it. Both of its sleeves had been badly burned, so she had torn them off at the shoulders. The bottom portion of the wrap shirt had been ripped open from one of Shaya's claws, and Meera had cut the ragged bit off, leaving her with a shirt that only reached to her waist. Several inches of her stomach showed between her cropped shirt and low-riding pants, but it was the best she could do.

She took some extra time twisting back the fronts of her hair and tying them in a knot behind her head. Her hair was getting rather long and hung past the end of her shirt down her back. She put on her trusty brown leather boots; they looked extremely worn but were still holding together. Then she donned Shael's black leather riding jacket and her sword, swung her nearly empty bag over her shoulder, and left the cave without a backward glance.

She wasn't leaving forever, she assured herself; she planned to return soon to restock the food stores she had eaten during her months on the mountainside. She liked knowing the cave would always be there—preserved—for her to return to if she needed it, and she mentally thanked Aegwren for the sanctuary and the sword. Her chest clenched at the thought of the man she felt she knew but would never meet, but she shook off the past and walked toward Shaya and her future.

Their flight was several hours long but peaceful. Meera kept herself warm by stilling the wind around her and occasionally summoning fire to her palms to warm her bubble. Shaya moved steadily beneath her and, thankfully, did not try to toss Meera from her back or attempt any last-minute training. As they left the mountains behind them, Meera felt the weather warm and was surprised to find that Levisade winters were hardly any colder than Levisade falls.

Finally, the peninsula appeared beneath them. Shaya circled overhead several times to give the raeken below the chance to become aware of her presence and recognize that she was not attacking. Meera looked down at Hadjal's house with a flutter in her stomach. She had envisioned this moment so many times— the moment in which she would leap from Shaya's back and run into Shael's arms, home at last—but now that it was here, she felt nervous and shy.

She could see the riders below gathering at Hadjal's and looking up at her. It was sometime between when they usually ate breakfast and lunch. The thought of food made Meera's stomach rumble, and she hoped Sodhu was cooking something good. Then she took a deep breath and sent Shaya a mental image of them landing. Her raek leaned forward and dove for the grassy slope below, unusually obedient.

Once Shaya landed, Meera released the air shape-shield she had been maintaining around herself and hopped gracefully down into the grass. She looked toward Hadjal's house where the riders were gathered—watching—and her eyes fixed on the new table standing where Hadjal's precious, ancient table had been. She cringed, knowing she still needed to apologize for burning the rider relic and hesitated at Shaya's side. But when her gaze landed on Shael, she walked toward him—butterflies flapping in her chest.

As Meera drew closer to the others, she saw a mixture of joy and trepidation on their faces. Shael's was a blank mask of stone. Her feet slowed at the sight of his guarded expression and cool gaze, but then she ran forward and threw her arms around his neck, hugging him to her. She waited one moment, then another, but Shael did not return her embrace. Releasing her grip on him, she dropped back onto her heels, and the butterflies in her chest plummeted into the fiery pit of her stomach, igniting and disintegrating.

"I missed you," she said, searching his grey-green eyes for some sign that he was glad to see her—some reciprocation of her feelings. She couldn't find anything. She stepped back like he had struck her. This was not the reunion she had imagined.

"Meera is back!" Soleille exclaimed, coming around the house and seeing her for the first time. Soleille stepped toward her, but Hadjal held out an arm as if to hold her back. The tension in the air was palpable.

"Welcome back, Meera," Isbaen said into the silence. She smiled at him and looked around for her father.

"He is fishing with Florean," Isbaen supplied.

Meera nodded, and it was then she noticed the man standing near Shael. His dark red hair was long and free over his shoulders, and he had it pushed behind his ears, which were both covered in intricate metal cuffs. His wrists and fingers also bore metal jewelry. "You must be Kennick," she said, continuing to look the man over: his clothes were dark but clearly very fine, he was slightly taller than Shael with somewhat narrower shoulders, and he stood with one of his hips popped out in a way that struck Meera as almost feminine.

Kennick tucked his ring-bedecked hands into his pant pockets as she gazed at him. "You must be Meera," he replied evenly. He did not smile exactly, but a humorous light glinted in his nearly black eyes. She saw his gleaming eyes travel over her, lingering on her raek fire scar.

"Meera," Hadjal interjected, drawing her attention back to the older knell woman. She stood stroking her thick braid and looking uncharacteristically wary. "I have given this a lot of thought ... I am sorry, but I must ask you to step back."

Meera stared at her blankly. "Step back?" she asked, as if she had not heard correctly.

"Yes. The safety of the riders is my priority and responsibility, and I must ask that you remain distant from us until we can be sure that you are safe," Hadjal replied. Everyone looked somewhat startled by her declaration, but no one objected—not even Shael, who continued to look coolly at Meera like he was observing someone he didn't know.

Meera swallowed but didn't move. Shaya sensed her emotion and slashed her tail in agitation behind her. "I'm safe," Meera asserted. "That's why I'm back." Resisting the urge to fidget with the edge of Shael's leather jacket, she stood still and certain; she was proud of all she had accomplished in her training, after all, and she was in complete control of herself. Her eyes flitted to

Shael. He looked back at her, expressionless, and she glanced away again. What was happening?

"Hadjal, Meera left of her own free will. If she has returned, I am sure it is because she is in control of her shaping," Isbaen finally said. Meera looked at the silver-haired man with gratitude. She had missed Isbaen.

"I need you to step away," Hadjal insisted, ignoring Isbaen and staring at Meera. "You could burn us all with one stray emotion. Then there would be no riders left to protect Levisade."

Meera bristled inwardly, but she took several large steps back —away from her fellow riders. She almost corrected Hadjal and asserted that the riders were formed to create peace between the races—not to protect Levisade—but she didn't want to cause more of a rift. "Hadjal, I am very sorry about your table, but I promise you, I wouldn't be here if I thought I might hurt anyone," she said quietly.

She felt Shaya approach behind her and could sense the raek's rising irritation. "What is happening?" Shaya asked in her mind, mimicking Meera's own confused thoughts.

"They aren't sure I'm safe to have at the peninsula," Meera replied mentally, feeling the sting of each word. This was not how she had envisioned returning to the riders. This was not the greeting she had expected after months away. Her hurt feelings mingled with Shaya's anger. Shaya seemed to think the riders were questioning Meera's abilities and thereby, questioning her judgment. "It's alright," Meera assured her in her mind. "Stay calm."

"Everyone, this is Shaya," she said aloud, as her raek approached behind her. Meera saw everyone's eyes shift to Shaya and how nervous the extremely large, wild raek made them. This was not going well, she thought.

"These people are supposed to be your kin," Shaya said. "Why do they not welcome you back? Why have they pushed you from their circle?"

"They're just nervous, that's all," Meera replied mentally.

"Do they not see that you are a warrior?" Shaya asked indignantly. She lifted her head and parted her mouth somewhat, scenting the air menacingly.

Meera held her hands up placatingly to her raek. "It's okay. They just need time to feel comfortable around me," she said in her mind.

Shaya ignored her. "We will show them what kind of warrior you are," she replied, flashing images into Meera's mind of the two of them fighting.

"No!" Meera shouted aloud, startling the other riders, who seemed aware that she and Shaya were conversing, if confused. "Shaya, don't!" Panic started to bubble up in Meera's stomach. The last thing she needed was to put on a frightening display of abilities, but she had never had any success getting Shaya to listen to her before. Her raek rumbled a low hum that made Falkai and Cerun nearby raise their heads and rumble as well.

"What is going on, Meera?" Isbaen asked, sounding sharper and more alarmed than his usual calm self.

"It's okay," she told him. "Shaya is just a little upset, but she won't hurt anyone."

Shaya raised one of her massive, clawed feet and slammed it down on the ground in disagreement.

"Shaya, go! Please!" Meera shouted aloud, feeling her raek readying herself for action. It was no use. Meera clasped her hands on either side of her head in frustration. "Everything's fine!" she told the other riders, waving them off. "Just stay out of it!" She saw the utter confusion and alarm on their angular, knell faces before she turned and sprinted away from Hadjal's house, passing Shaya and attempting to lead her raek away from everyone else. She dumped her bag and sword on the ground as she ran.

Meera was near Shaya's tail when her raek turned with fire in her maw and lunged for her, shouting, "I will show them that I chose a warrior for myself!" in her mind.

Meera easily blocked and redirected the fire, but she knew it was only a ruse; Shaya whipped her long, feathered tail at her in an attempt to knock her over. Meera jumped into the air, avoiding Shaya's tail, and when she landed, she ran further afield, away from the others. "Stop it, Shaya!" she shouted to no avail. The raek could not even hear her through her own frenzied determination to prove Meera's worth. Meera might have been flattered if she weren't so embarrassed by Shaya's behavior.

Shaya continued to attack, swiping at Meera with her claws, biting at her, blinding her with raek fire, and slashing her tail. There were no rocks for her to throw in the field, so she took to ripping up clods of dirt and throwing those just to add to the confusion. Meera dodged and blocked the assaults however she could, all the while trying not to display too much of her abilities; she didn't want to frighten the riders more than they already were. She continued to plead with her raek to stop, but Shaya didn't slow or hesitate in her attacks.

Finally, Meera lost her patience. She disoriented Shaya by surrounding her head with harmless pale raek fire, then she brought a powerful gust of wind down on the raek, flattening her to the ground. Once Shaya was pressed to the field, Meera shaped the dirt under her to rise up and encase the raek's legs and wings. She found the soft dirt of the field was actually easier for her to manipulate than the hard rock of the mountains. Compressing the dirt until Shaya could not move, she leapt on top of her raek in victory.

"There! I win! Are you happy now?" she shouted. Once Shaya

stopped struggling, Meera released her from the dirt and jumped back down, sensing her raek's satisfaction with her performance. She stormed several feet away before whirling back around, yelling, "Go! Just get out of here, you stupid, useless, winged rat!"

Shaya shook excess dirt from her feathers with a dignified raise to her head, and Meera could sense the raek was content with the display she had forced out of her. Then Shaya leapt into the air and flew out over the lake for a drink of water, proceeding to settle herself on the far cliff to preen her soiled feathers.

Meera stared at the destruction they had caused in the grassy field, which was now a churned-up heap of dirt. She shaped the dirt back into place but could do nothing to restore the grasses and flowers that normally grew in the now-bald patches. Hanging her head, she turned toward the riders and approached them once more. She could barely stand to look at their astonished faces. Even her father stood away from her and gaped—Florean at his side as if to protect the human man from his own daughter.

Meera shut her eyes briefly and reminded herself that she was not a destructive person by nature—that she could control her abilities and her body and her emotions. When she opened them, she saw her father step toward her, but Florean held him back. She gave them both a forced smile, attempting to look harmless; she hated being gawped at like some sort of raging monster. "It's good to see you, Father," she said quietly, then she raised her voice slightly: "I'm sorry for Shaya. She means well."

"Meera, that was remarkable," Isbaen said. "Did you shape the air and ground in addition to the raek fire?"

Meera nodded stiffly.

"... not natural," she heard Florean mutter.

Ignoring him, she looked to Hadjal, waiting for the woman to accept her or denounce her. Hadjal appeared uncertain. Meera glanced again at Shael, but he remained stone still and expressionless. Striding over to him, she removed his jacket and thrust it into his gut, forcing him to take it. She wanted to shake him—to shout—but she didn't want to cause more of a scene. "Thank you for the jacket," she said, then quieter, she added, "I came home, Shael ..."

He didn't respond. Swallowing, Meera turned and walked back away from Hadjal's table. She pushed her pain down to process at a later time, trying to appear calm and competent.

"Meera, do you want me to heal you?" Soleille asked.

Meera stared at her in confusion. "Heal me?" she asked, thinking for an irrational moment that Soleille was offering to heal her broken heart. Then she looked down at the bare skin of her stomach and arms—where her sweat was drying in the cool air and little chilled bumps were rising—and she registered the many bruises and scrapes she had amassed over time from sparring with Shaya. "Sure," she replied, standing still while Soleille shaped her small injuries away.

Meera hadn't really processed how sore she had been until her body was refreshed. "Thank you," she said to Soleille, who nodded, unusually reserved. "Why are you being so quiet?" Meera asked her. "I've been here a whole twenty minutes, and you haven't teased me once."

"I am taking in the new you," Soleille replied with an odd look on her face. Meera wondered what she meant by that; she was stronger and more confident, but she was still the same person.

"I like your new look," Katrea said. Meera assumed she was poking fun at her scraps of clothing.

"This is all I have left," she admitted, fingering the ends of her torn shirt.

"Not the clothes," Katrea amended. "Muscle looks good on you."

With a start, Meera realized Katrea was being serious, not

insulting her. Looking down at herself again, she supposed she did have a decent amount of visible muscle. She shrugged, unsure of how to respond.

"You appear to have worked extremely hard while you were gone," Isbaen said approvingly.

Before Meera could reply, Shael finally spoke. "You were gone a long time," he said, his voice wavering slightly, belying the indifference on his face.

"What's five months in a thousand-year lifetime?" Meera asked rhetorically, eyeing him. He looked well enough; his dark hair was shiny and clean, and he had filled out again since she had last seen him. She compressed her lips, so they wouldn't tremble and wished he would just hug her and tell her he had missed her instead of using his feelings as a shield and a sword through her heart.

"It was six months, actually," Isbaen said unhelpfully.

Meera supposed it was just about spring. Then she stood there awkwardly—apart from the other riders—wondering if they would ever invite her to sit and eat with them. She was starving. She kept glancing at Hadjal, but the knell woman continued to look like she was thinking or in pain or both. Meera shifted from foot to foot and wondered what else there was to say.

"So, can you use that sword?" Kennick asked, his hands still casually in his pockets. Everyone looked at Meera's sword on the ground, herself included.

"Maybe," she said truthfully. She hadn't actually sparred with another person.

Kennick grinned. "Want to find out?" he asked with a mischievous look in his dark eyes and a disarming smile.

Meera frowned at him; she found charming people inherently suspicious after dealing with Prince Phineas. Kennick had the handsome, confident look of a person who had always had everything he'd ever needed and always got whatever he wanted. Meera didn't want to trust him despite knowing he was Shael's best friend, but the offer to spar was tempting.

"Absolutely not," Hadjal said before she could answer. "Kennick, you will not spar with Meera. She is not safe."

Meera stiffened. She supposed her display of abilities hadn't done anything to ease Hadjal's concerns.

"She seems safe enough," Kennick replied with loose nonchalance. One of his ringed hands left its pocket and twitched at his side like he was itching for action.

"What do I have to do?" Meera asked Hadjal.

Hadjal sighed. "It will take time for us to know whether you can handle being around other people," she replied.

Meera had already given herself time—six months of time training and pushing herself so that she could return home to the other riders. Now she wondered if she even had a home. Shael and her father stood right there and didn't defend her—didn't greet her properly. Staring at Hadjal's new table, she thought maybe she didn't belong on the peninsula.

17

KENNICK

Kennick studied the newest rider with keen interest. When Hadjal had written to him months ago to let him know that Shael was back in Levisade—freed by a human woman he had brought with him—Kennick had assumed two things: a human woman had fallen in love with Shael for his looks (as the stereotype goes), and Shael had brought her with him out of a sense of duty that Kennick expected from his friend. It had never occurred to him that Shael might love the human in return, and he had certainly never considered the possibility of a wild raek turning the human woman into the most powerful shaper he had ever seen.

Shael's interest alone made Meera fascinating to Kennick, but the woman before him was not at all how he had imagined her. After learning more about Meera, Kennick had imagined her ambitious and conniving; he had assumed she had ensnared Shael with her love and convinced a wild raek to give her the body of a knell all in the name of power. He had observed his friend's anger with the human woman and had adopted the sentiment as his own, believing the worst in her. Now he realized how wrong he had been.

The dejected looking woman before him did not appear to take any pleasure in her power or indeed, have any notion of how remarkable her shaping was. Kennick had never seen anything like it. She also seemed to have genuine affection for his friend and was clearly hurt by Shael's cold reception. Kennick had heard what Meera had whispered when handing Shael his jacket, and he sympathized with her; Shael's obstinate silences could be immensely frustrating.

Despite Shael's rejection and Hadjal's banishment, Meera still stood before them all with her heart in her big, brown eyes. Her clothing was in tatters, and Kennick could see the goosebumps raised on her skin. Yet, she did not rub her arms or plead for clothes. He assumed she was hungry after her ridiculously impressive display of strength and shaping, but she did not ask for food. Meera stood before them all seeking acceptance—something Kennick had also once sought from the riders—and he, for one, felt willing to offer her some.

"How about I take on the risk for all of us? I will spar with Meera and find out whether she is safe to have around," he said, stepping forward and retrieving his sword from where he had left it by the table. He thought Meera had displayed an abundance of control fending off her raek and was not overly concerned about her roasting him. He could also feel a sense of ancient energy emanating from her sword and was eager to see if she could use it.

"No, Kennick," Hadjal said, puffing up like a mother hen and swinging her thick braid over her shoulder like she meant business.

Kennick had the deepest respect for his mentor, but he was growing extremely weary of her telling him what to do. "Hadjal, this is something I can and will do, assuming Meera is willing," he said evenly, hoping Hadjal would not be too offended. She acted like their leader and did lead them all, in a sense, but the riders each had their own free will. Kennick was determined to exercise his.

Hadjal opened her mouth as if to argue, but she shut it and merely looked aside, unable to stop him. Kennick felt a pang, seeing the fear in her golden eyes, but it was not a fear he shared.

"Meera, where did you get that sword?" Soleille asked uncertainly. "Where have you been?" Judging from Soleille's behavior, Kennick got the impression Meera was much changed since the riders had last seen her. The thought only made him more curious about the light brown-skinned, round-faced human woman.

Meera retrieved her sword from the ground before she answered, and as she did, she held it almost reverently. "Shaya took me to a place where Aegwren used to stay. This was his sword, and I intend to use it to help unite raeken and humans once more as he would have wanted," she replied.

Kennick felt just as shocked as everyone else seemed to be. Aegwren's sword? He had not known that the first rider's sword still existed. "How do you know what Aegwren would have wanted?" he asked challengingly.

She regarded him, dropping her eyes to his own fine sword— one from his family's collection. "I don't know what the grown Aegwren would have wanted," she replied, "But I do know that young Aegwren would not have begrudged a new warrior any blade she could get her hands on." She grinned and unsheathed the sword, a summons Kennick was eager to meet even if he did not understand her answer.

"Meera, Kennick is very skilled with a sword. You have exceeded my expectations in what you have accomplished with your shaping these past six months, but no one can learn to sword fight all alone," Isbaen said, the voice of reason. Even so, Kennick thought that he, too, looked curious.

"Then I guess he'll beat me," Meera replied, unconcerned.

"No shaping," Kennick said, drawing his own blade with a thrill of anticipation. They both walked out into the open field, and the others gathered nearby to watch them. Shael trailed behind somewhat begrudgingly.

"I can't make any promises," Meera replied. "Often I shape by reflex, but if I do, then I forfeit."

"Fair enough," Kennick said, hoping that reflex did not involve raek fire. He caught sight of Meera's father, standing to the side and looking overwhelmed. Kennick had not spoken much with the man, but he had seen enough of war to understand the far-off look that was often in his eyes. "Do not worry, Orson! I will go easy on her," he called over.

"Life has not been easy for my Meera," Orson replied, "But she weathers every blow and deals one back."

Kennick grinned at the odd man, then he turned to Meera. "I will dull our blades," he said. He dulled his own with a thought and reached out for her sword even though he did not need to touch it—he wanted to hold Aegwren's ancient blade.

Meera walked toward him and held out her sword, but the look on her face changed. "Right ..." she said. "You're Shael's best friend who can shape metal—the one who left him to rot in an iron cage." Her eyes flashed at him dangerously, and the steel in her voice was not steel Kennick could easily dull. He felt her words pierce his skin even though he had thought he had come to terms with his decisions regarding Shael's capture.

"About that ... thank you for picking up my slack," he replied with a wink. The wink may have been a bit much; Meera looked like she might roast him after all. His gaze traveled from the fire in her eyes back down to the fascinatingly intricate scar on her neck, and he wondered what else no one had thought to tell him about this human woman.

"Kennick ..." Hadjal said warningly, clearly worried that he might actually push Meera into burning him.

"I am meant to be testing her, am I not?" he asked with a grin and a loose shrug.

"Alright, test away," Meera said, holding out her hand for her sword.

Kennick quickly dulled her blade, wishing he had had more time to sense the energy captured within the steel, and handed it back to her. She took several steps away from him, rolled her shoulders back, and held her sword loosely in her right hand. "I'm ready when you are," she said. Then, perplexingly, she shut her eyes.

Kennick tied back his hair and eyed Meera. She looked calm, steady, and serious. He lifted his own sword, hesitated a moment, then moved toward her with a simple attack. She quickly lifted her blade and parried him, a small smile appearing on her lips. She must be able to sense him through the air, he thought. Kennick's own lips curled before he stepped and attacked again and again. Meera met each maneuver easily, holding her long sword in both hands. Every time Kennick backed away, she let her sword fall back to her side idly. It was both unconventional and extremely taunting, and Kennick was not one to let a taunt go unanswered.

He continued to intensify his attacks until they were both whirling and moving continually—their swords clanging off of one another in a symphony that sang in his soul. Meera's smile slowly spread until she was openly grinning. Her teeth flashed in the light of the high sun, and she laughed, blocking yet another of Kennick's blows. She continued to block and defend but not attack herself. "You know, you smile before you move," she said. "It gives you away."

"How can you tell?" Kennick asked, laughing as he feigned to her right and struck at her left. With some difficulty, he wiped the smile from his face and attacked Meera in earnest, ready to finally break through her defense. She fought admirably, even waging some offense in order to allow herself time to prepare for her next defensive maneuver. However, eventually Kennick saw his opening and took it, swinging for her exposed chest. Suddenly, his sword was torn from his grip and flew up into the air. He broke his movement and watched with amazement as it landed ten feet away. Then he stood with an open mouth and an open hand.

"Oops! You win," Meera said, opening her eyes and blinking at him.

Realizing she had deflected his blow by shaping the air, Kennick shut his gaping mouth. He sensed his sword in his mind, lifted it from the ground, and flew it back into his open hand. Meera's face darkened, clearly associating his metal shaping with his failure to save Shael. Kennick looked to Shael, wondering why his friend did not run and embrace this woman, who clearly cared so deeply for him. Shael's face was smooth, but his eyes looked troubled.

"That was excellent, Meera!" Isbaen said, walking toward them.

"How did you learn to fight?" Shael asked, sounding suspicious.

Kennick caught the hurt in Meera's face before she looked down at the ground. "I told you all before that Shaya is a memory keeper for the raeken," she said—a fact that Kennick had not known. "I trained with Aegwren in his memories. I learned from his Uncle Fendwren." She sounded sad like she missed these figures from the past.

Isbaen looked as if he had many questions, but he restrained himself.

"You must be hungry," Kennick remarked to Meera, knowing what a physical toll that much shaping and sparring could take.

"I am," she replied, touching her stomach reflexively.

Kennick could not help but admire the muscles of her stomach that showed between her ragged pants and shirt. Meera looked to Hadjal, clearly waiting for an invitation to her table. Hadjal appeared torn. Kennick wondered what was going on with his mentor; he had never known her to be so fearful and unwelcoming.

Isbaen stepped forward and embraced Meera. "Welcome home. You have done an extraordinary job training in a short time."

Soleille also stepped up to officially hug Meera and welcome her back, as did her father, Sodhu, and—to Kennick's amazement—Katrea and Florean. Only Shael and Hadjal did not embrace Meera in welcome and acceptance. Kennick stepped forward and offered her his hand in the human style. She took it, though she looked reluctant. "You fight better than you dress," he teased.

"Thanks," she replied unenthusiastically. Then she looked back at Hadjal. Kennick's mentor did not spurn Meera or turn away from her, but she did not extend a hand or embrace her either. Finally, Meera sighed. "I guess I'll go into town to eat and buy new clothes," she said, heading toward where her sheath and bag sat on the ground.

With both slung across her shoulder, she pulled her father aside, and Kennick watched. He could not hear what they said, but he suspected she was asking him for money. Then he saw Orson shake his head. Regardless, Meera turned for the woods and walked toward town, and Kennick wondered if she even had any money for food. The other riders were left looking awkward in her absence—Shael especially. Kennick approached him. "Shael, I know you are hurting, but Meera clearly cares for you. You should follow her," he said to his friend.

Shael shook his head. "I barely recognize her," he replied, sounding forlorn. "What she can do …" Kennick knew Shael had always been insecure about his inability to shape, and he wondered if his friend resented Meera for her own powerful magic.

"You love this woman, Shael," Kennick reminded him, wanting to see his friend happy. He wished he had been there to see Shael propose—to see him smiling and in love and hopeful. He hated that his friend's joy had been so short-lived.

Shael stared toward the forest and nodded, but he did not move.

"I will make sure she has money for food," Kennick said finally, trotting after Meera without waiting for Shael's reply. Kennick knew Shael was prone to moods and long silences, but he felt a little disgusted with his friend for not defending the woman he loved or making sure she had clothes on her back and food in her stomach. Still, he had to admit that he was glad of an excuse to follow Meera into town; he was curious to learn more about her. Kennick felt he had missed so much during his absence, and she was the key to all that had transpired without him.

18

MEERA

Meera trudged through the woods with a determined gait that belied her crumbling insides. She was starving, for one, and felt like her stomach was breaking apart and eating itself, but mostly, she was fracturing from Shael's and Hadjal's rejection. She had trained as hard as she could to return to them and be safe to sit and eat with—safe to hug. She had fought her way toward them—sweating and fending off an enormous raek—and they wouldn't take one step in her direction.

Tears slid down her cheeks and tickled the skin of her neck. Brushing them away, she walked onto the main road into town. Meera was barely presentable in her ragged clothes, but she would not fall so low as to be seen crying in public. While she'd been planning to go straight to the bakery, she elicited enough horrified stares and dramatic gasps on her way past other shoppers to veer toward the clothing shop instead. Her stomach could wait; she had known worse hunger.

Entering the shop, she didn't bother acknowledging the sour, middle-aged woman who worked behind the counter. She heard the woman's intake of breath and low curses when she saw her, but the shop worker didn't seem inclined to run her out of the store. Not that she could, Meera thought smugly; she might have very little money left, almost no possessions, and only the ghost of a family member, but she had her strength.

She strode purposefully through the premade portion of the store until she found the shirt and pant sets similar to those she had destroyed in her training. The bell on the front door tinkled as someone else entered the shop, but she didn't look up. Fingering a blue shirt in her usual size, she lifted it in deliberation. Then she paused, sensing the shape of a man approaching behind her. Her heart leapt. For a moment, she thought it might be Shael, but the man's proportions were not quite right.

"That will not fit you," a voice said. Meera turned to find Kennick just behind her, looking over her shoulder.

"Sure it will," she replied, holding the shirt up to herself. Had he followed her? Did he think she needed help shopping? He looked that arrogant ...

Kennick laughed, his hands tucked casually in his pockets. "When was the last time you looked in a mirror?" he asked with a smirk.

Meera wanted to argue with the smug look on his face, but she supposed it had been a long time since she had last seen herself. He gestured toward a mirror on a far wall, and she sighed, dropped the blue shirt back onto the table, and approached her reflection warily. Meera expected her hair was a mess and her eyes were puffy from crying. She did not, however, expect the shock she felt when she finally beheld her reflection after six months of training and hard living.

Standing in front of the floor-length mirror, her lips parted in surprise at what she saw. She had known she had lost some weight and gained some muscle, but she had not fully realized how drastically her body had changed. Gone were her soft feminine curves, her full hips, her large breasts. Her scraps of clothing hung on her—not just from being worn-out—but from being far too big. She fingered the muscles that showed on her exposed strip of stomach. They looked different straight on than they did from above.

Holding out one of her lean, toned arms, Meera saw how her muscles bulged when she moved. Now that she thought about it, she supposed her arms and thighs had been chafing less when she ran—she tried to focus on that positive because the absence of her curves felt like another blow on an already difficult day. Then she resisted the urge to touch her diminished breasts, reminding herself that she was not alone. Her eyes darted to Kennick, who stood watching her, but when she looked back at herself, she noticed her face—it was still round, but her cheeks were less full, accentuating her cheekbones more. She still looked human but in a less obvious way.

"That different, huh?" Kennick asked.

Meera regarded him next to her and was struck by how her body resembled his in some ways; they had drastically different coloring and hair textures, but there was a similarity in their muscled bodies. She supposed it was the look of a warrior—someone who trained hard enough for it to show. Still, the similarities between them disturbed her. "I look like ... you!" she cried with an expression of disgust on her face.

Kennick laughed, seemingly unperturbed by her tone. "Not quite," he replied. "Definitely not in that outfit."

Meera noticed again how fine his clothes were. They were simple and dark, but the fabric of his shirt rippled with luxury, and his pants were tailored to fit him impeccably. She shrugged. She just needed clothes to cover herself decently; she didn't need anything fine or fancy. Returning to the table, she held some smaller sizes up to herself, settling on three sets. Then she walked her choices up to the counter, hoping she had enough money left for the clothes and food.

A jacket would have to wait, she decided; she didn't have enough money for one, but it really wasn't all that cold for winter anyway. Plus, spring was about to bloom, she thought. Then she turned her attention to the woman behind the counter. The woman merely glared in return, apparently unwilling to speak to her. Meera put her money down and waited for her change, drumming her fingers on the counter impatiently just to irritate the sour-faced worker.

Sensing Kennick watching with amusement, she wondered why he was still there—why he had followed her in the first place, for that matter. She tensed, expecting him to say something to the woman—to show Meera how knell could exert their dominance over humans—but he did no such thing. Meera wanted to ask him what he was doing there, but she wasn't willing to break her staring contest with the sour woman to do so. Finally, the woman made a sound of disgust, pulled Meera's money toward her like it was covered in dung, weighed it, and pushed back her change.

"Thank you," Meera said automatically, shoving her new clothes into her bag. She reserved one of the shirts to pull on over her tattered one, and she left the store, not bothering to look at Kennick on her way past him. He followed her onto the street and waited while she went into the bakery.

When Meera emerged with her baked goods and bit into her giant raspberry jam pastry, the rest of the world fell away. She didn't care that Kennick was following her. She didn't care that Hadjal hated her, and Shael was angry with her. There was nothing more important in the whole world than the flaky, buttery, jam-filled pastry in her hands. "Mmmmmhhh," she intoned, bouncing with delight as she chewed. It was the most beautiful thing she had ever tasted. She had forgotten food could be so good after eating grain mush, old preserves, and mountain goat for so long.

Meandering the cobbled street of town, she took bite after bite, oblivious to the knell around her who stared. Jam dripped over her fingers, and she caught the precious red globs with her tongue before they could hit the ground. Then she laughed, thinking that if some did hit the ground, she might bend down to lick it off.

"What is so funny?" Kennick asked, jarring her from her jam reverie.

"Hmm?" Meera pretended she didn't know what he was talking about, unwilling to stop eating to answer him. A knell man passing by greeted Kennick, and he nodded back. The man shot Meera a bewildered look, so she waved her sticky fingers at him with a smile.

"That good, huh?" Kennick asked, eyeing her pastry with a gleam in his eyes.

Meera shielded her prized pastry with her body. "Get your own, Moneybags!" she replied, cramming the rest into her mouth. Even though she had a bag with several more, she wasn't sharing; she had used the last of her money to buy the goodies, and Kennick looked like he could more than afford to buy his own food.

Continuing to wander through town, she sucked stray jam from her knuckles unashamedly. For a moment, she felt completely at peace. However, she wasn't looking or sensing where she was going and stubbed the toe of her boot against a protruding cobblestone. Gasping, Meera looked down; her trusty, brown leather boot had finally ripped open. The leather upper hung detached from the bottom sole, and she gaped, horrified, at her ruined shoe. Her boots had seen her through a lot and were one of the few things she had from her life in Terratelle. Bending to inspect the damage, she wondered if she could sew it back together somehow.

"Your boots have taken their last walk," Kennick remarked.

Meera's previous jammy bliss was forgotten, and she rounded on the knell man. "What are you doing here? Why did you follow me?" she asked, both irritated and suspicious. Had Hadjal sent him to keep an eye on her?

Kennick shrugged, his hands in his pants pockets again, and Meera wondered at that—she hadn't seen knell pants with pockets before. "I did not think you had enough money to buy food," he replied.

Meera stared into Kennick's face, unsure if he was being kind or if he was jabbing at her poverty. His dark, almost black eyes always had a humorous gleam in them, making it hard for her to tell if he was being genuine or not. When he smiled with his lips closed, a single pointed canine tooth showed over his lower lip. She stared at the tooth and furrowed her eyebrows. Finally, she decided he wasn't being nasty, and she sighed. "Well, I did, but I don't have enough to buy boots," she lamented, looking down at her boots sadly. She hated breaking in new shoes, but she supposed she wouldn't have to—she was going to have to walk around barefoot like the beggar she was.

"I will buy you a pair," Kennick said casually.

"Why?" she asked, squinting at him.

"Because I can," he replied.

Meera rolled her eyes. Then she wondered if she had seemed that obnoxious when she had started working at the palace. If so, she almost couldn't blame the other servants for tormenting her. "I'll go barefoot," she announced, kicking off her boots. With a sad sigh, she ignited them with raek fire and watched them be devoured by the pale flames in her palms. A human shop worker passing by shouted with fear and ran away, and she looked after them, cringing. Shaking the leftover boot dust from her hands, she proceeded down the street barefoot, Kennick walking doggedly at her side.

"You can just create the raek fire?" he asked.

Meera "mmhmmed" absently.

"But it does not burn you?" he persisted.

"It only burns what I want it to burn ... now, anyway," she replied, thinking of Shael. She looked in the window as they passed the cobbler's shop.

"Let me buy you new boots," Kennick insisted, stopping and leaning against the shop window.

"Why?" she asked. "And don't say 'because I can,'" she added, mimicking his low, confident voice.

Kennick's pointy tooth appeared on his lip in amusement. "I figure I owe you since you freed Shael," he replied.

She considered him.

"Really," he added, his smile disappearing for once. "I am extremely grateful to you for helping Shael escape. Buying you boots is the least I can do."

Meera crossed her arms over her chest and considered him. After a long moment, she gave in. "Fine," she huffed. Then she fished in her bakery bag and pulled out a pastry, handing it to Kennick begrudgingly. He took her offering with another of his smug smiles, and they entered the shoe store. When they left, Meera was wearing her shiny new brown boots, which came slightly higher up her calves than her old ones and felt horribly unfamiliar.

"I hate them!" she exclaimed as they walked down the street. She was aware of each and every place the boots touched her feet

—extra aware with her irritatingly acute knell senses. Every step was uncomfortable and distracting.

"I guess I still owe you, then" Kennick replied with a mischievous glint in his eyes.

Meera had no idea what game he was playing. She didn't understand why he had followed her or was taking a particular interest in her. She felt compelled not to like him, knowing he hadn't rescued Shael from the dungeon. But she supposed he was at least trying to be friendly toward her, which was more than she could say for some of the other riders at the moment ... "I don't need anything else," she said, and she made for the path in the woods.

As she walked, her mind kept churning on the subject of Shael's rescue. Now that she had a knell body and magic, she could imagine how easy it would have been for Kennick to get into the Altus Palace and free his friend. He could have walked right in, bending down the swords of those who stood against him and opening Shael's cell with a single thought. He probably could have freed Cerun just flying overhead on his own raek at night when no one would have seen. Why hadn't he?

"It would have been so easy for you," she muttered bitterly. "They were locked in iron—metal that you could have shaped away for them! Do you even know what he went through?" she asked, her voice rising. She glared at Kennick, trying to read his expression, but she couldn't help but notice that the ridiculous metal cuffs on his ears had feathers etched into them.

Kennick looked back at her. His mocking expression was gone, but he still appeared unconcerned. "Sodhu said he was tortured," he replied calmly.

Meera couldn't tell if it was a question or a statement. She wished she could show him like she would with Shaya; she wished she could conjure the image to her mind and force it into his, but she couldn't. Instead, she tried to paint him a picture with her words: "His back was burned repeatedly with a hot poker, his butt and thighs were whipped bloody so he couldn't sit down, there were nails embedded in his calves, and ... words—horrible words—cut into his front ... " she said trailing off, suddenly unsure of whether Shael would want his friend to know all of this.

Kennick was silent for a moment, and Meera could hear him swallow. "You really love him," he said. Again, she wasn't sure if it was a question or a statement.

She nodded.

"You missed his birthday, you know. I could give you money to get him something," he offered.

Meera was annoyed that Kennick dismissed the subject of Shael's imprisonment, but he still succeeded in distracting her. "I guess I missed my own birthday too," she said thoughtfully.

"How old are you?" he asked.

"Why? How old are you? Five-hundred?" she asked in return.

"Twenty-seven."

"So, I was right—you're old," she said.

Kennick chuckled. Everything Meera said seemed to amuse him; she couldn't manage to get under his skin like he got under hers. Then she sighed. She had been gone for six months and missed Shael's birthday. Was that really too long? What was six months in the scheme of their long lives? Why was he so upset with her?

"You know," she said ponderously, "I do love Shael. I think I love him more than he loves himself." She wasn't sure why she was sharing this with someone she barely knew, but she didn't exactly have anyone else to talk to about it—or talk to at all, lately.

"What do you mean?" Kennick asked.

"He couldn't understand why I had to leave because ... he doesn't see himself as someone worth protecting. I didn't want to hurt him, but he didn't get that—he didn't seem to think it mattered if he got burned," she said, working out her thoughts as she spoke.

Kennick nodded. "Sounds like Shael," he said.

Meera sighed in frustration. "I can't do it," she said, stopping in the path. Kennick stopped with her and waited for her to elaborate. "I can't make him see that I love him if he can't see that he's worth loving. And I ... I can't keep bouncing back after he pushes me away. It's too hard ..." she said feebly. Despite her newfound strength of body and mind, she couldn't handle the thought of Shael rejecting her again. And again. She couldn't keep loving him and reaching out to him when he kept drawing away and shutting her out. Was that it? Was she done with Shael?

Meera's newly full stomach ached just at the thought. How could she be done with Shael? She loved him ... He was her person; he was the person she wanted to spend her time with, who was there for her when she needed him. Well, he was there when she really needed him, she thought; he often wasn't there for her otherwise. Trudging onward, she stared down at the path in front of her, her inner turmoil absorbing her enough for her to momentarily forget the discomfort of her new boots.

"You must have made him see some things," Kennick said. "He asked you to marry him. He put aside his vow for you." He sounded so sure of his statements that Meera had a hard time shaking her head in negation. Kennick raised his dark red brows at her.

"Shael asked me to marry him because my father told him to, and ... he didn't put aside his vow," she said awkwardly, wondering why she always had to discuss these things with the other riders.

Kennick looked genuinely surprised. "He planned to keep his vow, but you agreed to marry him?" he asked in disbelief.

"Of course!" she snapped defensively. "You've never been in love, have you?"

"No," he said quietly. "Why? What does it feel like?"

Meera wasn't sure how she had entered into this conversation, but she wanted out of it. "It makes you willing to overlook things like race, lifespans, and vows," she said tersely. "But I'm starting to wonder if I've overlooked too much."

Kennick didn't answer, and Meera avoided looking at him. When they reached the peninsula, she thanked him stiffly for the boots and walked away, wishing she hadn't told him so much of her feelings when he had told her so little about himself. She was embarrassed. Besides, Shael was the person she should be sharing with—not Kennick. Why hadn't Shael followed her into town? Why didn't he seem to care that she was back? Turning away from Kennick's inquisitive dark eyes, Meera walked back into the woods toward Shael's house, hoping to find him there.

19

SHAEL

When Kennick entered the woods after Meera, Shael stormed off as well, crashing aimlessly through the trees until he eventually ended up at his house. Meera was back. Meera was finally back, and he had just stood there and stared at her. He had been so angry with her lately that he had not actually considered what he would say to her if she returned. Meera was back, but ... she was so different. And even if she was back, she would leave him again. Of that, he was certain.

Shael paced his house, unsure of what to do. Should he have followed her into town? Should he have hugged her and kissed her and told her how much he had missed her? Should he have yelled at her for leaving? He did not know what he should have done, but he wished he had done something. He felt endlessly frustrated that his default reaction was passivity; he was a man of inaction. Slumping forcefully into his reading chair, he hung his head.

He was still holding the leather riding jacket Meera had returned to him in his clenched fists, and he reached into the pockets and found a now empty jar that had once contained lip balm, a few matches, and the slip of paper he had left for her. He pulled it out, unfolded it, and stared at the note. He could see how worn it was: the creases were flimsy and thin from being unfolded and refolded, the ink was faded, and he thought one splotchy area might have even been made by a tear. Shael supposed he had not stopped to consider what six months alone in the mountains may have been like for Meera. Leaning back in his chair, he shut his eyes against his confusion.

Sometime later, the door to his house opened slowly and quietly. He sat up straight and turned to find Meera in the door-way. She was still wearing her ripped pants, but she had on a new shirt and new boots. The light behind her accentuated the little stray hairs framing her face, and her large eyes made her look incredibly sheepish peering around the doorframe at him. The site almost made him forget the great power she held in her body —almost.

"Can I come in?" she asked.

Shael stood and nodded. Okay, he thought; he had not managed to speak, but nodding was something.

Meera stepped inside and shut the door behind her. "Shael, I ... don't know what to say," she finished lamely, looking down at the floor. He could sympathize. "I guess I'm angry," she said, glancing up at him. "I left for a reason—a good one, even if you didn't agree—I did what I set out to do, and I came back. You said you would wait for me. You said you loved me—but here I am! Here I am, and you couldn't even welcome me back! Do you have anything to say to me?"

Her voice slowly rose in volume and passion as she spoke until Shael crossed his arms over his chest, feeling attacked. Staring down at the floorboards, he tried to think of what to say.

"Say something!" she cried. "Do something! Tell me to get out or kiss me or something! I can't take this silence anymore!"

Shael stepped forward, seized Meera's face in his hands and kissed her, but his heart was not in it. She could tell. She pulled away.

"You are just so different—so changed," he stammered in explanation, and she drew back as if he had struck her.

"Seriously? I've lost my curves, so you've lost your interest?" she asked, tears filling her eyes under knitted brows.

"No! It is not that," Shael said, though the change in her figure had not escaped his notice. She did not look like his soft, clumsy, human Meera anymore.

"What is it then? You don't like that I'm stronger?" she asked. "That's what I left to do!"

"No!" he shouted, his anger rising. "You left to control your raek fire, and you did much, much more than that. How long ago could you have come back and controlled your abilities? How long did you stay in the mountains and train when you could have come back and trained with me? How hard would it have been to visit, or send a note, or otherwise let me know you were alive?" He was yelling, venting some of his frustration from his long months of waiting.

"I—" Meera floundered to explain. "I wanted to finish what I had started on my own! Is that so unreasonable? It was only six months!"

"I had no idea where you were or whether you were okay! Why didn't you at least visit?" he asked.

"I couldn't! If I had come back, I wouldn't have been able to leave again. I couldn't have left you again! It was hard enough the first time! But I—I wanted to become a warrior on my own," she said. She took a step toward him with her hands outstretched. "Shael, I love you. I just needed some time to myself—to find

myself and get stronger." She placed her hands on his chest, and
he could feel his heart accelerate under them.

He gazed into Meera's almond-shaped eyes. Her eyes were the
same; they held the same warmth, the same love, they drew him
nearer. Reaching up, he touched one of her cheeks. It was less full
but still Meera. He looked at her pouting lips. They were the same
lips, and they parted slightly under his scrutiny. Leaning forward,
he claimed her mouth with his own, closing his eyes and kissing
her to find his way back to her. She kissed him in return. Then she
grasped his shoulders with a firm grip and yanked him closer
to her.

Shael pulled away, stepping out of her grasp. Meera stared at
him, her eyes wide with surprise then confusion. They were his
Meera's warm eyes—except his Meera did not have such a strong
grasp. His Meera did not reach out with so much confidence.
Shael's eyes fell on the sword hilt peeking up over her shoulder.
His Meera did not want to fight or hurt anyone; she was soft and
uncertain and ...

"You don't like that I'm stronger," she said with new realization. She took a step back from him and barked a humorless
laugh. "That's it, isn't it? You liked me weak. It made you feel like a
big, strong man when I cried and stumbled and could barely run
—a big strong *knell* man. Is that it?" Shael just stared at her. Was
she right? Was he upset because her strength made him question
his own?

He shook his head, but he did not actually open his mouth
and tell her she was wrong. He was not sure she was wrong. He
had liked how Meera had always made him feel—it was part of
what he loved about her—but he also loved her for who she was.
At least, he thought he did. Why was he so confused? Of course,
he loved Meera! Her absence had torn him apart. He had missed
her with every muscle in his body.

However, a thought nagged at Shael's mind: could he have only missed the way she made him feel? Could he have only missed being her protector in this new knell world? He did not think so. He had missed Meera's warmth, her playful energy, and her joy. He had missed her silent companionship when they walked and flew together ... Or had her soft human body next to his make him feel stronger and less pathetic? His head spun and spun, and all the while he stood still and silent.

"I can't do this anymore," Meera said quietly, shaking her head back and forth. "How can I ever be certain of your feelings if you don't look certain? I can't be with you, Shael—I can't." Her voice cracked, and she turned and retreated into her old bedroom. He heard a quiet sob escape her when she was out of sight, but she returned moments later with her earrings, ring, and purple beaded bracelet clasped in her hand. She did not give the ring back to him—it was not his.

Instead, she turned toward the door and gave him a last sad look before she left. "Goodbye," she whispered, and she was gone. She had left again. Shael was alone again, without even Cerun in his mind for company. He had pushed his raek away so many times lately, that even Cerun had grown weary of Shael's moods and had left on an extended hunting trip.

Shael's legs buckled under him, and he fell to his knees. He had always known Meera would leave him, and she had—twice. But now he could not help but wonder if she had only left because he had pushed her away. He did not know why he put up walls, why he fell silent, why he pushed away those he loved, but he did. Scrubbing his face hard with his palms, he wondered if he was too broken for the world—if he should just end his life and his misery.

There was a soft knock on the door, and Kennick walked in. Kennick, who Shael had never managed to push away despite his tempers and his silences. Kennick held up a bottle of Sodhu's fruity wine in question. Shael did not normally allow himself to drink alcohol, but he smiled at his friend. If anyone could break his hard exterior and rigid thoughts, it was Kennick. Shael had even wondered if he could love Kennick as more than a friend, but he already did in a way—he loved him like a brother. Rising from the floor, he found two cups in his pantry.

"No need to pull out the fancy glasses for me," Kennick said before popping the top off the wine and taking a drink. He handed the bottle to Shael, who took a swig. Shael knew it would affect his training the next day, but he did not care. Kennick proceeded to roll up his sleeves, sit at the table, and challenge him to an arm-wrestling match. Shael laughed and acquiesced, knowing his friend would have to have a lot more to drink for him to have a chance at winning.

20

MEERA

Meera rushed away from Shael's house and didn't look back. She waited until she was a good distance away before she allowed herself to cry and fall to the forest floor. Then she heaved deep sobs and tried not to relive Shael pulling away from her—again—but it was no use. Once more, he had moved away from her touch, withdrawn from her love as if disgusted—as if burned by her hands.

Meera gasped and shook with her grief. She hated the way Shael made her feel; she had returned to the peninsula strong and confident, and he had reduced her to a shuddering puddle on the ground with just a look and a step back. Never again, she told herself, wiping her nose on her sleeve and using a nearby sapling to pull herself up. She wouldn't let Shael hurt her again. She wouldn't give him the chance, she decided. It was over. Done.

The thought was both comforting and deeply unsettling. Meera felt like she was taking control of her life—exerting her independence—and yet, Shael was all she had ... When did independence become isolation? Where was the line between being capable of living on her own and just being sad and alone?

She was not alone, she told herself; she had her father—what was left of him—she had the other riders even if Hadjal was wary of her at the moment, and she had Shaya. Meera reached out to Shaya mentally but couldn't feel her raek nearby. Stumbling through the woods toward her father's cabin, she hoped to find a friendly face and a comforting embrace when she got there. However, when she reached the small cabin, it was empty.

Dropping her bag and her sword, she reacquainted herself with the space. Thankfully, her cot still stood at the far end, and she threw herself down on it. It was only the afternoon, but Meera had had enough for the day; it had been long and exhausting, and she didn't relish seeing anyone else before it was over. Kicking off her new boots, she rubbed the sore skin of her feet. Then she lay down in her bed without changing; she hadn't bought a new nightgown and had burned her last one. Closing her eyes, she tried not to think about that night—or think about Shael at all. Why couldn't they just be happy together? Why was everything with Shael so hard? She pushed her thoughts aside and practiced clearing her mind; she found the practice much easier now than it had been six months ago.

Meera fell asleep before her father returned from his dinner, and she woke up the next morning after he had left to go fishing. She rose, changed, and ate a pastry from her bakery bag rather than attempting to join the others for breakfast. Then she set out to run and train—alone. She should feel used to isolation, she thought, but it was somehow harder to be alone with the people nearby than it had been in the mountains. She continued to reach out toward Shaya, but her raek was nowhere to be seen or sensed nearby.

Meera successfully avoided the other riders for most of the day, but by the time dinner came around, she was hungry and out of both pastries and money. She sidled up near Hadjal's table, feeling extremely uncomfortable. Most of the others were already sitting down—including Shael—and Hadjal and Sodhu could be heard clanking dishes inside the house. Meera moseyed over slowly, unsure if she was welcome or not. Then she loitered several feet away from the table until Isbaen noticed her. "Meera, there you are!" he said cheerfully.

She took another couple of steps forward. "Hello," she said to everyone and received several greetings in reply. Shael didn't turn around, and she tried not to look directly at him. Hadjal and Sodhu came out of their house carrying food. "Can I help?" Meera asked Hadjal, who had stopped at the sight of her. What she was really asking was whether she was welcome and could stay and eat.

Hadjal sighed. "Yes, of course, Meera," she replied, looking sad.

Meera smiled uncertainly and went into the house to retrieve more dishes. Hadjal followed her in. "I am sorry, Meera," she said, freeing her hands and putting them on Meera's shoulders. "You are one of us—you have been for some time—and I should have treated you with more trust than I did yesterday. I know you would not be here if you thought you would hurt us. I just ... worry."

Meera felt tears prick her eyes, and she nodded at the older knell woman, at a loss for words. Hadjal was one of the few mother figures she had ever had, and Meera had felt sick thinking she wouldn't forgive her for burning her table. "Thank you," she finally managed, and Hadjal gave her a tight squeeze. Then they both carried food out to the table.

Hadjal's new table had benches on either side rather than

chairs. Regardless, everyone was seated in their usual places. Kennick sat on Isbaen's left across from where Meera usually sat ... next to Shael. She hesitated a moment, unsure of what to do. She supposed she could insert herself elsewhere, but she didn't want to be dramatic when her usual seat was wide open. She and Shael would need to learn to coexist anyway, so she figured they may as well start now. Stepping over the bench, she sat down and avoided looking to her left.

Sitting so close to Shael and not feeling like she could talk to him or touch him was almost unbearable. How had they gone from engaged to nothing so quickly? Why couldn't he have accepted her the way she was? Meera's raw hurt was already festering into anger; she didn't think she had done anything wrong and resented how much Shael had toyed with her emotions. And yet, she could smell him and feel his warmth next to her and wished he would take her hand and apologize—propose again, even. If he did, would she forgive him? She had told herself never again, but if Shael wanted her again, could she really refuse him?

"Oh, Meera, this came for you," Sodhu said, handing her a rolled piece of paper and ripping her from her thoughts. Meera took the paper and stared at it, at a complete loss for who would write to her. She broke the seal and unrolled it, reading:

Meera,

You have surprised me once again. Sodhu tells me you have returned from your hiatus in control of your extraordinary abilities. As you may know, all new riders must present themselves before my council to be accepted and sworn in as official riders. It is a matter of service and loyalty.

I will expect you and your raek at the Levisade Estate at your earliest convenience.

Your Servant,
Darreal

Meera read through the letter several times. She smiled at Darreal's send-off, knowing it was in reference to a conversation they had once had about her role as queen. However, every time she read the note, her eyes snagged on the word *loyalty*. She wasn't sure she felt comfortable pledging her loyalty to Darreal and the knell. She had become a rider to try to end the war with Shaya—a mission that may require them to break with rider tradition and forge their own path.

"Is that from Darreal?" Soleille asked. "I bet she is chomping at the bit to see what you can do."

"Is that what the meeting is about?" Meera asked. "Will they be determining if I'm fit to be a rider?"

"Normally, it is more of a formality than anything," Isbaen replied. "However, seeing as you are human and Terratellen, there may be considerable debate as to whether you should be sworn in as one of Levisade's riders. Not all of the council members approved of Shael because of his upbringing."

Shael stiffened next to her. Meera had already known how the council felt about Shael, so she assumed they would hate her. "They're not going to swear me in," she said confidently.

"Meera, they have to," Hadjal warned her. "Otherwise, you may not reside on the peninsula and train as a rider. You are only assigned a mentor once you are sworn in."

"What will they do to me if I'm not?" she asked. No one answered. Apparently, it had never happened before.

"Speaking of ..." Hadjal said, raising her voice. "Everyone, I would like to officially announce that Kennick has completed his training." Everyone clapped and cheered for Kennick, Meera somewhat half-heartedly. "On that note," Hadjal continued, "Meera, if you are sworn in as a rider, Kennick will be your mentor."

Meera gaped at her.

"Kennick?" Soleille asked for her. "When he has only just completed his own training?" She was clearly bristling at not being selected herself.

"Seeing as Meera has elemental abilities, I think it is best that either Kennick or I mentor her, and I do not think I am the best person for the job," Hadjal said quietly, looking down at her plate. Meera wondered why Hadjal was behaving oddly; the older knell woman clearly felt bad for how she had treated her the day before, but what else was going on?

"I am sure Kennick will do a fine job," Isbaen said with calm assuredness as if to put the topic to bed.

"I don't think it'll work," Meera remarked bluntly. "I mean, I don't think the council will swear me in to begin with, but if they do, I don't think Kennick should be my mentor."

"Why is that, Meera?" Hadjal asked, looking shocked.

"Aren't mentees supposed to respect their mentors?" Meera asked, glaring at Kennick unabashedly.

He looked back at her, seemingly unfazed. Katrea sniggered at the end of the table. "I will train, Meera," she offered. "I like her more and more." This was glowing praise from Katrea, and Meera grinned at the frightening woman.

Hadjal looked uncharacteristically taken aback. "Uh, you may of course assist in training Meera, Katrea, but Meera, I ... do not know what to say to that. Kennick is extremely skilled at shaping, hand-to-hand combat, and sword fighting. I believe he is the best mentor for you."

"Do not worry, Hadjal," Kennick said. "I am up for the challenge." He pierced Meera with his liquid black eyes and his pointy canine tooth showed on his lower lip. Once again, he appeared amused by her disdain.

Meera scowled at him. If Kennick liked a challenge, he should have rescued Shael. But she didn't say anything—she still thought it was a moot point; the council would never accept her.

"You should go soon and get it over with," Soleille suggested to her.

"I will go whenever Shaya returns from wherever she flew off to," Meera replied, annoyed that her raek hadn't bothered to communicate about her departure.

MEERA WOULD HAVE LEFT for the Levisade Estate when Shaya returned, except Shaya didn't return. For two weeks, Meera trained with the other riders and waited for her raek. She couldn't so much as feel where Shaya was in her mind and grew extremely frustrated. She continued to avoid Shael—even though he was often right beside her—and she never had to decide whether she would accept his apology or not because he never apologized—he never so much as spoke to her.

In addition, Meera's father prepared to leave for the estate, saying that he was ready to begin his scholarly research again and would see her when she visited, and even though they shared the small cabin together, they barely interacted. Meera continued to feel alone, but she forged ahead, training and eating her meals with everyone.

One day when they were all having lunch, an unexpected visitor arrived at the peninsula: Farrah. The stout, sandy-colored horse that had carried Meera up the mountain, gotten spooked, thrown her, and left her there, arrived on the grassy slope next to Hadjal's. She was wearing a saddle and carrying a note.

"You!" Meera exclaimed when the horse plodded up to the table. Farrah snorted and gave her a disdainful look.

Isbaen rose and read the note attached to the horse's saddle. "Orson, Darreal has sent you her horse to ride to the estate. She says she will be very pleased to have you organize the estate's manuscripts," he explained.

Meera spluttered at the thought. "Absolutely not! This horse isn't taking my father anywhere," she said, eyeing Farrah distrustfully.

Kennick gave her a bemused look. "My mentee is afraid of horses. Training you might be more difficult than I thought," he said with a sly smile.

She glowered at him. "This horse cannot be trusted!" she insisted.

Soleille laughed like it was a joke. It was not a joke.

"Meera's right. I would not ride this horse anywhere," Shael said to her amazement. He had not so much as acknowledged her in weeks, and she felt a little thrill that he agreed with her. Then she chastised herself inwardly; she should be able to count on Shael for more than agreement about an untrustworthy horse. He had not so much as tried to apologize for his behavior or tried to reconcile with her, and she wouldn't throw herself at him for the vaguest friendly gesture. She avoided looking at him and looked instead at her father.

Orson appeared entirely unconcerned by Meera's thoughts on Farrah. He stood and approached the horse. Meera opened her mouth to warn him that Farrah bites, but then she shut it incredulously when Farrah whinnied a friendly hello to her father and closed her eyes in pleasure as he scratched her jaw. "I think she'll do just fine," Orson said, feeding Farrah fruit from the table. "Looks like I'm leaving."

Meera glanced away. She was still trying to get her father back, and he was leaving her. She didn't have Shael, she didn't have Shaya, and now she wouldn't have him. Biting her lip to hold back her emotion, she stared down at her lap. She noticed Shael's hand twitch on the bench next to her and wondered for a moment if he thought to take her hand. He didn't, which only added fuel to the flaming pit in her stomach. Regardless, Meera swallowed her feelings and stood to hug her father.

"I'll miss you and see you soon," she said, squeezing him tightly. Farrah snapped at her when she strayed close to the horse's head, and Meera had to resist the urge to give the horse a display of her new shaping abilities. "You take care of my father, or I'll come for you," she told Farrah, and she could have sworn the horse's whinny sounded like a laugh.

"Tell Darreal I'll come as soon as Shaya returns," she told her father. She hoped Darreal and the council weren't too upset about waiting for her.

Orson retrieved his possessions and clambered awkwardly onto Farrah's back, and the two hobbled away, disappearing into the forest long before Meera felt ready to see them go.

"Meera, your father is gone just in time!" Soleille exclaimed excitedly.

Meera had no idea what she was talking about. "For?" she asked.

"For the Spring Equinox! I assume you wouldn't have wanted him to see you dressed so scantily," Soleille replied as if what she said had any meaning to Meera whatsoever.

"Should I know what you're talking about?" she asked warily.

"The Spring Equinox is next week," Isbaen explained. "We knell will join together in the forest to celebrate life and birth."

"And I will be scantily dressed because ...?" Meera persisted.

"Because everyone will be!" Soleille exclaimed, sounding ecstatic about the prospect. "Everyone puts on special Equinox attire and dances and ... you know, celebrates new life and possibility," she said with a meaningful look.

Meera gaped at her. She had an inkling of what Soleille was trying to tell her but wasn't sure about the details. Either way, she didn't think it sounded like her kind of celebration. "I don't know ..." she started to say.

"You have to come! Everyone is going! It is too late for you to have anything made, but you can borrow something of mine to wear," Soleille insisted.

Meera wasn't entirely convinced that she wanted to go to the celebration, but the prospect of Soleille lending her clothes and helping her get ready felt almost sisterly to her—a feeling she couldn't resist. "Okay. Why not?" she said. She saw Shael's fist clench next to her and averted her eyes. She would not approach him during the celebration, and she would not let him hurt her again, she told herself.

Hadjal shifted in her seat, drawing Meera's attention. "Are you going to the celebration?" she asked the older knell woman, still trying to smooth over their relationship.

"Hadjal and I are planning our own private celebration," Sodhu interjected.

Meera smiled at her but quickly returned her focus to Hadjal, sensing she wanted to say something. They locked eyes, and Meera willed her silently to speak. "Meera, please be careful at the celebration," Hadjal said finally. "I do not want you to drink anything or inhale anything. You do not know how your magic might be affected."

Meera stiffened. Hadjal still seemed to think she was going to hurt people. "I will be careful," she said—she always was. She did not, however, make any specific promises about what she would or wouldn't do at the celebration.

21

MEERA

Meera felt slightly lost without Shael, Shaya, and her father, so she spent more time with some of the other riders over the next week. She ran several times with Soleille and learned that Soleille did her best to avoid combat training. Rather, she spent her time flying around to commune with other healers, teaching what she knew and learning from others. Meera wished she could do something useful and beneficial like heal someone with her magic, but try as she might, she could not sense or shape the living.

Katrea, on the other hand, spent most of her time exercising and building muscle. One day, Meera asked Katrea if she could join her for training, and the red-haired woman agreed with a somewhat ominous grin. They started by running, but rather than running for distance, Katrea trained in short bursts with weights strapped to her ankles. Meera panted and did her best to keep up, but even her knell body could barely move with the enormous iron weights attached to her legs.

"Push, Meera! Push!" Katrea yelled.

After their sprints, they lifted weights. Meera was used to lifting and carrying the large rocks strew around her mountainside valley, but she didn't know anything about weightlifting form. Katrea was kind and patient when she explained form and technique, but the moment Meera actually began doing her repetitions, Katrea continued shouting in her ear. "Come on! You can do it! Push, Meera!"

After they lifted weights, Meera could barely move, let alone practice hand-to-hand. Regardless, Katrea insisted they spar for several rounds. Meera shook with fatigue and moved through the familiar maneuvers she had learned with Aegwren—doing her best to avoid Katrea at all costs—but the second the larger woman got her hands on her, the fight was over; Meera couldn't do anything to break free from the bigger woman's iron grip. Katrea, at least, refrained from battering Meera bloody and bruised. She usually let her go once it was clear she couldn't move.

Eventually, Meera fell to the ground and didn't get back up. She gasped and trembled, and every muscle in her body screamed for rest.

"Come on, Meera! You have to push!" Katrea shouted again, grinning down at her and swiping her short hair behind her ears.

"No," Meera said breathlessly, "You have to pull!" She reached out her hands pitifully and said with a smile, "Come on, Katrea! Pull me to food! You can do it!"

Katrea laughed and shocked Meera by actually bending down, grabbing her, and hoisting her over her shoulder.

Meera laughed even though it was difficult to do with her stomach pressed into Katrea's shoulder. Her arms dangled uselessly, and blood rushed to her head. "Haha! Okay, you can let me down now!" she called.

"Nope! I am taking you to food," Katrea said jovially, clearly enjoying herself.

Meera struggled, but she couldn't break free of Katrea's grip. She didn't actually want to arrive at dinner tossed over another woman's shoulder. "Come on!" she pleaded. "That's enough!"

"Get free if you have had enough," Katrea replied smugly.

"I'm never training with you again!" Meera wailed, half-serious.

Katrea only laughed and whistled a tune Meera had heard Florean play on his instrument before. Finally, she swung Meera upright and deposited her in her usual spot at the table. For a second, her head spun so much she couldn't see. When she could see again, she wished she couldn't; all of the other riders were giving her entertained looks.

"Would you still prefer Katrea as your mentor?" Kennick asked with a glint in his dark eyes.

Meera scowled at him. "I suppose anyone would be better than Shaya," she admitted. She felt frustrated not knowing where Shaya was, but it was also a relief not to have the enormous raek attacking her at every opportunity.

"Do you know if she is coming back soon? You should really be going to the estate," Sodhu said anxiously.

"No idea," Meera replied. "Shael, where's Cerun? I still haven't seen him since I've been back." She spoke without thinking before realizing that it was the first time she had directly addressed Shael since ending things with him. Then she considered that he may no longer want her to have any sort of relationship with his raek. She tensed, unsure how he would answer her or if he would answer at all, but her fear turned out to be unfounded.

"He and Endu went on an extended hunting trip, but they should be back soon," he replied calmly, even making fleeting eye-contact with her.

Meera nodded, speechless. She assumed Endu was Kennick's raek.

Hadjal handed her a full plate of food, and she thanked her and smiled. Hadjal had been going out of her way lately to be kind to her. Meera appreciated it but didn't feel like it was necessary. If anything, she wished Hadjal would just treat her like everyone else. She started to eat, but picking up her fork felt like an immense effort, and getting it to her mouth was almost too hard. She wasn't sure if she wanted to laugh or cry about the state Katrea had put her in.

"Meera, I thought we could spar with our swords tomorrow," Kennick said from directly across from her.

Meera chewed her food and regarded him, still unsure of what she thought of Shael's best friend. She supposed he was just taking his possible role as mentor seriously, and—she admitted to herself—she had really enjoyed their first fight together. Even so, she doubted she'd be able to move the next day. "Tomorrow? Hmmm ... I'm not sure I'll be capable tomorrow," she admitted with a laugh that jostled her tired muscles. Everyone laughed with her.

"I will make you a tea for soreness," Soleille told her. "I do not believe in speeding the healing of muscles with shaping unless it is necessary, but the tea should help you move easier tomorrow." Meera thanked her warmly. She felt more and more like a member of the riders' little family.

"Do not go too hard on her, Kennick. She should be able to dance at the equinox," Soleille warned.

"I don't really know how to dance," Meera said with a side-long glance at Shael. He had taught her the only dances she knew.

"There really is not anything to know," Kennick told her. She hated the look on his face; it was like he always knew something she didn't know or was secretly laughing at her. The way his eyes gleamed and his lips were always turned up in a smile irked her. She couldn't tell if he was trying to put her at ease or intimidate her, and she found his confidence combined with his good-looks inherently suspicious.

"It is not like human dancing," Shael explained. Meera nodded, unsure of what that meant. She supposed she would just have to find out.

THE NEXT DAY, Meera sparred with Kennick. Soleille's tea had worked wonders, and she felt as fast and strong as ever. Even so, she could not win against Kennick no matter how hard she tried. At least, she couldn't win without shaping, which she repeatedly did by accident whenever his sword came close to hitting her. After their fifth match, she began to get frustrated and found the smug look on Kennick's face even more irritating than usual.

"Okay, fine," she said, while they both caught their breath. "Go ahead and mentor me. What am I doing wrong?" She hated to ask, but she wanted to know.

"You are not doing anything wrong. You are just being too nice," he replied with his usual easy smile. Meera wondered at that: too nice? What did that even mean? Was he being serious or putting her on?

"Okay ... How can I be less nice, you son-of-a-butt-licking-donkey?" she asked.

Kennick chuckled and took a drink from his water bladder before responding. "You are always defending and rarely attacking. If I am the only one attacking, eventually I will break through your defenses. You need to actually try to hit me in order to win," he said. He was grinning at her like she was a moron, and Meera thought she wouldn't mind smacking the look off his face. Still, she shifted from foot to foot, uncomfortable with the prospect of actually trying to stab Kennick with her sword. "What is it?" he asked.

"I guess I don't really want to hit you—anyone, I mean," she admitted. She played with a single curl that had fallen forward over her shoulder and averted her eyes from him. She had hurt people before without even trying, and she definitely didn't want to try to hurt anyone.

"You have to pretend this is a real fight," Kennick said. "You do not just want to win—you have to win. If you do not win, you die." He was still smiling, but she didn't think he was mocking her. She couldn't argue with what he said, either—except that if losing was dying, then winning was killing. She didn't want to kill.

Meera sat down suddenly in the grass. She had been enjoying the fun of training—of growing stronger and better with her sword—and she had forgotten her initial reluctance to learn how to use a weapon. Shaya had convinced her it was for defense, but Kennick was saying that defense wasn't enough. Now Meera wondered whether she even needed to defend herself with a weapon when she could blast people away with the wind or cover them in dirt or threaten them with raek fire. Fendwren had said that swords were a great responsibility because it was so easy to hurt people accidentally with them, and she didn't want to hurt anyone—anyone else.

When she blinked and came out of her reverie, Kennick was also sitting in the grass, observing her. His usual smug expression was gone; he looked curious, concerned even.

"I think I should hang up my sword," Meera said sadly. She really did love practicing with her sword and would miss it.

"For good?" Kennick asked, eyebrows raising.

She nodded.

"Wow, I really am a terrible mentor! One day with me and you're done fighting," he said, his smile returning.

"You said that like a human," she pointed out, noticing his contraction.

"I have spent a lot of time around humans lately," Kennick replied, unperturbed. "Meera, are you really going to stop sword training because you do not want to hit me?"

"You? No! I want to hit you," she said. "I just ... don't think killing people is a skill I want or need."

"You may not always be able to rely on your shaping. Sometimes magical energy is depleted, and sometimes we are not in the right mental space to shape," he said seriously.

"Then I'll run away really fast," Meera replied, wishing he would drop the conversation. She looked away, but Kennick continued to regard her in the still, calm way that knell had—the one she found difficult to emulate. She looked back at him but had trouble meeting his eyes and focused instead on the intricate metal cuffs he wore on both ears. Today they depicted little branches and leaves. His normally loose dark red hair was braided back for their sparring. Since they were clearly done for the day, he undid his braid while continuing to observe her and contemplate her feelings.

"If the options are kill or be killed, would you not rather kill?" he asked, shaping the metal clasp that had held his braid into another ring on one of his fingers.

Meera considered his question. She knew her answer should be obvious, but it wasn't. Who was she to decide if someone was worth killing? Wasn't that why she had freed Shael? The person trying to kill her might think that they had a good reason, too. Who was she to say that her reason was better? She wasn't sure she wanted to fight violence with violence ... "Not necessarily," she said finally, picking at some grass next to her.

"Why?" Kennick asked, sounding more curious than incredulous.

Meera wondered how she had ended up in yet another discussion of her most intimate thoughts and feelings with this man. She considered deflecting the question and ending the conversation, but she needed someone to talk to. "What makes me more important than anyone else?" she asked.

Kennick was silent a moment. He just sat still and thoughtful. Meera tried to stop fidgeting but couldn't manage it. She picked another blade of grass and split it into long strips.

"You have to believe in yourself—that you are doing what is right and good. Anyone who is trying to stop you or hurt you, is acting against what you believe in. It can be about saving yourself, but it can also be about protecting what matters to you," Kennick said quietly. He sounded like he was speaking from experience, and she wondered what he had been doing at the border. She didn't ask, though.

"I don't always do what's right and good," Meera replied matter-of-factly. She had made plenty of poor decisions.

"Don't you value your life?" he asked.

"Of course! I even bargained for a longer one," she said jokingly. She'd had enough; she wished he would just drop the subject and stop digging into her mind. Maybe her feelings were logical and maybe they weren't, but she didn't want to hurt people even if she might get hurt instead.

"You did?" Kennick asked with sudden intensity. "What did Shaya want from you in return?"

"I agreed to help her end the war," Meera replied, surprised he didn't already know. For some reason, she would have thought the other riders would have told him.

Kennick continued to look intense; there was no humor left in his dark eyes. "Why? For a longer life and abilities?" he asked.

"No," she explained, "Because it's the right thing to do—for the humans of Terratelle, the humans of Aegorn, and the wild raeken. I'm not going to sit here at the peninsula and train for my entire life if I can help so many people. That's why Darreal and her council aren't going to let me be a rider, so don't worry about failing as a mentor." She smiled, trying to lighten the mood, but Kennick didn't smile in return. He looked troubled.

"I am not worried about failing as a mentor," he said finally. "I am worried that I will be tempted to break my oaths as a rider for a second time."

"What do you mean?" she asked.

"When Shael was captured, going after him would have broken my oaths to the riders and Levisade. As you know, I did not go. If you left to try to end the war, and I thought that I could help—"

"You're worried you would break your oaths and follow me?" Meera asked incredulously.

"I am worried that I wouldn't," Kennick replied.

Meera's mouth gaped open a moment before she realized and shut it. The grass in her fingers hung limp and forgotten. "Why?" she asked breathlessly, leaning toward him.

"Because I want to do what I believe is right even if it is not what I am told to do," he said with creases between his brows.

Meera laughed suddenly. "I've been there," she said.

After that, their discussion evolved. Meera explained to Kennick how she had been torn between following the orders of King Bartro and following her own conscience. She shared with him the poor decisions she had made leading up to Shael's escape and her regrets, and she found that Kennick was actually a good listener and a sympathetic one when he wasn't grinning smugly at her.

She also found that he was extremely handsome, a fact that she had registered before but had never really allowed herself to acknowledge. Sitting and talking in the grass with him, she allowed herself a brief acknowledgement. Then she sat up straighter to lean slightly away from the attractive knell man; she knew better than to trust anyone as charming and disarming as Kennick, even if he said the right things and seemed to see the world in the same way as she did.

When Meera heard the others gathering for lunch, she realized they had been sitting in the grass talking for a long time. She stood quickly, feeling embarrassed that everyone had seen her and Kennick lounging when they were supposed to have been training. Picking up her sword, she sheathed it lovingly and wondered whether she should really stop training with it or not.

"You should keep training," Kennick said, watching her. "You're a fighter, Meera. You fight for what you believe in. Fighters need weapons."

Meera rolled her eyes; she would do whatever she wanted to do—with or without Kennick's would-be-mentor speeches. Although, his words touched her, and against her better judgment, she was actually starting to like him. "Maybe I will keep training. I do really, really want to hit you," she said, not bothering to look to see what he thought of that. Then she charged ahead for the table.

"You call that training?" Katrea asked Kennick when he approached from behind Meera. "Look at her! She is not even sore! What were you two doing? Braiding each other's hair?"

"I was instructing Kennick in the fine art of treason," Meera said jokingly.

Hadjal dropped a platter to the table with a clang, looking flustered.

"Everything okay?" Isbaen asked her. She nodded and headed back into the house. Meera noticed Isbaen and Kennick exchange a look and wondered, again, what was going on with Hadjal.

Just then, a shadow blocked the sun, and she could sense two raeken flying overhead. She squinted up at them and saw that Cerun had finally returned. She couldn't help but grin; she had missed her friend. The raeken landed in the field where she and Kennick had just been sitting, and Meera beheld Kennick's raek, Endu, for the first time. She felt a tickle in her stomach, then the tickle grew to a burble, which exploded into laughter that she could not repress. Doubling over, she clutched her gut and cackled: Endu was the exact same color as Kennick's distinctive, dark red hair.

"You match!" she gasped. Forgetting herself, she clutched Shael's shoulder and rocked him back and forth on the bench a few times. "You didn't tell me they matched!" she said to him. Shael's eyes widened slightly, and he smiled at her.

Meera could tell how vain Kennick was about his appearance and thought it was hilarious that he and his raek were coordinated. Some of the other riders laughed with her, and Kennick grinned, apparently unoffended. "Do you get him dyed that color, or is he just as vain as you are?" she asked.

"Do not let him hear you say that," Kennick warned.

"Please, I've handled a bigger raek," she replied.

Then Meera remembered Cerun and sprinted away across the grass to greet him. She didn't care if her relationship with Shael was strained; she had been friends with Cerun first, and she was determined to continue to be friends with him. "I missed you," she said, hugging his scaly snout and looking into his intelligent blue eyes.

Cerun hummed affectionately. Meera could only assume that Shael had already filled him in on everything. She knew Cerun probably wouldn't speak to her directly out of a sense of raeken propriety toward his rider, but she could and would still talk to him if she felt like it. "You know," she said. "My raek's a pain in my butt. I prefer your company. Just don't tell her I said that."

Cerun blinked in response.

"I know, I know," Meera replied. "Shael's a giant pain in your butt too, and you wish that I were your rider. I can't blame you." She sighed dramatically. "Oh well, I guess we're each stuck with what we've got."

Cerun blinked again, and Meera could have sworn his rumble sounded like a laugh.

22

MEERA

The next day, all anyone could talk about was the Spring Equinox celebration, and Meera oscillated between excitement and anxiety; she wanted to celebrate a knell holiday but had no idea what to expect. Finally, after dinner, Soleille and Katrea herded her to Soleille's house to get ready. Soleille lived about two miles into the woods, directly behind Hadjal's. Her house was slightly bigger than Shael's and made of stone. Its dominating characteristic, however, was that inside and out, it was completely overgrown with all manner of plants.

"I forgot that shaping living things could mean something other than healing," Meera said, admiring the many strange plants. "Do you use these for your teas?"

"I do!" Soleille cried brightly. She was in an especially good mood leading up to the celebration. "I know they are a bit much," she said, gesturing to the green and multi-colored vines over-taking her walls and some of her furniture, "But I keep acquiring more and cannot bring myself to get rid of any." Meera supposed that could be a real problem if you lived for hundreds of years. So far, she could still fit her meager possessions in a single bag.

Katrea flopped down comfortably on the sofa like she had spent plenty of time in Soleille's house. Meera remained standing and gawping at everything.

"Okay," Soleille said, clapping her hands together and getting down to business. "I know what I will wear, Katrea has what she is wearing, so that leaves you, Meera." She disappeared into another room and reappeared with a bundle of clothing in her arms, dumping it onto the sofa next to Katrea. "These are some of my past Spring Equinox outfits for you to pick from," she said.

"Some of them?" Meera asked in astonishment. She owned three outfits and rotated them. She still hadn't even bought a nightgown. "How old are you?" she asked Soleille, wondering for the first time.

"Oh, forty-something," Soleille replied absently, sorting through the pile. "I think this would be nice!" She held up something stringy and green that barely resembled a bra wrap to Meera, let alone a dress.

Katrea nodded. "Everyone wears green now," she said.

"I ... don't know," Meera said. "Can I see what you'll be wearing?" She was still trying to get an idea of what this event would be like.

Soleille and Katrea both went into Soleille's bedroom to change, and Meera began rifling through the pile on the sofa. Many of the garments looked like nightclothes to her, and none of them looked acceptable for public consumption. When Soleille and Katrea returned, her jaw just about hit the floor: they were naked—practically anyway.

"We look good, right?" asked Soleille, misunderstanding Meera's expression.

"I can see your nipples!" Meera exclaimed, not managing to filter her reaction with a polite response.

Soleille merely laughed. Her dress consisted of a pale green mesh that was draped several times over her private areas but not enough to be entirely opaque. Katrea was somewhat more covered in that her dark green mesh ensemble had pants and a fabric lining to cover her breasts.

Soleille then bustled into her kitchen and retrieved three flower crowns, placing one on her own head and handing Katrea and Meera the others. "I had these made for us by a friend who specializes in flowers!" she exclaimed.

"They're beautiful," Meera said, admiring the white flowers all around her crown. Each one was perfect and looked freshly clipped.

"What have you picked?" Katrea asked her.

"I ..." Meera looked back down at the pile of clothes. She rifled through it once more and tried to find something that wasn't see-through. Her hand landed on a light purple silk, and she pulled the dress out from the others and held it up. It looked to her like an immodest nightgown with little straps for sleeves and lace covering the delicate triangles that were meant to contain her breasts.

"A bit outdated, but it would look nice on you," Soleille said.

Uncertainly, Meera peeled off her clothes—all of them—and donned the scrap of silk. It fell past her knees because she was shorter than Soleille, but otherwise, she felt completely exposed. The neckline plunged between her breasts, which were not at all held in place by the flimsy silk fabric. The rest of the dress skimmed her body, and a slit bared her leg to the thigh.

"Very nice!" Katrea said approvingly.

"Really?" Meera asked. "I don't know ... I can't go out like this."

"Everyone dresses like this for the equinox," Soleille assured her. Then she stepped forward and undid the twists Meera had holding her hair back. "And everyone wears their hair down too."

With her long curly hair hanging down over her chest, Meera felt slightly less exposed, at least. Then Katrea placed her flower crown on her head and pointed her toward a mirror half-covered in vines on the far wall. Meera gazed at her reflection, barely recognizing herself. She was still getting used to seeing her new compact body in place of the luscious curves she used to have. Her initial reaction was always to cringe; she felt like she'd lost a lot of her femininity. But she was trying to embrace the function of her slimmer, more muscular body and not be overly concerned with her appearance.

Even so, she turned and inspected herself in Soleille's outfit. She supposed the dress skimmed her subtle curves nicely, and her small breasts weren't too unruly without any support. Her hair coiled wild and long, falling to her waist, and she arranged it to hide some of her body self-consciously. Then she met her own eyes, which stood out as large on her small, round face. Meera couldn't help but wonder if she was becoming who she was meant to be or pretending to be someone she wasn't. She didn't know if she liked herself in the skimpy dress; she didn't even know if she wanted to go to the celebration.

"Come on, Meera!" Katrea called, holding the front door open for her to follow and distracting her from her thoughts. Meera turned away from the mirror and followed. How would she know whether it was for her if she never tried it?

The three women walked through the woods barefoot. Meera shivered as the sun went down, wondering whether she should have brought more layers. She had been experimenting with letting some of the heat of her raek fire through to her skin, and she summoned it now on her arms.

"There will be a large bonfire at the celebration," Soleille assured her. "Or you can choose a man to keep you warm and take him somewhere private. That is what I will do."

Meera choked a laugh.

"Do you have anyone in mind?" Katrea asked.

"No ... I hope there will be some new faces tonight. The last few gatherings I attended all consisted of the same group," Soleille replied.

"Are you interested in anyone?" Meera asked Katrea curiously.

Katrea laughed. "I am too involved with myself to be bothered with anyone else," she replied.

"Isbaen is always on the hunt, and even Florean disappeared with someone last year," Soleille said. Meera wondered whether Darroah would be there but didn't want to ask because of how strangely Soleille had acted around him.

"Do not forget Kennick," Katrea added. "No one has sampled more of the knell population than he has." Meera didn't find that difficult to believe, considering Kennick's handsome face and easy smile; he exuded a calm self-assuredness that spoke to him being comfortable with himself and with others.

"Is Shael going?" she asked, embarrassed to ask and wondering whether she wanted him to be there or not. Not, she told herself. She did not want them stumbling into one another half-dressed, and she definitely did not want to see him with anyone else.

"I doubt it," Soleille said. "What is going on between you two anyway?" Meera wasn't surprised by the question. If anything, she was surprised that none of the other riders had brought it up with her sooner. Soleille, especially, had been uncharacteristically quiet on the matter.

Still, she sighed and wished she hadn't mentioned Shael. "Nothing. There is nothing going on between us. We are not together—certainly not engaged—and we don't even seem to be friends anymore. We're two riders who sit next to each other at mealtimes and are very careful not to rub elbows," Meera responded.

Soleille gave her a pitying look. "It is too bad. Especially, since —you know, you are both not quite human and not quite knell ... You might not have many other options," she said knowingly.

Meera bristled and tried not to snap in response. It wasn't very nice of Soleille to make her sound so undesirable, not that she was concerned with meeting anyone else. "I hardly think that's a reason to be together," she said sourly.

"Do not start with this, Soleille. Remember when you tried to set me up with that knell man from Gandry just because he had more muscle than me? He was seven hundred years old and ate everything with his hands—everything! I still cannot stomach Sodhu's squash soup. You need to focus on yourself and stay out of other people's affairs," Katrea rebuked her.

Just then, Meera started to hear music up ahead and nerves swarmed in her stomach. The celebration had begun. The sun was down, and the moon shone on them from directly above. As they drew closer, Meera heard voices and felt the rhythm of the music in her body as unseen musicians banged drums. The three women broke through the tree line together, but she shied back, hiding herself behind Soleille and Katrea, who moved forward confidently.

"There you all are," said a voice Meera recognized as Isbaen's. She peered around Soleille and clapped a hand over her mouth; Isbaen was completely naked except for a small covering made of leaves and flowers over his groin. Meera immediately clapped her other hand over her eyes. She didn't know if she should laugh or run away.

"I see you are already enjoying yourself, Meera," said Kennick from next to Isbaen, and she could hear the grin in his voice without even looking. Everyone was laughing at her. Slowly, she peeked between two of her fingers, grimacing preemptively. Kennick, at least, was somewhat modestly dressed in dark green pants and a mesh shirt. He also had a crown of flowers on his head, and his dark red hair fell over his shoulders as it usually did. His ear cuffs, bracelets and rings were all shaped into various floral scenes.

Meera lowered her hands from her face and smiled sheepishly at Isbaen and Kennick, resisting the urge to cover her body with her hands. Then she looked around the clearing and found it filling up with knell in similar levels of undress. A large bonfire burned in the center of everything, and musicians played on the far end. People seemed to be milling around greeting friends and sharing food and drinks with one another. Other than the outfits, it seemed like a relatively tame celebration, she thought.

"It will begin soon," Soleille told her.

"Begin?" Meera asked, but Soleille had already glided away to embrace someone she knew. The other riders were soon also similarly occupied, leaving Meera standing alone and exposed. Sidling over to a log near the fire, she sat down to observe everyone—an old habit that hadn't seemed to have deserted her entirely.

When people looked at her they often did a double take, noticing that she was human. Her massive amounts of curly hair gave her away in the dim light if nothing else, but no one approached her or told her to leave. She caught a glimpse of Florean, who was—thankfully—fully dressed. He was smiling broadly, and she gaped, having never seen him look so happy. She found herself smiling at the sight and sat back on her log to enjoy the celebration from afar.

It wasn't long before the music paused then began again with a new intensity. Everyone in the clearing stilled and waited expectantly, and through a gap in the trees, a procession of people appeared carrying some sort of platform. To Meera's utter surprise, on top of the platform was a very pregnant knell woman, who was entirely naked. The crowd cheered, and as the woman neared the bonfire, everyone in the clearing began to move and sway with the music, gathering around her in reverence.

Meera gaped as her fellow riders and the knell she didn't know danced like she had never seen before. There didn't appear to be steps or counting; they just swayed their bodies in loose, flowing movements. It was mesmerizing and beautiful to see everyone moving differently and yet pulsing as one. She stared transfixed as the pregnant woman was lowered to the ground and joined the throng of dancers. People lightly touched her protruding stomach as she passed. Meera supposed this was what the riders had meant when they had said the Spring Equinox celebrated life.

After a while, people began to break away from the dancing: taking seats, talking, sharing drinks, and wandering away into the forest. There remained a throng of dancers in the center, but Meera was no longer the only person not partaking. She saw vapors being passed around and a lot of flirtatious gestures and touches between the revelers. Soleille danced with two men at once in a manner that made Meera blush to watch, and Katrea and Florean stood talking to people.

Kennick eventually broke away from the dancers with a beautiful knell woman with jet black hair. They sat together and talked, and the woman draped herself on his shoulder, whispering into his ear and touching his chest. Meera wondered if Kennick knew the woman or if he just got what he wanted that quickly. Rolling her eyes inwardly, she looked back at the dancers.

Her chill was soon forgotten sitting near the fire. She felt like she thrummed with life and warmth, and she smiled, enjoying herself. She swayed gently to the music but didn't rise to her feet or engage. A knell man broke free from the dancers and put on a performance. He moved and flipped in a way that amazed her, and she clapped along with everyone else when he finished and stepped away. Looking around for the other riders, she caught sight of Isbaen leaving the dancing throng with another man.

Suddenly, Soleille appeared next to her, sweating and grinning. "Are you alright, Meera?" she asked over the music.

Meera nodded. "Who is that with Isbaen?" she asked before the men could disappear together into the woods.

Soleille looked where she gestured. "Oh! That is Gendryl!" she said, sounding pleased.

"Do you know him?" Meera asked. She was curious and couldn't help but hope that Isbaen would find the love he had been searching for.

"I assisted with his transition last year," Soleille said. Seeing Meera's confusion, she explained. "Gendryl was born with a female body but last year transitioned to be male."

Meera's eyes widened with shock and confusion. "You made him into a man?" she asked.

"We shaped his body to reflect who he is on the inside," Soleille explained.

Meera nodded as if she understood even though she was bursting with questions.

"Will you be okay on your own if I leave for a while?" Soleille asked.

"Go! Have fun!" Meera cried, noticing the man standing a short distance away waiting for Soleille. The two went into the woods together, and Meera sat once more on her log, alone. She didn't have long to feel her loneliness, however. A woman soon stepped into the light of the bonfire, drawing her attention. The performer invited the pregnant woman forward, who stepped into the light with her. Then she shaped water out of a bladder she carried and proceeded to swirl the water around the pregnant knell's body in a dance of magic and worship. Meera watched, intrigued, as she had never seen shaping used for performance before.

When a man bent in front of her and offered her a glass pipe, she wasn't sure what it was at first, but he showed her how to inhale the vapors. She hesitated for a moment, remembering Hadjal's warning, but then she leaned forward and did as he had done. At first, she didn't feel anything, but then a glowing lightness spread through her. She smiled at the man, and he smiled back, moving on to someone else.

Meera continued to sway on her log, but she felt like the music was inside of her now—beating in her blood and moving in her muscles. Her initial trepidation at joining the other dancers felt distant and unimportant. There was only her and the music and the bonfire. She watched the fire dip and shimmy, and she stood and danced with it. Someone near her approached the fire as well, and holding up their hands, the person changed the colors of the flames from orangey reds to greens and blues. Meera gasped with the crowd and applauded. Continuing to dance, she stepped closer and closer to the colorful fire until she was standing in the center of the clearing where the other performers had stood.

Suddenly, the music changed, and she felt the change like it called to her—like it sang in the fibers of her being. She lifted her right hand into the air, and out of her hand grew a pale, flaming raek made of her fire. She heard people exclaiming around her, but she didn't look at them; all that existed was her and her raek. She raised her hand higher and released the miniature flaming raek into air, watching as it flew up above her and circled. She circled with it, twirling and waving her arms over her head rhythmically.

The music changed again, and Meera lifted her other hand with the beat of the drum. From that hand grew another raek—an orange one. She beamed at her creation; she hadn't known she could do that. There were cheers and exclamations from the crowd again, and she raised her hand and released the raek to circle above with the other. As she danced, the raeken swirled and intertwined. They were pure joy, and she laughed with them.

As she did a rotation, her eyes flitted across the pregnant knell woman, and she beckoned to her. The woman stepped forward looking slightly nervous, but Meera smiled at her and held out her hands. The woman placed her hands in Meera's, and Meera positioned them in a cup in front of her protruding stomach. Then she summoned her flying raeken to swirl around the woman like fish swimming through water.

The woman's eyes grew large, but she stayed where she was with her hands outstretched. As the drumming rose in a fast, steady beat, Meera brought the raeken together, head-to-head over the woman's hands. Pale bluish white flame collided with orange flame for a chaotic moment, then both raeken vanished, and in their place was a flaming pink egg in the woman's hands. The woman smiled down at the fiery egg before her, and everyone stilled, watching.

The music slowed, and Meera's movements slowed with it. Then, very slowly, the flaming pink egg cracked open, and a tiny pink raek head emerged and nuzzled the woman's face. The woman laughed, and tears streamed from her eyes. The crowd awed and pressed forward to see. The music increased in speed once more. Meera raised both of her hands, and as she did, the tiny raek broke free of its egg and shot into the air. When it spread its wings for the first time, it burst into a thousand tiny pink embers that rained down harmlessly on the partygoers.

Everyone erupted in dance, and Meera found herself hoisted

onto the shoulders of two knell men and paraded around the clearing. She laughed and continued to sway and move from above until they put her down. Then, at last, she joined the main body of dancers. She threw back her head and let her masses of hair fall behind her shoulders and off her sweaty neck; she no longer cared what parts of her body were visible because she was beautiful! Everyone was beautiful! They were beautiful and free!

Meera danced and danced. Her hips rolled in new ways, and she found herself moving with people she didn't know, putting her hands around their necks and feeling their hands on her waist —men and women. Occasionally, someone would try to lead her away into the woods, but she just shook her head and kept danc-ing. She had never felt so alive and so on fire even though her fire lay dormant within her. She burned and burned until, eventually, she stumbled out of the dancing crowd, gasping for air.

23

KENNICK

K ennick kept an eye on Meera all night. He told himself he was looking out for her, but really, he just could not seem to look away. Her performance had dazzled him like everyone else, but even after that, he kept watching. His eyes were drawn to her purple dress in the sea of green, and he struggled to concentrate on the woman running her hands along his chest and whispering low into his ear.

Eventually, he dismissed the woman: he told her that night was not their night and left her, placing his flower crown on her head. She shrugged gracefully and moved away to seek other companionship. Kennick watched her go, wondering what he was thinking. Then he spent the rest of the night on the outskirts of the dancing as a silent observer.

When Meera stumbled out of the pulsing mob looking flustered, he was immediately by her side. "Are you alright?" he asked over the loud drums.

Meera fixed her eyes on his with some difficulty, blinking several times. He could see that her pupils were dilated, and she was not entirely herself. "I'm hot!" she shouted, shaking her arms like she could shake the heat from her body.

"Let me take you home," he suggested. She looked confused, scrunching her brows at him and swaying slightly. "To your cabin," he clarified, and her expression cleared somewhat. She nodded, and he led her into the forest.

He walked slowly and carefully since neither of them wore shoes. Meandering through the trees toward the peninsula, he felt slightly unsettled; he occasionally developed infatuations with women and felt the need to watch and pursue them, but he did not usually feel any qualms about those feelings as he did now. He could not pursue Meera considering that he might be her mentor soon and considering the condition she was in. He wondered what was drawing him to her. Could it be in part due to the horror his parents would feel if they knew he had his eye on another human woman? He did not think so.

Kennick felt more himself as they left behind the thumping, pounding music; his body could move loosely without the added reverberations tensing his muscles. Sighing, he swung his arms easily, smiling down at Meera next to him. He was just looking out for his mentee and would walk her home. "You looked like you enjoyed yourself," he said.

She seemed to have forgotten he was there and glanced up at him with surprise. "Where is your lady friend?" she asked.

He shrugged.

She shut her eyes, still walking. "Everything looks strange," she said.

"Your eyes are closed," Kennick told her, suppressing a grin.

Eyes still closed, Meera reached out and touched a tree limb. Then she turned on him and poked his nose.

"Can you see better with your eyes closed?" he asked.

"No, why?" she asked, sounding perplexed even though she continued to walk and touch things with her eyes shut tight.

"You fight with them closed most of the time," he reminded her.

"When I'm fighting, something is either coming toward me or it's not, but my eyes see everything—it's distracting. I'm used to fighting with Aegwren with my eyes closed in my body and open in his. But he doesn't see as much anyway because he's human," she explained.

Kennick studied her face in the moonlight, feeling like he could do so since her eyes were closed, though he knew she could sense his attention. Meera's face was round and soft like a human, but she was not unsymmetrical nor unattractive. Her scar glinted slightly in the moonlight, drawing his eyes to its swirling mass. She opened her eyes then, but he continued to regard her. Looking up at him, she teetered slightly and put a hand to her head. "I'm a little dizzy," she admitted.

"I think the vapors affected you strongly, either because you are human or because you are not used to them," he replied. Kennick was struck then by the fact that Meera had just referred to Aegwren's eyesight as being different because he was human, whereas he had made assumptions about her being different because she was human. He wondered how human she really was anymore.

Just then, they broke through the tree line right in front of the lake. The beach and Hadjal's house were a short distance to their right, and the forest drew right up along the lake where they stood. They both paused, looking out over the water at the high moon's reflection on its surface. "Meera, do you consider yourself more human or more knell?" Kennick asked. He studied her, but she remained staring upward.

"She doesn't care what she is called," Meera said, pointing up at the moon, which Kennick noticed was the same silvery white as the scar swirling up her neck.

"Does she not?" he asked with a smile.

"No," Meera said, spreading her hands up above her. "She shines down on us no matter what we call her, night after night." She stepped forward, still looking up, still reaching for the moon.

Kennick assumed she would stop when her feet entered the cold water of the lake, but instead of stopping, Meera stepped onto the lake's surface. As he watched in amazement, she ran toward the center of the lake, her feet leaving ripples across the surface of the water but not breaching it. Then, she was not just walking on water—she was dancing; she whirled around in the light of the moon, and his eyes traveled from her feet on the lake's surface up her body to her face, which was tilted up and full of wonder. He could have watched her all night.

Eventually, she wandered back toward him. When she stepped off of the water and onto land, she peered down at her feet in confusion. "Kennick, I lost your boots!" she exclaimed.

"This way," he said calmly, trying to lead her along the lake toward the cabin. When she did not immediately follow, he put a light hand on the small of her back and directed her with his touch.

She began to walk but still looked concerned. "But I lost the boots you bought me. I hate them ... but still ..." she said, large eyes peering up at him with remorse.

"Everything is okay. You will find your boots tomorrow," he assured her, giving her a small smile.

She smiled too and reached up and poked the tooth that tended to show over his lip, saying, "Boop!" That made Kennick really grin.

As they reached her cabin, Meera stopped and looked at her

feet once more. "Where are my boots?" she asked again, sounding small and concerned.

"We will find them tomorrow," he told her, casually reaching up and brushing some stray hair from her face, adding it to the coiling masses that hung down her back. The moonlight shone in Meera's eyes, and Kennick began to think that she really was quite beautiful.

Just as he lowered his hand, Shael stepped out of the cabin's shadow. "Meera?" he asked, gaping at her equinox outfit. Then his eyes landed on Kennick, full of accusation. "What are you doing?" he asked in a dark, predatory voice. Kennick could see his friend's shoulders tensing and mind racing behind his eyes.

He shrugged his own shoulders loosely and put his hands in his pockets. "I walked Meera home from the celebration," he replied calmly. "The vapors affected her strongly." Looking into Shael's eyes evenly, he waited for his friend to remember who he was—to recall that he was not a man who preyed on vulnerable women.

Shael released a breath and deflated slightly. He nodded. "Meera, I wanted to talk to you," he said, stepping closer to her.

The look in Meera's eyes turned to something like fear. "No!" she shouted, shaking her head vigorously and stepping back. Shael looked like he had been slapped. Meera began to claw at her bare arms.

"She is not herself," Kennick explained, turning to her. "Meera, we are at your cabin. Do you want to go to sleep?"

"Sleep? I can't! It isn't safe! He'll come!" she cried, pointing to Shael, who looked dumbfounded.

"Shael is leaving," Kennick said, not understanding what was going through her mind. "No one will bother you."

Suddenly, Meera lunged for him and grabbed his mesh shirt. Kennick put his hands on her arms to steady her and looked into her eyes to help her calm down. She was starting to hyperventi-late, her chest rising and falling in rapid movements. One of her thin straps fell off her slight shoulder, and he caught it and put it back in its place. Her breathing started to slow. "Where are we?" she asked. "We're not there, are we?"

"Where?" he asked, releasing his grip on her.

"Meera, this is not the Forest of Shayan. You are on the penin-sula. You are safe," Shael said, coming forward.

Understanding dawned on Kennick. He knew something of what Shael had experienced in the Forest of Shayan, and he had heard that Meera had also crossed through the enchanted forest. Meera looked at Shael but then glanced back at Kennick for confirmation. "This is not the Forest of Shayan," he told her evenly.

She nodded, swallowing visibly.

"You should get some sleep," Shael said to her. "We can talk tomorrow."

Meera shook her head once more. "No," she said again, this time sounding more like herself. "No, Shael. I will not follow you over a cliff—not *there* and not here." She walked toward him as she spoke until she stood directly in front of him. Then she rose up onto her tip-toes, brushed a featherlight kiss to his lips and walked away, entering the cabin.

Kennick wondered at what she had said, but Shael dug his fingers into his hair with a moan of pain, distracting him. "Come on," Kennick told his friend, moving away from the cabin. Shael followed, and they wound automatically down to the beach before speaking.

"Why were you waiting for Meera?" Kennick asked.

"Why were you walking her home when you could have been ... otherwise engaged?" Shael asked in return.

Kennick did not answer. He still was not entirely sure what he had hoped to gain by walking Meera to her cabin. After all, Levisade was so safe that she could have lain down and slept next to the bonfire like many surely would that night and found her way home in the morning. No one would have bothered her.

"How was the celebration?" Shael finally asked after a long silence.

"You would have hated it," Kennick said with a smirk.

"And Meera?" Shael asked. Kennick knew what he meant.

"She performed with her raek fire. It was incredible. Then she danced and danced. You would have hated that too," he replied.

Shael sighed and ran his hands through his hair. "I don't know what I'm doing," he said, tiredly. "Meera loved me, and I pushed her away. Now that she's done with me, I want her back. Am I just a glutton for pain?"

"You are a fool," Kennick said honestly.

Shael laughed.

Kennick supposed he was also a fool.

———

THE NEXT MORNING, Kennick arrived at breakfast earlier than the others. Hadjal alone was sitting at her table, holding what appeared to be a long-cold mug of tea. Kennick was glad to get a chance to speak to his mentor. He did not feel like he had spent much time with her since returning and something was clearly bothering Hadjal. "Good morning," he said, sitting across from her and blocking her view of the lake.

"Oh, good morning," she said, somewhat startled by his appearance.

"Long night?" he asked, noticing the tired lines around her still youthful eyes.

Hadjal leaned toward him, whispering so Sodhu would not

hear from inside. "Sodhu planned a nice evening for us, and I ruined it—I just could not focus on her. My mind is all over the place, lately," she admitted, sighing.

"You have not been acting like yourself," Kennick agreed. Then he waited. He would not ask Hadjal what was wrong, but he hoped she would confide in him. It felt like something of a role-reversal after so many years of her mentoring him, and yet, it felt right—like they could be proper friends now that his training was complete. At least, he hoped she would confide in him as a friend.

For a long while, Hadjal said nothing. Then she sighed again. "I have been a rider for a long time," she began, looking deep into her mug. "And since the massacre, everything has been relatively steady, peaceful. But lately ... I do not know ... I feel a change coming. It is Meera. I see her breaking new ground and forging her own way with no regard for tradition, and it frightens me. I suddenly feel old for the first time—like a creature from the past, being left in the past."

Kennick observed her seriously. "What do you fear will happen?" he asked.

"I fear this long-held peace will end," she said. "I fear Meera will bring it to an end."

"I do not think Meera seeks power for herself," he assured her.

"No, she does not. She is more dangerous than that—she is willful and idealistic, and I fear she will lead you all to your dooms," Hadjal said, piercing him with her look.

Kennick did not know what to say. He had already admitted to Meera that he would be tempted to follow her if she sought to end the war. "Not all change is doom," he said. He knew his mentor had faced horrible tragedies in her past and was set in her ways, but the world turned and moved ever onward. Levisade often felt timeless with its mild seasons and ageless occupants, but how long could Levisade remain a cloudless sky when storms raged on all sides? Maybe Meera would be the gust of wind to disrupt Levisade's endlessly blue sky, but Kennick was not sure that would be a bad thing.

"Perhaps I am too old, too far gone," Hadjal replied, sounding miserable.

"Hadjal, you are just old enough to provide us all with the much-needed perspective of the past, but you must also be willing to consider new perspectives. Why do you not spend some time training Meera? She would be glad to learn from you," he said. He thought to mention that Meera might need her help developing her new water shaping, but he decided to wait and let Meera tell Hadjal. He hoped their water shaping might forge a stronger connection between them.

"I suppose you are right," Hadjal sighed. "Perhaps I will train her in the rider histories after she sees the council. You are very wise, Kennick; I must have trained you well," she added, reaching across the table to put her hand on his face affectionately.

He touched her hand against his cheek. Then Hadjal rose and entered her house to get a fresh mug of tea. Kennick moved to his usual seat just as others began to arrive groggily to the table after their late-night celebrations. Sodhu came out with food, and they all began to fill their stomachs in preparation for the day.

24

MEERA

Meera awoke the next morning startled by how bright the cabin already was. Rising quickly from her bed, she became dizzy and fell to her knees on the wood floor. Then she grabbed her bedframe to haul herself back up and wiped drool from the corner of her mouth. Slowly, she recalled that she had been out late at the Spring Equinox celebration. Her head and face throbbed, and she already regretted the vapors she had inhaled.

Looking down, she found she was still wearing Soleille's purple silk dress, so she slipped it off and rifled the cabin for one of her three outfits. As she dressed and attempted to make her hair orderly, she pieced together what she could from the night before. She remembered her performance and dancing, and she recalled some horrifying dreams about the Forest of Shayan. She couldn't remember much else.

Meera left the cabin bootless and stumbled to Hadjal's table, desperate for something to eat and drink even though it was certainly later than everyone usually ate breakfast. Regardless, the others were still at the table—she wasn't the only one who had slept in late. Plopping down in her usual seat next to Shael, she ignored everyone, reaching for bread and water. She felt like her heart was beating in her temples. It occurred to Meera to wonder why Shael was eating his breakfast so late when he hadn't been at the celebration, but she didn't ask.

Kennick ate across from her and was giving her an even more infuriatingly smug look than usual. "What?" she asked him with an obvious edge.

He shrugged and smiled, not answering, which irritated her further. Just then, Soleille appeared and dropped Meera's boots and clothes from the previous day in front of her. Meera jumped at the sudden noise, then downed her cup of water; she felt like she had been trampled by stampeding horses. Soleille hummed with the self-satisfied air of the predator that had caused the horses to stampede. "Good morning," she said in a sing-song voice.

Meera scowled at her.

"It sounds as if you enjoyed your night," Hadjal said, coming out of the house with a mug of tea in her hands.

"Oh yes," Soleille replied with a coy smirk.

"Good," Hadjal said. "Meera, did you enjoy the celebration?"

Meera grunted noncommittally and rubbed her eyes.

"Meera was incredible!" Katrea said from down the table. "That was some performance!" Meera couldn't remember seeing much of Katrea at the celebration, but she must have stayed a while to see her perform.

"Performance?" Hadjal asked with an edge to her voice. She rounded on Meera, who was still holding a hand to her throbbing head and shoving food into her mouth. "Meera, why do you look like that?" she asked accusingly. "Did you drink something? Smoke something? I told you not to! You could have hurt someone!" The steam rising from Hadjal's mug seemed to intensify. Meera wondered whether the older knell woman was losing control of her own shaping at that moment, but she didn't mention it.

"I didn't hurt anyone," she said calmly. "Except myself, that is." She grimaced and made the mistake of glancing up at Kennick at the same time.

He was still smiling at her strangely. Hadjal looked angry, but before she could continue to berate Meera, Kennick spoke up. "Meera, you should tell Hadjal what happened on our walk home," he said, looking eager.

"Our walk home?" Meera asked blankly. She didn't remember walking home with Kennick. She didn't remember walking home at all. "Why? What happened?"

His eyes glinted with amusement. "Do you not remember?" he asked her teasingly, even though she clearly didn't.

"Should I?" she asked testily. She wracked her mind but couldn't recall her walk home. She remembered her dreams about the forest ... Shuddering, she pushed those thoughts aside. She looked at Kennick expectantly, but he continued to hold his tongue and smirk. "What? What did I do?" she asked. Her heart was starting to beat faster; she hoped she hadn't embarrassed herself. Why had Kennick walked her home, anyway? She glanced sideways at Shael, hoping he wouldn't get the wrong idea, but Shael was staring fixedly at his plate.

Kennick caught her glance and grinned wider. "Shael was there too, but not for the part I am referring to," he said vaguely. Shael was there? Meera had dreamt about Shael in the forest. Had that not been a dream?

"What did she do, Kennick?" Hadjal asked impatiently. "Why would I want to know?"

Kennick glanced at his mentor but held Meera's eyes when he said, "Meera walked on water—well, danced really."

Meera's stomach dropped. It wasn't what she had been afraid of him saying, but it was almost as bad. Staring obstinately at her plate, she began buttering more bread.

"Really?" Soleille asked, sounding amazed. Meera didn't look up to see Hadjal's reaction.

"You are not surprised," Kennick said, eyeing her. She glowered at him while she added jam to her bread. "You knew?" he asked.

She sighed and took a large bite of food, shrugging. She may have caused some ripples in water now and then over the past few weeks. She hadn't actually intended to acknowledge the new ability. Three elemental abilities were already more than anyone else had—more than enough. She didn't want to be any more bizarre, and she was annoyed with Kennick for blowing her secret—the one she hadn't really admitted to herself yet.

Meera tried not to look at him, but he was directly in front of her, and she couldn't help being aware of him. He sat tall and straight on the bench and ate with an annoying amount of dignity. The way he brought his food all the way up to his mouth instead of leaning down to eat it made her irrationally angry, and she slouched more and ate like more of a barbarian in response—tearing at her bread with her teeth like a coyote ripping into a carcass.

She could sense the other riders exchanging glances with one another, silently sharing their amazement that she had yet another ability. She didn't want to see their amazement and suddenly wished she'd done something embarrassing instead. After she finished eating, she pulled on her boots and stormed off on the pretense of training, though she really didn't feel up for training. She took her usual route for running around the lake, but she didn't run.

Kennick quickly caught up with her and fell into step at her side. She didn't look at him. "What now?" she asked.

"I apologize, Meera. It did not occur to me that you would not want others to know about your water abilities," he said calmly.

"Then why were you being so insufferably smug?" she asked with a sideways glance.

"Was I?" he asked, his pointy canine tooth poking over his lower lip.

Rolling her eyes at him, she kept walking. He kept walking with her.

"Do you really not remember getting home last night?" he asked.

"Obviously not," she replied shortly.

"Well, you should know that Shael was waiting for you outside your cabin," he said.

Meera felt a little thrill. She still loved Shael even if she had been suppressing her feelings, and she still wanted to hear that he loved her even if her rational mind knew that they shouldn't be together.

"He wanted to talk to you," Kennick continued. "You told him you would not follow him over a cliff."

"I thought that was a dream," Meera admitted. She supposed she had also kissed Shael, though Kennick didn't mention it. She sighed; she may have been delirious from vapors, but she stood by what she had said. It was the right thing to say, even if part of her wished she had listened to Shael's apologies and kissed him for real.

"I thought you should know in case ... you wanted to change your answer," Kennick ventured.

"No," she said simply, and he dropped the subject. When they crested the hill on the far side of the lake, Kennick suggested they do some hand-to-hand training and showed Meera to a small clearing nearby. They spent the rest of the morning training and talking, and she forgot her headache, she was having so much fun.

EVERY DAY THAT FOLLOWED, Meera spent most of her time training with Kennick: with swords and in hand-to-hand, near Hadjal's house and in their private clearing near the cliff. When she wasn't training with Kennick, she was wondering where Shaya was and fretting about what Darreal's council would decide about her. She received another note from Darreal—one in which she could sense the queen's impatience with her—and she only shared the note with Kennick, not wanting Hadjal to be even angrier with her.

"Do you think you should go without Shaya?" he asked.

"Maybe," she replied, puffing out her cheeks.

They had been sparring on the far side of the lake in the little clearing only they seemed to use. Meera sat heavily on the ground and lay back, looking up at the Shaya-colored sky. She tried to reach out to her raek, but as usual, she got no response. Then her mind strayed to Isbaen. She hadn't noticed his absence the morning after the Spring Equinox celebration, but he hadn't returned as the days had passed. She hoped he was somewhere with Gendryl, falling in love.

"What's the deal with two men being together?" she asked to distract herself from her worries. "It's like ... two swords and no sheaths," she said, lazily knocking her sword against Kennick's in the grass. Then she realized what she had just said, and she laughed and covered her face.

"Do you really want to know?" he asked. She could hear the grin in his voice and didn't look at him, too embarrassed.

"I'll wait and ask Gendryl when I meet him," she joked.

He laughed and reclined next to her on the grass. Then they both looked up at the bright sky and enjoyed the warming air of spring. For a time, they were silent. "Can I ask you something?" she asked finally.

"You already did," Kennick reminded her, his eyes glinting.

She ignored the comment. "What's your relationship with Endu like? I thought Shaya and I would be close—I thought we'd be friends and partners like Shael and Cerun—but I'm not even sure she cares about me. I'm not even sure she's capable ..." she said. Rolling onto her side, she propped her head on her hand and looked at Kennick.

He was lying on his back, fiddling with one of his rings—shaping and reshaping the metal. It moved like liquid between his fingers. At her question, he put the ring back on and, likewise, rolled to face her. "Endu and I used to be closer than we have been lately. We are still trying to find our way back to one another, but—I have changed, and he has not," he said, looking more serious than usual.

"How?" Meera asked quietly.

"Endu likes things a certain way. You know, I hate to admit this, but I think he chose me as his rider because I come from an Old Family—one of the oldest, wealthiest knell families—and because I have elemental abilities and am young and strong. He is very traditional and very proud ..." Kennick said, trailing off.

"You are still all of those things," Meera said, confused.

"Yes, but when Shael was captured, I wanted to go after him. I was willing to break my oaths and forsake the Riders' Code for my friend—a half-human one, at that. Endu refused to take me. He said he would not allow it, that he would not be the partner of an oath-breaker. I tried to go without him, but he would not let me pass. I am not quite as adept as you at fighting raeken," he said with a small smile. Meera was staring at him with open disbelief; she had thought he had chosen not to go to Shael—she had openly mocked and insulted him for it.

"For weeks, Endu and I fought about whether or not we should rescue Shael and Cerun. I admit, I was weak; breaking the Riders' Code was difficult enough for me without going against my raek. I could not change Endu's mind, so I did not go. I had lost my parent's acceptance long ago, but I could not bear to lose his as well. It was weakness hiding behind a facade of honor," Kennick explained, looking straight into Meera's eyes with a directness as piercing as his words.

"I have come to terms with the decision I made then," he continued, "But I also know that it is not one I would make again. That knowledge continues to divide Endu and I. He is ashamed of what he views as my sentimentality, and I am frustrated by his rigidity. I am not quite what he had hoped for in a rider, and yet, he will not suffer the embarrassment of breaking with me. And so, we are at an impasse. We go through the motions together but are not quite united in spirit."

Meera studied him, unsure of what to say. She hadn't realized quite how personal a question she had asked and was touched by how honest and vulnerable he was being with her. She considered apologizing for judging him so harshly when they had first met, but Kennick didn't seem overly concerned with the past. "You haven't completely changed, you know. You still eat like a stuck-up little rich boy," she told him.

Kennick threw back his head and laughed. His joy made him even more beautiful, and the soft light of the sun glinted off his dark red hair. Meera grinned with him then kicked out at his legs.

"Get up, lazy!" she said. "There's still time for one last round before dinner."

Isbaen wasn't at dinner, and he continued to be absent from the peninsula. While Meera was happy for him and hoped he was finding joy elsewhere—a sentiment shared by the other riders—his absence was also sorely felt by all; without Isbaen keeping him company every day and guiding him through meditations, Shael's mood quickly digressed.

Meera could sense the anguish emanating off of him at meals and struggled not to reach out to him in some way. She knew she was partly the cause of his misery, though she didn't quite understand his feelings. Slowly, he withdrew from the other riders, barely speaking and hardly eating. Even Kennick seemed to be struggling to break through his stony exterior. Eventually, Shael stopped coming to the peninsula altogether.

In some ways, it was a relief for Meera not to have to sit next to him and feel his pain—or be reminded of her own. But after he was absent for several days, she grew worried. "Should I go and talk to him?" she asked Kennick as they sheathed their swords after training. They hadn't been discussing Shael, but Meera didn't need to explain what she meant; they spent enough time together now to be able to follow one another's errant thoughts.

"I already tried to no avail," Kennick said. "Would you be willing to talk to him?"

"Of course! I will always care for Shael," she replied. She said "care," but she meant "love." She would always love Shael, even if she no longer wished to be with him—could no longer bear to be with him, more like. She hoped they could one day be friends again.

"I wish you luck," Kennick said with a small smile.

Meera looked at him and realized something: at some point, she and Kennick had become friends. They spent most of their time together and communicated easily. Meera had missed Shael and her father less spending time with Kennick, but she was also growing to appreciate him for who he was—his confident personality and subtle quirks. She found that while he was teasing and smug, he was genuine with her.

Though she tried to ignore it, she also felt a physical reaction to him at times when they trained together. When his hands landed on her body, her stomach fluttered. When they stepped close together during their sparring, her heart accelerated from something other than exertion. It was just lust, she told herself, and she disregarded those small moments. She had once felt similarly in King Bartro's presence, after all, and her feelings had not meant anything.

Meera told herself she still loved Shael—only Shael—and her feelings for Kennick were strictly physical. Kennick was handsome, and she was only human, after all—well, she supposed she wasn't *only* human, but she was a living breathing woman who could not expect herself to be entirely immune to his obvious charms. She did, however, expect herself to ignore her little thrills and flutters; she did not need to bungle another friendship.

Meera's mind strayed back to Shael, and she sighed, thrusting her sword into Kennick's hands. "Take this," she said. "I'm going now." Then she took a deep breath and trudged into the forest, taking the familiar winding path to Shael's house.

25

SHAEL

Without Isbaen on the peninsula to temper him, Shael quickly devolved into one of his deepest depressions yet. His thoughts spiraled into dark places and dragged him with them: he was weak and disgusting— a partial-breed that did not belong anywhere or with anyone. Meera saw how pathetic he was. Kennick only spent time with him out of pity. The other riders all secretly wished he would disappear and leave them alone, sick and tired of his moods.

Shael could not blame them, either; he was sick of himself. He was magicless and spineless and poor company. He had pushed Meera away, proving to himself and everyone else what a fool he was. He did not belong at the peninsula and never would. He would never regain the other's respect as a rider after his capture. He even began to believe that Cerun would be happier finding another rider. Cerun disagreed with him, argued with him, and tried desperately to distract him from his thoughts, but he could not be distracted.

Usually, Isbaen pointed out when Shael's thoughts were

distorted; he often reminded Shael that just because he thought something, did not mean it was true or that he had to believe it. It did not always help, but at the very least, having Isbaen's steady presence at his side everyday helped to calm Shael; he believed his mentor when his own senses sought to deceive him. But Isbaen was gone—probably driven away by his incessant neediness, Shael told himself.

Eventually, he stopped bothering to go to the peninsula. The other riders were better-off without him. He sat in his house, despondently, and let himself wither away—too weak to actually put an end to his useless life. Cerun remained nearby at all times, fretting over him like an overgrown mother hen, but Shael stayed in his house and shut out his raek as much as he could.

He was sitting in his reading chair one day, staring uncomprehendingly at a book in his lap, when he heard his door open. "What do you want?" he asked, assuming it was Kennick again.

"Shael?" called Meera's voice.

Shael spun around to look, fearing he was starting to hallucinate. But she was really there, standing in his doorway. He did not know why she was there; after all, she had made it fairly clear that she was finished with him. Meera stepped forward but did not shut the door behind her. Shael could not blame her. He had been keeping his windows shuttered; his house was dark and probably stale-smelling. He surely reeked and hoped she would stay away from him.

"Did Kennick send you?" he asked. He knew the two of them were spending all of their time together. He understood Meera's preference for a full-knell over him, and he understood Kennick's interest in Meera. He was not angry with either of them. He had been a fool, and now he was reaping the consequences.

"No," Meera said. "I'm worried about you."

"Why?" Shael asked disbelievingly. In that moment, he could

not comprehend why anyone would bother worrying about him —he was nothing.

"You're important to me, Shael," she replied. "Will you come outside and talk to me?"

He did not move. He did not speak. As he was wont to do, he seized up like stone. Meera walked over and extended her hand to him with a smile. It was their old gesture—the one he had used to lure her onto Cerun's back and out of Terratelle. Shael stared at her hand. Still, he did not move.

Seemingly unperturbed, Meera reached down and grasped one of his hands, yanking him to his feet with her new strength. "Come on," she said as she towed him behind her across the kitchen and through the front door.

Light and air slapped Shael in the face, knocking some life into him. Taking deep breaths, he squinted around at the new green in the trees. He had not realized spring had sprung so thoroughly. The forest smelled like rebirth. Meera turned on him, and he withered under her scrutiny, pushing his greasy hair behind his ears and wishing he had bathed. "What's going on? Where have you been?" she asked, her usual warmth and concern in her almond-shaped eyes.

"Nothing," he said defensively. "I have just been here, staying out of everyone's way."

She scrunched her brows at him, and he shrunk back. "What do you mean? You're not in anyone's way—"

"I am! I bring everyone down—I cause everyone pain! You know it! You know you are better-off without me, and so is everyone else!" he erupted, immediately regretting it and wishing he had kept his mouth shut. Meera looked at him with so much sadness and pity that he had to look away.

"Shael, look at me," she said, grasping his chin and waiting for him to meet her eyes. He did so reluctantly, and she let her hand fall to her side. "You hurt me when I got back, but that's behind us now. I love you—we all love you, and we want to see you every day. We want to train with you and eat with you. Not one of our lives would be better without you."

Shael looked into her sincere brown eyes and swallowed. He shook his head, at a loss for words. "I always knew you would be happier without me," he said quietly.

Now Meera was the one shaking her head adamantly. "No, Shael. I'm not. I need you in my life," she insisted.

"No—you left me!" he shouted back. "I knew you would leave me, and you did—twice!"

"Shael, I left to train because I couldn't stand the thought of hurting you—because I care about you—and I ... broke it off with you because I knew you would keep hurting me until you learned to love yourself. You say I'm better-off without you—that we all are—and you push us away even though it isn't true. That hurts, Shael! You were always stepping apart from me, saying you loved me then pulling away. You didn't think you were worth loving so you pushed and pushed just to prove it was true!" Meera cried.

"And it was!" Shael shouted. "You left!"

"I didn't leave, Shael. I'm right here! I still care for you, and I'll always be here for you—I just wasn't willing to be hurt by you anymore. There's a difference," she said, wiping tears from her eyes.

They were both silent for a moment, panting from their emotion. Shael stared at Meera and wondered at her words: were they true? He could not tell.

"No one is better-off without you," she said again, clasping her hands on his arms. Shael began to tremble. "Who?" she asked. "Who do you think is better-off without you? I'll go and get them, and they'll stand right here and tell you the same thing I'm telling you!"

He shook his head. Then, very quietly, barely a breath of air, he said, "Caleb."

"Who's Caleb?" Meera asked, still clutching his arms.

"I ... loved him," Shael said, shaking even more violently. This was not something he had ever admitted to anyone. This was his deepest, foulest secret.

"Like ... *loved* him?" she asked.

He nodded, irrationally expecting her to drop his arms and step away in disgust even though he knew Meera was not bothered by Isbaen's preferences.

"What happened?" she asked.

Shael had trouble forming words for a moment, but she waited him out. "I loved Caleb before I left Sangea. He ... said he didn't care if I was part-knell, but I left anyway—for his own good. He got married. His wife was pregnant last I heard. He's ... happier without me. I would have only caused him pain like I hurt you," he said, swallowing.

"Shael, Caleb didn't want you to leave, and you left anyway. That doesn't mean he's happier without you. He has made the best of his life without you in the human world because of a choice you made for him. He has a wife and a baby, but do you even know that he's happy?"

Shael stared at her. He had never considered that Caleb was not actually happy, and he supposed he had made the decision for both of them. When Meera phrased it, it all sounded ... different, somehow.

"Shael, Caleb loved you, and I love you, and the riders love you because you're worth loving. But the only opinion of you that really matters is your own. You need to find yourself worth loving," she said, squeezing his arms and letting them go.

He nodded. Everything she was saying made sense even if it sounded too simple, too easy, and yet ... too impossible. "How?"

he asked meekly. He was so used to despising himself, he did not think there was much hope for him.

"Why don't you visit Caleb?" she asked.

Shael stiffened. He was not sure he could handle that—seeing Caleb's perfect, happy human life. He nodded, even though he did not think he would go through with it.

"And Shael, you need to leave your house every day—get fresh air, go flying. At least your raek loves you," she said with a smile. "Mine attacks me randomly then disappears."

He nodded again.

"Come back to the peninsula. You can train with Kennick and I, or you can throw rocks at us while we spar just for the fun of it," she said looking up at him. He cracked the smallest hint of a smile. He was not sure he needed to see Kennick and Meera together. "We're your friends. All of us. We miss you."

"I miss you too," he managed to say through his tense jaw.

Meera gave him a big hug, squeezing him around the middle and shaking him lightly. He managed to return the hug briefly before dropping his stiff arms back to his sides.

"Now go bathe because you stink," she said, stepping away from him and making a face. "And I expect you next to me at dinner."

He nodded one final time, and Meera left, throwing a last look back at him over her shoulder.

"She is right," Cerun said in his mind. "I can smell you from over here." Shael had not even realized he had let his mental defenses down. He kept them down. It was not fair of him to block Cerun out. "Bathe, and we will fly before you eat. I need to stretch my wings."

Shael sighed out a breath of air and released some of the tension he was holding. When he went inside, he threw open all of the windows before scrubbing himself thoroughly and flying to dinner.

SHAEL DID NOT FEEL ENTIRELY BETTER after his conversation with Meera; he continued to have thought distortions, convincing himself that he was worthless and unloved. However, now when he did, he also pictured Meera dragging people in front of him to tell him otherwise, and the thought of her lining up everyone he knew to profess their love for him made him smile. He also felt lighter, having shared a part of himself he had been repressing for a very long time.

Meera, who was raised in a conservative human society similar to his own, did not appear to judge him for his romantic relationship with a man, and Shael began to wonder if he might be able to stop judging himself. He tried. Isbaen always told him to acknowledge his thoughts then let them drift away without internalizing them, but Shael found it easier said than done. It was much easier for him to stay in the present when he kept himself busy, so that was what he did: he resumed his training— often with Kennick and Meera.

One day, however, he woke up and did not feel like going to the peninsula. Meera's suggestion that he visit Caleb had continued to nag at him, so Shael put on his riding jacket and let Cerun know his plans. Cerun exalted at the prospect of a long flight, and they both enjoyed the warm spring weather on their journey despite Shael's ever-increasing nerves and anxiety.

He had known for a long while where he could find Caleb due to his mother's incessant gossiping. Cerun dropped him in their usual landing field in Sangea, and he walked the rest of the way. He tried to prepare something to say, but he could not put into words why he was going or what he hoped to find. Closure, he supposed; he wanted to see Caleb again to finally get the closure on their relationship he had never had.

Shael approached the quaint little home with the cheerfully painted yellow door and looked down at his knell attire. He hoped he would not frighten Caleb's wife or household. It took all of his nerve to knock on the door; he was buoyed mostly by the embarrassment he would feel if someone were watching him loiter on the doorstep. Then he heard footsteps approaching, and the door swung open.

Before him stood a pretty young woman with purple smudges under her eyes and her hair pulled back under a kerchief. She stared at him for a long moment, but before he could open his mouth to speak, she exclaimed, "Oh! You must be Shael!"

Shael felt his mouth drop open slightly, and he nodded.

"I'm Elise," she said. "Come in!" She backed up and beckoned him through the door. He followed. "I'm sorry for my appearance," she said, brushing at her dress, which he then noticed had something spilled down the front. "Twins! Twice the joy and twice the mess!" she chirped nervously.

"Congratulations," Shael said, digesting that bit of information. Caleb was a father. Caleb had a wife and twin babies. "What are their names?" he asked politely.

"Landon—for Caleb's father, of course—and Sophia," she said.

A boy and a girl, Shael thought, how perfect. Before he could inquire as to whether Caleb was there, Elise turned and called for him up the stairs.

"Coming!" they both heard him reply. Then they stood in awkward silence for a few seconds.

"I do not wish to keep you," Shael said, thinking that Elise looked like she had enough to deal with without babysitting him in the foyer.

"Oh, um, why don't you just wait through there in the drawing room," she said, gesturing to a door on their right.

Shael nodded and stepped into the small room. He could still hear Elise fidgeting in the foyer even though he had expected her to return to her children, and he wondered if his presence made her uncomfortable; she had almost certainly never met a knell before. Then he heard footsteps on the stairs. "Who's here, darling?" asked a male voice that he recognized as Caleb's with a jolt in his chest.

Elise whispered her answer, presumably not realizing that Shael could hear better than humans. To his surprise, she actually sounded excited: "It's your friend, Caleb! It's Shael! He finally came!"

"Really?" Caleb asked.

"He's in there!" Elise replied, ostensibly pointing to the drawing room.

Before Caleb even entered, Shael's heart lightened in his chest. They had discussed him—expected him all this time. He was *finally* there, and they sounded glad. That knowledge alone lifted some of the darkness from his past—freed him from some of his worst thoughts about himself. Being welcome in the happy little house where two babies lived made him feel more ... himself. He felt more like who he had been before human society had shunned him and he had shunned his human self in return.

When Caleb walked through the door, grinning at him, Shael stepped forward without hesitation and embraced his old friend. He congratulated him on his marriage and his children. Then they sat and spoke for a long while. Shael had thought that finding Caleb happy would prove that his old lover was better-off without him, but that was not how it felt; he was glad that Caleb seemed to truly love his wife and was obviously besotted by his children. He was glad Caleb was happy. It was the welcome Shael received that made all the difference.

When Elise brought the twins down from their nap and let Shael hold them, he felt one of the gaping wounds on his soul weld shut. He had not realized how much he had needed the acceptance of humans—not any humans or all humans—but the ones who had known and loved him before. He wondered if Meera was right—if he was the one standing in the way of his happiness, not his half-knell status or half-human status or lack of magical ability.

He looked at the chubby-cheeked baby boy in his lap and finally accepted that everyone came into the world innocent and perfect and worthy of love—himself included. He did not know who his biological father was or the circumstances of his conception, but he had been as bright-eyed and faultless as little Landon, who sucked on his knuckle. Tears filled his eyes, and he let them, not bothering to hold back his emotions among friends—not anymore. "Your little ones aren't in need of a god-father, are they?" he asked.

26

MEERA

When Shael didn't join them at the peninsula, Meera began to worry again. She assumed that he was once more shut up in his house, withdrawing from everyone. She wanted to go to him immediately, but she held back; she wanted to be his friend, but she also fretted that constantly showing up for him would give him the wrong idea. She still loved Shael—but with less urgency than she used to. She could actually imagine them being friends now, and she didn't want to ruin that by giving him false hope and letting him down again.

The next morning when he arrived at breakfast looking rested and happy, Meera was absolutely flabbergasted. He greeted everyone before taking his seat and grabbing a plate, and she just stared at him with her mouth hanging open. His hair was clean, his green eyes sparkled with life, and the shirt he wore was a lighter shade of blue than usual. When he politely asked her to pass the eggs, she nearly fell out of her chair.

Meera's first instinct was to demand to know what the

imposter had done with Shael. Her second was to ask him what had happened and whether he had visited Caleb. But she didn't act on either impulse; she opted for her third instinct, which was to accept Shael's well-being silently and respectfully so as not to make him uncomfortable. She did, however, raise her eyebrows at Kennick across the table and flick her eyes in Shael's direction. Kennick gave her a brief eyebrow raise in acknowledgement, and Meera smiled down at her food. She loved her little rider family.

SEVERAL DAYS LATER, Isbaen finally returned. He appeared at dinner with a bashful looking Gendryl tucked under his arm. Gendryl was slighter than Isbaen with a handsome face and honey-brown hair that reminded Meera of Linus. She fondled her bracelet as she always did when remembering her friend. Then she grinned at Isbaen and introduced herself to Gendryl, clasping his thin hand in her own.

"I was hoping Isbaen would bring you back with him," she told the man warmly. She already liked Gendryl a lot more than Darroah, though her opinion was based purely on how in love Isbaen and Gendryl looked sitting together and giving one-another tender glances. Gendryl smiled at her shyly, possibly the most timid knell Meera had ever met.

"Yes, Meera wanted to ask you something, Gendryl," Kennick said, joining them at the table. His dark eyes glinted at her mischievously.

Meera's own eyes widened, remembering her joke to Kennick about two swords. Stammering something unintelligible, she kicked his shin under the table and left to help Hadjal carry out food.

Hadjal had largely been behaving like her old self recently, and that, combined with Shael's good mood and Isbaen's return with Gendryl made the next few weeks of spring pass very comfortably. Meera barely even worried about meeting with Darreal's council or whether Shaya would return. She enjoyed her days with her family, surrounded by the fresh blossoms of spring.

Eventually, however, like all things, her period of bliss came to an end. Sodhu caught a messenger bird on her arm early one day that saw to that. She read the message silently to herself before turning to Meera, who was seated at the table. "Is this true?" she asked.

Meera stared at her. Sodhu was often silent and always friendly, but right now, she sounded angry. Meera didn't know what was happening, but when she saw the note in Sodhu's hand —written in Darreal's familiar handwriting—her stomach turned. "I—" she started to say.

"Meera, when the queen tells you to go in front of her council immediately, with or without your raek, you listen!" Sodhu said sharply. Everyone at the table gaped at Meera, Gendryl included, who was still hanging around and getting accustomed to the riders' interactions. "She says she summoned you weeks ago!"

Meera shrunk down in her seat. She had only told Kennick about the note she had ignored. Hadjal's golden eyes flashed at her dangerously, and even Soleille and Katrea looked concerned. Florean, who had been very quiet since her father had left, gave her a piercing stare. "If you wish to be a rider, you must respect the chain of authority," he told her.

Meera squirmed in her seat. She had not admitted to the others that she didn't actually want to be sworn in as a rider.

"You will write her a reply—now," Sodhu said, thrusting paper and a pen at her, "And you will give her an exact date for your council meeting. Someone will fly you to the estate if Shaya has not returned." Meera had never heard Sodhu be so forceful. She felt like she was finally getting a glimpse of the woman who had earned the respect of enough knell to be invited onto the Queen's Council—not that she ever seemed to participate in their meetings.

"Will you be there?" Meera asked her.

"I ... I no longer make decisions for others," Sodhu said quietly. Hadjal gave her a meaningful pat on the back, and Meera dropped the subject. Instead, she stared down at the blank paper in front of her.

"Meera, there is something I have been meaning to ask you, and I think now is a good time," Kennick said.

She glanced up at him quizzically. "Do you?" she asked. She couldn't imagine why now would be a good time to ask her anything, considering everyone was staring at her and pressuring her to go to the estate and do something she didn't want to do.

"My parents always host a Summer Solstice ball. Would you like to go with me?" he asked.

She stared at him blankly. Was he making some sort of joke? Was he trying to distract her from her concerns regarding the council? She looked down the table at Soleille like the blonde-haired woman might speak man better than she did. Soleille's eyes were bright, and she leaned forward, listening with intrigue. Meera immediately regretted looking at her. "Uh ... why?" she asked Kennick, studying him.

As usual, he appeared so relaxed and sure of himself, he might have been sitting on a cushioned throne instead of a wooden bench. "I am generally amused by your company, for one," he said.

Meera barked a laugh. "My, I've never been so flattered," she said dryly. "Am I blushing? I think I'll pass."

Katrea laughed. Kennick's pointy canine tooth showed over his lower lip, and there was humor in his eyes. "You would be doing me a favor. Your presence would deeply irritate my parents. Also, the queen and most of her council will be in attendance, so I thought you could arrange to meet with them at my parent's home the following day since they will all likely be staying the night regardless," he explained.

Ah, Meera thought, understanding why Kennick thought the invitation was relevant to her current predicament. "Or ..." she said, "I could go with you, not go to the ball, and meet with the council. I don't have anything to wear, and I don't have any money. I suppose I could get Shael's mother to send me my dress from her house ..." She considered the possibility. It wasn't a horrible dress by any means, though it wouldn't fit her anymore and brought back bad memories—as did the Summer Solstice for that matter.

"I will get you something to wear. Do not worry about that," Kennick said.

Meera looked down at his fine clothes and supposed he would likely choose something reasonably nice for her. Shrugging her acceptance of the plan, she quickly scribbled out a note to Darreal. As she wrote, she heard Soleille whisper to Katrea, "Meera is so lucky! I have never been to one of Kennick's family's balls. Only the most important knell are invited."

Meera sighed. She had no particular interest in the ball, but if Kennick wanted to parade her around to annoy his parents, she didn't especially mind. She also generally found Kennick's company amusing and figured they could enjoy any stuffy party together. Besides, she thought; she wouldn't be able to sleep before her meeting with the council anyway, so a ball might be a good distraction.

TIME BETWEEN KENNICK'S invitation and the Summer Solstice passed quickly, and before Meera knew it, she was standing on the grassy, flower-covered slope of the peninsula with her bag in her hand. She still didn't know what she was wearing that night as Kennick had assured her it would be awaiting her at his parent's house. She thought his parents must have a large house if so many people were spending the night.

Kennick also had a bag, which he was presently strapping to Endu's side. His body language was more tense than usual, and Meera wondered if he was arguing with Endu. She imagined—based on what Kennick had shared of his raek's personality—that Endu may not want a human to ride him. Even after Kennick finished his task, he continued to stand silently and stare at his raek, confirming to Meera that they were having a heated mental dialogue.

Shifting uncomfortably on her feet, she waited. The other riders had already wished her the best for her meeting with the council, and Shael had wished her luck—a human concept, as Darreal would remind her. Meera was not eager to tell the council that she did not actually intend to pledge herself to them or to the riders; she had no idea how they would react to such a statement. She was just beginning to wonder if it would be for the best if Endu refused to carry her when Kennick jumped onto his raek's back and beckoned her to follow.

"You sure?" she asked, stepping forward.

He nodded, looking more irritated than she had ever seen him. She smiled, knowing his irritation was not with her and leapt onto Endu's back, positioning herself behind Kennick. Endu took flight smoothly—much more smoothly than Shaya would have—and set off for Kennick's family home, which he assured her was not very far away.

The day was warm, and the sun beat down on them. Meera

did her best to put aside her worries and focus instead on the nice weather, which quickly made her drowsy. Reclining along Endu's back, she blocked the sun from her eyes with her hands and created a shape-shield around them to filter out the harshest winds. She let in a light breeze to cool them but didn't want to arrive in front of Kennick's parents with absurdly tousled hair. Sighing, she shut her eyes and spread her arms on either side of her.

"Are you going to fall asleep?" Kennick asked.

"Maybe," she replied, yawning for emphasis. He wrapped one of his hands around her ankle, which dangled by his side, and Meera smiled at the concerned touch. "I'm not going to fall," she assured him, "And if I did, I could catch myself." None of the riders had ever actually seen her catch herself from a fall because Shaya had not been around to throw her from her back mid-air.

Despite her protestations, Kennick kept his hand loosely wrapped around her ankle, and Meera tapped her booted foot absently against his thigh. She supposed she didn't hate the boots he had bought her anymore. They were thoroughly broken in and no longer irritated her—much like Kennick, she thought with a smile.

Meera dozed off for a while until Kennick squeezed her ankle. "We are almost there," he said. She sat up, stretched, and looked down. As Endu circled lower, she could see what looked like an enormous stone castle with a high wall around it, complete with several outbuildings. It looked more like the palace in Altus than the Levisade Estate did. "That's not a house—that's a castle!" she exclaimed.

Kennick shrugged in front of her. "My mother would certainly like to think so," he replied. Meera didn't know much about Kennick's parents, but they clearly didn't get along well if she was there to annoy them.

"Do you want to make an entrance?" she asked, bouncing eagerly. She was itching to free-fall. She had hated the sensation at first, but the more she did it, the more she enjoyed the feeling of falling through the air.

"What do you mean?" he asked.

"Let's jump!" she cried, grabbing his hand.

Kennick turned around and looked at her like she had lost her mind—his usual casual demeanor gone. "You want to jump?" he asked incredulously.

"I'll catch us! It'll be fun!" she said.

"Not this time," he replied, and Endu dove forward to land.

Meera considered jumping by herself, but she didn't want to alarm Kennick. She also supposed it wouldn't be a very nice way to arrive if the sight of her falling gave anyone below a heart attack. Puffing out her cheeks in frustration, she flicked one of his metal ear cuffs.

Endu landed in a spacious courtyard where—it seemed—an entire household of staff waited to greet them upon their arrival. Meera dismounted and looked around at the staff, who were all human and appeared extremely nervous in the large raek's presence. Kennick landed gracefully next to her just as a man and woman approached them from the middle of the gathered crowd.

Meera assumed the man and woman striding toward them were Kennick's parents, though it was incredibly strange to her that they barely looked older than him. The woman had his dark red hair, a severely angular face, and shrewd eyes. The man had extremely pale blonde hair and wore a friendly expression.

"Mother, you did not need to gather the entire household. Surely, they have enough to do preparing for the ball," Kennick said.

"Nonsense," the woman replied. "My son has finally returned home, and they will welcome him to his rightful place." Meera expected Kennick's parents to hug him, but they stopped in front of them instead.

"Mother, Father, this is Meera," Kennick said. Meera knew he had already written to them about her staying and about hosting the council meeting. Kennick's mother was, apparently, on the council, which Meera was starting to think might not be in her favor; the woman was regarding her with a look of unveiled distaste.

"We are Destin and Andreena," Kennick's father said with a vague smile.

"Hello," Meera replied. "Thank you for having me." Neither of them answered her.

"Well, that is enough of a spectacle, for now," Andreena said before turning and walking toward the front doors.

Meera and Kennick followed with their bags, and Endu sat in the courtyard preening himself.

"After you change, we will have lunch," Andreena said with a nasty look at Meera's clothes. Meera could change, but the woman wouldn't like either of her other two outfits any better, she thought. She looked to Kennick, who grinned at her and supposed she was doing an excellent job of irritating his mother, so far.

27

KENNICK

Kennick showed Meera to her room then went to his own in order to change for lunch. His mother always insisted they follow such formalities. He pitied the staff, who no doubt had an abundance to do that day in preparation for the ball and did not have time to stand in the courtyard to greet him. He knew his mother would never change, however, and he did not expect her to.

When Kennick knocked on Meera's door to retrieve her, he was delighted to find she had not bothered changing into one of her other few outfits. He looked her up and down, grinning, and she shrugged at him. "I'm here to annoy your mother, aren't I?" she asked, stepping into the hall.

Kennick had asked Meera to join him simply because he had wanted her there, but he did not bother to correct her. He showed her through the winding hallways and up the stairs to the dining room. "The dining room is upstairs?" she asked as they climbed. "Kitchens are usually on the main level. Do the servers have to carry the food up three flights of steps?"

"They do," he confirmed.

"Why?" she asked.

"I suppose my mother likes to look out over her domain while she eats," he replied. The question had never occurred to him before, though he remembered instances of servers dropping platters down the narrow serving stairs as a boy and having to face his mother's wrath. Meera laughed and rolled her eyes. Kennick had never described his mother to her, but he could tell that Meera already had a good understanding of Andreena's personality. Andreena could certainly make an impression.

His parents were already seated on opposite ends of their long dining table when they arrived. Kennick pulled out Meera's chair for her in the human style before walking all the way around to take his seat across from her. He saw her look at the view out the expansive window behind his father and gave her a pointed smile. Servers soon arrived with platters of light food, and they all began to eat with little conversation.

Kennick's parents were certainly not being friendly toward Meera. He had expected as much and would not have brought her if he had not thought she could handle it. Finally, his mother broke the silence: "Kennick, Flavian's daughter is coming tonight. I know the two of you have ... been acquainted in the past, and I thought you might occupy her at the ball this evening."

"That might be a little rude to Meera, Mother, as she is my date for this evening," he replied coolly.

His mother's fork froze midway between her plate and mouth. Then her eyes roved to Meera with a look of horror. "The human is your date?" she spat. "Kennick, housing her to be appraised by the council is one thing, but I would not have allowed you to bring her here if I had known you were up to this nonsense again!"

His mother's temper caused the candles in the wall sconces to flare and flicker, which amused him; he used to count how many times he could make her do that at any given meal. It was an old game but a good one. Kennick glanced at Meera, who did not look overly concerned by his mother's outburst and continued to pick at her food unenthusiastically.

"Destin–" Andreena said to her husband, commanding him to step in.

"Kennick, your mother is right," his father said meekly. "We were able to pass your previous foolishness off with our friends after you became a rider, and your tastes seemed to mature. We will not, however, be able to save your reputation again if you insist on parading this human around." Meera gave Kennick a curious look but continued to chew her food unconcernedly, apparently immune to being referred to so unfavorably.

"Father, Meera is beautiful and strong, and I enjoy her company immensely—there is no one I would rather parade around at your ball," Kennick replied evenly. At that, Meera did look a little shocked, which made him grin.

"We have heard rumors of the girl's abilities," his mother said, "But I seriously doubt her abilities will make up for her race in the eyes of most. Please, Kennick. Please be reasonable. If you brought her here to upset me then, fine! I am upset, and you got what you wanted. Please do not ruin your future because of our differences."

"Mother, despite what you may think, I am not concerned about your opinion or the opinions of others. I do whatever pleases me," he replied. Noticing Meera had stopped eating, he put down his own fork, hoping the meal and the conversation were over.

"Yes, we know you do whatever pleases you, Kennick. We are constantly reminded that our son is a whore. Would you please not embarrass us in this way as well?" Andreena asked.

Meera looked like she was about to show his mother that raek fire was scarier than regular fire, so Kennick stood. "Come on, Meera," he said. Instead of leading her out the way they had come, he took her down the servant's stairs to the kitchen to get her something else to eat. He knew she did not like the kind of cold fish and vegetable dishes that knell often favored for lunch.

Once they were enclosed in the confining staircase with the door shut behind them, Meera reached out and touched his shoulder. He turned to her. "I don't have to go tonight, you know. I won't be offended if—" she started to say.

"I want you to be my date to the ball," he told her. "I cannot wait to see you in the dress I had made."

Meera looked distinctly embarrassed, which pleased him. He led her down to the kitchen where their arrival caused the bustling commotion to come to a crashing halt. Kennick saw that his parents still employed the same cook, and he greeted her warmly. Then he asked her for some bread or pastries and turned to find Meera looking around the kitchen fondly.

"It looks just like the one where I worked," she declared. Some of the nearby staff gasped and exchanged looks. Many of them were gawping at Meera openly, staring at her scar and whispering to one another. Several gave Kennick disapproving looks, no doubt assuming that he was using his knell charms to prey on an innocent human girl. He ignored them.

"You worked in the kitchen in the palace?" he asked. He had known she had worked at the palace but had not known what her role was before she saw to Cerun and Shael—and spied.

She nodded. The cook held out a basket of pastries for Meera, which elicited a delighted smile from her in response. She bit into a cream-filled one and hummed in pleasure. Kennick enjoyed watching Meera eat sweets. He had always viewed food as more of a necessity than anything and had never derived as much pleasure from it as she seemed to.

After another bite, a bit of cream filling oozed onto her lower lip. He reached out with a finger and brushed the cream off. Then he licked the filling from his fingertip. Meera's eyes widened, and her pulse quickened at his touch. He grinned deviously; he enjoyed making her react to him. He could always tell when she got flustered or aroused even when she tried to hide it. In this case, she stuffed a large bite of pastry into her mouth and looked away from him while she chewed.

After she had eaten her fill, Kennick showed Meera around, enjoying her commentary about the different rooms and their ancient artwork. It was fun for him to see his childhood home through her eyes, and once the sugar she had eaten hit her bloodstream, she became very playful and silly. Finally, however, when they went outside to explore the grounds, she asked him the question he had been waiting for: "Kennick, what did your parents mean by your 'previous foolishness'? Am I not the first human you've brought home?" she asked, glancing at him while they walked.

"When I was a teenager, I became infatuated with one of the serving girls—a human. At a dinner party one night, I got angry at my mother for saying disparaging things about humans, so I announced that I was in love with the girl. Delia was her name. My parents were so mortified, they threw me out—right then and there in front of their guests," he explained. "When I became a rider, they started inviting me home again for holidays and parties. Sometimes I go ... sometimes I do not."

"You were in love with her?" Meera asked.

"Delia? No. I was infatuated with her, but I hardly knew her. I have not seen her again. My parents probably sent her away. I can only hope that she found another position elsewhere and that I did not ruin her life," he replied.

"Where did you go when they threw you out?" she asked.

"A clothing designer I knew took pity on me. Follaria let me stay in the room above her shop. We are still friends—she made your dress for tonight. Speaking of, we should probably go in and get ready." He pivoted back toward the house, and she followed.

They were both quiet and lost in their own thoughts on the way back to their rooms. Kennick had made sure Meera would have a room down the hall from him for convenience. "I have arranged for someone to come and style your hair and help you dress," he told her. "I will get you in about an hour."

"Okay, but if I don't like the dress, I'm wearing my own clothes. And I still expect you to parade me around," she warned with a smile.

"I will do so proudly," Kennick promised.

Meera slipped into her room, and he walked to his own. It did not take him long to get ready. He quickly dressed in the outfit Follaria had made for him; it was black with darkest green accents. He had already shaped himself a gold belt with a design in emeralds, as well as matching ear cuffs, which he donned. Then he switched out the rings he wore for some of yellow gold instead of platinum. As a finishing touch, he braided back his hair on either side of his head just above his ears and slicked the rest back, so it all hung behind his shoulders.

He was ready early. For a time, he tried to distract himself and dawdle, but he could not wait to see Meera. Suddenly, he felt nervous—something he did not experience often; he hoped she liked the dress he had commissioned for her and did not find him presumptuous. Kennick stashed the necklace he had made her in one of the human-style pockets he had insisted Follaria add to all of his pants when he had returned from the war. Then, without bothering to check his appearance in the mirror, he left his room and walked down the hall to Meera's.

28

MEERA

Meera found her dress hanging in a large, ornate wardrobe. It was covered in a protective cloth, and for a moment, she just stared at the cloth, too nervous to find out what she would be wearing to the ball. Then, in a rush of decision, she grabbed it to yank it free and accidentally broke the dress's hanger with her knell strength, reducing the garment to a puddle on the floor of the wardrobe. It landed next to a pair of shoes that sat waiting for her.

With a grunt of frustration, she bent and disentangled the dress from the cloth. It was a shimmery bluish white—very close in color to Shaya's feathers—but she could not decipher its shape. Quickly tearing off her clothes, she pulled the dress on. It was floor-length with sleeves, but the sleeves started below her shoulders. Her entire chest, neck, and shoulders were bare; the neckline cut in a straight line over her bust, and the sleeves only attached just under her arms.

Meera put on the delicate shoes that matched the dress and walked to the mirror. The dress hugged her slim shape perfectly down to her thighs, then it dropped to the floor with accents of floaty little feathers. It looked like silk but had some stretch to it and accentuated her subtle curves. She stood and stared at herself for a long time. She was struck by how this dress was almost similar to the one Shael's mother had procured for her: both were long and shades of white with long sleeves. However, while Shael's mother had sought to cover every inch of her scars, this dress left them almost entirely visible, somehow even accentuating their silvery sheen.

Meera felt exposed but not in a bad way—she felt seen; she felt like Kennick saw her and celebrated her with this dress. In addition to her silvery swirling scar showing in all of its horrific yet beautiful glory, her strength showed too in the muscles of her chest, arms and back. She looked strong, yet feminine—something she hadn't felt about herself since her body had changed. The dress was everything, or rather; she was everything in the dress. Or maybe, thought Meera, she had been everything all along, and the dress had made her see what Kennick already seemed to have seen. She found the thought both touching and unsettling.

Putting her hands to her face, she stared at her reflection and went through everything Kennick had said to her that day. Was this really a date, or was she there to annoy his mother? She wasn't sure. She knew she was attracted to him even though she tried not to be, but she couldn't tell what he might be thinking. Before she could give it any more thought, a knock sounded at the door, and a human woman pushed inside. "Good, you're dressed already," she said, walking toward Meera.

Without another word, the woman proceeded to push Meera down in a chair and started to sort through the coiling, snarled mess of her hair. She wasn't exactly gentle, either, but Meera sat quietly and patiently, assuming the woman could do a better job than she could. The woman quickly finished with her hair and started on her face, plucking a few stray hairs from her eyebrows and smearing some different creams on her skin. Finally, she stepped away and gestured briskly to the mirror. Meera stood and appraised herself once more; her hair was piled elegantly on the top of her head, and her cheekbones stood out more than usual and glowed slightly. Overall, she thought the effect was very flattering. She smiled at the woman and thanked her, and the woman had no sooner shut the door behind her when someone else knocked.

"Come in!" Meera called.

Kennick stepped through the door looking even more handsome and well-dressed than usual. His normally silver-toned jewelry was replaced with gold, and his belt and ear-cuffs glistened at her with jewels. Seeing him sparkle reminded Meera of her mother's earrings, and she fished them out of her bag, looping them into her ears. Then she kept her back turned to Kennick for a moment, almost too emotional to face him. The dress he had designed for her was flooding her with all sorts of feelings ... feelings she didn't quite understand or want to understand.

Finally, she turned to him. He stared at her, and there was no humor on his face—none of his usual smug smile or flashing eyes. "Well?" she asked, her heart beating like wings in her throat.

"What do you think?" he asked her.

"I think you keep buying me uncomfortable shoes," she said, deflecting her emotion and looking down at her feet. But she knew that wasn't fair to Kennick. Taking a deep breath, Meera racked up her courage and looked him in the face. "I've never felt so beautiful," she admitted.

He smiled. "Good. I have one last thing for you, though," he said. Walking over to her, he pulled something silver and shiny out of his pocket. He positioned her to face the mirror and stepped behind her, still smiling at her in the reflection. Then he wrapped a large necklace around her throat, shaping it together in the back. The necklace had swirls like her scar and was studded with diamonds. As she watched, he shaped the swirls to overlap the scars on the right side of her neck, and he shaped the left side in a continuation of them.

Meera stared at the necklace on her throat; it was beautiful and, once again, highlighted her body rather than covering her up. The necklace was large and stiff, and she doubted she would be able to look down. But it was spectacular.

"Is that comfortable?" Kennick asked.

"No, but I don't care," she said honestly, meeting his gaze in the mirror with a smile on her face—a radiant one, she thought.

"You will have to let me know when you want it off," he warned her. "It is shaped on."

"Thank you," she said, reaching up and touching the grand masterpiece.

"Ready to be paraded?" he asked, offering her his arm.

"Parade away!" she said, putting her hand in the crook of his elbow. Then they walked out of her room and through the halls.

"You know, I will make a clasp for the necklace when I take it off later, so you can wear it again," Kennick said absently as they walked.

"What? I can't keep this, Kennick! It's all diamonds!" Meera stuttered. She had thought he was lending her the materials for the night.

"Of course, you can keep it. I gave it to you," he insisted.

"No! It's too much. I can't accept it," she said. It really was too much; she had never seen so many diamonds in her life. She couldn't even buy a pastry with the amount of money she had left, so keeping the necklace seemed utterly ridiculous.

Kennick shrugged. "Consider it payment for rescuing my best friend if you want," he replied.

"You already bought me boots for that!"

"Keep it, or I will tell Shael that you think his life is only worth a pair of boots," he replied.

Meera laughed, and the sound of her joy echoed down the empty hallway. When they turned another corner, she started to hear the noise of other people. They could argue about the necklace later, she decided. "I was wondering where all the guests were," she said. "Is there anything I should know about knell balls before we go in?"

"Do you know how to curtsy? Formal balls are one of the few times knell bow and curtsy to the reigning monarch," he replied.

Meera gave him an approximation of the smug look he always gave her. "My curtsy has gotten me into trouble before," she said. Conjuring that memory reminded her that it was the Summer Solstice, and it had been a year since she had informed on the duke and gotten him killed. The thought sobered her good mood for a moment.

"Oh, really?" Kennick asked before noticing her shift in headspace. "Everything okay?"

"The Summer Solstice last year was not my finest day," Meera replied touching Linus's bracelet under her sleeve since he had given it to her that day.

"Hopefully this one will be better," Kennick said, squeezing her hand with his. They joined the throng of people filing into the ballroom. It was a slow procession because each guest had to greet the queen individually. Kennick held them back until everyone else had gone in.

"Are you nervous or something?" Meera asked.

He gave her his usual smile, his dark eyes like liquid in the candlelight. Then he leaned in toward her. "Rumor has it your curtsy is something to see, so I thought we should give everyone a chance to see it," he murmured. Meera felt her skin prickle where his warm breath touched her neck, and her heart sped up at his close proximity.

When it became their turn, they stepped into an expansive ballroom and walked toward Darreal, who sat in an ornate chair in the center of the room. Everyone else was fanned out on either side of the space, watching those that entered after them. Meera didn't recognize anyone other than Darreal and Kennick's parents.

She and Kennick stepped before the queen, and Meera dropped his arm and approached first. Darreal was wearing a gold dress to match the gold circlet she always wore upon her brow. Her light brown hair was twisted up on the top of her head, and her hands were clasped serenely in her lap. Her calm eyes fell upon Meera, and she smiled ever so slightly. "I am glad to see you actually came, Meera Hailship," she said.

Meera grimaced internally, not wanting to think about the council meeting the next day. Regardless, she held Darreal's eyes steadily. "Hello, Darreal," she said, and she curtsied.

As she had once done for King Bartro what felt like a lifetime ago, Meera extended her arms gracefully at her sides and bent her knees, lowering her body very slowly. She was able to do so with much more grace and finesse in her new muscular body than she had ever managed as a human. At the bottom of her dip, she bent her head ever so slightly in a show of respect for the queen. Her necklace dug into her skin somewhat from the movement, but she didn't let it show.

Meera held her pose for a long breath before slowly rising back to her full height. Keeping her shoulders back and down and her chin raised high, she bared the silvery scars on her skin to the room with pride. She held Darreal's gaze a moment before stepping away, and she could have sworn she saw a hint of a smile in their steady depths.

As she stood to the side and waited for Kennick to bow to the queen, whispers erupted all around her. She could not make out what anyone said particularly, but she could imagine: that is the human, the one who claims to be a rider, the one they say has abilities, did she come with Andreena's son, etc. Meera kept her chin up and looked only at Kennick, who positively beamed at her when he joined her. "You did not disappoint," he murmured in her ear. They were among the last to enter the ballroom, so Darreal shortly stood and announced that the ball should begin. The music started to play, and the people spread out, sampled food, greeted old friends, and danced.

Meera looked around and thought it looked more or less like the ball Shael's parents had held—except that the people were better looking, the ballroom was larger, and the decorations and outfits were far finer. The dance floor was so spacious there was a pond in the middle of it, covered in flowering lily pads. Meera's necklace was almost a trinket compared with what some of the knell women wore around their necks—not that she cared; she would choose the necklace Kennick had made her over any other necklace in the world.

Before she and Kennick could so much as make a lap around the room together, Andreena stepped up and whisked her son away, insisting someone or other wanted to speak with him. She did so several times, taking Kennick away from Meera for a few minutes at a time, until Kennick finally refused. However, when he refused, Andreena started bringing the person with her so that Kennick was forced to be polite to his many acquaintances and step away again. Meera knew his mother was keeping him away from her as much as possible. It irritated her, but she hadn't had any specific hopes for the ball, so she contented herself milling around alone, sampling the foods and watching the other people.

She garnered a lot of stares, which she ignored, and she amused herself pretending everyone stared because she was the most beautiful woman in the room, sweeping around as if it were true. No one dared speak to her until the queen did so: Darreal approached her with a true smile on her face and very large emerald earrings dangling from her ears. "Meera, I wish to tell you that your father is doing well. He has been combing through our histories and organizing our collections at the estate," she said.

Meera smiled. "Good. I'm sure he's happy there doing what he loves. Thank you for hosting him," she replied. She thought to say something to Darreal about her horse but decided not to; maybe if she was polite, the queen would side with her during the meeting the next day.

"There is one more thing I wish to say to you," Darreal added leadingly, her eyes wandering from Meera's face for a moment.

"Oh?" Meera intoned, heart racing, she hoped she wasn't in trouble in some way. She didn't dislike Darreal by any means, but the power monarchs possessed frightened her; she had reason enough from her past to fear their control and their wrath.

"If you are seeking to gain the respect of the knell who control Levisade, you might want to know that Kennick may not be the best person for you to use as a guide. He has something of a ... fraught reputation and is often viewed as a laughing matter," Darreal said airily.

Meera gaped at her, and before she could think of how to respond, the queen bid her good evening and swept away. Meera was left unsure if she should laugh or be angry. But before she could make up her mind about the matter, she was approached again, this time by a knell woman in purple. "Hello," the woman said. "My name is Ephream, and you are?

"Meera," she replied, smiling uncertainly at the woman, who had her hair pulled back in a severe way and wore a necklace of purple jewels to compliment her gown.

"Meera, I hope you will not take this amiss, but I saw you with Kennick. As you are ... new to Levisade, you may want to know that Kennick often shows interest in women, but his interest never holds for long. Enjoy the ball." With that, the woman walked away, and Meera was left once more gaping after her.

The woman in purple was not the last to give Meera vague warnings about Kennick; several more women approached her in the time that Kennick was with his mother. By the time he finally broke away and returned to her, Meera didn't know what to think. She had already known from Soleille and Katrea that Kennick was free with his body, but she was beginning to feel like he had slept with every woman at the ball. She wasn't sure that had anything to do with her, as—so far—she and Kennick were only friends, but it was still unsettling. She couldn't help but wonder if he had made them feel as seen and beautiful as he had made her feel that night and then lost interest in them soon after. Had he broken these women's hearts?

"Are you having an okay time?" Kennick asked her. "I promise I will not let my mother pull me away again. In fact, we should dance! She cannot interrupt us on the dance floor." He took her arm and tried to lead her to the dance floor, but she didn't budge.

"I don't think that's a good idea," she said, studying his face.

"No?" he asked with a smile. "Not as confident about your dancing as you are about your curtsying?"

Meera bit her lip uncomfortably. "If we dance, I'm afraid a crowd of women might interject to defend my honor," she said.

"What?"

"Kennick, women keep approaching me and warning me about you ..." she said, shifting from foot to foot. She watched as some of the humor left his face, though he still didn't look overly concerned. "Have you slept with every woman here?" she asked.

"Not every woman," he said with a shrug.

"Well, did you break their hearts or something? Why are they all trying to protect me from you?" she asked. She felt like she needed to know, but she also hoped Kennick wouldn't read too much into her questions. Meera had just been engaged, after all, and had almost lost Shael's friendship because of it. She wasn't sure she would risk her friendship with Kennick to try to be with him, whether or not it seemed likely that he would take her to bed then grow bored of her.

"I have not broken anyone's heart, Meera. They are warning you because you are human, and I am knell. They think you are naive and easily led astray. They also seem to think that I am preying on you in some way. Ignore them. They are acting on age-old stereotypes," he replied.

Meera thought about what he had said and felt slightly better. She remembered first meeting Darreal, and the queen's assumption that Shael had charmed her into saving him. That said, she still didn't quite know what to think about Kennick ... He was her friend, she told herself; he was her friend, and she trusted him not to lie to her or mislead her. She certainly trusted him for a dance. Taking his hand, she led him to the dance floor so no one could accuse him of pressuring her into anything. They were certainly getting a lot of stares.

"Everyone's watching," she said quietly. "Do you think they'll draw weapons if you put your hands on me?"

Kennick grinned. "Let them. I like a good fight," he replied, putting one hand on her waist and taking her right hand with the other. "Are you uncomfortable?" he asked, catching her glancing around at the staring knell.

"No," she lied.

"Yes, you are," he said.

"Well now I am since we're standing here not dancing," Meera said. Everyone else was moving around them, and they were the only pair standing still. "Come on!" she cried. "I don't know this dance; you'll have to lead me."

"Will I?" Kennick asked, his eyes sparking. He started to move his feet, but he didn't direct Meera in any way, leaving her standing still and looking ridiculous.

She laughed to mask her embarrassment. "Kennick, come on!" she pleaded, but he continued to grin and move in small steps without her. "If you lead me, I'll make it worth your while," she said desperately, not even sure what she meant by that.

His eyebrows shot up on his forehead. "How?" he asked.

Meera looked to the side, thinking, and noticed the pond set into the dance floor nearby. "We'll dance on the water," she replied.

"Can you do that?" he asked.

"I have no idea," she said with a laugh.

Grinning, he swept her properly into his arms and lead her through the unfamiliar dance. As he stepped and twirled, he also inched them toward the pond, and Meera cringed, thinking they were about to get very wet and look very foolish. She closed her eyes as they neared and focused on sensing her feet, the floor, and the pond—she tried to, anyway; she found it extremely difficult to focus on anything other than Kennick's hands on her body and his tall, fine figure standing right in front of her.

Meera completely lost focus on the floor and opened her eyes to tell Kennick she couldn't do it—to lead them away—but he was grinning down at her delightedly. "You are doing it, Meera!" he said.

"I am?" she asked, looking into his dark eyes. She was too afraid to look down. It still felt like they were dancing on the floor, but then she heard gasps and exclamations from around the room. "Are we trampling the flowers?" she asked, grinning back at him.

He didn't answer and spun her out for a twirl. Meera lifted her arm in her best approximation of grace and drama before he spun her back toward him and held her closely. Then he led them off the pond before the song could end. There was a smattering of applause for them when the song finished; knell clearly appreciated performances and displays of magic. Kennick took Meera's hand and drew her off the dance floor.

"Well, we didn't fall in the pond, and no one attacked you!" she said, laughing. She was finally enjoying herself.

"Do you want to get some fresh air?" he asked.

Meera nodded, though she wasn't sure why he wanted to go outside. They had only danced one dance and certainly weren't out of breath. It also wouldn't be any cooler in the night air. She followed him all the same—unconcerned that she would miss anything at the ball—and as they exited through one of the open back doors to the garden, she tried not to notice people's stares.

29

MEERA

There were other knell standing and talking in groups on the patio outside the ballroom, but Kennick didn't pause; he continued to lead her across the patio and into his parent's incredibly lush garden. Meera stopped occasionally to admire flowers in the light of the moon. "These are all incredible!" she exclaimed, gently cupping a flower larger than her face.

"My father grows them. He can shape the living like Soleille but chooses to focus on plants rather than people," Kennick explained. He took a step away then another, and Meera followed him, beginning to wonder where they were going and what they were doing.

The looks people had given them when they were leaving clearly suggested to Meera what they thought she and Kennick would be doing in the garden, but she had already made it clear that she didn't want to be another one of his many women—hadn't she? She tried to remember exactly how their conversation had gone but couldn't, too distracted by the possibility that

Kennick might be leading her away to put his hands on her. Her mind was saying that she only wanted to be friends with him, but her body was turning to tremulous liquid at the thought that he might want more.

"Kennick, what are we doing out here?" Meera finally asked, stopping next to a rose bush full of pink blooms. She hoped her question sounded casual, but she could feel her heart thudding wildly in her chest and suspected that he was aware of it as well.

Kennick's own demeanor was as infuriatingly calm and relaxed as ever. He stepped closer to her, his hands in his pockets and a smile on his lips. "Well, I wanted to kiss you in the ballroom, but you seemed worried that overzealous bystanders might interfere. So, I brought you out here to kiss you, instead," he explained with a steady confidence that might have rankled Meera, were she not struggling to maintain her composure.

She took a breath through her mouth to say something, but before she could think what to say or make any words, Kennick bent toward her and met her lips with his own in a kiss both gentle and alarmingly sensuous. Meera's body won the battle over her mind for a moment, and she shut her eyes and leaned into the soft pressure of his mouth, parting her mouth to his tongue as it swept over her lower lip.

She started to reach her hands for him to pull him toward her, but she caught herself and shoved him roughly instead. Kennick stumbled back, removing his hands from his pockets. His eyebrows were slightly raised, but he looked otherwise unperturbed. "What are you doing?" Meera asked, suddenly angry. She was breathing rapidly, and her hands were curling into fists in front of her. Her necklace started to feel too tight.

"I have been wanting to kiss you all night, Meera. I have been wanting to kiss you for weeks," Kennick said quietly, his dark eyes still fixed on her with desire.

"Well, I don't want to be another woman in the long string of women that you take to bed then get bored of!" Meera cried, groping at the swirling points of her necklace that were digging into her skin. "We're supposed to be friends, Kennick! How could you do this?" she asked, her voice sounding strangled. She hated to think their friendship meant so little to him that he was willing to throw it away for sex.

"It is not like that, Meera," he said, still infuriatingly calm. "I have never felt this way before. I—I think I love you," he stuttered, his steady exterior finally cracking.

Meera shook her head violently, causing her necklace to jab her even more. "No, you don't!" she said rather forcefully. "You're just used to getting what you want and can't stand that I've rejected you—or you hope that someone will see and tell your mother that you kissed a human. Don't be ridiculous!" she shouted. Suddenly, she really couldn't breathe and clawed at her necklace in desperation.

"Here, let me," Kennick said, stepping forward, but she flinched back and away from him. She yanked at the necklace again, and it inexplicably turned to a putty-like texture, tearing free from her neck. Her movement was so forceful that the necklace flew from her grip, landing on the ground near Kennick's feet. Meera vaguely registered the surprise on his face before she turned and fled.

Running through the garden, she took turn after turn, desperate to put some bushes between herself and Kennick so she could think—so she could use her mind without the constant pull of his body. She didn't think he had followed her, so finally, she came to a crashing halt on a wooden bench. She was shaking and gasping from her emotion more so than her run, and it took several minutes for her to calm herself enough to think rationally again.

Once Meera could reflect, she felt awful. She couldn't believe what she had done—not the kiss, that she could believe; she couldn't believe she had shoved Kennick away and yelled at him when he had been vulnerable with her. She had behaved just as Shael had toward her, she realized. She was in yet another garden after yet another ball, only this time, it was she who had stepped away from a kiss—from the offer of love—and had flown away.

Why? She sat and asked herself why she had behaved so abominably even though she had suspected the moment was coming. Kennick had done and said everything right, after all; he had told her she wasn't just another woman—that he had true feelings for her. Meera put her face in her hands and let herself feel whatever it was she was hiding from. She knew her anger had reared up only to protect her from some deeper emotion: it was fear.

She had opened herself up to love once before and been hurt, and she was afraid of being hurt again—she was afraid of losing another important friend for a few heated kisses. She loved Kennick—of course, she loved Kennick. She loved him so much, she was afraid of losing him. He was her friend, her sparring partner. He was also ridiculously attractive and a heartbreakingly good kisser, but Meera felt she could ignore those things; she would rather ignore her attraction to Kennick than risk losing him. That is, if she hadn't already.

Rising from her bench, she quickly retraced her steps back to the pink rosebush where they had stood together. Kennick was no longer there. Wiping under her eyes, Meera gathered herself together as much as she could before entering the ballroom again. She walked around the floor several times, but Kennick wasn't there, either. Leaving the ballroom, she wound around the absurdly grand house until she found their hallway and approached his door. She knocked quietly and tentatively. "Can I come in?" she asked against the door.

"Come in!" he called.

Meera cracked open the door and peeked inside. She hadn't been in his room yet. The large room was decorated in a color very similar to Kennick's hair. She would have poked fun at him for it if she weren't there to apologize. There was a bed with canopies against the back wall, but Kennick sat on a red sofa in a little sitting area in front of the bed. He had already undressed from the party and was wearing a black silk robe and pants.

"Are you alone?" Meera asked with mock suspicion. Kennick gave her a look and waved her in through the door. She stepped inside and shut it behind her, suddenly feeling ridiculously over-dressed in her gown. Walking to the sofa, she kicked off her shoes, and plopped down next to him, looking at him uncertainly all the while. "I'm so sorry, Kennick," she said without preamble. "I was awful. I was mean. You—" she broke-off, putting a hand up to her face. She wished she had prepared a better speech.

Looking into Kennick's eyes, she tried to gauge how he was feeling. If he was upset, she couldn't tell. Then her gaze snagged on his ear, which was bare—free of one of the cuffs that always covered it. The sight completely distracted her, and she grinned. "How am I supposed to concentrate when you're naked?" she asked, poking Kennick's ear with her finger.

He laughed and reached up his hands to cover both ears. "Better?" he asked. It actually wasn't because in doing so, the front of his robe spread open to reveal his chest, and Meera had to try very hard not to look at it.

She playfully batted his hands away from his ears. Then she took a deep breath to center herself and try again. "Kennick, I feel like I just did this," she said. "I just blew up my friendship with Shael trying to make us into something more, and I'm scared I

would lose you. I—I can't lose you; you're too important to me."
She looked at him pleadingly, willing him to understand—willing
him to still be her friend.

"You will not lose me, Meera. I am right here," he said, taking
her hand and squeezing it.

She smiled at him and sighed out a deep breath. But there was
one more thing she felt the need to say even if it embarrassed her
immensely, and she cleared her throat awkwardly. "You know,
when ... um—whenever Shael pulled away from me like that I, uh
... I couldn't help but assume he found me repulsive ..." she
paused and swallowed before continuing, "I just—not that I think
you lack any confidence in the matter—but, just so you know, I
don't ... find you repulsive, that is."

She glanced up at Kennick's face, cringing and found his dark
eyes flashing with humor. "I know," was all he said.

"Good," Meera said, looking around the room, searching for
a way to change the subject. Kennick seemed content to let her
keep rambling on and on. Her eyes fell on her mangled necklace
on the table next to him, and she leaned over him to pick him
up, trying not to focus on how close their bodies were or how
good he smelled. Then she inspected the bent, misshapen
necklace.

"Was that your first time shaping metal?" he asked.

"So, I did this?" she asked. She had suspected as much but
hadn't been sure. Kennick nodded. "Well, I'm sorry for this too,"
she said, miserably.

"I will fix it for you," he assured her. "I'll make it more
comfortable and add clasps on the back."

Meera gave him a look. "I still can't accept this," she told him,
handing the necklace back. He didn't argue with her this time,
and she sat back and scratched at her head—her hairdo was
starting to feel tight and irritating as she grew tired.

"Let me," Kennick said, and he shaped the pins out of her hair all at once, collecting them in a pile on the table.

Meera's hair flopped suddenly, and she shook her head and rubbed her scalp to loosen the twisted and clumped curls, sighing in relief. Then she leaned back again and observed Kennick silently, while he looked at her in return. Now what? She wondered whether their friendship would ever really be the same after this.

"Shael was a fool, by the way," Kennick said, finally.

Meera looked down and away in embarrassment. "You know, that makes me the fool in this scenario," she said, wondering if she really was being stupid.

"You said it, not me," he replied with a grin.

Meera laughed—he could always make her laugh. "It all might be a moot point," she said soberly. "The council might not let me live after what I have to tell them tomorrow ..." Her stomach soured at the thought. The meeting was tomorrow— today, even; she wasn't sure what time it was. She didn't know what the council would do when she told them she wouldn't pledge herself to them.

"Worrying about it will not change the outcome," Kennick said, clearly not taking the possibility of the council killing her seriously.

She nodded but bit her lip and continued to fret.

"Meera, do you still love Shael?" Kennick asked suddenly, jarring her from her thoughts.

"I will always love Shael, but we cannot be together," she replied honestly.

"Even now that he is doing better?" he asked. She considered the question. Shael had been doing better, and yet, it had not occurred to her to try their relationship again. She did love him still but in a different way—a less urgent way. Kennick might even have something to do with her change in feelings, she admitted to herself.

"No," Meera said certainly. "I no longer want to be with Shael."

Kennick regarded her seriously, but he only dipped his chin in acknowledgement. Meera slid further down on the couch, exhausted by their conversation and all of the emotions swirling within her, terrified to face the next day. "Can I stay here a while?" she asked. She didn't want to be alone with her thoughts in her room.

"As long as you want," Kennick said.

They both reclined on the couch in silent contemplation until finally Meera could barely keep her eyes open anymore and stood to go to her own room. She said "goodnight," picked up her shoes, and padded to the door.

"Meera, wait. There are people in the hall. They will see you and get the wrong idea," Kennick cautioned.

She shrugged. Of all the reasons she had pushed Kennick away, being embarrassed to be seen with him wasn't one of them. "I don't care," she said, putting her hand on the doorknob, "But I'll wait if you want me to." She could also hear the footsteps in the hall and sounds of two people talking drunkenly.

He shook his head, so she left, passing the two knell as she walked to her room down the hall.

30

KENNICK

Kennick watched Meera go with a smile. The night had not ended how he had hoped it would, but he felt content. Meera may not be ready for them to have a physical relationship, but he could wait. He would wait for her. He had been with plenty of women—and some men—and had never felt this way before. While he had always enjoyed his short-lived trysts, he wondered now whether he had been searching for something more and not finding it; he wondered whether he had found it with Meera.

He may not have lured her into his bed, but he felt somehow more deeply satisfied knowing how much she cared for him. She had said he was important to her—too important to her for her to risk losing him. He had been rejected before but certainly never for a reason so meaningful. Kennick also valued Meera's friendship, but he had never loved and been hurt before as she had; he was all hope and ambition. He would wait for her to be ready even if she continued to push him away. He would be a sly and stealthy predator in constant pursuit, yet hidden—watching, waiting. He would let her come to him.

THE NEXT MORNING, Kennick sought Meera for breakfast but could not find her in her room or anywhere else he thought to look. Eventually, he caved and ate breakfast alone with his parents. His mother and father continued to berate him for taking Meera to the ball and were also aware that she had left his room late at night, disheveled. Kennick ignored them. He had grown up trying to please his parents—trying to live up to their goals for him—but he was not that boy anymore.

When his parents had thrown him out, they had hurt him, but they had also freed him. The worst had happened, yet he had found himself happier than ever with a new, makeshift family than he had ever been with his own parents. Now he truly did not care what they thought or what anyone else thought of him; Kennick lived his life for his own pleasures and his own goals, occasionally visiting his childhood home but not internalizing the pressure his parents put on him.

After breakfast, he looked and still could not find Meera. He waited outside her room for a long time, expecting her to return there before the council meeting, but she did not return. He hurriedly changed into finer clothes and hastened back to the dining room for the meeting. He was not on the council, of course, but since his mother had offered to host the meeting, Darreal had agreed to allow his presence as well as his father's. Stepping back into the dining room, he found it already full of council members. His mother sat at one end of the long table, and Darreal sat at the other. Meera was not there.

Kennick nodded a greeting to those who looked up at him and

took his seat next to his mother at the end. There was now one more seat available, vacant and awaiting Meera. Kennick was not usually a nervous person, but his stomach flipped over, wondering whether she had made a run for it. He understood why she was anxious. He, too, had no idea how the council would react to what she had to say. However, he also knew that Meera valued the other riders and her life on the peninsula and found it hard to believe she would have left.

"Rider Kennick, will Meera be joining us today?" Darreal asked him down the table.

"I assume so, but I have not seen her," Kennick replied.

Darreal looked almost amused, but the other council members did not seem to share her attitude. "If the human cannot even appear in front of the council in a respectable way and timely manner, then I cannot see how she can hope to be named a rider," Odon said predictably. He was always the most unpleasant and outspoken of the council.

"Perhaps she does not hope to be named a rider," Darreal said airily, surprising Kennick as well as some of the council, who gave one another looks.

Andreena waved to a nearby server to bring refreshments, taking it upon herself as hostess to make sure everyone was comfortable if they had to wait. Kennick wondered how much delight his mother would get in watching the council rip Meera to shreds if she ever turned up.

"Kennick, have you seen the supposed wild raek that took Meera as her rider and changed her?" Odon asked him.

"I have," Kennick replied shortly. The old knell would have to work if he wanted any information from him.

"I have already had descriptions of the wild raek from Sodhu as you well-know, Odon," Darreal said calmly. "Whether or not the raek exists is not in question. Not to mention, most of us were in attendance at the ball last night and witnessed Meera shape water. Am I right to assume that was Meera's doing and not your own, Kennick?" she asked him.

Kennick nodded and ignored his mother's glare; he was sure she had not enjoyed watching her son dance with a human no matter how well she had shaped. "That was Meera. She is much more powerful than I," Kennick replied just to further annoy his mother, who tensed next to him. He watched the candles on the wall sconces to see if he had angered her enough to make them flicker, and they twitched ever so slightly. Many of the council members appeared disconcerted by his statement.

"Darreal, I really think this new magic could be a threat to our race," said a woman whose name he could never remember. "I do not think this is a matter of whether or not the human should be sworn in as a rider, rather, I think this is a question of whether wild raeken bestowing abilities on humans should be permitted at all. This could destroy us."

Kennick took a quelling breath to keep himself calm. Meera may have been right to think some of the council might actually wish her harm. Where was she? How could she hope to defend herself if she never arrived? He would gladly defend her on her behalf, but he doubted his word would sway anyone.

"I have already heard your thoughts on the matter—and yours, Odon," Darreal replied smoothly, cutting the man off before he could add his opinion. "We will not be able to decide anything until we have heard from Meera."

Kennick was relieved that the queen seemed to respect Meera. He suspected if her uncle were still alive, he would not have bothered to invite a human to a meeting about their own future. Catching a look pass between his mother and the woman who had spoken against Meera, he wondered what it was about. He saw his mother nod ever so slightly to the woman. His mother would not seek to harm Meera, would she? Andreena was cunning and opinionated, but he doubted even she would risk openly acting against the queen in any way. Darreal's word was still final even if she took her council members' opinions into consideration.

Observing the troubled, even hostile faces around him, Kennick was starting to wonder whether Darreal might be Meera's only hope. His father, alone, looked relatively calm and unconcerned, but Kennick assumed that was because his mind was on his plants or a bug in the room. Destin enjoyed controlling the small living things around him that he could exert power over because he had long since given the rule of his own life and actions over to his wife.

A tense silence fell over the room, and Kennick had to resist the urge to shift in his seat; his nerves were affecting him more than usual. Where was Meera? What would happen to her if she did not join the meeting? Would she have to leave Levisade? Would he go with her? Before he could give the question serious thought, he heard hurried footsteps running up the servant's staircase. Then the serving door to the dining room burst open, and Meera walked in.

Kennick's immediate relief turned to confusion at the sight of her: she was wearing her dark blue outfit, but she was covered all over in grey sludge and dust. It was on her shirtfront, her hands, and a smear of it blemished her cheek. She was coming up from the kitchen, but he did not think the substance was food; it had an earthy smell. Aside from her mysterious grey coating, Meera looked blazing mad.

31

MEERA

Meera awoke the next morning full of anxiety. She was expected in the dining room at 11 for her meeting with the queen and the Queen's Council. Getting up, she dressed quickly, twisting back her hair. She considered going to Kennick's room, but after their extended awkwardness the night before, she decided not to; she wasn't sure she could handle any more stress that day. Instead, she left the house to run around the grounds.

Running helped Meera shed some of her excess emotion and center herself. Even if she didn't think she would ever really feel ready for the meeting, she at least felt ready to face Kennick on this new day. She was running on the edge of his parent's property —skirting the outer wall—when she noticed some human workers patching a crumbling section of wall up ahead. She watched as the workers climbed a rickety ladder to the top, carrying buckets of mortar and large rocks before balancing precariously to do their work.

Cringing at their lack of safety measures, she paused to

observe. She watched how the men below mixed the mortar, adding water until it reached the right consistency. Then they handed it over to one of the climbing men, who ascended the ladder. They had already built a wooden frame to fill the patch of broken wall and were adding rocks and mortar into its gaps. Meera wondered why the men didn't use ropes or anything to secure themselves to the wall when they were so high up, but they all looked sure-footed enough.

She turned away, ready to find her breakfast in the kitchen, when she sensed a smaller figure taking the next batch of mortar up the ladder. Whipping her head back around, she found that the worker was just a young boy. His thin frame could barely support the heavy bucket and climb at the same time, and he teetered precariously on the ladder. When he reached the top, he took several unsteady steps toward another man with outstretched hands, but the heavy bucket unbalanced him. The boy fell over the edge of the wall.

In a rush of instinct, Meera reached out with her hands and her senses and shaped the air into a swirl to slow the boy's forty-foot drop. He came to a stop just above the ground—hovering for a moment—before she released the air and let him plop into the grass. The men in the area were all staring at the boy and at her with a mixture of fear and relief. They ought to be scared of her, Meera thought, marching up to the nearest man. "What do you think you're doing letting a boy climb up there without any safety equipment?" she shouted.

The burly human man took a step back from her and fiddled nervously with his bushy beard. "This's the way it's done, missus," the man said, eyes widening. The other men gathered around their companion to back him up, but they looked distinctly afraid.

Meera deflated somewhat. She didn't actually want to scare these men; she just wanted them to be more careful. "He's just a boy," she said, gesturing to the kid, who was hauling himself up from the ground. Meera could see that he'd peed himself in the fall, and she averted her eyes from the wet spot spreading through his pants. The men were brushing the boy off and asking him if he was alright. She could see that they genuinely cared for him, but if so, what was he doing out here? One of the men whispered in the boy's ear and pointed to her.

With round, button eyes, the boy stepped toward her. "Thank you, missus," he said bashfully.

"How old are you?" she asked.

"Ten," he answered, puffing up his chest like he was trying to look taller.

Meera glared at the men around the boy. "What kind of men let a ten-year-old boy climb up a forty-foot wall without protective ropes?" she snarled. If she had not happened to be there, the boy would have died or at least broken his back.

"The kind what don't want to see him and his family starve," said one of the men, stepping forward bravely. "Ned needs work like the rest of us, and he has a right to do it to provide for his mother. This is the way the work's done. Ropes slow us down too much, and the masters said this has to get done today."

Meera contemplated his response. She was struck by the boy's name: Ned; he had the same name as the Duke of Harring-bay, and she wondered at how she had ended the life of one Ned and saved the life of another. Was this how the world balanced itself? Could she feel redeemed in some way? No, she thought. Life wasn't that simple. A life saved didn't make up for another one lost. This boy should not have been endangered in the first place.

"Where is your father?" she asked Ned.

"Died, missus," he said, looking at his feet.

"And by masters, you mean the knell that own this property?"

she asked the man. He nodded, looking uncomfortable to be talking about Andreena and Destin. Meera couldn't blame him.

"Did your father work here too, Ned?" she asked the boy. He nodded.

Meera knew the knell used human laborers, but she thought it was unspeakably cruel of Andreena and Destin not to provide the boy with food to eat if his father had worked for them until his death. To force the men to work in a way that valued speed over safety was also inexcusable—especially since the knell could have probably shaped the wall back together themselves in less time and with no risk to themselves. She shook her head disgustedly; it was wanton disregard for human life.

"Ned, why don't you go to the kitchen and get something to eat," she suggested. "I'll stand in for you." Ned looked delighted, but the other men looked shocked and suspicious.

"You want to help us work, missus?" the man with the bushy beard asked.

"I want to help you finish your task without anyone falling to their death," Meera replied with a shrug. "Let's get going." She didn't know what time it was, but she couldn't in good conscience leave the men to continue on as they had been. With luck, they would all be fine, but if she went to her meeting and later learned that one of them had fallen and died ... Well, she wasn't going to let that happen. She didn't need any more lives on her conscience.

She would help them work to speed it along, and she would catch them if they fell. Picking up a bucket of mortar, she climbed quickly to the top of the ladder, handing it to the man who still crouched at the top of the wall. He looked at her with such astonishment, she feared her presence would send him over the edge, but he stayed steady and took the mortar. She descended the ladder, grabbed two bags of rocks, and scurried back up.

For several minutes, the men just watched Meera in disbelief.

But when they realized how quickly progress was being made, their moods lightened, and they joined her in her efforts. Meera actually enjoyed the work; it was like training but with more company than usual and, she admitted to herself, she had missed the company of humans. There was something louder and less refined about her race. When the men started singing a working song, she quickly picked up the words and added her voice to the medley.

When the wall was finished, they all stood back and admired their work, Meera included. She had never accomplished anything like it before and swelled with the feeling of being useful and capable. Then she helped the men pack up their supplies. Did they need her help for that? No, but she was having such a good time, she didn't want to leave. "I'm starving," she announced after they were packed. "Let's get something to eat!"

The men cheered and followed her to the kitchen. Meera had probably saved them all from a very long, very hard day of work, and they seemed to have all warmed up to her. The bearded man even shook her hand and thanked her for her help and for saving Ned. "We didn't want him out here, missus, but we don't have enough to spare to give to him," he explained.

Meera nodded sadly. "Please, call me Meera," she said. "And I'm sorry you don't have better employers. I'll do something for Ned if I can." She wondered whether the boy could read and thought to send him to her father at the Levisade Estate. Darreal was paying him for his work, and she was sure he could use some young eyes to help him.

When they reached the kitchen, Meera gladly ate the plain bread and cheese given to the men by the kitchen staff—forgetting her meeting entirely until a serving woman came down the stairs from the dining room, looked at her, and whispered something to the cook. "Miss, you're wanted in the dining room!" the cook exclaimed.

Meera swallowed and felt her heart accelerate. "Ned, can you read?" she called over to the boy, who was being fussed over by some kindly laundresses.

He nodded.

"I'm going to set you up as my father's apprentice. Expect a letter or something," she said before hastening up the stairs.

The young boy's pee-stained pants reignited the fury in her chest, and her anger with Andreena and Destin built as she climbed the ridiculous stairs they made their servers carry their food up. Her raek fire flickered just under the surface of her skin in contained readiness. Council or no council, she was going to have words with Andreena about the way she treated humans. Meera burst into the dining room ready to tear into Kennick's parents.

When she emerged, the entire council gaped at her—Kennick included. Meera caught his eyes rove over her shirt and hands, so she quickly ignited both in raek fire to burn off the mortar clinging to her. A few of the council members gasped at the display. Putting her fire out, she went to take her seat—the only empty one, which was midway down the table. However, she shot Andreena several angry looks on her way, barely containing the verbal fury that wanted to burst out of her. Next to his mother, Kennick caught her eye and pointed to his cheek. Meera reached up a hand, felt the mortar stuck to her face and burned that off too.

"Hello, Meera. Thank you for joining us," Darreal said calmly. Meera looked at Darreal, who sat in front of the large, picturesque window. She wanted to be gracious and respectful toward the queen, but the sight of the wall through the window only stoked her anger with Kennick's parents.

After gazing into the queen's bemused golden-brown eyes for a moment, Meera whipped her head to face the opposite end of the long table where Andreena sat with her chin up and rubies dripping off of her like she herself were queen. "Have you no regard whatsoever for human life?" she shouted, causing some of the council members to jump.

"Girl, I do not know what you are talking about, but clearly, you have no regard whatsoever for the time of this council," Andreena replied icily. Some of the council tittered with appreciation. Meera avoided Kennick's eye; he was staring at her in bewilderment.

"I don't know what the laws are in Levisade," she said, "But your friends might find it interesting to know that you employ children for men's work and pressure all of your laborers into working without proper safety measures. Just now, a ten-year-old boy would have fallen to his death had I not been running by!"

"Is that what you were covered in? Human filth?" Andreena asked, making a face that elicited more laughter from her peers. "I employ humans for all manner of work. It is up to them to do their work properly. Besides, one less human is no great loss," she added, eyeing Meera pointedly.

Meera was so angry, she could hear her blood rushing in her ears. She was barely containing the flames that licked under her skin. Then she saw Kennick eyeing his mother with the same disgust and hatred that she felt, and his comradery calmed her somewhat. Taking a deep breath, she turned toward Darreal. Meera found the knell's disregard for humans deplorable and thought it was about time they did something to help the other occupants of Aegorn. It was time, she decided, to announce her true purpose for becoming a rider:

"Darreal, you once told me that it is your burden to serve the people of this land. I am not here today to hear whether you think

I am fit to be a rider. I am here today to implore you to serve all of your people—humans and raeken included—by helping me end the war between Aegorn and Terratelle," Meera paused in her speech and waited for Darreal's permission to continue. The room was so silent, she could hear the serving girl in the corner swallow. Darreal raised her eyebrows at Meera and gave her a very slight nod, so she faced the table at large.

"The wild raek I ride is called Shaya. She is a memory keeper for her race and has shown me many things in addition to changing my body and giving me abilities. She was able to turn my human body into that of a knell by imbuing me with magic because that is all that knell are—knell are the descendants of humans, imbued with raek magic." Several council members guffawed and exchanged looks, and Meera waited until they quieted down.

"Thousands of years ago, humans and raeken fought in a seemingly endless war against one another. But it did end; it ended when the human warrior Aegwren and the raek Isabael partnered together to show that their races could live in peace. They and the other riders patrolled the skies to prevent violence. As they absorbed their raeken's magic and changed, they lived together with those who did not have magic and remained unchanged.

"At some point, however, those with magic separated themselves from the other humans in Aegorn and sequestered themselves in Levisade. You are their descendants." The council members all stared at her with varying degrees of contempt, but Darreal looked intrigued. Meera soldiered on: "Shaya changed my body because we share a goal; we seek to end the war. She tells me the wild raek population is dwindling without the ability to migrate safely to their brethren in the north in their usual mating patterns." Some of the council looked genuinely concerned by that bit of information.

"I am here today to beseech all of you to finally step in and end the war. Your people are dying," she said, turning to Darreal. "The borders have not changed in this long struggle, and the people of Aegorn—the knell included—have nothing to gain by the continued fighting. The raeken that made you what you are suffer, and I see no reason why your mighty race should not bring peace to both lands," she finished. Then she waited, trying not to squirm. Meera hadn't actually intended to give a grand speech, but she wasn't overly embarrassed by her attempt.

"That was very well said," Darreal replied approvingly. Meera squinted at the queen and wondered whether that meant she was on her side. "I would just like to add that Meera's father has been combing through our histories and has found several documents that add validity to the notion that we knell were once humans."

"No matter what we once were," Odon spat. "We are not humans anymore!" Several council members nodded with him.

"No, Odon, we are not, but we do share this land with them and owe them our consideration. We also owe the raeken of Aegorn our respect," Darreal said calmly. There was some agreement to her statement around the table, which gave Meera hope.

"If the girl does not seek to become a rider, then she is a foreigner with powers that we do not understand but are clearly dangerous. She admitted that she will not pledge her loyalties to Levisade, so I do not see how we can let her leave this room," Andreena said. "I motion that we detain the girl."

Meera's stomach lurched; she had thought something like this might happen. Every time Hadjal had looked at her with fear, she had wondered how long it would take for others to see her as a threat to their way of life. She did her best to remain calm and unmoving in her seat. Kennick's eyes were boring into her as if waiting for her signal, and somehow, she knew in her gut that he would fight with her if it came to it. She hoped it wouldn't.

"Meera has been in Levisade with my permission and under my protection," Darreal protested, an edge creeping into her usually airy voice. Meera's shoulders sagged slightly in relief.

"That was before she changed," said a woman Meera didn't recognize. "Darreal, you may be our queen, but we have the right to stand against you if we think you are endangering our people."

Meera didn't like the sound of that and found herself wishing Shaya were nearby to fly her away. At the thought, she automatically felt for Shaya—as she had been doing multiple times every day since she had last seen her—and to her complete amazement, she felt her raek in her mind—Shaya was nearby. Meera sent a silent plea down their tether. Shaya was coming for her, she thought, and the thought gave her hope.

"You always have the right to speak against me," Darreal replied, "But you do not have the right to stand against me. I know our laws." The bite in her voice was deadly. Meera had never heard the queen lose her calm demeanor before.

Then Meera noticed Andreena nod at the woman who had spoked against her, and suddenly, the marble floor of the dining room was moving under her seat. The marble rose up over her ankles and clamped down, rooting her to the spot. She looked down at it in shock, but she didn't panic—the marble was stone, so she assumed she could shape it. She didn't try to shape it off, however; she waited; she needed to bide her time until Shaya reached her. Meera simply laughed. "Is that all?" she asked tauntingly, looking at Andreena.

The woman's face turned almost as red as her hair, and suddenly Meera was surrounded by fire. It swirled around her in an enclosure but didn't touch her skin. That was fine, she thought; she couldn't shape regular fire, but she could suffocate it. She quickly shaped the air to extinguish the flames before her, feeling sweat prickle her skin from their heat. Andreena looked livid.

In the next instant, utensils flew from the table and morphed to form a chain around Meera's torso and her chair. The chain broke and reformed several times. Meera saw the concentration on Kennick's face and knew he was fighting whoever sought to bind her; she couldn't tell who the other metal shaper was. After several tense moments, Kennick won, and the chain fell to the floor with a clang.

"That is enough!" Darreal cried, raising her voice above the commotion.

"Yes, it is," Meera said as she felt Shaya nearby. Standing, she sensed the marble restrains around her ankles. The marble felt different than the rocks and dirt she was used to shaping. For a moment, she couldn't quite grasp the substance with her mind, and her heart raced as she wondered if she was caught. But with a desperate thrust of energy, she shaped the marble off of her. Stepping out of the rubble, she turned to the glass windowpane and ignited it in pale flames, melting the glass onto the window ledge. Then she ran for the window, deflecting bits of rock and metal that flew toward her with deadly accuracy. Without looking back, she jumped.

Meera fell through the air with the wind whipping at her limbs and hair. For a breath, she enjoyed the sensation of falling, reveling in her freedom. Then, with a powerful swirling gust, she caught herself and propelled her body out and away from the house, across the front courtyard. When she was twenty feet from the ground, Shaya swept down from the sky above and plucked her from the air with her enormous feet, holding her delicately in her claws. The raek flapped her mighty wings until they were both out of sight above the clouds.

Meera automatically sent Shaya an image of her unclasping

her claws. Shaya obeyed, and Meera clung on to her scaly feet and hauled herself up her raek's legs. Using Shaya's feathers, Meera climbed onto her back, stilling the air around her. Finally, she slumped on the raek's shoulders and breathed a sigh of relief; she was safe—already far from the Queen's Council.

"Well, I don't know where you've been, but you showed up just in time," Meera said mentally, letting her words ooze with exasperation.

"I felt you battle last night and came as fast as I could," Shaya responded levelly. Meera didn't know what she meant by that. "You were being strangled," the raek explained.

Confused, Meera thought back to the night before. She remembered feeling like she couldn't breathe before ripping off the necklace Kennick had made her. Was that what Shaya meant? Throwing her head back, she laughed with abandon. Maybe she should have kept the necklace after all, she thought; it turned out to have been more than a statement piece. Then she felt a pang, having left Kennick behind. He would be okay, though; his parents were awful, but they would not let harm befall their own son.

"Where are we going?" Shaya asked.

"Home," Meera said, sending her raek an image of the peninsula. She didn't know what the council would try next, but she would not give up her home so easily. She was a raek rider, with or without oaths, and she belonged at the peninsula with her family.

As they flew above Levisade, Meera looked out across the horizon and realized she was ready—she was ready to end the war and the suffering of so many humans. She was ready to use her abilities to enact good in the world. She was ready to fight.

A FLIGHT OF FANCY

BOOK 4 OF THE RAEK RIDERS SERIES IS AVAILABLE NOW!

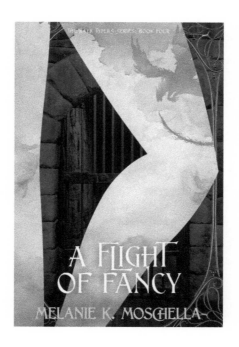

Read on for a preview...

CHAPTER 1

MEERA

EVERY NERVE IN MEERA'S BODY sparked with tension on her way back to the peninsula from Kennick's family home. Being on edge made the relatively short flight feel eternally long, but eventually, Shaya landed on the grassy slope, crushing flowers beneath her massive, clawed feet. Meera leapt from her back, charged and ready to fight an enemy that was not there. As she released the shape-shield she was using to block out the wind, a warm summer's breeze buffeted her face half-heartedly, and white lace flowers beat ineffectually at her shins. She was otherwise unaccosted.

Taking a deep breath, she tried to calm herself after the council's attack. Meera had no idea what to expect now that the majority of the Queen's Council had declared her a threat to Levisade and had sought to detain or kill her, but she refused to run and hide; the Riders' Holt was her home—whether she was an official rider or not—and she wouldn't abandon it so easily.

Hadjal and Sodhu emerged from their ancient wooden house and waved to her. They appeared mildly intrigued by Shaya's arrival, considering Meera had not seen or heard from her raek in weeks. Shaya, of course, was not at all remorseful for her long absence. Rather, she seemed quite pleased with herself for showing up right when she had been needed. Meera ignored the smugness emanating from the raek as Shaya began to lick and preen her already spotlessly glossy feathers. Then she took another steadying breath and loped easily through the thick grass to tell her family her news.

"Well?" Hadjal asked, wondering whether Darreal's council had accepted Meera as the newest Raek Rider of Levisade.

Meera hadn't actually told the others—except for Kennick—that she'd had no intention of swearing an oath to the riders or to Levisade. She had already pledged herself to helping Shaya end the war; her loyalties were spoken for. Beyond that, she felt compelled to maintain her autonomy and the ability to act on her own conscience. She had been a traitor once to free Shael and didn't relish the idea of being one again. "They tried to kill me!" she announced without preamble. Then she sat at the table and helped herself to some fruit, having barely eaten anything that day.

Neither Hadjal nor Sodhu moved for several seconds; they stood staring at Meera and processing what she had said. Sodhu, who flinched from conflict of any sort, looked like she wanted to wrap her two long braids around her face and hide from the world, but Hadjal's golden-hued eyes were calculating. Finally, she sighed. "Before you explain, let me get the others," she replied, walking away to drag her fellow riders from their training. It was mid-afternoon, and they wouldn't normally gather for dinner for several more hours.

Meera squished a palmful of grapes between her teeth all at once and regarded Sodhu. "It's alright," she told the older knell woman. "You can tell Darreal I'm here." She knew Sodhu regularly reported to the queen. It seemed to be how she fulfilled her role as a council member even though she never attended meetings. Sodhu nodded and went into the house, presumably to write a letter and send it with her carrier bird.

Meera dug her fingernails into the vibrant peel of an orange, but after several attempts at removing the fruit from its waxy armor, she grew frustrated and ignited the orange in pale flames, burning away the peel and leaving the inner fruit intact. When Isbaen approached the table, she handed him a slice, which he took with a friendly smile. He didn't ask her what was going on; he knew she would explain soon enough. Isbaen, as usual, had the calm patience of a heron waiting for fish.

"Where's Gendryl?" Meera asked, inquiring after his new partner. Gendryl had been spending a lot of time on the peninsula lately. Meera was still trying to get to know the shy knell man, but she enjoyed seeing him with Isbaen—their joy in one another radiated off of them, often lightening her mood.

"He returned to his farm to make sure everything was running smoothly in his absence and to visit the animals," Isbaen replied. At Meera's confused look, he explained, "Gendryl has a dairy farm. Cheesemaking is his passion."

Meera nodded and wondered how she had not known that. She loved cheese, so this bit of information only made her like Gendryl even more.

After several minutes, Katrea and Florean arrived at the table together looking wary. Then Shael appeared, sweaty from whatever he had been doing. He broke a slice off of Meera's orange and crammed it into his mouth before sitting in his usual seat next to her, and the casual interaction eased some of Meera's tension; she felt like she and Shael were truly on their way to being friends again after their short-lived, misbegotten romance.

Finally, Hadjal returned with a scowling Soleille. "This had better be good, Meera," Soleille spat, clearly disgruntled from being interrupted. Her stormy face was at odds with her sunny blonde hair.

"Define good," Meera replied tonelessly. All of the other riders were gathered except for Kennick—who she hoped wasn't having a hard time cleaning up after her hasty departure—and they all looked at her expectantly. "So ... I should maybe tell you all that I never actually wanted the council to make me a rider ..." she began awkwardly, grimacing at the looks of shock and confusion around her.

"Instead, I asked them to consider helping Shaya and I end the war. Darreal seemed receptive to the idea, but ... well, the other council members declared that I was a threat to Levisade and tried to detain me against Darreal's wishes. When they couldn't detain me, they tried to kill me, so I jumped out the window and left." Meera told her story in an undignified flurry of words before looking down at the table and drumming her fingers against the wood.

"The council acted against Darreal's orders?" Sodhu asked, sounding alarmed.

Meera nodded.

"Where is Kennick?" Shael asked.

"He's still there, I guess," she replied. Glancing up at the sky, she hoped to see Endu any moment.

"Why did you not tell us your plan, Meera? We thought you wanted to be accepted as a rider," Isbaen said.

Meera felt shame churn in her gut as she appraised the sincere expression on his handsome, angular face. "I do—I mean, I want to be one of you, I just don't want to swear any oaths that I can't keep," she explained.

Isbaen hummed in understanding, but Meera refrained from comparing him to his brother. Then she glanced at Hadjal, who looked extremely tired and didn't meet her gaze. Hadjal was the unofficial leader of the riders, and she and Meera had been struggling to coexist lately. Meera wondered if the older knell woman would now see fit to cast her out entirely—she had not been swift to accept Meera's abilities, after all.

Hadjal took a deep breath and looked up at everyone. "All we can do is wait and see what will happen next," she said. "If Darreal did not want Meera captured, then there is no reason we cannot continue to shelter her and train with her. I do not know how Darreal will regain her authority, but there is nothing we need to do unless called upon."

Everyone nodded their agreement. Meera felt relieved that she wouldn't be thrown out of her cabin, but she didn't much like the idea of waiting around for news. Just then, Shaya squawked as Endu descended from the clouds above and landed on the slope. Standing from the bench, Meera ran for Kennick, surging with relief. He leapt gracefully from his raek and caught her as she pummeled into him. She didn't hug him, exactly, but she grabbed his waist and held him steady to inspect him for damage. "Are you okay?" she asked. "The council didn't turn on you, did they?"

"No," he replied.

Realizing, she was still clutching him, she dropped her hands to her sides. Kennick was gazing down at her without any of his usual humor; his dark eyes looked troubled. "I was worried you would be far away. I did not know if you would come back here," he admitted.

Meera shrugged. "This is my home," she said. Looking up at him, she wanted to tell him that he was her family, but she didn't. The night before had left things unsettled between them.

"You did not need to run. I would have fought with you," he said. Meera gazed at him; she had never actually seen Kennick upset before and thought that this might be it—subtle as it was. His arms were crossed instead of loose, and a very slight crease showed between his eyebrows.

"You did fight with me," she replied. Then, quieter, she added, "I'm sorry I left you there—I shouldn't have."

With a shake of his head, Kennick's momentary anger subsided just like that, and his arms uncrossed. "You needed to leave," he said with a loose shrug. Then he turned and started untying two bags from Endu's straps.

"What happened after I left?" Meera asked.

"There was a lot of confusion, which was made worse when my mother's temper flared, and she set the walls on fire. Everyone ran out of the room. The last I saw of Darreal, she was striding down the hallway, alone. I summoned Endu, packed our bags, and left. I had hoped to catch you in the air, but you were much too fast," he replied with his back turned to her.

Meera nodded dully even though he couldn't see her. She was feeling worse and worse for leaving him there. He turned and handed her her bag, which looked fuller than she remembered. Peering inside, she found her dress and shoes from the ball. The ball felt like it had been weeks ago. "Thank you. Your mother probably would have burned my stuff if you hadn't gotten it," she said.

For a moment, they both stood with their bags slung over their shoulders and regarded each other awkwardly. Meera felt like there was something she still needed to say, but she wasn't sure what it was. She wanted the usual gleam to return to Kennick's eyes and for his pointy canine tooth to make an appearance when he smirked.

Shaya was still in the clearing, and she shifted her weight to observe Kennick and Endu. Endu shifted in return and some sort of raek show-down ensued. Meera hoped they wouldn't start fighting. "Is this your new mate?" Shaya asked her.

"No!" Meera replied mentally, feeling blood rush to her face even though she knew Kennick couldn't hear them.

"He has better plumage than the last one," Shaya commented.

Meera felt laughter bubble in her stomach, but she pushed it down. "Not too gaudy for you?" she asked her raek.

Shaya puffed a bit of smoke. "No, but maybe it is the summer air talking," she replied.

Meera did laugh then, realizing her raek was feeling lustful. She wondered whether Shaya was appraising Kennick's plumage or Endu's.

Kennick had been looking between the two raeken with caution, but his attention moved to Meera in curiosity. "What?" he asked.

She was still laughing and wiped a stray tear from her eye. "Shaya likes your plumage," she said, which made Kennick grin. "Also, we might want to leave these two alone," she added, gesturing to their raeken with a pointed look.

Kennick's eyes widened, and his eyebrows rose in understanding. He laughed with her, and they walked to Hadjal's table. Everyone greeted him, relieved that he had returned safely. Then Hadjal, Isbaen, and Florean questioned Kennick about what had happened even though he didn't have anything new to add to Meera's story. After a while, the questions ran dry, and the riders all sat for several moments in silence together, each individually digesting the current situation.

"So, since no one is in imminent danger ... Meera, how was the ball?" Soleille asked, leaning forward excitedly. Her earlier irritation at being interrupted was obviously forgotten. "I want to know everything!" she continued before Meera could even answer. "In fact, I want to see the dress! You have the dress, right?" Soleille rose from her bench and went around the table to grab Meera, hauling her to her feet and dragging her toward the cabin.

"Seriously?" Meera asked. "Right now?"

"Right now!" Soleille chirped.

"I want to see it!" Katrea said, getting up and following them.

"You do?" Meera asked, baffled.

"No, but I do not want to miss anything," Katrea said honestly, making Meera laugh.

Wrenching her arm free of Soleille's surprisingly strong grip, she walked toward her cabin with the other two female riders—the young-ish ones, anyway. Once they were all stuffed into the small space together, Soleille continued her stream of enthusiasm: "I want to know everything! Who was there, what they were wearing, who they danced with—did you dance? What happened with Kennick? Oh! Start there!"

Meera had started pulling out her dress and shoes, but at that, she stopped and gaped at Soleille. "With Kennick?" she asked in mock confusion. "Nothing happened ..."

"Meera, you are a terrible liar," Katrea intoned. The large, muscular woman was sitting on what had been Meera's father's bed and making it look doll-sized.

"What happened?" Soleille gasped, leaning so close to Meera that she flinched away.

Meera wanted to bond with these women, but she also didn't quite feel comfortable discussing Kennick with them. He was her friend, too, and she didn't want to betray his trust. Soleille was like a prying older sister who, Meera suspected, might blab her secrets to anyone who would listen the second she walked away. "Nothing—really," she lied.

Soleille looked annoyed, but she let the matter drop. "Well, let us see the dress!" she chirped.

Meera pulled out the dress, which was carefully folded, and as she unfolded the shimmering bluish white fabric, the necklace Kennick had made her fell out onto her bed. She smiled at it, unsurprised that he had tried once more to make her keep the extravagant piece of jewelry. Picking it up, she saw that he had fixed the damage she had caused, made it more pliable with little hinges, and added clasps to the back.

"Oooh, what is that?" Katrea asked, eyes drawn to the sparkling diamonds.

"Turn around, and I'll show you!" Meera said forcefully.

Both Katrea and Soleille turned their backs to her impatiently. Meera hadn't actually needed privacy to change; she just didn't want them staring at her while she sorted through the emotions her outfit from the night before caused her. Now that it was the light of day and she had survived her meeting with the council, she wondered whether she had made the right decision. She couldn't exactly lie to herself about the fluttering feelings Kennick caused in her stomach.

Changing into her dress, she put on her shoes and necklace, leaving her hair half-back as it was. She didn't have a large mirror in the tiny cabin, but she didn't need one; the feel of the dress on her body and the swirling necklace overlaying her silvery scars brought back how beautiful she had felt the previous evening. Meera tried not to also think about the feeling of Kennick's lips on hers, but she was unsuccessful. "Okay," she said.

Soleille and Katrea both turned in unison and gasped. Soleille, for once, seemed speechless—at first, anyway. "Kennick gave you that dress and that necklace, and he did not try to take you to bed with him?" she finally asked, sounding incredulous.

Meera rolled her eyes.

Katrea whistled low. "I have never seen so many diamonds," she said, staring at the necklace. Meera had had the same thought the night before, and she sighed; she really shouldn't keep it, but she really wanted to.

"Come on! Hadjal and Sodhu have to see this," Soleille said before once more grabbing Meera's arm and hauling her away. "No! Soleille, stop," Meera argued as they rounded Hadjal's house. She felt like she had already made enough of a spectacle of herself that day—and every other day—and didn't need to be paraded around in her new finery.

Soleille was deaf to her pleas, however; she dragged Meera up to the table, where the other riders still loitered. Katrea followed behind them. "Tada!" Soleille cried, as if she had something to do with making Meera look so good.

Meera rolled her eyes again. Unfortunately, she then looked straight into Shael's pained face and quickly averted her gaze. Hadjal and Sodhu both fussed over how pretty she looked, and even Florean gave her a compliment. "This is some fine work you did," Soleille said to Kennick, who already looked pleased enough with himself. "I expect you to do the same for me next summer," she added threateningly.

He laughed. "I could not possibly dress you better than you dress yourself, Soleille," he said flatteringly.

Soleille practically purred, and Meera found herself wondering whether the two of them had ever slept together. But she pushed the thought aside. Feeling like the show was over, she unclasped the necklace from her neck and held it out for Kennick. He put his hands obstinately behind his back. Undeterred, she stepped forward, wrenched one of his hands from behind his back with her knell strength, and dropped the necklace into it.

At first, Meera worried he would be offended, but Kennick merely laughed like they were playing his favorite game. "You know, you did that with a lot more pizazz last time," he said, referring to her impromptu metal shaping. He slipped the necklace into one of his human-style pockets, but Meera had a feeling she would see it again. The feeling tickled her stomach and made her smile.

"Funny story about that," she said. "Shaya came back because she thought someone was strangling me," she told him.

He laughed with her, and everyone else looked confused—

except Shael, who was staring down at the table like he might die if he looked anywhere else. At the sight of him, Meera gave everyone a mock curtsy and hurried away to change. She had thought she and Shael were ready to be friends, but the look on his face told her otherwise; he was clearly not over his feelings for her. The thought was extremely confusing because all Meera had wanted weeks ago was to have proof of Shael's love for her. Now, it was written all over his face, and she wished that it wasn't. Was she flighty? Had she flitted from Shael to Kennick too easily?

She felt tempted to judge her feelings, but she didn't actually think she was being unreasonable. She couldn't help how she felt. Besides, she had returned from her training ready to be with Shael, and he had pushed her away—not for the first time, either. Shael had hurt her, and Kennick never had—not yet anyway. Kennick made her feel seen and heard and understood and beautiful. He made her laugh.

Meera sighed. Then there was the fact that Kennick had confessed his feelings for her, and she had turned him down. Why had she done that? She remembered her reasons, but at that moment, she couldn't remember why she had thought they outweighed the possibility of love. What if she could be with Kennick and not have it end in disaster? If she never tried, wouldn't she always wonder? She probably would.

THE COMPLETED
RAEK RIDERS SERIES

Milton Keynes UK
Ingram Content Group UK Ltd.
UKHW040133130324
439347UK00003B/52